A PLACE WITH DRAGONS

Book I
A City With Seven Gates Novel

STEVEN L. LOVETT

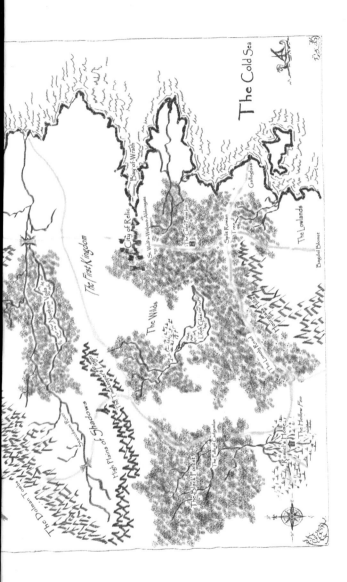

A PLACE WITH DRAGONS

Book I
A City With Seven Gates Novel

STEVEN L. LOVETT

ISBN 978-1-988256-81-8

www.dragonmoonpress.com

DEDICA

To Emery, who believes in fai
dragons, and to Selayoa,

Telluric Grand

ACKNOWLEDGMENTS

A first doff of my hat goes to my nephew Joshua L. At a family gathering some time ago, I handed him the first (very rough) ten chapters of this book and asked if he'd like to read them. He finished later that same afternoon and asked me where the rest of the story was. So I kept writing.

I'd also like to kindly thank Lelan and Christina D., who kindly agreed to read an only-slightly-more-improved first draft of the first fourteen chapters. They did so by spending their evenings reading aloud to each other while creating "voices" for each of the characters. They said it was good and "couldn't wait for the movie." So I kept writing.

Oh, and for the hours I spent listening to the energetic or mournful strains of violins, violas, French horns, oboes, and sundry other orchestral instruments, I extend a heartfelt thank you to the London Symphony Orchestra and the City of Prague Philharmonics. There is music—sometimes light, sometimes dark—interwoven throughout the book.

My heartfelt appreciation goes out to Gwen Gades of Dragon Moon Press, who took an energetic gamble on an unknown and untried author. You and I both hope it pays off. And to Sandra Nguyen, you were as much of an enthusiastic reader as you were an editor. Thank you!

Most especially, however, I'd like to express my eternal gratitude—sincerely, humbly, and lovingly—to my wife and daughter. They tolerated the endless hours I spent outside inside a little shop behind our house, wrestling with bog worms and ogres, meeting giants and Wisps, and carefully walking the landscape of the First Kingdom and Telluric Grand. My wonderful girls patiently refilled my propane heater for cold winter days, listened to me read (and, sometimes begrudgingly, edit) chapters to them in the evenings, constantly urged me to "go write," and faithfully offered to fix me "special" drinks at the end of many long writing days.

Any insufficiencies, oversights, or mistakes are mine alone.

PROLOGUE

Nicolas stared at the overlord dragon. He stared blankly into the face of timeless Death and no longer cared. His thoughts drifted away from the knot of anguish swelling up inside of him, wandering back to the Saturday morning, long ago—to when he first saw the crow.

It seemed ages ago.

———◆———

The sum of his entire life surged up inside of him. Like a last trembling draught of breath before plunging into a cold pool of water, Nicolas' life up to this point—its safe sense of *who* he was and *what* he was—crowded inside him until all he could see were cataracts of greyish memories. He knew nothing would ever be the same. Life would never again be defined by the kinds of things most boys busy themselves with before they unwarily stumble into manhood.

The knife Nicolas held in his hand—its blade and spine awash with thick, wet, dark blood—had made sure of that. The thin blade had done what no amount of youthful experiences could have. In the traitorous twist of a single moment, it had severed—*murdered*, really—Nicolas' past; laid his memories to rest inside a hateful coffin of sudden violence. And like a soul-empty survivor at a funeral wake, Nicolas now looked hard at those memories—especially the memories of that frosty Saturday morning long ago—struggling to memorize them, relive them, if only for a moment. But with each heavy drop of blood from the sodden knife, he felt them fade. They weakened

9

and withered and shrank away until, finally, they were gone.

Now empty, his soft grey eyes slowly adjusted once again. He stared at the enormous demon. Into timeless Death.

And in that small moment, Nicolas knew—he truly *knew*— he had become a Wren. *The king of birds.*

CHAPTER 1

A PECULIAR MORNING

Even before he got out of bed, Nicolas Bennett knew this was going to be strange day. A strange day indeed.

It was Saturday, and it was the 31st of October. Halloween. And, as it so happened, it was also Nicolas' birthday. His twelfth birthday.

But those things weren't strange. The strangeness was how the day *began*. And how it began—bizarrely and in a most unexpected, peculiar way—was with a shadow.

After waking, Nicolas yawned and lay quietly in his bed, watching the paleness of the early morning light cast sleepy silhouettes against his attic bedroom's walls. Over the high lip of his bed's footboard, Nicolas could see his room's single, small, round window. Sparkling frost trimmed its panes and made the comforting weight of his bed's tattered old quilt feel especially warm and safe.

On most weekend mornings, Nicolas loved to lie still in bed and spy on the world as it woke up. Bright sunrays would slip through the gloomy shades of the woods beyond his home, and birds would begin to chat busily with each other as if discussing the past week's news. Nicolas would feel the wall behind his headboard gently rattle as his father, Peter Bennett, strode from the house to "shake out his legs" with an early morning stroll. Nicolas' mum, Sarah Bennett, would sing softly to herself, bustling about their small kitchen and making a "fry up," a scrumptious breakfast of thick bacon, poached eggs, fried tomatoes and mushrooms, fried bread with butter, Cumberland sausage, and hot mugs of tea. The family's cat, Thomas (which his father called "Sir Thomas More"), would be scolding the family's dog, Jasper (which his father called "Jasper Carrot"), for lying across the threshold of the side door, waiting for father's return, and blocking Thomas' way of escaping to the outside world. On most weekend mornings, Nicolas loved to lie still in bed and let the world wake up around him.

But this morning felt different. *Peculiar.*

The night before, a suspicious, cold fog had crawled into the nearby woods. Now, as the dawn slowly awoke, the fog's chilly fingers lingered, groping through the hedgerow at the edge of the family's small sheep pasture. A snap of early winter weather had blown in from the darkness of the Irish Sea, and the birds were keeping quiet in their nests. Nicolas' father hadn't left the house yet, and Nicolas couldn't hear his mum bustling about the small kitchen making breakfast. The small farmhouse felt especially hushed. Silent.

Nicolas lay in his bed, looking out at the early morning, the wintry fog, and the dreary sky. He imagined he was all alone.

A shadow suddenly filled his room's small window. It bobbed and jerked about in shudders and shakes, blocking out most of the morning's first light. And, with startlingly force, the shadow began striking the window's glass.

The flurry of violent strikes on the glass made Nicolas jump. He was sure the window was going to break, and for a moment, he even imagined he heard a loud pop and crack. The noise was thunderous in the small attic bedroom, as if someone was throwing stones at the small window. Nicolas was gripped by an overwhelming urge to plug his ears and dive safely under his bed's thick quilt.

But he didn't. Nicolas didn't plug his ears. He didn't hide. Instead, cautiously, he sat up. Straight up.

He stared at the window. The part of Nicolas that made him sit up was deeply curious, and his eyes seemed to be in control of the rest of his body. In spite of the unease twisting in his stomach, he wanted to know what had landed so unexpectedly on his windowsill and was beating so loudly on the frost-encrusted glass panes.

Then, as abruptly as it had begun, the frenzied attack stopped. The jerking shadow twitched, nodded, and became still.

Nicolas' heart was thumping. He took small, nervous gulps of air.

The attic bedroom was extra quiet. "As quiet as a tomb," he unexpectedly whispered to himself, but even at a whisper his voice sounded loud.

Hesitantly—carefully—he pushed back his warm blankets, and with wary movements, swung his legs over the side of his bed.

The shadow in the window didn't move.

Without taking his eyes away from the window, Nicolas fished around for his slippers and wriggled his feet inside. Gingerly, he stood up. His small attic room was cold, unusually cold, but Nicolas didn't bother putting on the green-checked bathrobe his mum had given to him for his birthday last year. Instead, he took a few, careful steps toward the window. When he was within a few inches of it, he stopped.

Nicolas now stood so close, he could look through the window's unfrosted middle and off to the side of the windowsill. Whatever was casting the shadow was sitting there, unmoving and hidden.

Nicolas, holding his breath, leaned forward for a look.

The thing moved. It cocked its large head to one side and filled the middle of the small, round window with a cruel beak and

13

a wild crest of jet black feathers. Nicolas froze in place. He was staring into the beady, dark eyes of an unusually enormous crow. Each of its eyes were like smooth drops of marbled glass. They had smoky swirls of deep red, like the last trace of a dying sunset.

Seconds stretched as they passed by.

Then, with a last angry rap on the glass, the giant crow thrust away from the windowsill and flew off. The shadow and the crow were gone.

<hr />

Suddenly, dazzling rays of sunlight streamed through the empty window. Nicolas blinked. The sun had made its way above the horizon, and the fog's slinking fingers had shrunk back into the cover of the woods.

A sparkling web of fine cracks now bejeweled the window's middle pane of glass.

"Stone the crows!" said Nicolas.

He reached out and touched the cold glass. The tips of his fingers could feel the cracks' faint traces. *That'll make dad hoppin' mad*, he thought with a shake of his head.

He slipped the window's latch and with a light bump, spun it open on its axle hinge. A gust of frigid morning air leapt into the room and sent a long shiver along Nicolas' shoulders. He ducked his head a bit to get a look out of the lower half of the window. There, lying precariously on the thin ledge of the sill where the crow had perched, sat an odd-looking leaf. It had a broad, flat shape and was almost as thin as a piece of parchment paper. Tiny veins fanning out from its middle were the color of brightly burnished bronze. The rest of the leaf had a coppery color with edges trimmed in a dull patina of loamy green. Except for the wooden twig jutting out of its base, the leaf looked like it was metal. Nicolas picked it up, slowly turning it, and watching as the sun's warm beams gathered and bounced off its metallic surface. He squeezed the copper leaf between his fingers. It felt brittle, but strong at the same time. He'd never seen anything like it before.

"How strange." Nicolas traced the leaf's bronze veins with his finger. "What a very strange thing to leave behind." Warily, he looked out across the sky, half-expecting to catch sight of the ominous crow somewhere in the distance. "What a strange way to begin my birthday." The boy shivered, absently refastening the window. Nicolas walked to where his bathrobe lay draped over one of his bedposts. He laid the leaf on his bed, shrugged on his robe, and stood staring at the odd object while rubbing some warmth back into his arms.

"How strange," he said again.

<hr/>

"Thomas!" The cat leapt onto Nicolas' bed, startling him. It sat there looking idly at him for a moment and then began to clean its spotted paws. The soft licking was loud in the stillness of the small bedroom. "Where is everyone, Thomas?" Nicolas quietly asked. Thomas paused from licking himself but didn't look up. "Where *is* everyone, Thomas?" he asked again. The cat simply yawned and curled into a tight ball.

Perhaps they're planning to surprise me, Nicolas thought hopefully. He reached down and kindly tucked his heavy quilt over the cat. Thomas, promptly agitated by the charitable gesture, walked to the other side of Nicolas' bed and curled up again into a tight ball of tabby fur and whiskers.

Nicolas, fixated on thoughts about his birthday, ignored the cat and imagined walking down the narrow stairs from his room and into the kitchen, where his father would flip the light switch, and his mum would sing out, "Happy birthday!" and give him a big hug. Every year, he looked forward to his birthday. In previous years, Nicolas' father had carefully collected chestnuts in

15

early October from a horse chestnut tree in preparation for his birthday games. His mum made homemade invitations, carefully telling Nicolas to give them out after school since not all of his classmates could be invited. The invitations would always say something neat like, "You are warmly invited to celebrate Nicolas Bennett's birthday and his ninth trip around the sun at 4 o'clock sharp, on Wednesday, 31st October." As Nicolas' friends would arrive on the big day, his father would have each child repeat after him, "Oddly oddly onker, my first conker," before giving them each a "conker," a single chestnut with a string threaded through it and a knot tied at one end to keep the chestnut in place. Shortly after the last guest arrived, the "Great Birthday Conker Tournament" would begin. The children would go at it energetically with shouts of "strings!" and "no stamps!" and the sharp crack of conkers as the chestnuts struck each other, flying noisily around the Bennetts' small yard until Mr. Bennett, with all the seriousness of a headmaster, would examine each child's conker and (even if the conkers weren't entirely broken) solemnly announce the tournament's winner as "this year's Conker King!" Other birthday games, like pass-the-parcel and "Queenie, Queenie, who's got the ball?" (which only the girls wanted to play), would follow, and because Nicolas' shared his birthday with Halloween, each year his parents would spend extra money to hire a face painter so everyone could run around looking like mummies and vampires and witches and ghouls (although the girls always insisted on being fairy princesses). As a customary finish, the children would play Nicolas' favorite game, "What's the Time, Mr. Wolf?" They would form a long line in the Bennetts' small pasture, and the recently crowned "Conker King" would be first to play Mr. Wolf. Mr. Wolf would call out "3 o'clock" or "9 o'clock" or "7 o'clock" when the other children would ask, "What time is it, Mr. Wolf?" With each answer, the children would all take three or nine or seven steps toward Mr. Wolf, until Mr. Wolf would suddenly shout, "It's dinner time!" Girls would scream, and boys would yell, as they all made a mad dash back to their starting mark, trying to avoid being caught by the pursuing Mr. Wolf. Then, when all the children were exhausted and out of breath, Nicolas' mum would sing out "cake time!" from a table set up in the yard.

Every year, only a single lighted candle would decorate the middle of Nicolas' favorite dessert. "After all," his mum would tell him with a sly wink, "we're only celebrating one year each year. Last year, we celebrated last year's birthday." Nicolas would shut his eyes tight, always a bit little light-headed after being hunted down by Mr. Wolf, and whisper to himself one big wish before blowing out the candle. Each child would then stand in line to receive a thick slice of homemade salted caramel toffee swirl cheesecake with a small ball of vanilla bean ice cream on the side. Nicolas' previous birthdays were always a smash, and each October, while other kids were talking about trick-or-treating and Halloween parties, Nicolas anxiously waited for his birthday celebration to arrive.

But this year, on Nicolas' twelfth birthday, there would be no party.

The week before, Nicolas had asked his mum about birthday invitations. She had gently said, "Not this year, my love. Your dad and I aren't in a good place right now, and money is a tad tight." It was hard for Nicolas to remember any occasion when his lovely mum didn't look happy. Her rosy cheeks were always lifted high in a wonderful smile, and her green Irish eyes sparkled, always merry and a trace mischievous. But when she had said that, her soft eyes were troubled, and Nicolas didn't ask anything more.

On Friday, the day before his birthday, Nicolas' parents both seemed distracted and distant. When Nicolas' father arrived home from work, he ate a quick bite of supper and spent the rest of the evening sitting in front of the television, watching the Penrith Rugby Union Football Club play a close match in Winter's Park. Nicolas' mum spent most of her late afternoon and evening talking on the telephone with his great aunt, Harriet Loretta Cheesebottom, who lived over in Carlisle. For as long as Nicolas could remember, Aunt Harriet always seemed to be sick with something and to never get any better. Every time she visited, or every time Nicolas heard his mum talking with her on the telephone, all conversations seemed to revolve around a never-ending list of Aunt Harriet's complaints and ghastly ailments: painful corns on her toes, newly discovered moles on her incredibly fat neck, aches in her back (caused by a lifetime of slouching, Nicolas' father always said), gout in her joints (which sounded nasty even though Nicolas didn't know what "gout" actually was), and an appalling wart on her left index finger's second knuckle, which never seemed to go away.

No one had said much about any birthday celebration. Nicolas' father, a typically cheerful man who was known for sweeping up his wife and son in tremendous bear hugs for no reason, kept to himself that evening. During supper, when Nicolas asked his father whether he had gathered any chestnuts this year, secretly hoping his father might say something about last minute party arrangements, Mr. Bennett had folded his fingers together and simply said, "Tomorrow's your birthday, Nicolas. We can't have a party this year, but your mother and I know it's a special day, and we do 'ave plans. We thought it might be nice for the three of us to have a spot of lunch in Penrith and then take ya to the medieval fair in the Yanwath Wood." The fair sounded nice, but it wasn't a birthday party.

Nicolas respectfully nodded his head and had finished eating his cooked peas.

——•——

Now it was the morning of his birthday, and Thomas the cat seemed to be the only other member of the family who was up and about.

Nicolas took off his bathrobe and dressed. With the late October cold, Nicolas decided on a pair of old wool socks, hiking boots, long trousers, a t-shirt, and a dark green Guernsey, a fisherman's sweater his mother had knitted for him during the summer months. "Well, Thomas," he said cheerily, holding his arms out, "how do I look?" The cat glanced up, blinked, and yawned its sleepy approval. Nicolas took a quick look at himself in the modest mirror hung just above his single chest of drawers. *Mum will say I'm a mess, but*, he thought, *it is my birthday after all.* And with that, Nicolas pulled his shoulders back and smiled at himself.

Spinning on the ball of his foot, he went to the old travel trunk at the foot of his bed. Nicolas unlatched the two thick leather buckles and lifted its heavy lid. Inside were some of his most important, and most private, things. His great grandmother's silver sewing thimble, which Nicolas sometimes imagined was a beer mug for fairies, sat precariously atop a wooden soldier's head, as if the soldier had placed it there as a convenient helmet. He sometimes carried it for good luck. Nicolas dropped the thimble into his pocket.

The toy soldier—more precisely, but importantly to Nicolas, a member of the Queen's Guard—had been his father's when he was young. The scarlet red of the soldier's tunic was chipped and worn away, but Nicolas thought he looked stately, and in his imagination, had commanded many a British regiment in many a war. Sitting solemnly next to the wooden guard stood the Tower of London, a model Nicolas' father had made out of a stout chunk of Yew wood three years ago as a Christmas present. Nicolas ran his fingers along the castle's seven huge towers: the Salt, Broad Arrow, Constable, Martin, "Royal Beasts", Bowyer, and Flint Tower. In the middle of the Tower castle were six black buttons, which Nicolas pretended were the Tower's resident ravens. As he often did, Nicolas softly repeated his father's warning three years ago as Nicolas unwrapped his new Tower castle, "If the ravens leave the Tower, the kingdom will fall."

Nicolas carefully moved the Tower to one corner of the old trunk before continuing his search. Among other odds and ends, he found a short bit of braided string made of a blue string, a red string, and a gold string, which also made its way into his pocket. Finally, he scooped up a canvas coin purse that jingled as he set it on the floor. With a single pull, Nicolas opened the drawstring and out spilled a modest plunder of old coins: three farthings, a haypenny, a penny, a thrupenny bit, sixpence, two shillings, a two bob bit, two half crowns, and the most prized of all, a 1935 "rocking horse" crown coin. The "rocking horse" design was a picture of St. George slaying a dragon. Nicolas often placed this large silver coin in his Tower castle as if it was royal treasure. Today, for some reason, he took a long moment to rub the smooth crown coin between his thumb and finger and dropped the crown coin into his pocket, along with the thimble and string.

In spite of the majesty of the crown coin, he actually liked the simple farthing coins the most. Each farthing had the profile of King George V on one side and on the other was a picture of a little bird with short wings and an upright tail. The little bird was a wren. It had always fascinated Nicolas that such a kindly looking bird would have been chosen to share a coin with the faces of kings and queens. When Nicolas had asked his father about the bird a few years before, his father told him the ancient story about the "election of the king of birds." His father said whichever bird could fly to the highest altitude was to be made King of Birds. Naturally, the eagle out-flew all other birds and soared to great heights high above the clouds. But even so, the eagle was beaten by a very small bird, the wren, that had hidden itself in the eagle's feathers. At the last moment, it sprang from its hiding place and flew higher than the eagle. Because of this, the wren was crowned *King of Birds*. "Even the least can surprise everyone and become the greatest," his father had told him with a knowing wink.

Nicolas took one of the farthing coins and let it slide into his pocket. He heard it clink happily against his great grand-mother's silver thimble and the "rocking horse" crown coin. He carefully put the other coins back in the canvas bag and re-turned the bag to the trunk. With that, Nicolas dropped the lid of the trunk down, re-buckled its straps, and stood up. Point-ing a determined finger at the sleeping cat, Nicolas said, "Even if there *isn't* a party today, I'm still happy it's my birthday." Thomas didn't stir.

Nicolas lifted his chin and shoved out his jaw. "I'm a wren today," he said firmly, feeling funny, but good, as the words came out of his mouth.

Nicolas ran his fingers through his untidy, curly hair, and pulled a warm knit cap over his head. Just as he did, a shadow again fell across the room. Quickly looking out his window, Nicolas could see a grey cloud drifting in front of the sun. He let out a breath of relief. Nicolas glanced at the strange copper leaf sitting on his bed. For no particular reason, he scooped it up and dropped it inside his trouser pocket.

Stepping quietly out of his bedroom door and down the nar-row stairs, he left Thomas the cat curled fast asleep on his bed.

CHAPTER 2

A Place with Dragons

The kitchen was empty.

Nicolas stood in the doorway for a moment. Deep down, he hadn't truly expected a surprise greeting, but there was still a twinge of disappointment. "I'm a *wren* today," he said again, but it didn't feel quite as good this time.

Nicolas considered what to do next. He had always loved his family's small farm kitchen with its chipped block-wood table, mismatched chairs, rustic and stained cabinets, sooty inglenook fireplace, and great black stove. His mum, who was usually hurrying about, baking and cooking, always made the kitchen an inviting place to be. Indeed, the rest of the Bennetts' small cottage seemed to hum around this room like spokes on the hub of a wheel.

But not this morning.

This Saturday morning, the kitchen was empty. Quiet and empty.

"Nicolas?" As gentle as his father's voice usually was, its deep bass was a "presence of its own," as his mum often said.

Nicolas walked across the kitchen's flagstone floor and under an archway, which led through a cubby boot room, and into his father's study. Nicolas' father—a lean and bookish sort of Englishman who grew up in a coal-mining family from Haydock, England—was sitting in his favorite reading chair with the Saturday edition of the Cumberland and Westmorland Herald spread out across his knees. His father's socked feet were propped up on an overstuffed stool in front of the fireplace where flames were happily bobbing around three splits of wood.

The cozy study was well-lit even in the amber tints of early morning light. A single large window—like an enormous picture in a picture frame—took up most of the study's wall to the east. Nicolas would sometimes sit with a pillow in the window seat, reading his favorite book, *Cue for Treason* by Geoffrey Trease. He would gaze outside, across the lawn, and out beyond the family's sheep pasture, imagining what a great adventure it would be if he were the main character, Peter Brownrigg, a fourteen-year-old boy who had run away from his medieval village by hiding inside a "prop coffin" used by a band of traveling actors. The bookshelves were filled with such wonderful books, as well as assorted statuettes of English mastiffs, a single cast-iron bulldog, a modest collection of aged clocks (most of which still ticked happily away), a multitude of worn magazines and trade papers, and an unopened bottle of Grand Old Parr Real Antique and Rare Old DeLuxe Scotch Whiskey ("aged older than this house," his father would proudly say to guests). Above the archway hung an iron doorknocker fashioned as a stag's head next to an old, and absurdly large, iron key. And above the fireplace's thick mantle hung a carving of an English wych elm tree, something Nicolas thought must have taken years to make. Beneath the carving, propped against the wall, was a smooth square of knotted elm wood with a piece of parchment lacquered onto its surface. Written in dark ink were the words, "...a comrade, bending over the house, strength and adventure in its roots." Nicolas knew the words were taken from one of his father's favorite novels, but he fuddled the title whenever he tried to think of it.

"Yes, Dad?" Nicolas responded.

"Come here, lad."

Nicolas moved over to his father's chair and put his hand on Mr. Bennett's forearm.

"Happy birthday, my boy," said his father clapping his rough hand on top of Nicolas'. "Today, you're twelve years old. Am I right?"

Nicolas nodded. "Yes, sir."

"Grand," his father said with a big smile. "That's grand." He paused, looked out the window for a moment and then back at Nicolas. "Your mother left early this morning to pop in on Aunt Harriet. She shouldn't be gone too long, and then we'll begin our day. We're light on breakfast this mornin', lad. There's still a flat loaf of the barley bannock your mum griddled yesterday. You can warm it up on the stove and eat as much jam as you'd like." Nicolas' father smiled warmly and winked a conspirator's wink. "It's your birthday, my boy. Can't have too much jam on your birthday."

"Yes!" exclaimed Nicolas. He was halfway through the cubby boot room when he abruptly stopped and turned back toward his father's study.

"Dad?"

His father looked up from his paper and pushed his glasses back up his long nose. "Yes?"

Nicolas started to say, "something happened this morning," but he changed his mind at the last minute, and a jumble of words came out instead. "Something...something... I have something in my pocket."

His father chuckled. "Okay! And what might 'something' in your pocket have to do with me and my mornin' paper?"

"I thought you might be able to tell me what it is." Nicolas reached in his pocket, pushed his coins and thimble out of the way, and pulled out the coppery leaf.

His father tilted his chin up and took a long look at the leaf through the lower half of his glasses. As luck would have it, Mr. Bennett happened to be an arboriculture professor at the Askham Bryan College's agricultural campus just outside Penrith at Newton Rigg—"just an English chap who loves trees," as he sometimes described himself. Many of the books and magazines in his study were devoted to the planting, transplanting, pruning, diagnosing of various diseases and parasites, and all other sorts of issues involving trees. He loved teaching and was a well-known member of the Royal Forestry Society, having proudly hosted various woodland field conferences over the past several years.

The odd, coppery leaf Nicolas held in front of him was perplexing. "Hmph," he said and wrinkled his nose. He swung his head from side to side, inspecting each side of the leaf. "Hmph," he said again. Mr. Bennett sat back in his chair and spread the morning's copy of the Herald smoothly across his knees. "Let me see that, Nicolas."

Nicolas placed the leaf on his father's newspaper. Mr. Bennett leaned over it, wrinkling his nose again and repeatedly pushing his glasses back up the bridge of his nose. He gently poked the leaf and finally held it up, lightly rubbing its veiny surface. Cocking an eyebrow and throwing a glance over the top of his glasses, Mr. Bennett asked, "Where did you get this, my boy?"

"A crow…um, well, I, um… It was on my windowsill." He meant to tell his father about the crow but suddenly felt silly saying anything about it. "I found it on my windowsill."

Mr. Bennett looked closely at Nicolas. "Your windowsill?"

"Yes, sir."

Mr. Bennett nodded. "And how do you suppose it got on your windowsill, lad?"

Nicolas paused but finally said, "A crow put it there this morning."

"A crow *put* it there?"

"Yes, sir."

Mr. Bennett sat back in his chair and looked out the large picture window. "Was it a large crow?" came the soft question.

"Yes, sir," Nicolas said, a little surprised at his father's guess.

Mr. Bennett nodded but kept looking out the window. "And did it rap on your window?"

"Yes, sir!" Nicolas, now even more surprised but also relieved, quickly explained, "It just appeared, and tapped on the glass very hard, and cracked it."

Mr. Bennett took a deep breath and sighed. "Hmmm" was all he said.

Several moments passed in silence.

"I want to show you something, Nicolas. Go get me that book." His father pointed toward a large book on the bottom shelf of one of the bookcases. Several other books were stacked on top of it. It looked as if it were very old and was bound in dark green leather. An unusual picture was engraved on its front cover, depicting a creature with the body of a lion and the head of a man. Its mouth was open, and the creature looked as if it had several rows of sharp teeth.

Mr. Bennett took the book and handed the coppery leaf to Nicolas. He opened the large book and began turning its thick pages. "This," he said without looking up, "is a book your grandfather gave to me years ago, before he passed away. He told me his father had given it to him before that, and that it had been passed down in our family for several generations." After turning several more pages, Mr. Bennett stopped and pulled out an even older-looking sheet of folded paper from inside the book. "It is a strange book, lad. A priest named Edward Topsell wrote it several hundred years ago. Much of it talks about common animals, like tigers and elephants and apes, but it also contains descriptions of creatures most people think do not exist. Amazing creatures like gorgons, unicorns, sphinxes, and serpent-women that eat children." Mr. Bennett looked at Nicolas. He took off his glasses. "When my father gave me this book, he told me that sometimes there are things in life we don't understand. Things that seem peculiar and unbelievable."

Slowly, he unfolded the paper he'd taken out of the book. Inside, flattened by the press of the book, was a large leaf. A coppery leaf. A coppery leaf which very much looked like the leaf Nicolas held in his hand. "My father told me about a time when he was very young. At the time, he lived with his family on a small farm along England's northern border. He told me about waking one morning to find a huge crow rapping violently on his window. When it had flown off, your grandfather found this leaf as if it had been left behind." Mr. Bennett picked up the flattened coppery leaf and held it up next to the leaf in Nicolas' hand. He then pointed down at the open book on his lap. There, under his pointing finger, was a large picture of a black and white engraving. It was a picture of a monstrous dragon. "He told me," Mr. Bennett continued, "this leaf came from some other place. A place with dragons."

Nicolas stood there silently. His father seemed uncharacteristically concerned, and naturally, this concerned Nicolas.

"Nicolas, my boy," Mr. Bennett said, "I don't know *where* these leaves come from. But wherever they come from…," he paused and returned the flattened leaf to the paper, gently refolded it, tucked it back inside the large, dark green book, and slowly closed it. "Wherever they come from," he repeated in a barely audible whisper, "is a place with *dragons*."

Nicolas' mum returned home at half past eleven. By then, Nicolas had consumed all of the strawberry jam (with a last, delicious spoonful even after the bread was gone), brushed his teeth, finished his morning chores, and sat on the floor in the family room, reading the graphic comic novel, *Fables: 1001 Nights of Snowfall*. Except for occasionally reaching into his pocket to touch the coppery leaf, Nicolas didn't think too much more about what his father had told him. The fact that it was his birthday, after all, left him too preoccupied to think of much else.

When his mum walked in the room, Nicolas had just begun to re-read the Chapter entitled "Fencing Lessons," imagining what it must be like to be in a real sword fight. His mum rushed over and nearly sat on top of him, giving him a big hug and loudly kissing his cheeks twelve times. She squeezed his face and said "Happy birthday!" at least half a dozen times before getting up to walk into the study still wearing her mittens and coat.

After a few minutes, Nicolas could hear his parents arguing in low voices. He caught the words, "Aunt Harriet," "money," and his father grumbling, "this *always* happens, Sarah." These arguments seemed to occur more frequently, and Nicolas felt the strain in the Bennetts' home. For the most part, his parents didn't argue in front of him, but Nicolas could see it in their faces. He could hear it in the tone of their voices, and much of the laughter which had always been a fixture in their warm home was gone.

Peter Bennett strode into the family room. "Grab yer jacket," he said sharply. Nicolas nodded and quickly hopped to his feet. "Wait." Nicolas stopped and looked at his father. Mr. Bennett's eyes had softened. "I'm sorry, lad. I didn't mean to snap at you. Go grab your jacket. Your mum's ready to go, and I'm hungry, even if you're stuffed with jam." Mr. Bennett winked. "Let's get a bit of birthday lunch and then go see about the fair."

Nicolas grinned. "It's alright, Dad. And I'm hungry, too."

The Bennetts' cottage was part of Plumpton Head, close to the small village of Plumpton, which was situated in the north ward of Penrith, England, not too far east from the cold Irish Sea and a bit south of the Scottish borders. The drive from Nicolas' home to the town of Penrith usually took about fifteen minutes, and Mr. Bennett would typically drive along, chatting happily about the unique characteristics of some tree they were passing or about some stand of trees in the distance. But on this Saturday morning, Nicolas' father didn't say a word. His mum, who usually hummed gently to herself while his father carried on about trees, was also uncomfortably quiet.

Nicolas peered out the window as pastures, low stone walls, and thick hedgerows passed by. *I'm a wren*, he thought again, and looked up at the grey sky, thinking how cold it must be so high up in the clouds.

Before too long, the Bennetts' twenty-year-old Land Rover 110 rolled into Penrith down Stricklandgate, where Nicolas' father was able to find a parking spot off of Devonshire Street. With collars turned up against the late October wind, the Bennetts walked southeast, past Castlegate, until they arrived at the Four and Twenty eatery at 42 King Street.

Inside the restaurant, it smelled delicious. Nicolas picked out a table near a window and rubbed his hands together while he read the menu. His parents were still mostly quiet, although Nicolas' mum had said, "Whew! The wind!" when they'd first stepped out onto the sidewalk, and his father had "hmphed" in agreement, pulling his big scarf up over his chin.

"What may I have?" Nicolas asked, with a quick look to his mum and father.

"Anything you like, my sweet," said Mrs. Bennett. "Dad said you ate up all our jam, but I don't suppose that's hurt your appetite." She gave him a delightful smile. "You're twelve, and twelve-year-olds eat like lords." His mum had actually been saying that since Nicolas turned ten, and as true as it seemed then, it seemed even truer now. He was starving.

"What'll you have?" asked their waitress, a pen at the ready.

Nicolas blurted out, "I'd like the roast turkey, please." The plate came with something called "forcemeat," pigs in blankets, shredded sprouts, and gravy. He wasn't sure what "forcemeat" was, but anything with pigs in blankets and gravy had to be good. Mr. Bennett ordered a turkey and beef club sandwich with a salad and home-cut chips, and Mrs. Bennett ordered "moussaka," a lasagna-like dish made with lentils. Nicolas grimaced. His mum stuck her tongue out at him, which made him laugh.

Nicolas finished his lunch with sticky toffee pudding, while his parents ordered another cup of tea. "I've no idea where you put all that food," Mr. Bennett said. "You're skinny as a pole, lad."

Nicolas smiled and shrugged, popped the last bite of pudding in his mouth, licked his spoon, and said, "Where to now?"

"Where shall we go, love?" said Nicolas' father to his mum. Nicolas thought his father's face looked kind, but slightly hurt, too. He hoped his parents wouldn't have another argument.

"Well," said his mum thoughtfully, "with this snap of cold, I'd say we head out to the fair for a few hours. If we get back home in time this evening, we can watch a scary movie, and yer Dad can tell us the story of the ghost of Bailiff Wood before bed." Her beautiful Irish smile made her cheeks dance, and she raised her eyebrows in a teasing way. "Perhaps it won't be as frightening this year."

Nicolas playfully smirked back at his mum. "I'm not scared anymore!" He remembered the first time his father told him the story about the sad ghost of a white-skinned young woman, dressed in an old-fashioned nightdress, with short dark hair, who haunted the Bailiff Wood area. She would appear to people at night, usually in their bedrooms, and ask, "Who has murdered me?" Nicolas had been so scared the first time he heard the story, he left his desk lamp on all night. His father told him the young woman's body had been found deep within the lake, weighed down with heavy stones. Her murderer had never been discovered. It had become Nicolas' favorite Halloween story.

"Are you sure, lad?" His father chuckled. "The first time I told you that story, ya nearly papped yer pants."

"No I didn't!" laughed Nicolas as he put his coat on.

A few minutes later, the Bennetts were piled back in their truck and heading southeast on Bridge Lane to the A6, over the River Eamont with its "Giant's Caves," and south through long necks of woods which bordered Earl Henry's Drive.

The day still felt peculiar to Nicolas. Even if it didn't seem like a birthday, he was excited all the same. He pressed his smiling face against the window, watching the deep autumn woods race by.

I'm a wren, he thought again, *and there's a place with dragons.*

CHAPTER 3

✝HE FOO✝PA✝H

The Will-o'-the-Wisp Medieval Fair is situated in the Yanwath Wood, north of Arkham Hall, and bordered to the east by the River Lowther. Once a year, from the twenty-fifth of September through Halloween, the secluded road running through the quiet woodland is opened by the good Earl of Lonsdale, Viscount Lowther, Baron of Whitehaven and Lord of the Manor of Threlkeld.

The fair provides a "living history" of medieval England, but with a bit of amusement and liveliness, too. Dancers, magicians, jugglers, musicians, beggars, singers, rogues, peasants, priests, and princesses are everywhere, talking, laughing, eating, and rabble-rousing as they stroll down enchantingly named paths, such as "Castlerigg Lane," "Brigand Alley," and "King Richard's Avenue." They devour sweet oat cakes with jelly, hot shepherd's pies, warm doughnut twists blanketed with snow-white sugar, an assortment of roasted meats, sausages, and cheeses, and freshly baked bread. They swig and gulp draughts of beer, apple cider, wine, and cinnamon tea. They purchase velvet cloaks, flower garlands for maidens' hair, hand-carved walking canes, glass-blown artwork, witches' brooms, parchments with colorful coats-of-arms, puzzle rings, magical charms, pewter mugs, and long swords. They entertain themselves with stage plays, falconry shows, axe throwing, archery, barrel tosses, and games of cups, tug-of-war, drench-a-wench, and soak-a-bloke. Round-bellied donkeys, plodding tamely behind portly friars, carry laughing children (who each pay a penny), while waves of cheers rise and fall as knights joust and men-at-arms fight valiantly with sword and shield in the Falkirk Amphitheater. Musicians join in elegant string quartets, or wind their way through the woodland playing silly songs on wooden flutes or mournful melodies on Scottish bag pipes. Artisans and journeymen in gloves, leather aprons, and tall boots practice and display their trades in open stalls. Coopers, or barrel makers, hammer iron hoops around wooden barrel staves. Blacksmiths heat their forges with leather hand bellows, hot enough for metal pokers to glow red. Potters shape wet clay on turning wheels. Ropemakers twist together lengths of hawser-laid rope. Chandlers, or candle makers, hang long wicks over molds full of wax. And wheelwrights force wooden spokes into wooden hubs with wooden mallets.

Along with its impressive spectacle of food, fun, and adventure, the Will-o'-the-Wisp Medieval Fair exposes its most morbid and well-known feature as it comes to its end on 31st October, All Hallow's Eve. On the fair's dying day, the weeks of silly merriment quickly fade into a sinister tradition called the "Piper's Procession of Ghouls and Goblins."

In the gloom of twilight, glowing and ghastly faces, which have been carved wickedly out of large pumpkins and Scottish mangelwurzels, are stabbed onto the sharp points of spears and long pikes carried by several dark-robed priests. Then a funeral parade, led by the fair's "Pied Piper," winds its way through the fairgrounds' darkened streets and alleyways while the Piper plays sorrowful notes on a flute recorder of yellowed bone. The fair's shops, stands, and booths all close as if to keep out the evil spirits who are passing by. Every year, enthusiastic spectators— the brave few people who haven't yet left the fair and trudged out to their cars to drive home—join in the funeral march, intermingling themselves with the dark-robed priests and carrying watchmen's lanterns, candles, and torches to help light the way. After a dozen mournful twists and turns, the ominous procession finally reaches its end—the "Hanging Tree," a giant and shadowy ash tree, which stands alone in a clearing at the center of the fairgrounds. There, in the flicker of crude torchlight and lanterns, the dark-robed priests silently mount the low platform under the Hanging Tree. They remove the carved jack-o'-lanterns from the points of the spears and pikes and arrange them for the gathered crowd of onlookers to see. The procession's Pied Piper, dressed in a blood-red leather waistcoat and with the black hood of an executioner placed over his head, chooses two of the best-carved jack-o'-lanterns as the procession's victims. The Piper then turns to the crowd, and in a nasty but rhythmic voice, chants the ancient "Piper's Curse."

In 1284,
The Piper did appear,
Clothed in pied colours,
And grinning ear to ear.
Children born in Hamelin
Loved his piping sound.
Those charmed by his playing,
Now lie buried in the ground.

Pumpkin heads and vigil prayers
To spare the axe and noose,
Fail to keep you safe, you see,
When the Piper's on the loose.
So dig your grave with haste,
And bow your mournful head.
The Piper's just approaching,
And the Piper wants you dead!

The Piper then lifts the two chosen jack-o'-lanterns high into the air, one at a time, for all to see. The excited spectators "condemn" both lanterns to grisly fates with shouts of "give it the rope!" for one and "give it the axe!" for the other. For the sad ghoul doomed to be "hung," the shrouded Piper runs a knotted rope through its carved face, tosses the rope's other end over a lofty limb of the Hanging Tree and hoists it up, until the unlucky ghoul is twisting and turning high above the wooden platform. Suddenly, the Piper lets the rope go. The plummeting jack-o'-lantern smashes open its skull on the hard planks below. The crowd cheers. For the ghoul sentenced to the axe, the Piper sets its bodiless head on a knee-high block of grey cork oak, takes up a stained, two-handed woodman's axe, and brutally chops the grinning head to pieces.

Even before the slaughter is finished, those in the crowd who faithfully remember begin wildly reciting a medieval chant:

Onto the Dead go all estates,
Princes, prelates, and potentates!
Both rich and poor of all degree,
The fear of death disturbeth thee!

Indeed, as the marketing brochures for the Will-o'-the-Wisp Medieval Fair claim, "Fair maidens beware! All was not always merry in merry old England."

Nicolas Bennett had been to the Will-o'-the-Wisp Medieval Fair once.

The year before, after Nicolas' birthday party finished at 3 o'clock, Mr. Bennett had taken Nicolas and one of his schoolmates, Jonathan Cranston, to the fair, and they stayed for the Piper's Procession of Ghouls. The spectacle had been frightening but exciting at the same time. Now, as the Bennett family drove quietly through the autumn woods and south along Earl Henry's Drive, Nicolas imagined the Piper's iron axe crashing again and again through the madly grinning pumpkin head while the crowd repeated, *Onto the Dead go all estates…*

Delightful chills ran up his spine as the Bennetts' truck pulled into a grassy parking area. He wondered if they would stay long enough to watch the Piper's Procession again this year.

His parents' long silence on the drive out to the fair had felt uneasy. After the brief bit of laughter at the end of lunch, they hadn't said anything to each other or to him. Nicolas couldn't remember a time when his father and mother weren't constantly talking and laughing with each other, but as of late, their conversations had become progressively shorter and more tense. They always seemed to be arguing about Aunt Harriet or money. Nicolas often felt lonely and worried. Now, as the Bennetts wound their way through other parked cars on their way to the ticket gate, Nicolas wished he could have at least brought Jonathan. Someone to talk to and run around with.

After a brief wait in line behind an elfish princess and her parents (an elfish princess wearing a less-than-elfish pink pair of muck boots, woolen mittens, a scarf, and an earflap hat resembling a pink penguin), the Bennetts made their way through the "Olde Castle Gate" and into the fairgrounds. A large outdoor fountain, the so-called "Fountain of Fairies," stood in front of them with lanes leading to the left and to the right. A troupe of spangled gypsies was clapping their hands and dancing wildly for a small crowd. A colorfully costumed court jester was alternatingly a juggling act with passing out parchment-style papers, entitled "Mappe of Will-o'-the-Wisp Medieval Faire," to passers-by.

"Dad, can I have one?" asked Nicolas.

"Sure. Grab one for yer mum and me, too."

Nicolas waited until the jester had caught all three juggling pins and then asked for two maps. He handed one to his mum and began scanning the other for things to do. "We've just eaten," she said. "So maybe something fun to do?" She looked at him. "Would ya like to try your hand at the archery butts, my boy?" She pulled back an imaginary bow and said, "Pow!" with a quick wink and a smile.

Mr. Bennett interrupted before Nicolas could say anything. "I think they charge per arrow, Sarah."

"Oh," she said, and dropped her imaginary bow in defeat. "Well, maybe not archery, then." They all stood there quietly for a few moments. He didn't want to, but Nicolas suddenly felt cross. He felt frustrated. He felt like his twelfth birthday was meaningless. He felt like going home. He stared at the gypsies, wishing he could join them. Wishing he could disappear.

Nicolas caught his father looking at him.

Peter Bennett's face was slightly drawn and anxious. "Perhaps we can catch the show at 2 o'clock at the Lancaster Castle stage," he said gently, pointing to the map's schedule of events. "It says three Pendle Witches will be on trial for heresy and murder, and," he added a bit sheepishly, "I think it's a free show." Nicolas could sense his father's embarrassment.

As suddenly as he'd felt angry, he now felt sorry. Perhaps today had been somewhat strange. Perhaps his birthday wasn't all that great this year, and perhaps there wasn't enough money for a party, but he hated to see his father look hurt. "Sounds good, dad," he said.

"Yeah?" His father lifted his eyebrows.

"It'll be smashing, Dad," Nicolas said as cheerily as he could. "Besides," he added with a sly look, "*this* is a place with dragons, right?"

Oddly, Mr. Bennett's face darkened for a brief moment. "Right," he said hesitantly. "Right. A place with dragons."

Mrs. Bennett was looking curiously at her husband and son, but neither said anything more. "Nicolas?"

"Yes, mum?"

"What would *you* like to do?" She was smiling her wonderful Irish smile again.

"Well…," he mumbled while drumming his fingers on his lips. Given the chance, Nicolas wanted to run around, watch knights joust, try on a shiny coat of mail in one of the armorer's shops, look at the swords and daggers made by the bladesmiths, eat a bowl of sliced apples and cheese, and drink mulberry ale (which was really sweetened mulberry juice). He didn't want to start an argument, but he wanted to have fun. *It's my birthday*, he thought, which made him a little sad. A moment later, he thought, *I'm a wren*, and he smiled back at his mum. "May I go look at the swords?" Before his parents could answer, Nicolas added, "I can meet you and Dad later, okay?"

His mother looked at him and nodded slightly. She seemed to understand. "Okay," she said. "Peter, do ya think that'll be okay?"

"Sure," his father said in agreement. Suddenly, Mr. Bennett tilted his head slightly, put his hand on Nicolas' shoulder, and took a long look at him. He took in a deep breath as if he was about to say something of great importance. "Ya know what, son? You go and have a good time." He held out a five-pound note. "It's yer birthday, lad, and I'm having trouble remembering that today. Yer mum and I will walk about and see what there is ta see. You go and 'ave fun." He glanced at Nicolas' mother, and she nodded her head in return. "Go and 'ave fun, son, and we'll plan on meetin' you back here at about 5 o'clock for the Piper's Procession. How does that sound?"

"Smashing, dad!" Nicolas stuffed the five-pound note in his

trouser pocket and rolled up his parchment map in one hand. "Back here at five," he repeated over his shoulder as he took off at a brisk walk.

"And be careful!" Mr. Bennett called after him, but Nicolas was already gone.

———●●———

Nicolas didn't have a specific plan in mind, but taking a look at the bladesmiths' swords and daggers *did* sound like a good start. He took a quick left near Longshank's Stage and headed up Alewife's Alley in the direction of the bladesmith shops on Robin's Row. A crowd, gathering outside the Cock & Bull Pub while waiting in line for "pints of bitter" and cheese and pickle sandwiches made with thick "doorstop" slices of toasted bread, blocked his progress. Nicolas pulled up near a "Lucky Post," a ten-foot post of silver birch which passers-by would touch or knock for good luck. The line for the pub was rapidly slowing down the press of people walking up and down Alewife's Alley, and the resulting mob seemed too thick to push through. Nicolas lifted his woolen cap and pulled his fingers through his corkscrew hair. *Stone the crows*, Nicolas thought. *Wish I was bigger.* His wiry frame was great for a footrace, but it wasn't much for pushing through crowds of grown-ups. He looked around for another way to go.

To his right was an off-set fence with a sign nailed on it, declaring in painted, red letters, "The Merry King's Staff ONLY." Nicolas looked to his left. There was a thick stand of wild crabapple trees crammed between two shops. From walks he had taken with his father, Nicolas knew the trees were likely to have thorns, and besides, there didn't look to be any way through them. Except...

Nicolas narrowed his eyes and looked more closely.

He hadn't seen it at first, but branches from two of the trees formed a natural arch. It appeared as if a faint footpath lay between them.

Nicolas looked around. No one else seemed to notice the footpath. Everyone was doing their jolly best to jostle through the muddling crowd of people heaving about outside the Cock & Bull Pub. Nicolas glanced back at the footpath. He blinked a few times. The footpath disappeared, but after a few seconds, he could make it out again even more clearly than before.

Suddenly, it occurred to him to take a look at the map still gripped tightly in his right hand. He quickly shook it open and turned it around a few different ways, looking carefully at all the street names, and at the shops located on Alewife's Alley. At one point, the map was almost stripped out of his hands when a passing lord's cloak caught its corner. After several wasted minutes, Nicolas finally gave up. The footpath wasn't on the map.

Well, he said to himself, summoning up a sense of adventure, *it looks about right for a wren.*

He waited for a pause in the slapdash rush of people and practically leapt from the comparative safety of his spot by the Lucky Post. He stayed light on his toes and managed to evade being squashed by two bearded men wearing horned helmets, who were recklessly banging together their shields as they strode along. A second later, he ducked his head just in time before becoming wrapped up in a long scarlet banner, which was being energetically waved about by a knight, loudly announcing his victory at the Battle of St. James. Finally, within a few feet of the footpath, Nicolas made a desperate lunge forward, nearly catching a face full of thorny branches and leaves in return. He dodged left at the last minute as his feet carried him from Alewife's Alley, through the arched limbs, and to the safety of the footpath beyond.

Nicolas jogged a few more steps, stopped, and looked over his shoulder. The footpath's opening appeared even smaller from this vantage. The stand of thorny crabapple trees was curiously dense, and it gave the effect of a narrow tunnel. Nicolas watched as half a dozen people strode by the opening, but no one followed him. They didn't give any pause to the footpath he had found.

Nicolas turned his head and looked further up the path. It was relatively clear of underbrush, and the press of trees seemed to open up a bit a little further on. *A few steps more, and Bob's your uncle,* he thought, snapping his fingers crisply, *I'll be walking up Robin's Row.*

Wanting to make the most of the shortcut he'd discovered, he set off at a gentle trot.

***

Nicolas' hiking boots were an old pair of Malhams his father had bought a few years before from a boot maker in Yorkshire. Their sturdy rubber soles were always fairly quiet, but within the muffle of the woodland trees, and along the footpath's bed of loamy soil, damp leaves, and spongy moss, his boots didn't make any sound at all. Out of a habit borrowed from his father, Nicolas instinctively named the different trees as he soundlessly passed them by. Slender alder trees with brilliant yellow and orange leaves. Robinson crabapple trees with remarkably pink blooms. Wild cherry trees with purplish-brown bark. Blackthorn trees with clusters of blue-black berries. And moor birch trees papered with stiff curls of dull, greyish-white bark.

He had taken only fifty strides or so before the footpath took a sharp right turn. Fifteen paces further on, it slowly began to curve back to the left. Just as the trees began to thin, the footpath wended its way through thickly growing bracken ferns. The ferns grew almost as high as Nicolas' waist. The denseness

41

of their broad, triangular fronds forced him to slow his pace to a walk to avoid losing sight of the path underneath. At one point, he had to leap forward, narrowly avoiding tromping through a shallow brook of water which crossed the path. A few steps later, Nicolas almost bolted in the opposite direction. A grey squirrel raced out from the undergrowth, chattering angrily before it disappeared just as quickly back into the cover of the ferns.

The footpath continued to switch back and forth, and by now, Nicolas wasn't entirely sure he was still headed toward Robin's Row. Eventually, the undergrowth of thick ferns came to an end, and Nicolas trudged up a slight rise. On the downhill side, he could see the path bend to the right and disappear again into another thick stand of trees.

This patch of woods seemed far larger and deeper than it should've been if it was only a thin ribbon of trees between Alewife's Alley and Robin's Row. The map of the fair had shown a stretch of woods between the two lanes, even though it hadn't shown the footpath, but Nicolas felt like he'd been walking for at least twenty minutes. Frowning, he looked back. Because the thicket of ferns hid the footpath, and because he hadn't looked up very much as he'd been walking through them, he wasn't exactly sure of the direction from which he'd just come. This made him feel slightly nervous. *Like the breadcrumbs are gone*, he thought. To add to his growing uneasiness, he now realized how quiet the woods were. He couldn't hear any voices, or the shuffle of any feet, or any of the sounds associated with the fair. They had simply disappeared.

Something didn't feel right.

Stone the crows, Nicolas thought for the second time that day, *now what?*

He looked back up the path toward the thick stand of trees.

He stood there for a moment, debating whether to turn back or to carry on when his eye caught something moving along the ground. More pointedly, it was hopping on the path. Curious, Nicolas took a few cautious steps down the slope to have a better look.

It was a bird.

Instinctively, Nicolas flinched and immediately looked skyward. It was empty. Not a bird, not a crow, in sight. He let out a nervous laugh. "Guess that ol' crow made me a bit jumpy," he muttered quietly. He took in a deep breath and let it out. He looked down the footpath.

The bird stood there, cocking its head from side to side. It had pale brown upperparts, a dirty-white chin and throat, and black spots on its mottled underside. A small sprig of lime-green mistletoe was clenched in its short, pointed beak, which triggered Nicolas' memory. The bird, he realized, was a mistle thrush. It took a few more hops forward, and then, in a very odd fashion, stopped and looked back at him. Nicolas took another few steps forward, and the bird repeated its bizarre mannerism, hopping forward, and stopping to look back at him.

"Do you want me to follow you?"

The bird again tilted its head from side-to-side and hopped forward again. Its glossy, black eyes stared back at Nicolas.

"Alright," said Nicolas. "You have the lead, Mr. Thrush."

What a strange, strange birthday, he thought to himself as he slowly followed the bird down the footpath. *A thrush leading a lost wren*. Nicolas couldn't help but smile, and he promptly felt better. A few hops and steps later, the bird and boy faded into the deep shadows of the great canopy overhead.

CHAPTER 4

A Cottage in
the Woods

s far back as Nicolas could remember, he felt at home in the woods. When he was still a "wee lively lad" (as his father often said), he would join his father for walks through the stretch of woodlands bordering the Bennetts' small sheep pasture. He came to know them well, and those woods had become a second home for Nicolas. They were a place he could go to be alone and feel free at the same time. Two years ago, when his parents had transferred Nicolas from the North Lakes School to Hunter Hall, an esteemed preparatory school situated in Frenchfield Farm outside of Penrith, Nicolas had spent time in the woods almost every day after school. The initial stress of missing old friends, the awkwardness of trying to make new ones, and the uncertainty of new surroundings, had been difficult for him. Eventually, he had come to love Hunter Hall, but in the beginning, the sanctuary of the woodlands had given him a private refuge where he could have time to be alone, to think, and to be himself.

In the thick of the trees, anything could happen. Nicolas would pretend to be Little John, daring to fight Robin Hood with wooden quarter-staffs over the little brook which meandered through the woods. He would be the brave Lord Gilpin, saving terrified villagers by hunting down and killing the ferocious, wild boar of Westmorland. He would take a crooked stick in his hand and become the mysterious wizard, who was said to live in the woods outside the Cheshire village of Alderley, ready to summon King Arthur and his valiant knights out of eternal sleep to defend England from destruction.

But just as often as pursuing games of swordplay and wizardry, Nicolas would simply sit quietly, leaning against the enormous trunk of his favorite English elm tree—a tree his father had named the "Red Deer Tree" because of a small herd of does and fawns he had once spotted gathering under its branches. "They came there to visit and rest," his father had told him with a serious voice. "A tree like that has become rare in England, my boy, and the animals know how special 'tis." As Nicolas would relax against the elm's corky bark, he would close his eyes. He could listen to the calls of conversing swallows, the extravagant songs of flying larks, and the chirps of busy bush warblers. He imagined he was a crafty red fox, skillfully hunting rabbits through the trees, or a sharp-toothed pine marten, running expertly along high branches on the hunt for birds, berries, or honey. He listened to tens of thousands of leaves, rustling, cracking, and whispering to each other in gentle breezes. More than once, Nicolas had fallen asleep in the woods, curled up fitfully on a litterfall of small twigs, rotten leaves, and old bark. The vague calls of his mum, telling him supper was ready, would wake him up and hurry him home.

Now, as he walked down the footpath behind the hopping mistle thrush, Nicolas found himself relishing the cool and quiet of these woods, too. The stand of trees they'd entered was mostly made of grand English Oaks. The trees each had colossal trunks and vast crowns of craggy and rugged branches. Their bark was mossy grey and covered with leafy and shrubby lichen, which made the trees look as if they were sporting ragged beards. Their leaves, still deep green, created an impenetrable canopy overhead, which caused Nicolas' eyes to have to adjust

45

to the wood's gloominess. Nicolas noticed the ground on either side of the footpath was almost entirely covered with thick, spongy moss. It looked like an endless heavy carpet, rising and falling with the odd-shaped bulges, swells, knobs, lumps, and bumps caused by roots, rocks, and burrows lying underneath. English ivy dressed the base of some of the trees and in other places entirely hid old stumps. The footpath, while not quite muddy, appeared to be damper under the trees, and after a few yards, it also became narrower. Nicolas found himself almost needing to place one foot immediately in front of the other to stay on its slender course.

Eventually, the slope of the ground led them down to a dry streambed. Nicolas paused while the thrush deftly hopped its way over the shallow channel, up the opposing bank, and over the lip of another gentle rise. The autumn air was even cooler inside the shaded woods. Nicolas turned up the collar of his waxed cotton jacket and pulled his knit cap further down over his ears. He stood there with his arms over his chest for a moment to capture a bit of warmth and watched his warm breath puff out in quickly fading clouds. "For queen and country," he said amusingly to himself and jabbed his right arm into the air as he charged over the streambed and scrambled up the embankment to catch up to the bird.

By this time, the thrush was confidently hopping along, no longer pausing to see if Nicolas was trailing behind. It had kept the sprig of mistletoe in its beak and occasionally wiggled it in such a way, it made Nicolas think of Thomas, the Bennetts' cat, wiggling its nose.

What a funny bird, thought Nicolas. *It seems to have a better idea of where it's going than I do.* No sooner had he thought this than the thrush flew into the air and came to rest on a crooked oak branch. For a second, Nicolas thought his guide might fly away, but the thrush just sat there and wriggled its sprig of mistletoe one more time.

"Are we there yet?" asked Nicolas cheerily.

The thrush looked back at him silently, and to his utter surprise, bobbed its head as if nodding.

"Ha!" Nicolas laughed aloud. "You are a sharp little thing, aren't you?" he said, shoving his hands in his jacket pockets. "Alright, Mr. Thrush, *where* are we?"

The bird canted its head to the left and stared down at Nicolas with its shiny left eye for several ticks. It then drew itself up, hopped two feet along the branch, and vanished inside a large, weathered birdhouse. The birdhouse was partially hidden in a fork of several smaller branches. A birdhouse, nestled away in a giant oak, hidden deep within a dark stretch of woods, and occupied by an extraordinarily peculiar bird, was the last thing Nicolas expected to see.

Until he saw the sign.

As Nicolas stared at the weather-beaten birdhouse, a worn and battered sign materialized just below it. In fact, the craggy sign hung almost directly over the footpath, but like the birdhouse, it seemed to blend in with the trees. It consisted of a single cracked board, about the size of a license plate, suspended from the birdhouse branch only by what appeared to be several thick braids of ivy vines. An abundance of small greenish-yellow flowers along the ivy vines further masked the split gray board.

Nicolas took a couple of steps toward the sign to see whether he could read anything written on it. After several moments of straining his eyes, several letters began to appear, carved into its surface. Nicolas glanced around his feet and found a fallen branch. Using it to lift away the ivy's blooms, he could see two exposed words.

"The Knothole," he read aloud.

He didn't recall seeing any shop named The Knothole on the map of the Will-o'-the-Wisp fair, but then a simple idea struck him and gave him some relief. Perhaps the fairgrounds included this footpath once upon a time, and perhaps there had been a shop called The Knothole in this same place. Once the shop was abandoned, perhaps it had rotted and fallen apart, and eventually been covered by the moss, leaving only its old shop-sign as a sort of gravestone. The birdhouse, Nicolas guessed, must've been built long ago by the shop's keeper.

He jammed his hands deeper into the warmth of his pockets, pleased with his detective work. The time it had taken to walk from Alewife's Alley to this stand of gloomy woods still didn't make much sense, but that now seemed to be a minor point. Nicolas felt confident he would find Robin's Row soon enough if he kept to the footpath.

"What do you think, Mr. Thrush?" Nicolas asked, looking back at the birdhouse. The thrush poked its head out, took a sharp look at Nicolas, and ducked inside again. *No worries,* thought Nicolas, looking back at the sign, *at least I don't feel so lost anymore.*

"Are you coming with me," he called out, "or have you arrived home for the evening?" The thrush didn't pop his head out this time, and Nicolas pressed his lips together. "Well," he said with a polite nod to his feathered companion, "thank you all the same for your company, Mr. Thrush."

Nothing for it but to press on, he thought and began walking once again down the footpath.

After another fifty paces, he could see the footpath bend to the right, leading around the mammoth trunk of a dark and twisted tree. As Nicolas trudged around the turn, the most surprising thing—out of an already peculiar day—lay about one hundred feet in front of him. In fact, he stopped so abruptly in mid-stride, he nearly lost his balance. A mere one hundred paces away, the footpath came to a sudden, and bewildering, end. Instead of turning out to be an unused shortcut to Robin's Row, the wily footpath simply came to a dead stop—like a short sidewalk leading to a front door—at a rickety-looking, slapdash, haphazard set of old, wooden steps, which zigged, then zagged, ten feet up into the air, arriving unexpectedly at the front of a small cottage, which had somehow been built into the broad fork of the most gigantic and knobby-knobbed oak tree Nicolas had ever seen.

The cottage was ramshackle and awkwardly constructed. It had a narrow, covered porch with curled floorboards and an unruly railing of entwined branches and dried vines. On it sat a little rocking chair also made of woven branches. The cottage's doorway—an odd door painted with shiny red paint—was partially open, and Nicolas could see a faint glow coming from inside. Its roof was covered by a blanket of moss much like what covered the forest floor. A smooth rock chimney rose up crookedly out of the mossy roof with soft tendrils of greyish white smoke floating out of it. The entire cottage seemed to lean a little to the left, while the tree in which it sat was so bulbous and contorted, it looked more like a colossal mushroom with branches and leaves.

Nicolas honestly did not know what to do. For several seconds, he kept gawking at the treehouse cottage in confusion. *Stone the crows!* he finally thought in frustration… for the third time that day. *What is this place?* Before he could think anything more, much less decide what to do, he heard singing, coming from behind the gigantic, gnarled tree.

How far is it to Babylon?

How far away you say?
Is the distance a thousand leagues,
Or is it but an inch away?

How far is it to Babylon?
How far away you say?
Why would you walk a thousand leagues,
When it's three barleycorn away?!

On the last line, "when it's three barleycorn away" (which was more shouted than sung), a little man appeared, strolling merrily around the foot of the tree. He was bald and wearing an eyepiece—a gentleman's monocle—over his right eye, which was secured by a slender, golden cord to the hefty, loop of a silver earring, dangling from the outer edge of his right ear. His nose was large and hovered imperiously over a most extraordinary moustache. The ends of the moustache, which must've been at least two feet long, were braided, and small silver bells were tied to each of the braids' ends. The miniature bells rang freely as he walked, but instead of the high tin-like jingle one might expect, they each gave off a deeper, melodious sound.

The little man was shirtless, although he wore a cloak fastened around his neck and draped down his back, which looked to be made of goatskin. For his size—no more than Nicolas' own height—he appeared to have broad, muscular shoulders, a stout, hairless chest, and a belly that was clearly strong even though it was also very round. Across the equatorial curve of his belly was a colorful and strange-looking tattoo, which immediately reminded Nicolas of the face of the antique, brass compass his father always kept on a watch-chain in his pocket. The little man's burly forearms were hairy, and his fists looked to be the size of small hams. In his right one, he carried a bulging burlap sack, and in his left, he carried a stout-looking spade.

He had a thick leather belt around his waist, buckled with a substantial bit of black metal. The belt held up trousers which were tucked into a pair of stocky boots. Nicolas took all this in within a few moments as the little man made his way over the mossy forest floor and to the foot of the rickety stairway.

◆━◆━◆

Still frozen where he stood, Nicolas watched the little man plant his right foot firmly on the first step and calmly looked over his shoulder.

"I'm fairly puckled, lad," the little man said in an odd, but Scottish-like, accent. He pointed with his spade in the direction of the cottage's doorway. "Thar's a warm fire inside, and if yer so inclined, ye can falla me in."

Nicolas, in spite of his good manners, couldn't think of how to respond. He just stood there with wide eyes, staring at the little man, the peculiar cottage, the rickety stairs, and the fantastically fat tree. The little man stared back. After several long moments, Nicolas (with eyes still wide) finally managed to nod his head.

"A nod," the little man said, "is only as good as winkin' at a blind harse. Doos yer noddin' mean yer comin'?"

Nicolas' throat felt a bit dry. He swallowed. "I'm sorry, sir. I… I don't know…." his voice faded away.

The little man nodded thoughtfully, turned, and began climbing the stairs. "Quit standin' thar noddin' yer head, lad, an' c'mon." He reached the top of the stairs and turned around. The little man waved his arm. "C'mon, laddy. I got us a bag o' taddies ta fry oop with some onion, butter, an' griddle cakes." He smiled a great smile beneath his extraordinary moustache. "An' as delicious as it sounds, ye can tek my word fer it, it's better when it's in yer belly." The little man laughed.

Nicolas took a deep breath. Almost with a mind of their own, his feet began walking toward the rickety stairs. When Nicolas

51

got there, he stopped. It wasn't so much the ramshackle-look of the stairway that made him hesitate. (After all, twelve-year-old boys don't give much pause for safety's sake). He hesitated out of *disbelief.* Even though they were sitting in front of him, the existence of the rickety stairs, and the cottage perched in the tree, and the little bespectacled man were so strange, so remarkably peculiar, Nicolas felt as if they all might vanish.

"Dinnae worry," laughed the little man. "These stairs are nothin' fer a malinky longlegs lak *you.*" When he said the word, *you,* the little man pushed his lips out from underneath his abundant moustache and left them there for a moment, puckering them. He stared keenly through his monocle at Nicolas, and then, almost too quietly to hear, whispered, "Adventure always begins by takin' a wee step far'ard, lad."

Nicolas looked down at the old wooden step in front of him and then up at the little man. *I'm a wren, and today,* he thought with a sudden sense of majestic resolve, *I'm a king.*

The idea felt a little foolish, but foolish or not, it gave Nicolas a warm sense of daring. He stood on the first step. Then another. And one by one, he climbed to the top.

"Aha! Looks like ye 'ave company, lad," said the little man, looking past Nicolas, as he reached the top step. The boy turned his head and looked back down the rickety stairs. There, three steps down, stood the Mistle Thrush.

"Mr. Thrush!" said Nicolas in cheery surprise. The bird bobbed its head and looked back at him with its shiny black eyes.

"What, what?" asked the little man. "No, no, laddy. T'ain't no thrush. That wee thing is Magnus Mungo Macaroobie, tho' I jess call 'im Magnus because it puckles me ta say his 'ole name. He's a *kelpie,* lad, a water spirit who came outta the dry stream ye crossed back along ta path. When it dried oop, Magnus shifted inta a baird, an' now e's stuck thatta way." The little man put the back of his hand to the side of his mouth and said, "I think 'e meant ta change inta a harse, but knowin' Magnus, 'e got lazy an' dinnae keep shiftin'." This last sentence was a loud whisper, which clearly Magnus the thrush heard. It hopped up and down and rapped its small beak indignantly against the wooden step until it had wedged it firmly into a crack. The irritated bird wiggled back and forth and eventually sprang itself free.

"A t'ousand pardons, Magnus," said the little man gravely, bowing with a sweep of his arm, but as he said this, he winked slyly at Nicolas and began laughing until he was wiping tears from his eyes. "C'mon to ya both!" he called out as he ducked merrily inside the cottage. "These taddies woont fry themselves without a pan and a hot fire!"

In spite of himself, and in spite of the absurdity of it all, Nicolas couldn't help but laugh, too. A few hops and steps later, the boy and bird also ducked inside the little man's merry tree cottage, as the woods outside fell quiet and dark in the gloom of an early twilight.

———◆———

A malevolent shadow, unseen by the boy, the bird, or the little man, sat perched high up in the mammoth, dark and twisted tree just down the narrow path. Faint sounds of laughter wended their way through the forest's murky nightfall. It beat its black wings, glowering at the merry tree cottage with beady eyes.

The shadow cracked its sharp beak against the tree in anger. Its warning had been ignored. The boy-king had found the door.

CHAPTER 5

✝HE IROn DOOR

Inside the happy cottage, supper was as the little man promised—ruddy potatoes, sliced and fried in butter with sweet
onions, tiny leaves of thyme, and coarse ground salt and pepper, all of which was swimming in a delicious bacon gravy.

The little man busied himself, skipping about his cottage,
stoking the fire, and nursing the deep iron skillet that sat over
a grate in the small cottage's fireplace. The entire time, he kept
Nicolas—and Magnus the thrush, who sat contentedly next
to Nicolas on a low bench near the hearth—entertained with
wild stories about the woods, here and there interrupted by
silly jokes, which always seemed to make the little man laugh
until tears trickled down his crimson-tinged cheeks. He served
up supper in tin plates with flat griddle cakes, that could be
broken apart to use as dippers and scoops. Magnus enjoyably
pecked away at a pile of assorted seeds the little man set next to
him, then hopped onto the little man's lap when the last seed
had been swallowed. Nicolas, who hadn't realized how hungry
he was until the smell of frying onions and potatoes had filled
the cottage, tucked into the warm food as if he hadn't had a
bite all day.

After supper was eaten—with three steaming helpings for
Nicolas—and the empty plates were tossed into the skillet, the
little man poured hot apple cider into two clay mugs, spiced
them with sticks of cinnamon, and sat back in a small armchair
by the fire. He kicked off his boots, propped up his feet on a

stool, and waggled his fat toes while quietly sipping his drink. For the first time that evening, he fell silent.

Nicolas sat on a low wooden bench pulled near the fire, listening to the cold breeze outside rustle and swish through the great oak's branches, and watching the fire's hot flames spark and crackle, slowly breaking apart the charring logs one at a time. The pleasant fire reminded him of the fireplace in his father's study, and with a start, he sat up, worried about the late hour.

The little man turned his head and gave Nicolas a knowing look. "Dunna worry aboot yer home, lad," he said steadily. "It'll stay wer it always was, an' it'll still be thar fer ye when ye return." He leaned back and gazed into the flames. "*Time*, ya see, flows a bit different in these woods."

Nicolas didn't reply. He slowly settled back onto the bench, baffled by the little man's comment, a comment that had seemed to read his mind. *I don't suppose it's really* that *late. I can't have been here too long*, he thought. Nicolas looked out of the cottage's dirty windows. It was dark outside, and little could be seen. *Must be storm clouds*, he mused. *It can't be that late*, he thought again, but this time, he couldn't help but feel a bit more worried.

"I'm not readin' yer mind," said the little man matter-of-factly, as if that was exactly what he was doing. "It's easy ta guess what yer thinkin', lad, but ya needn't be troubled. Ye are *where* yer supposed ta be an' *when* yer supposed ta be, but …," he paused thoughtfully and reached for a pipe lying on a shelf close by, "I imagine that'll merit some explainin'."

He packed his pipe carefully, lit it with a glowing twig plucked from the fire, and eased back, puffing away until pipe-smoke gently circled his bald head. "The fact is, lad, I was expectin' ye fer supper. I asked Magnus," and here, the bird looked up and bowed its small head at Nicolas, "ta make sure ye found yer way here. Ta path narrows a bit, and these woods can be a bit dark an' dodgy at times. In any case," he gave his pipe three good puffs, "yer here now, an' lak I said, that merits some explanation." The little man paused, puffed his pipe a bit more, and looked at Nicolas as if waiting for a reply.

***

Nicolas' mum, Sarah Bennett, had always said one of Nicolas' most admirable traits was that he kept his mouth shut until he had something to say. "An unusual quality for children," she'd say to him with her delightful smile, cupping his face in her warm hands. This evening, as he sat listening to the remarkable little man, Nicolas stayed true to form. He couldn't think of anything to say, so he kept quiet.

After a few moments had passed, the little man slowly nodded his head and continued. "I am Baatunde, which means," he paused for full effect, "*Return of the Father.*" Baatunde leaned forward and stuck out his hand. Politely, Nicolas shook it.

"I'm Nicolas."

"Well, 'o course yer Nicolas!" laughed the little man. "Who *else* would ye be?" He settled back, chuckling to himself and puffing his pipe. "Ma name is Baatunde and that is who I am," he said again, as if it were the beginning of a story, "an' I'm not from 'ere, although I've been 'ere, in yer world, a long, long time. I arrived aboot seventy-two years ago, long before ye were even baern." He waved his hand about. The pipe smoke swept away and gathered itself among the ceiling's eaves. "I arrived long before much was 'ere, 'cept these woods an' ta footpath. I 'aven't had too many visitors, my boy, but," he chuckled, "I keep ma own time, an' I daenna mind ma own company." Saying this, Baatunde stared into the fire for a long time, sometimes muttering to himself and sometimes puffing vigorously on his pipe.

Finally, Magnus pecked at the little man's hand. "Ouch!" He winced, glancing over at Nicolas. "Apologies, ma boy. I'm not the lively young man I used ta be. Sometimes ma t'oughts choose thar own path." Sighing, he said with a smile, "These past eleven years an' a day, I've been waitin' fer *you*, Nicolas, ta arrive fer supper."

As bewildered as Nicolas felt, he also, curiously, felt safe.

"Ya see, ma boy, I'm a *Gatekeeper* o' sorts, like ta rest o' me family, an' it's long been our job ta look after t'ings, an' ta make sure ta right t'ings pass troo ta Iron Door, an' ta wrong t'ings stay put. Yer world, like ma own, has *doors* in it, so ta speak, an' t'ings can travel troo those doors." He took several gulps of cider and puffed his pipe briskly, softly ringing the silver bells at the end of his moustache.

Nicolas didn't want to sound dumb, but finally, he spoke. "I don't think I understand, Mr. Baatunde. What '*doors*'?"

"Hmmm," Baatunde pondered , "well, 'doors' is per'aps not ta best word, but…." He interrupted himself, pouring more hot cider into his mug. "I 'ave ta admit, lad, I 'aven't 'ad ta explain it before this." Saying that, Baatunde threw his bald head back and laughed. "I guess it all sounds a bit daff. Here, let me try it another way. Imagine two worlds, lad. They sit next ta each other, like two lovebirds cleverly holdin' hands. They're different, but what affects one affects the other. If one lovebird cries, ta other lovebird cries. If one laughs, ta other laughs. If one sneezes, ta other gets wet. Thar separate but tangled, ya see? An' that's 'ow yer world an' ma world exist, like lovebirds 'oldin' 'ands."

At this, Baatunde stuck his pipe in his mouth and linked his hands together. "A door is lak these 'ands," he said through clenched teeth, "an' t'ings can move between ta worlds, lak a squeeze through a finger." He grabbed the bowl of his pipe with one hand and waved the other between Nicolas and himself. "So ya see, lad, ye an' I are sitting on ta tips o' one o' them fingers." His smile was so big, and self-gratifying, Nicolas couldn't help but smile back and nod his head, as if it all made sense.

"So," offered Nicolas hesitantly, "these woods are like a 'door' to another world."

"Not exactly," replied Baatunde, pursing his lips. "More precisely, ta door sitting over in that corner is *the* door, an' it doesn't jus' lead ta just any other world. It leads, my boy, ta *Telluric Grand.*"

When Baatunde said, "*Telluric Grand,*" he waved both his hands reverently in the air, as if he were actually going to conjure a strange world right out of the pipe-smoke hanging above him. Magnus stood up in Baatunde's lap, bobbed its head, shook out its tail-feathers, and settled back down.

Nicolas looked over Baatunde's shoulder for the door.

Shadowed silhouettes danced among the cottage's clutter of pots, a spare pair of boots, a woodsman's axe, a stack of ancient-looking books, a hunting knife stuck in a whittling stick, a loop of rope, a dented storm lantern, a large water pail, and Baatunde's cloak, among other odds and ends, all of which were hanging on pegs, or sitting on bowed shelves, or piled on the floor. Hidden partially behind the hanging cloak, Nicolas finally spotted the door. It wasn't really a proper door, set in a frame with a knob and hinges, but more like an oval hatch one might find aboard a ship. It was hard to see in the dim light, but the door looked to be made of thick, pitted black iron, reminding Nicolas of the deep cast-iron skillet in which his mum would make soft biscuits or fry up sausage or bacon. A single hinge—as large as a loaf of bread—was bolted to the wall. Four large bars crisscrossed the door in different directions and came together in its center. Engraved into each bar, and written with gold, Nicolas could see some kind of scrolled writing in bizarre letters. Where the bars crossed, like the hub of a wheel, was a thick-plated gear with six points. Like the bars, it also had a scrolled engraving inlaid with gold, but Nicolas could see this engraving more clearly, and its lettering was familiar. *Suthron,* he read silently to himself, although he didn't know what it meant.

"Oh," Nicolas finally said as he looked meekly back at Baatunde, who now had a strange look in his eye.

"Hmph," muttered Baatunde and began briskly puffing his pipe. After a few minutes passed, Baatunde pulled his pipe from his mouth and pointed its stem at Nicolas. "Ye 'ave no idea, do ya, lad?"

Perplexed, Nicolas asked, "What do you mean?"

"Ye 'ave been starin' at that t'ing fer at least an *hour*, lad!"

Nicolas tucked in his chin. "I have not!" he replied. "I only glanced at it."

"Glancin' suggests a short amount o' time, lad, boot ta t'ing aboot *Time* is that it can *stretch* from short ta long dependin' on *where* ye are."

"That makes no sense," said Nicolas. "I've been sitting right here!"

"Ha!" hooted Baatunde. "I know ya been sittin' right 'ere, boot that dinnae mean *Time* dinnae *stretch*." He wrinkled up his face and spread his little arms as far apart as they would go. "In a manner o' speakin', lad, jes ba lookin' at ta door, ye were in a place where Time slows down. It stretches out!" he exclaimed as he wiggled the tips of his fingers.

Nicolas' eyes were wide. He still didn't really understand what the little man was saying. "Have *I* stretched out?" he asked nervously.

"No! Bless ye!" roared Baatunde, who began slapping his knees in hearty peals of laughter. "Bless yer innocent 'art, lad!" He laughed so hard, the bells at the ends of his moustache suddenly became tangled. He tried to undo them in between guffaws, but by this time, he was nearly blind from the flood of tears, and he managed to make all of it worse by accidentally weaving his pipestem into the moustache's braids. By trying to disentangle his pipe, he showered hot embers all over his lap. Magnus, who had become alarmed when Baatunde began slapping his knees, now shot straight into the air, and beat its wings about Baatunde's bald head, squawking loudly with indignation. Baatunde leapt up, shaking the burning embers out of his lap and tried to ward off Magnus' battering. Almost instantly, the tangled ends of Baatunde's moustache caught the corner of his armchair, throwing him off balance. The little man crashed over the furniture into a heap of smoke, ashes, bells, and moustache braids.

"Codswallup!" Nicolas heard him declare in aggravation. Then, in a much more mournful voice, "I broke ma pipe. I broke ma pipe." Baatunde rolled over and slowly sat up, glumly showing Nicolas the pipe stem in one hand and the pipe bowl in the other. Nicolas helped the little man back up to his feet. He uprighted the overturned armchair into which Baatunde promptly plopped back down. Magnus, perhaps the wiser, perched on the thick mantle and preened his feathers.

"I'm sorry about your pipe," said Nicolas. He tried not to laugh himself when Baatunde had been flailing about and falling all over himself. But he was sorry the little man broke his pipe. "Do you have another?"

Baatunde's eyes lit up. "I do!" he shouted triumphantly and slammed a clenched fist into the palm of his hand. He hopped out of his seat and began rummaging through a beat-up tin that sat on a shelf near the mantle. Before long, he was proudly waving another pipe in the air. "Tickety-boo!" he shouted. "Tickety-boo! As long as I 'ave a pipe, ta laughter was worth ta misfortune."

Shortly, Baatunde had mushrooms of smoke issuing from the bowl of his newfound pipe, and he turned to Nicolas once again. "I realize what I'm sayin' is na easy, lad. Time is like a landscape, rollin' and changin' with mountains an' crags an' tricky moors. Quit thinkin' aboot Time as a long straight line which takes us from mornin' ta nightfall. It isn't. Instead, Lord Time curves an' winds an' rambles endlessly on, lak uneven cobbles pavin' a king's road."

He paused, pushing a few more smoky mushrooms out of his pipe. "T'ink of Time lak ta footpath ye were on, my boy. It moved ye for'ard even tho' it turned ye right an' left." Baatunde said this while waving an arm back and forth, snapping his fingers. "Time is not a matter o' evenly measured days, lad. It's na even a matter o' *direction*. It's a matter of *distance*. Distance that grows larger and squeezes smaller." By this time, the pipe smoke had grown so thick, Baatunde seemed to disappear with the end of his last sentence.

Nicolas turned and stared blankly into the fire, trying to make sense of what the little man was saying. *How can time not measure ... time?* he thought with some exasperation.

Baatunde's eyes appeared through the smoke. They looked round as tea saucers, and Nicolas leaned back. With a cagey whisper, the little man said, "Careful, laddy. Time is not whot it seems ta be. Everythin' ta do with Time," he said as his eyes vanished back into whorls of smoke "...depends entirely on where your feet stand."

Nicolas was unsure of what to say next. He felt uncomfortable, and he didn't dare look at the mysterious iron door again. Suddenly, he sat upright. "You said you have been '*waiting*' for me. What did you mean by that?"

Baatunde waved his hand, clearing some of the smoke away. "I *did* say that, didn't I. Well, lad," he paused, knocking the ash out of his pipe and into the fire's coals. "Lak I also said, I'm a gatekeeper o' sorts, an' that thar," he pointed a thick finger at the iron door, "is ma gate. As a gatekeeper, I've got an idea aboot those t'ings which need to pass through ma gate, an' those t'ings which should nat pass through." He grinned mischievously and winked. "An' *you*, ma boy, are one o' those t'ings which are meant ta pass through."

"Pass through?" asked Nicolas. "You mean *I'm* supposed to go through the door?" He felt a knot in his stomach. Part nervous and part excited.

"Hmmm." Baatunde looked at him with a raised eyebrow and cocking his head to one side. "Yer not a kelpie, lak Magnus o'er there, lad." He paused and stood up, placing both hands on his hips. "Ye are a … *wren*. I know it!"

Nicolas sat there in astonishment. "That's what I've been telling myself!" he practically shouted.

"I know, lad, an' yer as right as spring rain!"

"I've been telling myself I'm a wren today," said Nicolas. Then, shyly, "it's my birthday, you know."

"I know, lad! I know!" replied the little man, dancing about. He waved his arms in the air and laughed. "An' now yer here lak ya should be."

Nicolas swallowed, feeling nervous again. "What's through the door, Baatunde?"

"Telluric Grand is thru ta door, jus' lak I said."

"But I don't have time," Nicolas said, thinking of his parents and wondering if he was already late.

"O' course ye don't 'ave time, lad! No one *has* Time!" exclaimed Baatunde. The little man stopped dancing about and looked closely at the boy. "Dinnae worry, ma boy. Ta door will *give* ye Time. I promise. When ye return, I'll be 'ere, an' Magnus will be 'ere." He hesitated, taking a deep breath. "What do ya say, lad?"

Nicolas looked down at his boots. *I'm a wren*, he thought earnestly. *I'm a wren.* He looked up. "What's it look like inside?"

Baatunde's face fell. He spoke slowly—grimly—emphasizing each word with his thick, Scottish-like accent. "I won't lie to ye, ma boy. Beyond ta door, it's as blak as the Earl o' Hell's waistcoat." The little man clasped his hands tightly together. His eyes narrowed, and he looked about the small cottage suspiciously as if someone, or something, might be spying on them from the shadows. "An'," he added, quietly through gritted teeth, "'tis a place with *dragons*."

Nicolas stood to his feet, his shoulders tense. A light sweat broke out on his forehead. He dug a hand into his pocket and pulled out the coppery leaf. He held it up in front of the little man. "Have you ever seen one of these?"

Baatunde looked bleakly but steadily at the strange leaf. "Aye," he said. "That I 'ave."

Nicolas swallowed. "Does this come from the land beyond the door?"

Baatunde nodded slowly. "Aye. It does."

Nicolas could think of only one other question. It was almost a whisper. "Did you know my grandfather?"

The little man stared at the boy for a moment, but he didn't answer the question right away. Instead, he asked his own. "Ye 'ave a king's coin in yer pocket. Am I right, lad?"

Nicolas thought about the rocking horse crown coin—the coin with an image of St. George slaying a dragon he had taken from the chest in his attic bedroom. "Yes," he replied. "I do."

"So too did yer gran' pappie, my boy," Baatunde said quietly. "Ye are a wee wren, Nicolas, but," he lifted his chest and stood a bit straighter, "ye may also be a *king*." His voice sounded slightly sad but solemn, too. As he spoke, Nicolas felt a warm wave of courage inside him.

Grandfather Bennett must've been here. He must have gone through the iron door. He must have gone to the place with dragons.

"Alright," he said firmly. "I'll go."

Baatunde relaxed and broke into a warm smile. He settled back in his armchair. "Yer a jammy duffer, lad," he said, winking at Nicolas. He hit his knee with one of his ham-sized fists. "Now listen carefully. This is what ye must do. Ta open ta door, turn that grimlock—that's ta gear-lookin' t'ing on ta front o' ta door—*anti*-clockwise. It'll open on its own. An' when *that* 'appens, step on t'roo lak it was yer own front door."

Nicolas nodded nervously.

Baatunde waved Nicolas closer and cupped his hand next to his mouth. In a whisper, he said, "When yer t'roo, set out ta find a man named Aldus Ward. Show 'im what ye 'ave in yer pocket. 'E'll explain t'ings to ye, an' he'll know what ta do." Baatunde turned and sank back down in his armchair as if he was exhausted, but he also looked peaceful again. His eyes were lost in the fireplace's glowing embers, but in a low and steady voice, the little man shared one last thought. "Dinnae worry, Nicolas. I'll be 'ere when ye return."

Nicolas took a deep breath. He looked up at Magnus. The thrush still sat perched on the mantle. It looked back at the boy with shiny black eyes and gave him a simple nod.

The boy laced his boots tight and stood up. Purposefully, he turned toward the iron door and took a few steps forward. The cold, pitted iron of the gear-lock filled his hand. He turned it counterclockwise and let go.

Silently, the door swung open.

Before there was time to take a last look at the little man sitting by the fire, the boy was through the door. And gone.

CHAPTER 6

THE TALL MAN AND THE DONKEY

Not far from Nicolas' home in Plumpton Head, the River Eamont pours merrily out of the ribbon lake of Ullswater at the point where the lake is overlooked by the wooded bluff of Dunmallard Hill on which sits an ancient fort. Once free of the lake's boundaries, the River Eamont makes its way through the gentle county of Cumbria in northwestern England.

In late spring, Peter Bennett would sometimes take Nicolas to a favorite fishing spot outside the small hamlet of Eamont Bridge, situated south of Penrith, along the River Eamont's peaceful banks. They would spend the day fishing for brown trout and eating a picnic Mrs. Bennett had made of thick roast beef sandwiches and Nicolas' favorite cheese, Wookey Hole Cave Aged Farmhouse cheddar from Dorset. Nicolas loved to watch the clear water babble over the river's smooth gravel bed, and if the trout weren't biting, he and his father would roll up their pants' legs and wade about, splashing each other with the icy water and laughing.

On one such visit the year before, Mr. Bennett and Nicolas had walked along the riverbank to the old stone bridge spanning the river's cold waters. They had stood there, watching the running water swirl and eddy around its time-worn stone pillars. After several minutes, his father had quietly said, "This small village is where Ealdred son of Ealdwulf met with other olden kings. They decided to form the Kingdom of England." He looked at his son. "Our country is like this river, lad. New waters flow inside its banks every day, but the rocks and banks and bends which make the river what it really is, are very old."

They had walked in thoughtful silence back to their fishing spot and waded out into the splashes and splatters of the River Eamont's running waters, Nicolas had imagined he was a feudal knight, crossing the river to assemble with other great kings, chieftains, and Lairds of old.

A moment later, a frigid splash of water from his father had shocked him out of his daydream, and laughing, he splashed his father back.

Now, as Nicolas stepped through the dark iron door inside Baatunde's tree cottage, he instantly thought about that day with his father. He thought about the quaint village of Eamont Bridge. About the cold waters swirling beneath the stone bridge.

These memories came to mind for a simple reason. It was the cruelness of the cold.

The first thing Nicolas felt as he stepped through the mysterious black door was a sense of terrible, fearsome cold.

It wasn't the kind of cold he had felt many times, trudging to school through grey winter mornings, bundled in cozy clothes, with only his green eyes peeping out over a snugly-knitted scarf. This cold—the cold beyond the door—was the kind he had felt when wading into the icy water of the River Eamont with his father. When the muscles in his bare legs tightened as painful iciness splashed and pushed against them. When his toes lost their feeling. When all the warmth in his body seemed to flow out from him and into the rippling, murmuring water. When his lips spluttered together, and he gasped as if his heart and lungs were going to stop working.

It was *that* kind of cold.

Stepping through the iron door, Nicolas felt as if he had fallen headfirst into the bitter cold water of the ancient River Eamont. And it was dark, too.

It was the inky darkness of his attic bedroom on a moonless night after everyone had gone to bed downstairs, and the world lay silent and asleep. It was the dreadful dark of the deep Irish Sea Nicolas' mum would tell him about, filled with stories of evil water wraiths with withered faces, who pulled down unlucky swimmers into the fathomless depths. It was the fearful dark of the nearby Penrith Castle ruins, where his father said a wiry, small, and wicked demon lived in deep shadows with rust-red iron claws and a scarlet bonnet dipped in the blood of its victims.

It was *that* kind of dark.

Stepping through the iron door was agonizing cold and nightmare dark.

———◆———

As Nicolas shook violently, gasping for breath, he curiously thought of his fishing trips to the River Eamont. His thoughts seemed to float away from his body. He once again imagined he was an elder-born knight, crossing a cold, dark river to meet with great kings, chieftains, and Lairds.

Suddenly, Nicolas could hear slurred whispers, but couldn't quite make out the words. They seemed urgent. Hissing. Rustling. He felt heavy, as if the black around him were pressing him down, pushing against his lungs, dragging at his ankles. Near panic, he thought the voices were some kind of water wraith, tearing at him and tempting him into a frightful, drowning death.

He now could see the muted wink of a vague light, like a ghost-lantern blinking far away on a lonely moor. Instinctively, he fought to reach his hand out to it. His outstretched fingers looked strangely long and wispy, like curls of smoke rising from a dying fire.

And then it was over.

The cold and the dark were gone. The blurred light grew brighter, the ominous whispers faded, and suddenly, he was falling through empty air. But just when he opened his mouth to cry out, he found himself standing again on solid ground.

All was quiet.

Nicolas held out his hands. They looked normal again, and he slowly squeezed them into fists, which felt normal, too. He patted the outside of his sweater, ran his fingers through his tussled hair, and jammed his hands into his pockets where his fingers quickly found the folded five-pound note, the braided bit of colored string, the rocking horse crown coin, the farthing coin, the coppery leaf, and his great grandmother's silver thimble. Satisfied everything was still in place and seemingly unaffected by his strange journey through the door, Nicolas tried to make sense of where he was standing. It seemed like a closet because he was standing in a closed space, but this didn't make much sense. A funny-looking doorway, somewhat in the shape of an irregular triangle, was in front of him. For a few moments, he just stood there. Then, gradually, he realized where he was. He stepped through the doorway and turned around to look.

He had just stepped out of a cavernous tree hollow at the base of an enormous tree. For a fleeting moment, Nicolas thought he might have exited through the back of the tree that held Baatunde's cottage, but the surrounding forest looked different, and a quick inspection showed him the other side of the tree was empty. Nicolas looked around. Very tall, straight trees, grew closely together, looking much like some kind of massive pines with reddish bark. The forest floor was covered in a thick carpet of brown needles, pine cones, and twigs. There was very little underbrush. The air felt cool with a touch of frost and smelled fresh and slightly sweet. Nicolas could hear the comforting chirp of birds and the swish of a slight breeze high above in the branches. These woods were not as gloomy as those around Baatunde's cottage, but the afternoon light was old and fading quickly into evening. Nicolas cautiously peeked back inside the tree hollow. The weakening light seemed unable to penetrate inside the tree, and he couldn't see anything. The tree hollow felt especially cold. Nicolas thought he felt a slight draft coming out of the silence within.

"Aldus Ward," he finally said aloud to himself, straightening himself up. "I'm to find Aldus Ward." He stepped back from the tree hollow and turned in a slow circle. Aside from the birds he could hear, the woods seemed empty, and there was not a road or pathway in sight. "Where do I find Aldus Ward?" he asked himself, trying his best to sound matter-of-fact, in spite of a sense of apprehension.

He noticed a slight running depression in front of him, almost as if he was standing in the middle of the dry bed of an old stream. *Well*, thought Nicolas as he looked down the length of the old streambed, *this direction's as good as any.*

"Off we go," he said to no one and struck out with a brisk walk.

Out of habit, he counted every time he set down his left foot. It was a simple way of measuring distance he'd learned from his father. Normally, Nicolas could count up to fifty-eight paces for every hundred yards he walked. He didn't know how far—or where for that matter—he needed to go, but counting paces was heartening, and besides, it couldn't hurt. At some point, Nicolas thought, he would need to return to the tree hollow.

The old streambed ran fairly straight for a few hundred yards then began a gentle bend to the right and widened out. As he came up to the bend, Nicolas paused his pace count (which was up to one hundred and twenty-three) and turned to look back from where he had started. The enormous tree now stood in deep shadows, and the tree hollow at its base was little more than a barely visible dark blot. From where he now stood, the enormous tree looked as if it sat near the crest of a hill. In the dwindling light, Nicolas couldn't really see anything past it. He shivered.

He heard a noise in the distance. It came from the direction in which the streambed bent, and Nicolas turned toward it, held his breath, and strained his ears to hear something more. A moment later, he heard it again but couldn't quite make it out, except that it mostly sounded like faint laughter punctuated by occasional shouts. He thought he could hear at least one man's loud voice. Nicolas began trotting along the bending streambed. (It was only much later he would realize he'd forgotten to resume his pace count.) There were other voices now, and more laughter, and it all sounded friendly enough. Nicolas picked up his pace, thinking Aldus Ward might be nearby.

As he went along, the streambed widened and became shallow, until it wasn't much more than a slight impression in the ground. Sapling trees had begun to grow in its broad channel, and in the twilight, Nicolas ran over a few of them by accident. The voices and laughter had abruptly become muffled, and he was afraid he might have missed whoever they were. He picked up his pace again, but in the gloaming woods, the deepening evening tricked him, and he didn't notice the streambed turning hard to the left. He ran headlong into a chest-high embankment, thick with various bushes and bramble.

Stone the crows! he thought as he rolled onto his back against the wall of the embankment, and lay there catching his breath and rubbing a sore elbow, *I didn't see that one comin'.*

"Hold yer water, ya miserable ninny! I'm comin'! I'm *comin'!*" shouted a man's grumpy voice a few feet away from where he lay.

Nicolas nearly jumped out of skin. He had no idea anyone was so close, and he'd no idea why anyone would be calling him a "miserable ninny" or sound cross with him at all. Unconsciously, he shrunk down in the dark bushes and held his breath, trying his best not to move.

"Hold yer water, ya flippity-flop! Hold yer flippity-floppin' water!" said the man.

A terrible urge overcame Nicolas. His nose tickled and was sure he was about to sneeze. He pinched his nose hard with one hand and held his other hand tightly over his mouth. Right before he was sure his eyes were going to pop out of his head, the torturous tickle in his nose won. "Aaaachoooooo!" The built-up force of his sneeze hurdled him forward, knocking him away from the protection of the embankment. He landed spread-eagled on his stomach in the old streambed, sniffing and coughing.

"Holy hair knots and ham fat!" Nicolas heard the man yell in surprise. "Who goes there?! I've a hayfork, so no funny business!"

Nicolas gathered himself up and brushed himself off. "Hello?" he said back.

"Who goes there?" asked the man again. "I'll have no mercy if you mean any harm."

"I don't, sir," said Nicolas in reply. "I don't mean any harm."

Mustering some courage, he scrambled up the embankment and pushed through the dry brambles and short hedge. Nicolas found himself looking across a muddy, rutted crossroads at an old inn. Its walls were mostly made of rough stone with strong timbers framing its corners and its large doorway, which was illuminated by a large lantern that hung from a great iron

71

hook. Below the hook was a battered sign with its few remaining chips of paint depicting a large barrel cider press. At the base of the cider press was an oversized apple, faded and dull, with a surprised face painted on it that reminded Nicolas of old pictures of the man in the moon. Beneath the apple were the carved words, "The Cider Press Inn." The inn had a second story, and out of its rooftop poked two chimney stacks, cheerfully emitting puffs of thick grey smoke. The two windows on the first floor, and the single, more narrow window on the second floor were lit from within, and Nicolas could hear several voices talking and laughing from inside. Attached to the left of the small inn was a partially enclosed stable, and it was here Nicolas saw the man with the hayfork.

Several horses were standing together under the stable's eaves, calmly chewing mouthfuls of hay out of a wooden hayrack. The front of the stable was fenced with split rails, and Nicolas could vaguely see a large cat perched on the top rail, lazily whisking its bushy tail left to right and grooming its front paws. At the end of the stable, furthest away from the inn, stood a tall man, holding a rustic-looking hayfork, and peering hard at Nicolas. Upon seeing him, Nicolas' first thought was the man also had come from the Will-o'-the-Wisp Medieval Fair. He was wearing a weather-stained hood and long cape, a rough-looking shirt tucked into a broad leather belt, and an old pair of trousers jammed inside a pair of boots that came up to his knees. To his right stood a barrel-bellied donkey with a single rope looped over its neck, tethered to the end-post of the stable's gate. The donkey lazily munched on its rope.

"Who are *you*?" asked the tall man.

"My name is Nicolas, sir."

"You're a boy?" The man leaned his head forward a bit and squinted his eyes. "You look like a boy."

"Yes, sir. I turned twelve today," said Nicolas, *and*, thought Nicolas bravely, *I'm a wren.*

"Hmmm." The man scratched at the dark stubble on his chin. "An' what would you say you were doin' in the bushes, lad? Have you run away?" His voice sounded friendly but suspicious.

"No, sir, I have not," said Nicolas. "I've... I've..." Nicolas was trying to think of what to say. *I came out of a tree*, didn't sound like a very believable thing to say. "I've come from the forest. From there," he finally said and pointed vaguely back in the direction from which he'd just come.

"Ninny knuckles," said the man with a gruff chuckle. "I *know* you've come outta the forest, lad. I can see that. I'm askin' you *why* you're comin' outta the forest."

Nicolas looked down for a moment and absent-mindedly pushed over a gummy swell of a mud rut with his boot. "Well," he began uncertainly, but then, not sure of what else would make sense, decided to say what he was thinking. "Baatunde sent me!" He looked earnestly at the man. "I'm looking for Aldus Ward. Are you Mr. Ward?"

The man's mouth opened slightly, then he snapped it shut. He had a slightly bewildered look on his face. He opened his mouth again as if to say something, but thinking better of it, shut it again. Nicolas glanced at the donkey. It had chewed its way through the rope and was now slowly eating the end connected to the loop around its neck. The rope reminded Nicolas of a long noodle of spaghetti.

"Aldus Ward?" repeated the man carefully. His voice was lower than before.

"Yes, sir," said Nicolas. "Are... are you him?"

"No, lad, I'm not him." The tall man glanced at the donkey. "Cherry Pit!" he said, noticing the chewed rope. "What 'ave I told you about chewin' your rope? Holy hair knot! Don't even know why I bother." He leaned over the stable's rail fence and forked a large clump of hay that had fallen out of the hayrack. He tossed it on the ground under the donkey's nose. "Here, ya dim-witted beast." He stroked the tussle of mane that fell between the donkey's long ears as it dropped the rope from its mouth and began munching on the hay. "Bless me, Cherry Pit," he said with deep affection, "I don't know why I keep you. You're nothin' but trouble." He stood there, stroking the donkey's mane and tugging gently at its long, soft ears. "Aldus Ward?" he asked again quietly. "Well, lad, I haven't heard of this Baatunde, but if someone has sent you to find the Laird of the First Gate, then I would say it must be important. And," he concluded matter-of-factly, "if you don't know who the Laird of the Gate is, then I suspect you must be from very far away indeed."

He glanced up past Nicolas, staring into the darkening woods for several moments. "Maybe you're from across the Cold Sea. Maybe from the Land Beyond the Fogs," he said more to himself than to Nicolas. The tall man paused and scratched again at his chin's grey and black stubble before looking directly at Nicolas. "And if you've come from far away, wherever that might be lad, then *that* must mean somethin' too." He stretched out a broad, strong-looking hand and tenderly patted the donkey's head. "Cherry Pit and I will see that you find who you're lookin' for."

The tall man struck Nicolas as a kind person in spite of his abruptness. "Thank you, sir," said Nicolas. "Is he nearby? Is Mr. Ward inside the inn?"

"No, lad, Laird Ward is not inside." The tall man leaned the hayfork against the stable's rails. "Inside are other men, an' they might feel inclined to ask more questions than I have." Even in the dim twilight, Nicolas could see a stern look come over the man's face, and he spoke in low tones. "These have become dark days, lad, and others might be inclined to ask their questions in a *hard* way, but," he added distastefully, "that ain't right, and that will not do."

Nicolas didn't know what to say. He had no idea what the man meant by questions being asked "in a *hard* way," but it made him shiver. "What… what should I do?" he asked cautiously.

"Well," said the man as if he had made up his mind. "You can make yourself useful, an' stand here and make sure Cherry Pit doesn't decide to wander off in search of somethin' sweeter than this moldy hay. I've got my kit back inside the inn. I thought I was goin' to stay here the night, but I need to go grab it now, an' toss the innkeep a few pecks. It doesn't look as if we'll be drinkin' our ale by a warm hearth tonight, lad." With that, he strode through the mud and quickly disappeared inside the inn.

Nicolas stood still, half-considering the idea of running back into the woods and following the old streambed back up to the tree hollow. The tall man had sounded sincere, but he was a stranger, and his grim words hadn't exactly been comforting. Nicolas looked over his shoulder. The trees and bushes were awash in long, deep shadows. The air around him was growing colder, and the thought of going back into the darkness of the forest spooked him. He looked at the fat donkey. The beast seemed untroubled and as unconcerned as when it had been idly chewing through its rope. It was difficult for Nicolas to think of the donkey's owner as being an unkind person. Perhaps he was a person Nicolas could trust.

"What do you think?" he whispered to Cherry Pit. The donkey, unaware its advice was desired, kept pleasantly munching on its hay and did not look up. Nicolas turned his eyes up and down the muddy roadway. Other than the light from the inn, the road lay dark and empty in both directions.

He didn't want to admit it, but he felt troubled and uncertain.

CHAPTER 7

S†. LLULF'S-LLI†HOU†-ALDERSGA†E

All the world *is home to a wandering man.*

The sound of Nicolas' father's strong voice popped into his head as clearly as if Mr. Bennett was standing right there beside him. He recalled the first time his father had taken him on one of his morning walks years before. Nicolas had felt as if they had walked forever, and he remembered feeling hungry and tired. "Can't we go home, Dad?" he'd asked. Mr. Bennett had smiled, and with a knowing look in his eye, he replied, "All the world is home to a wandering man, Nicolas."

"No, Dad," responded Nicolas impatiently, "I mean *our* home." His father had laughed. "Of course. Of course, my boy." Their walk back hadn't seemed to take as long, and by the time they were passing through the Bennetts' gate and into their yard, Nicolas could practically taste the warm hotcakes and sweet myrtleberry jam he was sure his mum had made for breakfast. "Nicolas," his father had said as they were taking off their muddy boots in the small boot room, "wherever ya go in this wide world, home is always where you want it to be. And all the world is home to a wandering man."

"This world can be home," Nicolas now said aloud to himself as he made his way across the muddy ruts in the road. He picked up the chewed end of the rope dangling from Cherry Pit's neck, and pushed some more hay together for the donkey to chew. Lamp light flooded the muddy road as the door to the inn suddenly flew open.

"An' you're no Talön Knight!" shouted the tall man to some unseen fellow inside. He slammed the wooden door shut behind him, muffling the wave of laughter from within. "Ninny knuckles and ham fat," grumbled the man to himself as he walked briskly toward Nicolas and the donkey. "Too many strangers these days, an' too few manners to go 'round. We're well-quit of the lot of them, lad. They would've been suspicious, and it might've gone hard on you." Saying this, he effortlessly hefted two large burlap sacks onto the donkey's back. They were tied together at their necks, and they hung over Cherry Pit's fat sides like bulky saddlebags, making the donkey look even rounder than before.

The tall man had a stout-looking staff slung over his right shoulder held by a thong of leather, and on his back was a leather pack with a rolled blanket wrapped in oiled sheepskin. "We'll make our way down the road a bit. I know of a rock overhang not far from here which will give us a roof and a bit of shelter for the night." He paused, arching a critical eyebrow and looking up into the late evening sky. "Fallow is fadin' into night, lad. We best be on our way. Quickly now."

Nicolas didn't know exactly what "fallow" was, but he took it to mean late evening. He nodded his head in silence and handed the donkey's rope to the man. "Where's your kit, lad?"

"My kit?" said Nicolas.

"Yes, your kit. Your stoof. Where's your belongin's?"

"Oh," Nicolas shook his head and shrugged his shoulders. "I haven't got any."

"Hmph," grunted the man. He cocked his head and stared at Nicolas. "You *are* a strange one, aren't ya, lad? Well," he said with a deep breath, straightening his broad shoulders, "you can share what I've got. We all have lean times now an' then."

He turned on his heel and gently pulled at the donkey's rope. Cherry Pit seemed reluctant to leave the last few stalks of hay lying on the ground. It just stood there, slowly rolling his teeth together. "Great gander gaffs!" said the man in exasperation. "If it wasn't for that giant belly, you'd think he was starvin'. C'mon, my Cherry Pit. There's sweet apples waiting down the road." He made this promise in a mock whisper and gave a quick wink to Nicolas, who smiled back. Surprisingly, the donkey lifted its head, and without any more urging, began following the man through the criss-cross of wheel ruts and piles of muck. Nicolas trailed along behind the donkey, uneasily glancing over his shoulder every now and then, while being careful not to run into Cherry Pit's hind quarters.

Nicolas didn't begin to feel better until the light from the inn had faded into the distance, and the sound of harsh laughter had been consumed by the forest's silence.

A short distance from the inn, the road became more passable. Muddy wheel grooves flattened out, and an even bed of damp, fallen leaves made their passing a relatively quiet affair. They moved along with an unspoken sense of haste. The earth underfoot was soggy in places, but the mud had mixed with pine needles, flakes of bark, rotting leaves, and twigs, creating a kind of cushion that kept boots and hooves from sinking. A fresh breeze had picked up since they'd left the inn, and Nicolas felt cold currents of air trying to creep under the thick defense of his woolen sweater.

By his pace count, they had covered about four miles before they unexpectedly came to a stop. The tall man didn't say anything. He just held up his hand and stood still in the middle of the dark road as if listening for something. The donkey and

Nicolas followed suit, and the three of them stood there silently. With night full upon them, they could hear forest noises murmur in the darkness around them. Nicolas could hear the breeze making its way through invisible branches, while the occasional rustle, or snap of a twig, gave away the scurrying movements of small, unseen animals, busying themselves with finding dinner or journeying back to the warmth of earthy burrows.

All at once the noises stopped. The wind stood still. But the cold deepened.

"The woods," whispered the tall man, "are no longer safe."

Nicolas could vaguely see his dim outline. He had not turned around. He did not seem to move at all.

Nicolas began to ask what was going on but barely had the first word out of his mouth when the man held out his hand. "*Something*," the tall man hissed in warning, "*...something is here.*" Nicolas wasn't sure what the man meant, or why everything had gone quiet, but Nicolas felt frightened. He thought of the safety of the warm light from the inn back down the road. Even if the men inside had been dangerous, Nicolas wished they'd stayed there.

Without a sound, the tall man carefully unslung the leather pack from his shoulders and dropped it to the ground near his feet. Quickly, he knelt down and from inside the rolled-up blanket, he took out a battle axe. Nicolas could see that the axe's shaft was about two feet long with a wrapped handle. In the paleness of shadowy moonbeams, the axe's head appeared smaller and somehow more vicious than what Nicolas had seen in movies or at the medieval fair. It wasn't shiny, but just enough light caught the scars where the metal had been scored by the cruelty of fierce combat. Its bladed edge curved downward, forming into a nasty point. The axe was brutal and savage. Nicolas shuddered and shrank behind Cherry Pit. In a moment of true dread, Nicolas realized this axe was an actual weapon. It was made to cleave through flesh, to splinter bone, and to kill brutally. And it had.

Slyly, the tall man stood up and slung the pack onto his broad back. "Stay close," he ordered.

Nicolas placed a hand on Cherry Pit's warm flank. The tall man drew up beside him. He smelled like wood smoke and vinegary oil. "These woods aren't what they used to be," the man muttered and glanced around. "The wilds are closin' in more an' more every day. Cave trolls, and fenris wolves, and tree blights, and such, are wanderin' more freely than they have in many years. But *this*…" His long, drawn face looked up at the dark sky. "Whatever is near us is something *different*."

Only a handful of stars were visible through the forest's upper canopy, and only a slender crescent of moon could be seen. High up, silhouetted branches reached up their bony fingers to the black heavens, and the forest felt even darker than before. Slowly, the tall man said, "'Tis a 'Tusk Moon' tonight. No clouds. That's good. Spirits are departing."

He dropped his chin and drew his face uncomfortably close to Nicolas. "Many say the dreaded War Crows are looking to cross the Cold Sea, an' treasonous giants have been seen again in the frosty peaks of the Dolmen Tombs. They say—" The tall man paused. His voice changed into an icy, bitter tone. "They say the *Shadow Thief* has come back." This last sentence was uttered so quietly, it was almost as if the tall man had said it to himself instead of Nicolas. Nicolas felt the tall man staring keenly at him. His voice changed. It almost sounded curious. "And with no king upon the throne, who's to say who will rule?"

Nicolas shivered. He felt his shoulders hunch down involuntarily. "Shadow Thief?" he asked hesitantly.

"Aye," the man nodded, "the *Shadow Thief.*" He gripped his hatchet tightly and raised it to point to the dark sky. His voice was hoarse, and the words were guttural, "Árnyék Tolvaj."

Genuinely frightened, Nicolas looked skyward. He strained to see anything, but there were only charcoal smudges of scattered clouds and sharp flickers of starlight. Nothing moved in the night sky. But Nicolas had a queer feeling something was going to. Something awful was about to happen. The longer he stared, the darker the clouds seemed to become, and the fewer stars he could see. Like some great coffin lid, the sky seemed to be closing down upon him. Nicolas felt entombed in the dark. Something wicked and terrible was about to race across the sky.

"Stay close!" The man's sudden order caused Nicolas to jump.

The tall man was leaning forward, staring intently into the dark forest. He crouched with his feet apart and his arms out from his sides. The terrible axe swung slightly in his hand.

Nicolas, now terrified, pressed close to the donkey. The mustiness of its thick winter coat, with its barnyard smell of hay, dirt, manure, and wood chips, filled his nose, giving him an instinctive sense of comfort. He peeked over the donkey's back but couldn't see anything in the forest. Crumpled wrinkles of tree bark absorbed grey hints of starlight, causing the trees closest to the road to vaguely contrast with the deeper ink of shadows further in the woods. This made the nearest trees look like giant, craggy ghosts.

And at that moment, one of the giant ghosts moved.

Just back from the side of the road and partially hidden by another immense tree, something enormous moved slightly back and to the left before it stopped and became absolutely still again.

Nicolas' entire body became as rigid as a corpse. He dared not breathe. He blinked his eyes rapidly, desperately trying to focus them in the surrounding darkness. But the shadows and shades only muddled what little light there was. Everything faded together. His mouth was dry. Nicolas didn't know if the tall man had seen what he'd seen, but he was too scared to say anything. *My eyes are playing tricks on me*, Nicolas thought desperately. *Trees can't move!*

"*Eeeeasy*," warned the tall man with a hissing breath. Nicolas noticed he was crouched still as a stone. "Easy."

Then, a hoarse voice, or something like a voice, sounding as if it was traveling through a long, hollow pipe somewhere in the hellish darkness, snarled, "*Alllllbrec Westenraaaa*."

For a second, everything was silent and still.

With a primal battle cry of "*Fire and Iron!*" the tall man lunged straight into the dreadful blackness, swinging his terrible, long-handled axe over his head in a great and murderous arc.

The moment he leapt, the dark thing—which was clearly not a tree—unfolded a giant span of wings, or threw open a giant black cloak (Nicolas couldn't tell which it was), and, with the violence of a locomotive roaring out of the mouth of a dreadful tunnel, it flew directly at them.

The tall man vanished into the blackness.

Nicolas barely had time to duck his head behind Cherry Pit before the demonic apparition was upon him. The air around him felt like wet frost, and strangely, smelled faintly of almonds and burned earth. Involuntarily, he cried out, and without really knowing what he was doing, Nicolas punched a fist into the thick of the enveloping blackness.

Just as quickly as everything had happened, it was over.
There was another snarl, and the apparition was gone.
It ceased to exist.

Timidly, Nicolas raised his head.

The woods still lay in deep shadows, but they no longer felt as oppressive or ominous as they had moments before. Cherry Pit, for his part, had remained remarkably still, and Nicolas patted him on the neck, feeling a flood of relief weaken his knees. He let out a nervous laugh. "Good boy, good boy," he said, congratulating his stoic companion. "Good boy." The donkey turned its kind head to look at Nicolas, and in the same way the kelpie thrush, Magnus, had done, Cherry Pit winked at him. Before a surprised Nicolas could react, there was a rustle of leaves and twigs, and the tall man reappeared out of the darkness.

"You're still here!" he said to Nicolas with a stern but distinct air of satisfaction. "Good! I thought you might've bolted or been struck dead." He walked over to the donkey and gently tugged at its long ears. "In fact," he said with a hint of curiosity, glancing at the boy, "that's quite amazing, really. Far greater men would have hidden and been soiling themselves behind some bush." The tall man looked keenly at Nicolas for several seconds. Nicolas didn't know what the tall man expected him to say, so he said nothing. Finally, the tall man asked, "Are you hurt, lad? Are you okay?" There was the same rough gentleness in his voice Nicolas had heard him use back at the inn.

"I'm fine," said Nicolas quietly, doing his best to sound normal. He couldn't help the slight quiver in his voice. "What *was* that? Was it the Shadow Thief?"

The tall man kept studying him for a moment in silence, then, to Nicolas' surprise, his face relaxed, and he laughed loudly. "No, my boy! *That* wasn't the Shadow Thief! Although, when it suits it, *that* can be *just* as dangerous." He chuckled quietly to himself for a minute or so. He sounded cheery, but he also sounded relieved.

Nicolas couldn't help it. He smiled back, confused but re-assured by the tall man's amusement. "I'll admit, lad, there's plenty of things which are ferocious and dark in this world, but I suspect you've just been introduced to one of the older and more powerful things. It was *Kohanim*."

"A what?"

"I suspect you've just met a thing called a *Wisp*, lad. They are good Kohanim—ancient creatures once belonging to two tribes. Long ago, the Kohanim's two tribes went to war against each other, and the good tribe prevailed. The Kohanim are not seen by people as often as they once were," the tall man said thoughtfully. "Most now live quietly in the mists of the moor lands, but there are a few—" Here, the tall man's deep voice dropped to a whisper, and he leaned in toward Nicolas. "There are a few of these creatures who still roam about, dangerous and unaccounted for. These wandering Kohanim are called *Shedu*—storm demons—homeless survivors of an ancient trib-al feud." He stood back upright. "But," he continued more lightly," if you can believe it, *this* one was a *friendly* one. I was afraid it might've been a Shedu, but if it had been, then you and I and ol' Cherry Pit would be in sorry shape indeed." The man looked around. "And *this* one spoke. A Shedu would not have been able to speak. At the end of the tribal war, the Wisps cut out the tongues of all Shedu."

The tall man said this without any emotion, but Nicolas felt a shiver run along his spine. "Why did it feel so … so *dark*?"

"Well, my boy, Kohanim are powerful. Magical. And I've always believed they come from an even more ancient power." He shrugged. "All power, both good and evil, possesses a sense of darkness. A sense of wrath is a better way to say it, I sup-pose." The tall man scanned the surrounding shadows. The for-est's night sounds had come back as if nothing had happened.

84

"Good Kohanim or no, I think it best if we keep movin'."

Nicolas didn't know who, or what, a Kohanim, a Shedu, or Wisp really was, and he didn't know what else to say, so he said the next most practical thing which came to mind. "How much further?"

"Eh? Oh, ah, well… I don't much care any longer to spend this fine evening tucked away somewhere in these woods. We might not be so lucky the next time. What say we push on a few miles more?" Nicolas couldn't see the man's face clearly in the gloom, but his voice sounded sure of itself. "What say we push on to the Laird's gate? I wouldn't usually like to approach a city gate at night, but I find myself wanting to put some stone walls around me, instead of the blackness o' these woods."

"I agree." Nicolas was grateful for the suggestion. Even if he still wasn't clear on who Aldus Ward was, or what a "Laird" of a city gate meant, the idea of being inside somewhere safe for the night, perhaps with a warm fire crackling happily away, sounded much better than making camp underneath a rock overhang deep in the forest's darkness.

"Then away we go, lad, and look sharp!"

The tall man balanced the handle of his axe across one shoulder, and the weary companions resumed their pace with a fresh purpose, keeping their thoughts and worries to themselves as they once more passed silently along the dark forest road.

———

"Whoa!"

For a second, Nicolas was confused. Before he could stop his feet, he'd walked blindly into Cherry Pit's hindquarters. The patient donkey seemed undisturbed and only swished its tail, which stung like thistles when it smacked Nicolas in the nose.

"Ow!" he said, blinking furiously at the sharp pain. With mild surprise, Nicolas realized he'd nearly fallen asleep as he'd been walking. He'd failed to realize the man and donkey had come to a stop, until the man's voice had broken the silence. Nicolas shook his head to clear his thoughts, and rubbed his nose, easing the sting of the donkey's tail. He and Cherry Pit were stopped in the middle of the road, but the tall man was off to its side, busily taking an unlit lantern down off a hook on a tall iron pole. With skill borne of having done it a thousand times before, the man set the lantern down, fished a small tinder kit out of some hidden pocket in his cloak, and struck a few sparks into a wad of oily cloth. As a flame appeared in the cloth wad, the man shoved it inside the lantern, lighting the lantern's wick. This quickly threw a warm, yellowed light across the roadway. Its glow made Nicolas feel safe. The man stood up, holding the lantern out in front of him, and turned back to look at the boy.

"We've reached an approach-light post, lad. The gatekeep's not far. Let's keep sharp, and look as normal as we can. 'Tis the first eve of Haligtide, and we don't want the High Chancellor's archers mistakin' us for a small band of mischievous hobgoblins." He smiled broadly, and his sturdy face looked kind. His eyes were bright and wide. "Hog's toes and radish rumps, lad! If you've never seen the gates of the City of Relic, then you're in for an eyeful."

The tall man held out a small drinking flask. Nicolas nodded and took a deep drink. He suddenly realized how thirsty he was. It occurred to him he hadn't had a drink since his supper with Baatunde. He gulped the warm liquid, which tasted bitter but with a hint of sweetness like honey. His throat burned, but the drink warmed his insides, and almost instantly, Nicolas felt better.

The man pushed his axe back into his pack and tugged at Cherry Pit's rope. "Off we go!" he said, and the three travelers started down the road once again. After another hundred yards, the road turned sharply left, and abruptly, the forest's thick copse came to an end.

The dark sky opened up, and a countless number of bright stars came into view.

Nicolas' mouth fell open, and, with memories of England's Windsor Castle now dwarfed in his head, he stood in awe of what appeared before him.

———————

The roadway sloped down before him across a treeless plain, winding its way among a field of rocky outcrops until it rose again to the largest castle gate Nicolas had ever seen.

St. Wulf's-Without-Aldersgate stood as a fortress unto itself. Rising two hundred feet into the air, with crenelated ramparts, slitted archers' ports, and horseshoe towers on each of its seven corners, it was one of the largest fortresses Nicolas had ever seen. It took Nicolas' eyes several moments to finally spot a covered bridge arching out of the back of the gate, then crossing a wide gorge and into the great, shadowy walls of the City of Relic.

Willing himself out of his momentary trance, Nicolas the Wren ran to catch up to his two companions, who were already picking their way along the open road with the lantern's cheery light bouncing from left to right.

CHAPTER 8

THE GATEKEEP

The further Nicolas moved away from the forest, the less tired he felt. The open plain, and the sudden expanse of night sky and fresh wind—as cold as it might have been—was a welcome relief from the closeness and darkness of the forest's enclosure.

Nicolas caught up with the tall man and the donkey after a hundred yards or so. He couldn't help but stare in awe at the quickly approaching fortress which made it hard to keep his eyes on the road. Occasionally, Nicolas had to leap to the side of the roadway to avoid running into the donkey's hind flanks as it ambled peacefully along behind its master.

———

St. Wulf's-Without-Aldersgate was massive.

The gatekeep eventually blocked Nicolas' view of the walled city, which lay in deeper shadows beyond the gate's immense size. The gate's entrance itself was unusually wide, perhaps wide enough for thirty men to walk through it together, shoulder to shoulder. The entrance looked deep, too, much more like a tunnel than the kind of thickened arch Nicolas had seen in most castle gates. Suspended just inside the gloomy opening, he spied the iron points of an impressive portcullis—woven bars of thick, black metal, ready to fall into place if the gatekeep was threatened. The dreadful, sharp teeth looked like they were waiting for an unsuspecting meal to wander inside.

On either side of the intimidating passageway were two lofty ramparts of angled bastions—bulwarks of gigantic stone block, rising fifty feet into the air—which, in the desperate straits of war, would give the gate's defenders an advantaged view of its entrance and natural fields of fire to rain arrows down on attacking forces. More mammoth stones, fitted together expertly in nearly seamless courses, created colossal walls looming far overhead. There were immense towers, too. Each rose dozens of stories into the night sky—stone watchmen of the gatekeep's seven corners. The towers were joined by lofty curtain walls. It was hard for Nicolas to imagine anyone wanting to assault the gatekeep, or how they could ever hope to overcome its tremendous defenses.

St. Wulf's-Without-Aldersgate, one of six impressive gatekeep entrances to the vast City of Relic, conveyed a sense of unconquerable strength, as if its stones were part of a supernatural mountain, scored and chiseled out of sheers of granite cliffs, growing out of the floor of the treeless plain.

About four hundred yards away from the entrance, the path narrowed and began a gradual upward climb. As the three travelers trudged slowly up its gravely scape, Nicolas was reminded of the winding and narrow path leading up to Dunnottar Castle, a lonely medieval castle along Scotland's northeast coast. He had once visited Dunnottar Castle while on holiday with his family, and he vaguely remembered his father telling him the Scottish crown jewels had been hidden there in a time of troubles long ago. At the time, looking out past the moss-bearded stones of Dunnottar's ruined walls and into the empty, grey expanse of the cold North Sea, Nicolas had a distinct sense of long-forgotten history. Now, as he, the tall man, and the homely donkey moved closer toward the imposing, fortified walls of St. Wulf's-Without-Aldersgate, that same sense of long-forgotten history came back to him in a rush… but it vanished almost as quickly as it had come.

To Nicolas, the great, shadowy blocks of stone of St. Wulf's-Without-Aldersgate seemed ancient but also *living*.

"Hail, the keep's Grimlock!"

The tall man had stopped about fifty yards from the gate's entrance and raised the lantern aloft, high above his head. His weathered cloak snapped in the wintry wind, but he stood completely still—a man who had become a light post. Vast copper bowls, burning radiantly like two immense lamps, were suspended on either side of the gate's entrance by chains made of enormous links which were held by great iron hooks. Nicolas felt exposed and wondered who, or what, might be staring down at them.

As if it knew what was expected, the tall man's donkey had also come to a stop and stood there patiently. Nicolas again stood close to his gentle friend and set his hand on the warm barrel-curve of its furry stomach. The echo of the tall man's deep shout was stripped away in a fresh bluster of wind, and Nicolas wondered if anyone had heard him. From the edge of the forest, Nicolas had been able to see the glittering of evening lights in the city beyond the gate, but aside from the immense lamps hanging on either side of its entrance, the gatekeep itself stood dark and silent.

For a moment, the chill of wind lessened.

Then it gusted again, causing a gout of bright orange flames to leap from the giant oil lamps and fly into the air as if they were trying to break free before they quickly vanished. Nicolas wished he were close enough to feel some of their heat, but he was too far away, and the bowls were hung too high.

Aside from the wind and the flames, nothing seemed to move. St. Wulf's-Without-Aldersgate lay asleep.

Or lay waiting.

Near the gatekeep's yawning entrance, a figure materialized from a hidden recess in the gate's deep shadows. In the feeble moonlight, it took several seconds, and several rapid blinks of his eyes, for Nicolas to see the faint outline of a false wall, which must have concealed an unseen sentry's entrance.

The figure which had emerged looked massive. It stood at least as high as the tall man and seemed twice as broad. Nicolas was reminded of the colossal competitors in the strong-man competitions his father would sometimes watch on television. He was sure this figure would have won all of them.

A heavy war helmet covered its head, hiding its entire face, except for a thin, horizontal slit from which it could see. Leather covered its arms and legs, on top of which were buckled metal cuffs and armor plates. The figure wore a long hooded sleeveless vest made of dark green velvet, stained but embroidered with golden thread. The vest hung to its knees and was belted at its waist with a sturdy chain of silver. Hanging from its neck, from an equally sturdy chain, was a large flat iron disc. The edges of the disc were scalloped, and teardrops of metal had been struck from its center. This adornment prompted Nicolas to think of the large gear on his bicycle, and just as quickly, of the gear-like dial that opened the iron door inside Baatunde's cottage.

With an unnerving speed and purpose, the menacing figure strode toward them. Its burly arms swung at its sides as it moved, while its beefy hands, now balled into mallet-like fists, acted as ballast weights at the end of powerful pendulums. The figure's iron-tipped boots slammed hard into the earth, causing Nicolas to imagine the distant beat of heavy hammers against a solid drum.

An arm's length behind the enormous figure was a creature about the size of the tall man's donkey. Nicolas, with some astonishment, suddenly realized what it was.

It was a dog.

But it was the largest dog Nicolas had ever seen.

The beast was covered with coarse red and white hair, and wore a heavy collar of beaten leather. It had narrow eyes and a long face which swayed slightly as it walked. Tuffs of fur curled along the seam of its mouth were glistening wet. The easiness of its pace—set with effortless strides of long, muscular legs—carried a sense of ready energy, as if the great dog could swiftly move from an idle walk to a full-blown attack. It was much like an enormous Irish Wolf Hound.

Oddly, it was the dog's casualness that intimidated Nicolas the most.

———◆◆———

The helmeted figure and its companion dog covered the ground between the gatekeep's entrance and the tall man in a mere matter of seconds, stopping just short of the wavering circle of light thrown out by the lantern.

"Good evening, Master Grimlock," said the tall man firmly, slightly nodding his head.

The large figure said nothing in return. Behind it, the huge canine raised its solid, grizzled muzzle and took in a loud, deep draught of air. It held the position for a moment, then dropped its head and nudged the back of the helmeted figure.

The enormous figure finally spoke in a deep voice. "You have the approval of Basileus. He doesn't often like strangers, and he especially doesn't like strangers in the dead of night. Name your business at the Gate," he growled.

The tall man slowly lowered his lantern. Like Nicolas, he kept a watchful eye on the great dog.

"Only one of us is a stranger, Master Grimlock. My name is Albrec Westenra. I am originally from the City of Relic—from the Dreggs—but I have long been away. I return on a simple errand. This," he said waving toward Cherry Pit, "is my donkey, and this boy here," he lowered his hand and lowered his voice, "is Nicolas. I met him several miles up the road outside the Cider Press Inn. He was alone and said he needs to see the Laird of the Gate. I believe he's an honest lad, but…" the tall man paused as if he were thinking of what else to say, "…he isn't *from* here."

The helmeted figure warily swung its eye-slit to look in Nicolas' direction when the tall man said this, as did the great dog, which curiously seemed to have understood what the tall man had just said.

"Come into the light, boy."

Nicolas stepped slowly around Cherry Pit, nervously rubbing the farthing coin in his pocket, and repeating to himself, *it'll be alright, it'll be alright.* He walked over to the tall man and stood there, feeling as if he'd been called to the front of his schoolroom to be scolded by his teacher. Stepping forward, the dog almost touched its huge muzzle to Nicolas' nose.

"Basileus!"

The dog turned its head and looked at the helmeted figure. With deliberate motion, it swung its head back in Nicolas' direction and looked him straight in the eye. Nicolas had no idea what to do, and part of him was sure he was about to become a late-night treat for the enormous beast. He did his best to look back at the dog, while trying to not look challenging. The boy and the dog stared at each other for several seconds. Shivering, Nicolas felt silly and afraid and daring all at the same time.

Finally, with a few quick sniffs, the dog backed up a few steps and sat down.

Nicolas, who'd been holding his breath, sucked in a few deep gulps of the cold night air.

The helmeted figure moved toward the seated dog and stretched out one of its massive hands to pat the beast on its head.

Without looking up, the figure lifted his other hand and pointed with a thick finger to the entrance of St. Wulf's-Without-Aldersgate. "You, Albrec Westenra, have the Master Grimlock's permission to enter. You may stable your donkey within the gatekeep and appear tomorrow before the King's First Bench."

"As you wish," replied the tall man and nodded his head in agreement.

"As for *you*," the great, helmeted figure turned to face Nicolas. "Basileus, an elder among his pack and a curse to all enemies of this keep, does not wish to *eat* you. And since he does not wish to eat you, you shall be a guest of the Laird of the Gate. However," the figure's voice became threatening, "I give you this warning, and you shall only be given this warning once. After shelter and food have been provided as our law requires, a *guest* may very well find he is *no longer* a guest, and Basileus may find he is hungry once again. A *guest*," he hissed, "remains only as safe as his actions permit him to be. You'd do well, *boy*, to remember that!"

A gust of cold wind roared among them.

"Go!" the helmeted figure commanded and pointed toward the gatekeep's dark entrance. "Go quickly!"

The tall man immediately motioned for Nicolas to follow him, and once again, the tall man, the donkey, and the boy set off toward the looming, colossal walls. Nicolas looked over his shoulder before disappearing into the darkness of the gate's mouth. The plain behind them was empty. The enormous helmeted figure and his great dog were gone.

Only a bitter wind and the sharp sickle of the tusk-like moon remained.

Quietly, the trio entered the gatekeep.

Aside from the light cast by the tall man's lantern, the gate's entranceway was dark. Its high ceiling, large enough for giants to walk without stooping, and its stone walls made it seem like a long cavern. Cherry Pit's hooves made soft noises, but no other sound could be heard. The entranceway's inky blackness seemed impenetrable, and it felt as if they were being watched by snooping eyes. After moving about ten yards inside the long tunnel, the tall man, who seemed to know what he was about, paused near three iron hooks bolted into the stone wall. Unlit lanterns occupied two of the hooks. He hung his lantern on the third hook.

He sighed heavily and slowly. "Now is when we part ways, lad." The tall man reached down and took two crude torches from a woven basket sitting on the ground under the hooks and lit them both. He handed one to Nicolas. "It must not feel like it, but you're safe here. No harm will come to you. I know the keep's Master Grimlock sounded a bit gruff, but you're here under his protection." The tall man bent down a bit to look Nicolas in the eye. "I don't mind saying that you feel... *different* to me—special, I think. Maybe just well-intentioned, and maybe being well-intentioned in these dark days is a special thing." He straightened up. "I imagine you'll be given an audience with Laird Aldus Ward. Take my advice, and be truthful and brave. Each of the gatekeep's lords is old and wise, but Laird Ward is an exceptionally just and clever man. Some say," he mused almost as an afterthought, "he can be dangerous, too." The tall man then gave Nicolas a kind look. "Do not be afraid. Laird Ward is the first, and the greatest, of the Commissioners of the Forfeited Gates. I haven't a clue as to why you need to see him, lad, and I don't need to know, but I'm sure he can help with whatever it is. I'm glad if I was of service to ye." He bowed his head.

Nicolas nodded and did his best to smile confidently. "Thank you, Mr. Westenra. I really appreciate your help." Privately, Nicolas didn't like the idea of the tall man and Cherry Pit leaving. "Where are you going?"

"I have some brief business in the Dreggs, lad. Dark business. The Dreggs are a place within the City. Tomorrow, I'll go there, and with any luck, be done with it quickly. Our Land has been at peace these many years, but…" his shadowed head shook gravely, "things have begun to change. Darkness is afoot, and it is said the *Shadow Thief* has awakened."

The tall man looked around as if suspecting someone, or something, to be there in the tunnel's blackness. The cold of a slight breeze found its way to them from the mouth of the gate, making the two torches flicker and blink. The tall man looked back at Nicolas. The torchlight cast eerie tricks across his weathered face. In a rough whisper, he said, "All I've ever known is 'Fire and Iron,' lad. This has been my fate. *You*—I see Fire and Iron in you, too, but there is also *more*. I am certain of it."

The tall man straightened up to his full height. "Beware the Fire!" he commanded suddenly in a loud voice. "And guard the *Iron!*" Without another word, the tall man spun on his heel and marched off, the light of his torch disappearing quickly into the gloom of the gate's long tunnel. Cherry Pit, with a long, curious last look at Nicolas, followed loyally at the heels of its master.

Nicolas, at last, was alone.

For a minute, twelve-year-old Nicolas Bennett stood there, looking after his parted companions.

He raised his torch, but the dimness of the tunnel seemed oddly resistant to the wavering light, and he was unable to see very far. He could now hear a faint, monotonous drip of water coming from somewhere else. The stone walls near him looked damp and cold. Nicolas shivered. At least the ground underneath his boots appeared to be dry and untroubling. It was a sodden mix of long, corded strips of fibrous wood and sand spread over cobbled stones.

Aldus Ward, Nicolas said to himself. In truth, he wasn't anymore sure than the tall man had been as to why he was here, or why Baatunde had sent him with instructions to see Aldus Ward, but he felt like Mr. Ward—or, *the Laird of the Gate*, he quickly corrected himself—would want to see him. Nicolas jammed a hand in his pocket, fishing for his coins and thimble. Instead, his hand first found the coppery leaf. Nicolas shuddered. *A place with dragons.* His fingers moved the leaf aside and found the crown coin of St. George. He rubbed it reassuringly.

"Show him what you have in your pocket," Baatunde had told him.

Bloody cheeky, thought Nicolas. *I suppose I'm to walk up to this Laird Aldus Ward, a* dangerous *man, and just say, look at what I've got in my pocket, sir. I've got a leaf, a thimble, and two coins. And look at this one, sir. It's such a fine coin, isn't it?* Nicolas began to laugh at how ridiculous all of it felt, but the sudden sound of laughter caught in his throat. He coughed instead.

With his cough, in the darkness beyond his torchlight, there came the rush of beating of wings. It was distant at first. Nicolas swallowed hard to stop his cough. He strained to hear, but the noise had stopped. His mouth was dry, and his tongue felt thick. He stood there quietly. He could hear the dim drip of water somewhere beyond the shadowed walls. Nicolas stretched out his arm, slowly waving the torch back and forth, but he couldn't see anything else in the gate's tunnel. A disturbing vision of the crow's frightening head appearing in his window filled Nicolas' imagination.

The boy took a few hesitant steps forward.

Immediately, there was another rush of beating wings. This time the sound didn't stop. It grew swiftly and sounded clearly as if it were coming toward him. Anxiously, his hands sweating, Nicolas stuck his chin forward and looked hard into the darkness just as a great raven suddenly materialized out of the blackness.

Startled, Nicolas reeled backward to avoid the bird.

His heel tripped over the lip of an uneven cobble, and he crashed hard onto his back. Nicolas managed to keep his hold on the torch, but before he could recover his breath, the raven leapt onto his chest. It adjusted its large, sharp talons slightly, sinking them into the thick wool of Nicolas' sweater. It lowered its long, black beak until its coal-black eyes were staring into Nicolas' own. The great bird felt like it weighed several pounds, enough that Nicolas didn't think he could easily dislodge it from his chest.

After several terrifying moments, the raven lifted its large head and uttered a distinctive and deep *prruk-prruk-prruk-prruk*. Satisfied, the bird looked back at Nicolas and cocked its head.

Nicolas heard soft steps and a deep grunt or two beyond him in the darkness.

He wanted desperately to look up, but he dared not lift his head. From the corner of his eye, he could see a vast shape emerging out of the blackness. Its enormity seemed to take up the entire tunnel. Slowly, with an ambling stride, the shape came into view. If he hadn't already been lying on his back, Nicolas was sure he would have fallen down out of sheer fright.

At his feet stood the nightmare of a colossal bear.

Its front legs looked like stout tree trunks covered in deep brown fur. Because of its size, Nicolas didn't have to lift his head to be able to see the bear's strangely short snout, or the bulk of its massive, muscular shoulders, or the orange hue of its eyes, staring curiously back at him. The bear's hugeness was shocking, but Nicolas' fear wasn't as great as it could have been.

The bear, he realized in wonder, was wearing *armor*.

A heavy-looking mask of grey metal went from its ears to its muzzle with hinged plates protecting the back of its cheeks, partially hiding its massive jaws. Straight out of the plate on the front of its face was a cruel-looking spike about a foot long. Three broad rings of the same grey metal looped around its neck and were joined together, along with the bear's face armor, by thick straps of leather. On its chest, strapped up around its shoulders, was another plate of metal. None of the armor looked fancy or decorative. Nicolas could see that it was scarred, scratched, and scraped. Only the metal spike seemed to be smooth and unmarked. Its tip looked needle-sharp.

The armored bear just stood there and seemed to do nothing more than give the air a few curious sniffs. Nicolas realized the raven—still standing astride Nicolas' chest—seemed completely unalarmed by the bear's presence. It had not even turned its large, black head when the gigantic creature had arrived.

With a final sniff and grunt, the beast gently nudged Nicolas' foot with one of its great paws. In any event, Nicolas presumed the bear had intended to nudge his foot, but the nudge actually pushed Nicolas' entire body, nearly causing him to lose his grip on his torch. The raven hopped from his chest, turned its curved beak to one side, then leapt into the air with a beat of its wings and neatly landed atop the bear's great shoulders.

Cautiously, Nicolas raised his head. The odd pair of animals kept looking at him, but they remained still. He slowly sat up, and when that also didn't prompt any reaction from either bear or raven, he pulled his feet beneath him, and with very deliberate movements, managed to stand up. Even now, at his full height, the bear's enormous head was still at least two feet higher than Nicolas'.

"Well," Nicolas asked in a voice more practical and less nervous-sounding than what he felt inside, "now what?"

The bear swung its armored head around and looked up at the raven. The bird looked back at the bear and pecked twice at one of the thick rings of metal beneath its claws. The bear sniffed the air again, as if in good measure, grunted, turned about, and began walking back in the direction from whence it had come.

Nicolas stood still for a moment.

For half a panicky second, he wondered if he shouldn't quietly run back out of the gate's tunnel, out onto the open plain, back along the forest road, and search for the hollow in the tree. He wasn't entirely sure if he'd again just escaped an awful and dreadful death… but for some inexplicable reason, he didn't *feel* that way. Like the great hound he'd faced outside the gatekeep, the raven and bear seemed more inquisitive than aggressive, and the fact he had just been face to face with another gigantic creature and had lived gave him a touch of courage.

The boy watched the bear and raven lumber off into the darkness, and—to his own surprise—Nicolas the Wren decided to follow after them.

———◆———

Eventually, Nicolas could see a greyness beyond the hulking shape of the bear, and he presumed the tunnel must be coming to an end. Not once during their quiet trek through the keep's long tunnel, did the raven or bear look back at Nicolas, but as they reached the mouth of the tunnel, the bear stopped. The raven alighted from its shoulder and landed on the ground, seeming to wait for Nicolas to come up even with it. As Nicolas did, the raven flew up onto his right shoulder, causing Nicolas to grunt from the bird's weight. The bird's curved talons dug deep into his sweater as it settled on its new perch. Nicolas was once again thankful for how thick his mum had knitted his sweater.

The tunnel exited into a large, round yard, perhaps a hundred yards across. Several arches and bays encircled the yard's perimeter. Bronze bowl-lamps hung from hooks between the archways. Because of this, and especially after the darkness of the gate's tunnel, the yard seemed well-lit. Nicolas could see a few men moving about, busy with various chores, while five others stood huddled together near the middle of the yard, warming outstretched hands over a blazing fire crackling away inside a large iron brazier. The brazier had a tall brick chimney built above it, which, Nicolas thought, must be intended to keep rain off the fire. Ghosts of white and black ash spiraled out of the chimney and were quickly swept away in the cold breeze above, soon lost in the sky's deep darkness.

Off to the left, Nicolas could hear the braying of a donkey and the whinny of a horse. He thought of Cherry Pit, wondering if the tall man's companion was stabled nearby. A handful of horses, sporting light saddles, were quietly standing in a small but open corral near the men by the brazier. They were busy munching on a trough which hung from the corral's fence, filled with oats. None of them appeared surprised at the presence of the giant bear, or the boy and his raven.

Nicolas, lost in a sudden excitement about finding himself inside a real-life castle, was brought quickly back to reality. The raven rapped its thick beak on his shoulder.

"Ow!"

The bird's beak hadn't really hurt, but it surprised him, and since he wasn't accustomed to his shoulder acting as a roost for a giant black bird, Nicolas took a few involuntary stutter-steps, hoping the raven would fly away. It didn't. Instead, the bird tugged at his right sleeve, and like before, Nicolas took another few steps. When he stopped, the raven tugged again. It suddenly struck Nicolas what his unwanted guest was doing.

"Do you want me to go this way?" he asked.

The raven cocked its head. Nicolas looked into the bird's glossy black eyes. "Okay," he said cautiously, "I'll go this way." He began taking a few short steps toward the right side of the courtyard. The raven, now content, rode along quietly. Nicolas felt surer of himself and began walking normally, looking ahead for where the two might be headed. As he neared a pair of arches, Nicolas could see one was blocked by a closed door, but the other had a lit torch mounted on the wall just inside, and appeared to contain a staircase leading upward.

"Which one shall I take?" he asked his raven-guide. The large bird leaned to its left, pushing its body against the side of Nicolas' head. "The staircase it is." Moments later, he stood at the first step.

Nicolas took a last look around. As he did so, he caught sight of the massive bear, which had stayed behind, turning back inside the gatekeep's long, gloomy tunnel. As it did this, the enormous creature stood on its thick hind legs. The bear must've been thirteen or fourteen feet tall, but its astonishing height wasn't what caught Nicolas' attention. Although Nicolas couldn't be sure in the courtyard's uncertain, flickering firelight, he thought the bear seemed to look remarkably like a giant man just before it disappeared entirely into the tunnel's obscurity.

Nicolas looked at the staircase before him. He took a deep breath. *A place with dragons*, he suddenly thought, and he plunged ahead.

CHAPTER 9

QUESTIONS AND
ANSWERS

The stairway was warmer than the cold, open air of the
courtyard.

Each step was made of flat, broad flagstones, which
made the climb relatively easy. The passage turned a number of
times, sometimes going up, sometimes going down, and sometimes leveling off for several paces. Every so often, he would
pass an alcove in the stone walls. Within each alcove stood
a statue, all of which appeared to be close to identical. Each
statue—all images of lean old men, covered almost entirely in
robes with long, vertical folds—towered over Nicolas, standing at least seven feet tall. Each figure was hooded, but when
Nicolas paused to take a closer look at the first one he came
across, he could see an exquisitely carved face set deep within
the stone hood. The face was wrinkled, with furrowed brows
and a stern look. The masonry work was in such marvelous
detail, the figure's face seemed uncomfortably life-like. It had a
lengthy beard spilling out of the stone-carved cloth and hanging far down its chest. In spite of himself, Nicolas reached up
to touch its petrified curls. Abruptly, he realized the statue's
black marble eyes were looking directly at him, and the reflec-
tive glint of the stairway's torchlight made them continue to
look at him even after he nervously had stepped away. Uneasy,
Nicolas lowered his own eyes to avoid the figure's stony stare.

Its arms were crossed over its chest atop its beard, and its
long, gaunt fingers grasped two objects. One was a large book

103

with hinged clasps. The hinges looked like they were made of very old, blemished metal. Nicolas touched one of the hinges with his finger, and when he took it away, it had a smudge of dark rust on its tip. The book's pebbled cover gave the impression of scoured leather. Its only decoration was a thick seal made of the same metal as the book's hinges, which was the size of a small salad plate. An ornate dragon's head had been forged into the strange seal. The dragon had a wicked face, and its brow was so deeply creased; Nicolas could barely see the glitter of green stones which had been inset for its eyes.

The statue's other hand held a hoop of iron from which hung a large iron key. The key looked similar to the old key hanging above the doorway to his father's study. Mr. Bennett's key and the stone figure's key were made for warded locks, with notches and slots of various lengths and thicknesses cut into their end. But unlike Mr. Bennett's key, the statue's key's notches and slots looked jagged and cruel-looking. They looked like tongues of iron flames, twisting and uncoiling in opposite directions. Nicolas lightly touched the bizarre key, watching it swing easily back and forth on its ring. Suddenly, he leaned forward to get a better look. Among the nasty shards of flames was the small—almost unnoticeably small—image of a man. It was hard to tell, but the small man looked as if his arms were raised in the air, and in a chilling way, Nicolas thought the man's eyes and mouth—created by pinholes—were elongated as if the man's face was melting or crying out in anguish.

Nicolas let go of the key. He backed out of the alcove and went back into the stairwell. The raven, which had never left his shoulder, was again looking at him with its head cocked to the side. Slowly, the bird turned, and by doing so, drew Nicolas' eyes to the base of the stone statue. Chiseled into the round base on which the figure stood was the name, *Apellus*. The letters sparkled with flecks of gold leaf within the stone. Nicolas hesitantly looked back up at the statue's lifeless face. The orbs of its black eyes stared back at him.

The raven sharply tugged on his sweater's sleeve, and Nicolas resumed his journey along the staircase. A few steps away, he looked back at the stone figure, which had almost entirely disappeared in the recess of its alcove. The bizarre iron key was still swinging slightly on its giant ring.

Nicolas encountered another ten stone statues, all hooded in long robes, all with heads bent, all with black eyes which seemed to follow him, and all with large books and iron keys. Each figure had a different name, a different face, and a different dragon carved or chiseled onto each book's seal—all with malignant, distorted faces, and green-gem eyes.

At long last, the stairway arrived at a solid oak door. Its wooden beams were old and rubbed smooth. Nicolas caught the faint smell of linseed oil as he inspected the door closely for some sort of handle or knob by which it could be opened. There was none.

Well that's daffy, he thought, running his hands along the seams where the door's beams were joined, but the tight seams yielded no secrets. Nicolas made a fist and rapped twice on the wood with his knuckles. The door seemed solid, and the sound of his quick knock only created a slight echo through the stairwell.

"Well," Nicolas declared to the raven, "I think we might have come all this way for nothing." He sighed and turned around. *What now?* He leaned back against the polished wood—and heard a soft click.

Turning, he could see the door begin to gradually swing open. When it finally came to rest, now wide open, the large raven startled Nicolas by suddenly alighting from his shoulder and flying off into the darkness beyond the door. Nicolas heard its wings beating and flapping for a moment, and then the sound faded, leaving him alone and in silence. Nicolas took a wary step forward. There was a distinctly musty and stuffy smell, which reminded Nicolas of the great library room in Muncaster Castle in Ravenglass, Cumbria, where his father had taken him for a visit during his summer break. It smelled of old books.

Stone the crows, Nicolas thought. He stood on the door's threshold, trying to decide what to do.

"Don't just stand there, boy," said a bodiless voice out of the blue-black dark beyond the door.

Nicolas jerked backward with fright and surprise. From the shadows stepped a figure nearly identical to the statues Nicolas had passed in the stairwell's numerous alcoves. The hooded figure loomed above him, grasping a similar great book in its crossed arms.

"You *are* Nicolas, are you not?" It said, stretching out one of its long arms and uncurling its thin fingers. "Come this way. I have eagerly awaited your arrival, my boy. There is much to discuss." With a slight bow, it said, "*I* am Aldus Ward."

Before Nicolas could recover, think of something to say, or decide to run as fast as he could in the other direction, the robed specter sank back into the dark passage and melted away. Were it not for the muted sound of shuffling feet, Nicolas might have believed the tall, stony-looking figure had disappeared entirely.

Its voice had sounded worn and gravelly, but not unkind. *It says it's Aldus Ward*, Nicolas reasoned with himself, *and it says it's been expecting me*. This last bit was unnerving, but because Baatunde had said much the same thing, Nicolas felt slightly better. He rubbed the coin in his pocket. *I've come too far to turn back now*, Nicolas thought sternly, as if giving himself an order.

And with that, he gave a good shudder all over, filled his lungs with air, and faded into the dark beyond the door.

Once out of the stairwell's torchlight, Nicolas' eyes slowly adjusted, and the darkness of the passage beyond the door did not seem so bad. If Nicolas squinted, he could see the vague outline of the robed figure walking several paces in front of him. For some reason, Nicolas felt the need to walk as quietly as he could—perhaps not wanting the stranger in front of him to realize he was following.

The passageway was silent, cool, and appeared undisturbed. There weren't any side doors or windows or alcoves. Aside from the presence of far too many cobwebs (which Nicolas quickly—almost frantically—tried to pull out of his hair and face, wondering why the robed figure moving in front of him hadn't run into them first), the passageway felt peculiarly empty, as if nothing and no one had been through it in a long time. Gradually, Nicolas began to see some sort of blue-white light far ahead. The light wasn't bright really, but it seemed—*clear*. The light didn't flicker like a torch or a lamp, and Nicolas guessed it signaled the presence of a doorway. As the figure in front of him moved closer to the source of light, the outlines of its robe and hood became more distinct, and in the confines of the narrow passage, the figure appeared even taller than it had before.

After another fifty paces, a door did come into view. It was wooden and had a simple, but low, stone archway. Nicolas thought the mysterious figure would continue shuffling through it, but instead, it stopped.

Hunching over at its shoulders and dropping its chin to its chest, the figure spoke three Latin words in a deliberate but hushed voice. "*Salus in arduis*" (a stronghold in difficulties). As soon as the words were spoken, the clear blue-white light from the foot of the door glowed more brightly, and Nicolas could see the figure's long, gaunt fingers unfold from somewhere inside its stiff cloak. They stretched out in front of it, and the robed figure gently waved them in the air. "*Domicilium in tempus pacis*" (home in a time of peace), it said in the same measured but subdued voice. Slowly, in the same way Nicolas had many times watched the morning sun push back a plum-colored night sky, the clear blue-white light transformed into a hospitable buttery glow—the familiar-looking radiance of roaring fireplaces and merrily burning lamps. A gentle warmth seeped into the passageway. Suddenly—oddly—Nicolas had the strangest sensation he was... *home.*

The boy followed the tall, robed figure through the archway and into the inviting light.

———•———

The odd sense of being at home was, strangely enough, the result of a distinct recipe of smells which filled Nicolas' nose. There was the slight tang of calf-skin vellum covers, a whiff of ligament-cord bindings, a hint of mildewed water stains, the mustiness of old and worn clothes, and the distinctive but indefinable scent of... age-old paper. Indeed, for a brief moment, what Nicolas' eyes saw was outdone by what his nose smelled.

He smelled *books.*

Tens of thousands of books, leather and papyrus parchments, scrolls of all sizes and thicknesses, broken and discarded binding cords, tallow-based and pungent glues, bitter inks and oils, and shabby dust-layered covers. For the first time in his life, Nicolas understood the subtle smells which filled his nose every time he walked into his father's study. The smells in his father's study weren't an overpowering assortment of aromas, and they couldn't compete with the kitchen's fragrant smells of baked bread or pot roast, but they were distinct, subtle, and a permanent part of his feeling of home. Like the smoky scent of charred wood in the fireplace and the cherry perfume of pipe smoke, the smell of books was a natural part of his father's study, and uniquely a natural part of his father.

Nicolas breathed in the smell of thousands of books and thought of his family's quiet home in the country outside of Penrith, England. And with that impression still lingering in his mind, his eyes took in the wonderful scene in front of him.

A scene teeming with books.

Thousands of books.

Tens of thousands of books. Seemingly endless shelves— some of which one would need a ladder to reach—were chockablock full of books. Books on top of bookcases. Books on the floor in heaps. Books leaning against each other in snakelike rows, as if they were dominoes. Books stacked crazily atop each other as tall as a man. Books with every possible variety of color, shape, size, and thickness, were packed, crammed, squeezed, stuffed, and crowded into almost every inch of space.

Nicolas looked around in awe.

An iron chandelier, lit with seven fat candles, hung from a chain in the vaulted ceiling above. To one side, amid the wonderful confusion of books were two high-backed chairs, facing a little fireplace. A blackened fire basket with a grate of three iron bars stood inside it, hosting the comforting snap and pop of a small fire. Through the flames, Nicolas could see a decorative metal fireback with a raised impression of a large tree. Half the tree's branches were full of leaves, while the other half was barren. Beneath it were strange words, written in the flow of a lovely script: *Llawenhewch, yn Dod y Brenin.*

"Welcome."

Nicolas gave a start. In the warm light of the fire and chandelier, he now saw that the tall robed figure was an old, grandfatherly man, dressed in a linen tunic and a dark green woolen cloak with silver leaves and vines embroidered along its hem and collar. Around his waist was a simple leather belt. The top of the old man's head was bald, but thick locks of pleasantly silver hair surrounded the rest of his head, reaching down past his shoulders. Roosting behind one of the old man's ears was a long reed pen with an ink-bit, looking very much like a small arrowhead. When the old man turned his head, the reed pen reminded Nicolas of a weathervane atop a barn, turning with the direction of the wind. The old man's wide forehead, high cheekbones, and untamed eyebrows caused his eyes to sit in a slight shadow. Even so, Nicolas could still see the bright blue color of the old man's right eye, which seemed to sparkle with specks of gold and emerald. The old man's left eye was entirely milky white and seemed sightless. From the lower lid of this eye, an uneven scar ran down his cheek for about two inches and eventually disappeared in one of the thickest and fullest beards Nicolas had ever seen. The old man stood there inquisitively, tugging gently at his beard's ample curls and staring intensely at Nicolas with his good eye.

"Come now, Master Bennett," he said, placing a kind hand on his shoulder, "let's have something to eat and drink, and a warm place to sit. You and I have much to discuss, I think, and not much time to do it in." The old man pointed to one of the chairs. "This room is part of my private chambers. Please make yourself comfortable."

Nicolas sat back in one of the chairs, his legs dangled a few inches off the floor, while the old man took the other. Both stared in silence into the fire for a few moments. A bubbling tea kettle hung over the flames on an iron swing-arm, with small clouds of steam lazily wafting out of its spout. It was then that Nicolas noticed the large raven had settled on the high back of the old man's chair. It was looking directly at him with its head cocked to the side.

"That one's name is *Kaha*," the old man explained, looking at the bird and the boy. "He's now one of the gatekeep's ravens, although," he paused and said quietly, "he's not entirely a raven, you know."

"Not entirely a raven?" repeated Nicolas.

"No, of course not. His kind are something special, Master Bennett. He's a Chatham raven—extinct where you come from, I think. Very large. Very smart. And they have a fascinating way of accommodating *ghosts*. The best I can tell, it's as if a Chatham raven has enough room inside itself for someone else. They're fairly picky, mind you, especially those within the any one of the Gates." He threw the raven a small bit of dried meat he'd taken from a pouch sitting on the end table, "This one here was especially selective. *Kaha* decided he had room for a Wisp."

A Wisp was something the tall man in the forest had called a Kohanim. "What's a Wisp?" Nicolas asked, and before the old man could answer, he asked, "What's a Kohanim?"

The old man sat back, cocked an eyebrow, and nodded his head in approval. "You're already learning, Master Bennett." He reached inside his robe and withdrew a pinch of green dust, which seemed to glow. He threw the dust in the fire, where it exploded with a mild pop. "As I said, you and I have much to discuss."

A slender sidedoor swung open, and in walked a boy several years older than Nicolas. The boy was pushing a pair of thick, round spectacles up his long, thin nose, but in spite of his efforts, the spectacles were still so far away from the boy's eyes, Nicolas thought it must be more work to try to see through them than it must be to not use them at all.

"Good evening, m'lord," the older boy said with a slight bow of his head to the old man. He was dressed in comfortable-looking leather slippers and a dark brown hooded cowl which was

bunched together at the waist with a braided cord of three colors—yellow, blue, and red—from which hung a metal ring and
several clanging keys of various sizes. His light brown hair was
cropped evenly around his head, and his fingers were stained
with ink. His thin nose kept twitching as if he were about to
sneeze, and he glanced quickly from Nicolas to the old man.

The older boy reminded Nicolas of a new book he'd recently
seen in his school library. It was about a young monk named
Theophane, who lived in a monastery in the Mourne Mountains of Northern Ireland. Theophane's job had been to make
ink for the other monks, and he discovered ways to make the
ink colorful. The book had been easy reading for Nicolas, and
illustrations had been bold and captivating. Nicolas had found
himself wondering what it would have been like to live in a
medieval monastery with its tall towers, stone walls, and its
monastic occupants. Now, in a most peculiar and remarkable
way, the book had come alive for him. Nicolas suddenly decided he liked the boy with the long thin nose.

"Good evening, Master Brooks!" said the old man exuber-
antly. "Would you please awaken Jotham and have him warm
some cakes and biscuits with jam? Master Bennett here looks
as if he hasn't had a proper bite to eat in quite some time, and I
feel much the same way. After all, dinner was several hours ago."
He winked and smiled at Nicolas as he said this. "See if Jotham
can trouble himself to find some of that wonderful apple butter
we indulged in yesterday morning. By the king's throne, that
was delicious!" The monkish boy named Brooks nodded and left
quickly to find Jotham, the gatekeep's head baker.

From somewhere inside one of the sleeves of his green cloak,
the old man drew out a slender straight-stemmed pipe, perhaps
two feet in length. Its long, delicate stem was made of darkly
marbled wood and was wrapped in two threads of copper and

silver, which coiled like snakes around the small bowl at the end of the pipe. Soon, gentle puffs of pipe smoke wafted into the air, filling the sitting room with sweet-smelling fragrances. Nicolas thought of the sweet-smelling pink azaleas, yellow buttercups, and pink dog roses, which his mum grew in the Bennetts' small garden.

The old man and the boy sat there quietly. A couple of times, the old man harrumphed and chuckled quietly to himself, but said nothing to Nicolas, who was beginning to feel sleepy.

To stay awake, Nicolas sat up on the edge of the soft cushions of his chair and watched pleasantly as the fire leapt and gyrated in the firebasket. His body felt tired, and he guessed it was well past midnight. He thought about the peculiar footpath which had taken him away from the Will-o'-the-Wisp Medieval Fair. He thought about the odd little fellow, Baatunde, and his odd little treehouse, and the frightening intensity of the cold he'd felt once he stepped through the iron door. Nicolas thought about the curious tree hollow which sat silently in the empty woods, and his journey through the dark forest with the grim tall man and Cherry Pit. He remembered fear he'd felt when the wraith-like creature ambushed them along the forest road, and he thought of how intimidating St. Wulf's-Without-Aldersgate had looked across the cold, treeless plain. He remembered how huge the Master Grimlock had been, and how huge Basileus, the dog, had been, and how exceptionally gigantic the bear in the tunnel had been. Nicolas thought about the stony sculptures of the tall, robed men, holding keys and books with dragon seals. And he thought about the remarkably peculiar old man sitting with him, merrily puffing his remarkably long pipe.

"Excuse me," Nicolas said, feeling a bit of determination to at last get some answers.

The old man laced his fingers along the pipe's slender stem

and withdrew it from his mouth. "Yes, Master Bennett?"

"I have a few questions I'd like to ask, if that's alright."

The old man smiled playfully. "Oh, I'd much rather begin with *answers* than with questions, my boy. Answers, after all, are tidier than questions because answers know where they belong. Questions—anyway, *most* questions—have no idea where they're going or where they belong. *You*, Master Bennett, have questions because you have no idea where you're going or where you belong. I, however, have *answers* because I *am* where I belong."

Nicolas thought about this for a moment, trying his best not to be confused, but feeling confused all the same. "Alright," he finally said, pushing his chin out slightly. "I'd like a few answers, please."

"And indeed, Nicolas the Wren," said the old man with deep satisfaction, "you should have them."

CHAPTER 10

A TERRIBLE INVITATION

Master Brooks, the older boy with the long, thin nose, suddenly reappeared through the sidedoor, bearing a sizeable covered basket. His head was tilted back to allow him to squint through his spectacles. From the basket, he withdrew two deep wooden bowls. Each contained a quarter-loaf of malted currant bread, soaked in warm milk and liberally sprinkled with crumbs of sugar. He then took out two plates, which held thick slices of steaming shepherd's pie, a few salted herring, and some pads of creamy cheese.

Aldus looked crestfallen. He stared into his bowl and trencher with his one good eye. "No apple butter, I suppose."

"No, m'lord. The head baker said… um—" the young man uncomfortably searched for the right words. "He said, if yer, um, *majesty* is so inclined as to, um, *desire* his, um, apple butter, then yer *majesty* can good an' well get it for 'imself.'"

Aldus scowled fiercely. He pushed his lips out, causing his great beard to rise and fall off his chest. "Our good baker said all *that*, did he?"

Even in the firelight, Nicolas could see the older boy turn red.

"No, m'lord. Well, *yes*, m'lord! Well, that was *some* of it anyway." The poor young man's shoulders slumped down in nervous defeat. His spectacles slid to the very end of his long, thin nose. "The head baker said it, um, more *colorfully*, m'lord."

For a moment, Aldus just sat there, scowling and wagging his beard. Suddenly, he turned to Nicolas, gave a great wink with his brilliant blue right eye, and laughed. "Well then, Mas-

ter Bennett, you'll simply have to try our marvelous apple butter when you return. Thank you kindly, Master Brooks. I shan't
be needing you the rest of the night."

"Thank you, m'lord," the older boy replied. He gave his
plunging spectacles a final shove up the bridge of his nose, and
with a final courteous bow—which promptly caused his spectacles to slide back down to where they had been—he disappeared back through the slender sidedoor.

Watching the door close, Aldus leaned over and whispered
to Nicolas, "Master Brooks is a fine fellow, really. Not sure how
he can ever see anything, but he *does* seem to manage." He
pointed to Nicolas' food. "Tuck into it, my boy. It's all best
when it's still hot."

The old man and boy chewed and dipped and gulped their
way through pie, bread, cheese, and fish. When Aldus had finished, he brushed crumbs of malted currant bread out of his
thick beard and tossed a last salted herring to *Kaha*, who ate it
in a single gulp.

"I shall begin with a few necessities," he said as Nicolas sa-
vored his last pad of creamed cheese. "We can then pick and
choose other things to discuss if there is any time left, but the
hour is late."

Aldus settled deeply into his chair and took a few thoughtful
puffs from his freshly lit pipe before beginning. "You, Master
Bennett, may call me Aldus, although most call me by other
names and titles. I am known as Laird of the First Gate and a
council member of the Commissioners of the Forfeited Gates.
My gatekeep, St. Wulf's-Without-Aldersgate, is, naturally, the
first of the Forfeited Gates of the City of Relic. As its Laird, I
am charged with its safekeeping and the disposition of all those
who enter it. I am also a judge of the King's First Bench. All
those who wish to enter the City of Relic must pass through

one of its outer gates, and to pass through one of its outer gates is to enter by permission of a judge of the King. Unless…" the old man leaned closer, arching an eyebrow over his milky, blind eye. "Unless a person enters by *invitation*. And *you*, Master Bennett," he emphasized, "are here by invitation." Aldus said this then stopped, waiting for a reaction.

"But I *haven't* been invited," Nicolas replied. "A little man in a woods near my home, named Baatunde, told me to find you, and I went through an iron door in his cottage, and came out of a tree, and I met Mr. Westenra, a man who helped me find my way here, where a huge man with a huge dog met us outside the gate's entrance, and told me to come inside." Nicolas had said all of this in a rush. He was out of breath, and he hoped Aldus would believe him. "*How* can I have been invited?"

"Aha!" exclaimed Aldus, and he thrust his finger in the air as if he'd just discovered something. "Aha!" he exclaimed again, although he didn't say anything else right away. Instead, he puffed his pipe thoughtfully and raised both eyebrows. "*How* were you invited, you say? I imagine you were *invited* through a *warning*, my dear boy, and by the king's throne, Master Bennett, I've been *waiting* on your arrival for years."

At this, Nicolas looked so honestly bewildered, Aldus laughed aloud and waved a hand in the air as if to shoo away the boy's confusion. "I thought we had agreed, Master Bennett. *You* shall keep your questions until *after* I provide answers."

Still chuckling, the old man stood up and plucked two worn and chipped mugs from the shelf of a cupboard near the fireplace. He poked around noisily within the sideboard underneath the cupboard and shortly withdrew his hand, grasping a fistful of rolled cinnamon sticks. The sticks were dropped into the mugs, along with the hot water from the hissing and spitting black kettle. To this was added sprigs of mint, a spoon of sugar, and some grated nutmeg Aldus had selected from blue glass jars sitting on the table near his chair. "Let it soak a minute, Master Bennett, then drink up! You've come a long way, and I daresay, you have a much longer way to go before you return. You'll need your energy." He paused. "You'll be leaving in the morning." He said this last bit more softly, as if it was a thought only meant for himself.

Nicolas wrapped his hands around his mug and blew on the hot drink. It smelled refreshing and pleasant. He took a first sip, trying his best not to slurp. And he waited.

The old man sat still. Unmoving, his drink went untouched. He stared absently at the bobbing licks of flame in the firebasket. Nicolas noticed deep lines of concern etching his scarred and ancient face.

Finally—quietly—Aldus said, "I spoke those same words to your grandfather many long years ago."

"You knew my grandfather?" Nicolas asked in shocked surprise. "Baatunde…" he began to say, but Aldus gently waved his hand in the air, and Nicolas fell silent.

Turning to face Nicolas, the old man smiled kindly. "That is how I know your name. In fact, your grandfather looked much like you do now, although his hair wasn't such a mess." He nodded his head slightly, as if remembering a memory from long past. The concern on his face was now gone. "I knew him briefly, but in that time, *much* happened. Much happened, and much of that leads to you."

Aldus suddenly twitched his nose, gulped his cinnamon tea loudly, and said, "But let's begin where it makes sense to begin. We'll begin with the *where* and move to the *why*."

The old man tugged at his long, thick beard. "*You* are not far from your home. To be more precise, in fact, you are next to it.

Your world and this one—this one called Telluric Grand—are *parallel* to each other. Indeed, these two worlds share the same sun and moon, and even some of the same earth and water. They are connected, even if the connections have not always been easy to see."

His eyes lit up, and he leaned forward with an excited look on his face. "Permit me to ask *you* a question or two, Master Bennett. Have you ever taken a quiet walk in a woods and thought you heard a voice even though no one was there?" Nicolas nodded. "Well," said the old man with smug approval, "someone *was* there. You see, there are places where the space between our worlds is *thin*." To demonstrate this, he quickly rubbed two fingers together and took a long puff on his pipe. "Have you ever visited a cave and felt like someone, or something, might be deep inside? Have you ever seen something moving in a fog, but when you looked closely, it had disappeared? Have you ever heard a floorboard mysteriously creak, or felt a queer current of cold air on a warm day?

"There are places and spaces we *share*. Old towns, old woods, old caves, old castles, old graveyards, and even old storm cellars. They are all places where Telluric Grand and your world *rub* together. And then of course," he said matter-of-factly, "there are *doors*. Most doors have long been forgotten or have been closed, but there are few which remain, and these few are closely guarded secrets. Even I do not know where they are. Doors, you see, are *dangerous*. Long, long ago, the ancients used them to pass more freely between Telluric Grand and your own world. They thought of it as adventurous, as a way to trade and to explore. But dark things also found the doors, and they, too, passed between the worlds. Dark things which were never meant to be shared found their way through.

"The ancients discovered this, and measures were taken to

restore things to their rightful place. Many doors were closed, tombs were sealed shut, and most dark things were hunted out of existence. Countless years have passed in your world since this took place, and now only a few still believe that dark things ever existed. Men in your world now scoff when the bones of giants are said to be unearthed. They dismiss primal powers such as sorcery and alchemy. They believe all magicians are simple tricksters, and they believe fairies are for bedtime stories and silly dreams. When they do find age-old books about devils and monsters and trolls, they call such things fables and myths and legends." As Aldus spoke, his face and his voice became grave.

"Once, long ago, your world held true knights and clever wizards. Your elders understood the deeper meanings of the stars, the tides, the trees, and…" The old man paused. He gazed at the flickering flames in the firebasket. "They *understood* fire and iron. They understood *dragons*."

With this, the old man slumped back in his chair. Quietly, he sat there, puffing his pipe, and staring distractedly into the firelight.

For his own part, Nicolas also sat back in his overstuffed chair, sipping his tea, and looking around the room, thinking about what Aldus had just told him. He looked at the marvelous stacks of books, and shelves crammed with books, and he wondered what amazing things they all might contain. He thought of the strange book his father had shown him. The one written by the priest, Edward Topsell, with its engraving of a fierce-looking dragon.

"My dad showed me an old book about animals and monsters," he said quietly.

Aldus looked knowingly at Nicolas with his piercing, blue eye. "I suppose he did. I also suppose you have a coin in your pocket. A coin with a knight and a dragon."

Carefully, Nicolas dug into his pocket and withdrew the rocking-horse crown coin. He handed it to Aldus. "Hmmmm," muttered the old man, turning the coin back and forth in the light. "The gatekeeper, Baatunde, sent word about you, Master Bennett."

"He did?" asked Nicolas.

"Oh yes. Baatunde is a Caledonii, although there are many other names for his race of people. They are a strange and ageless little folk. Some of their tribes live beyond the moor lands of the Hollow Fen, deep inside the Black Forest, just south of a treacherous strip of high crags called the Timekeeper's Finger. I do not know if the Caledonii have always been, but their kind seems to appear in almost all the old tales. Baatunde is one of their elders, and as such, he was chosen as a gatekeeper. I cannot say how they know the things they seem to know." He smiled to himself. "They *are* an odd, little folk. They generally love to laugh and are very kind, I believe, but they can be fierce and sturdy when it is called for. They do not often mix company with other races, and it is a unique thing to spend time among them. And," Aldus added thoughtfully, "they are *wise*. Very wise indeed."

"Oh," said Nicolas, realizing how little he knew about the peculiar fellow he had met with the cottage in the tree. It made him think of what else he had in his pocket. "I also have this," he volunteered, and he held up the farthing coin.

"Ah. Nicolas the Wren," declared the Laird of the First Gate, admiring the coin's image of the little bird. "The title suits you well."

"But that isn't my title," said Nicolas.

"Well, of course it is," replied Aldus. "That's what you've been calling yourself, isn't it?"

Nicolas smiled sheepishly and wondered what other information Baatunde had sent to Laird Ward, and he wondered *how* Baatunde had sent such information. Nicolas glanced up at the large raven still perched on the back of Aldus Ward's chair. It could have been a trick of the firelight, but for a moment, it looked as if Kaha was glaring intensely at him. Nicolas blinked. The bird blinked back at him and began preening its feathers. The bird's intense stare reminded Nicolas of something... *The crow!* thought Nicolas suddenly.

"There was a crow," he blurted out.

"A crow?" Aldus stopped puffing his pipe and bent forward. "A crow?" he asked again. "When? Where?"

"When I woke up this morning, er, I mean yesterday morning, or whenever it was, there was a crow at my window."

The old man's eyes narrowed, creating slits of indigo blue and milky white beneath the overhangs of bushy eyebrows. "And what happened?" he asked warily.

"Well, um, nothing," said Nicolas, who was not even sure why he'd mentioned it.

"Nothing?"

"No. Well, I mean, when I went to the window to see what it was, it saw me, and it flew away."

Aldus stared at him. "That was all?"

"Yes. I think so," replied Nicolas. "And I found this on my windowsill." Carefully, he pulled the coppery leaf out of his pocket and laid it on his lap.

The old man's blue eye seemed to change to a dark grey. "By the king's throne!" He said in a dreadful voice. His entire face drained of color, but he didn't reach for the leaf as Nicolas expected. Instead, the Laird of the First Gate hung his head and shook it back and forth. "This is worse than I imagined, my boy. This is a terrible warning. This is an omen of what is coming. What *may* come."

"What may come? Why is this a terrible warning?"

Aldus set his jaw with stern resolve, now sounding like a formidable judge of the King's First Bench. "This," he said pointing an accusing finger at the coppery leaf. "This was your 'invitation' that came as a warning. I had been hopeful the warning would have been something else. It *should* have been something else," he said grimly. "I knew the time had come. Time for a new…" he hesitated, clearly searching for the right words. "Time for *you* to come here, Master Bennett. I knew it was time because something has been changing in this land. The great city beyond this gatekeep, the City of Relic, the greatest city in Telluric Grand, has been at peace for a number of years, and peace has been kept in most of the kingdoms even far from its walls. But something has changed. Currents of fear are now rippling through the land. Rumors of war and destruction and of a coming darkness have begun to spread. The long peace has been threatened, and so I knew it was time for you to come. But this," he said, waving cheerlessly at the coppery leaf. "This is a *far* worse invitation than what I had imagined."

Nicolas looked down at the strange coppery leaf on his knees. He remembered the apprehension in his father's eyes when he had shown the leaf to him in his study. "A place with dragons," he muttered softly to himself.

The Laird of the First Gate looked solemnly at Nicolas. "Yes, my boy. *This* is a place with dragons."

Shadow Thief, the frightening name the tall man in the forest had spoken to Nicolas now came to his mind. Timidly, he asked, "Is it Shadow Thief?"

The old man looked sharply at Nicolas. "You listen well, Master Bennett, and that is a good thing. Yes, the threat to the long peace must be the dragon they call the Shadow Thief. There *are* other, lesser dragons—they are extremely dangerous, but not as destructive or as powerful. Shadow Thief is an overlord dragon, a direct descendent of *Komor Herceg*, the one called the First Prince."

The old man and the boy sat in silence.

A small log shifted and broke in the firebasket, sending up a gentle spray of red, firefly sparks. Nicolas was afraid, but he was sure Aldus Ward knew what could be done, and at the moment, it felt safe sitting in front of the fire surrounded by stacks of books and thick castle walls. He waited for Aldus to say something.

After several minutes had passed, the Laird of the First Gate sat up, grasped an andiron in his hand and stabbed its sharp end irritably into the fire. Several showers of sparks flew into the air. This time, none too gently.

Aldus spoke. "When I was much younger and still learning about such things, I sought out the wisdom of mystics and the science of alchemists. I studied under one of the few remaining ancients, and I learned many, many things from him. One of the many things I learned about was the Beginning, the Beginning of Telluric Grand, a beginning which, I believe, was in time with your own world's beginning."

He turned to face Nicolas. His good eye was gleaming. It was brilliant blue again. "There isn't much time, Master Bennett. You need to listen carefully to what I have to tell you. Dragons," he said firmly, "*weren't* always dragons."

CHAPTER 11

ᚈALᕮS OF DRAᏀOᏁS

In a time before time—before the oldest trees, before clouds carried rain, before much more than the wind moved beneath the sun, and even before the high mountains or the vast ocean knew the hard footprints or laboring oars of common men— the Thing-which-became-the-first-dragon was still a shapeless part of the vast and endless heavens. It may have not yet been a *dark* thing, but at some point in a time before time, the Thing-which-became-the-first-dragon grew to be *hungry*. And hunger invites *darkness*."

The Laird of the First Gate and the greatest among the Commissioners of the Forfeited Gates hesitated before going on. His face was troubled and his voice was dark. "To satisfy its hunger, the Thing-which-became-the-first-dragon devoured one third of all the heavens. Its frenzied feast left great holes in the vastness of the sky, and the once-whole light of the heavens was broken into the sun, the moon, and the stars. Because of its selfish gluttony, the Thing-which-became-the-first-dragon soon hardened into a great but fractured stone. The folds of its skin were like shards of flint. Its teeth were like granite daggers. Its eyes were like fragments of marble. And its long claws were like immense splinters of glass. It became a *dark* thing—perhaps the first of all dark things—and it fell out of the vast and endless heavens, plunging violently into the deepest waters of the Cold Sea.

"This *Thing*-which-became-the-first-dragon—this starving horror of darkness—leapt out of the Cold Sea and took in its first breath of air. The ancients of old said it was at this moment that it the thing became the First Dragon, *Komor Herceg*. An elemental fire ignited within its belly, and as it rose into the mists of the sky, it took the shape of a great winged worm."

In a faraway voice, the old man added quietly, "And then, it went looking for *food*."

———————◆◆◆———————

Kaha, the great raven, chose this moment to shake out its long, black feathers, startling Nicolas and causing him to spill some of his tea. The bird quivered as it stretched out its huge wings, casting terrifying shadows across the spines of thousands of books. It stabbed its neck forward and opened wide its sharp beak. Nicolas imagined a winged dragon flying among the flickering lights of a dying sky. The bird relaxed. It gathered its wings back into its body and shifted the grip of its talons on Aldus' high back chair in a more comfortable roost.

The old man continued his tale. "The ancients say there was a race of wicked giants which dwelled in enormous stone fortresses high in the wintry peaks of the Dolmen Tombs, a wild mountain range in the cold wastes far to the north. These wicked giants mined for gold and silver and iron, believing it was their right to take whatever they wanted from the earth. The great winged worm sought them out and struck a deal with these creatures. In exchange for letting them live, they agreed to provide it with food. Its food, Nicolas, was *iron*. Molten iron ran like honey inside its dark veins. When fresh air rushed over Komor Herceg's copper-like tongue, it mixed with the molten iron inside the dragon's belly, and in this way, its primal fire was sustained. Explosions and flames ripped from its jaws in jets of red-hot fire. And misery came with it."

Aldus Ward leaned back in his chair and pinched his eyes closed as if to blot out a nightmarish memory. Except for the cracks and pops of the fire in the firebasket, the room was silent. Nicolas could even hear his own heartbeat thumping inside his ears.

"Iron," Aldus finally said, "mined from the bowels of frozen mountains is sufficient for a time, but overlord dragons always prefer star iron, the elemental iron which sometimes falls from the heavens in the form of great stones. Star iron is more rare, and while the giants in the mountains kept the First Dragon satisfied for a time, soon Komor Herceg's craving for star iron caused it to begin marauding the kingdoms of Telluric Grand, searching for it. I think it missed the *taste* of the endless heavens."

The old man knocked ash out of his pipe bowl and refilled it with a fresh packing. He fished about in the fire with the andiron poker for a long stick. When he found one, unburned on one end, and with a glowing ember on the other end, he drew it out of the fire and lit his pipe. Nicolas took his last drink of the cinnamon tea and wished he had another bite of the malted currant bread.

The old man wiggled his nose amid the fog of pipe smoke and waved the air clear with a sweep of his hand. "*That*, Master Bennett, is the Beginning. The First Dragon was the evilest of curses across Telluric Grand, spoiling and destroying everything in its path with fire and hunger. But after a long time had passed, and after much suffering, a great war broke out. The Kohanim—Wisps, as you have been told—intervened, and Komor Herceg was defeated and buried deep within the earth." He looked at Nicolas. "I imagine you shall learn much more about this later, but for now, there are more pressing things for you to know."

Nicolas thought about what he'd been told. Secretly, he wanted to know what happened—about wars and giants and Wisps, which sounded frightening and exciting all at the same time— but he also wanted Laird Ward to think he was sensible and helpful. Nicolas said, "You said the Shadow Thief was a fourth generation dragon. If you like, please tell me about that dragon."

Aldus' blue eye twinkled, and he smiled. "You *are* a clever boy, Nicolas the Wren. Yes. I shall tell you about him."

———————◆———————

"Before Komor Herceg was brought down, the dragon managed, through dark sorcery and black powers beyond my learning, to conceive a second overlord dragon, one called *Külon Tuz*, or 'Separate Fire' in the common tongue. This dragon was even more *worm-ish* than Komor Herceg had been. I suspect it was made more of wet earth than stone. Külon Tuz was the first of the overlord dragons to learn to crawl along the ground on its legs and great claws. It favored the earth more than the sky, and it carved out a deep lair in the cliffs overlooking the murky waves of the Cold Sea. To this day, the War Crows—a dark race of savage warriors who come from across the Cold Sea—refer to Külon Tuz as the 'Worm of Crows.' They mistakenly thought they could parley with the dragon and join forces with it to defeat the City of Relic and the First Kingdom, but overlord dragons do not covet kingdoms. The emissary sent by the War Crows was roasted alive, and Külon Tuz took its time picking the War Crow's bones clean." The old man smiled grimly. "Overlord dragons desire only death and suffering—and iron.

"Eventually, Külon Tuz created a third dragon, named *Király Hazug*, or 'King Liar.' This overlord dragon proved to be exceedingly clever, and it was able to learn the speech of men. Mothers still tell their little children that if they hear a strange but gentle maiden calling their name, it is the King Liar disguising its voice. It is said anyone who heard this dragon speak had their skulls crushed as if their heads had been beaten by great hammers."

Nicolas' eyes went wide with alarm. "Was that true?"

The old man shrugged. "Perhaps, but I think that part of the legend was meant to scare little children into listening only for the sound of their mother's voice." He sighed. "But no one living can really say."

Nicolas tried to imagine what it must be like to have one's skull, much less *any* bone, broken to bits by a hammer. It was an awful thought.

"King Liar," Aldus said, continuing, "was the dragon which bore *Árnyék Tolvaj*, the fourth generation of overlord dragons. The one known as the Shadow Thief. This last dragon was even more clever than King Liar. It struck vile bargains with evil men and with outcast Wisps called Shedu. Like a colossal snake, it preferred to attack most of its victims through ambush and cunning, although, when hungry enough, it also did not mind burning alive all the inhabitants of outlying villages merely to eat the iron in their farming tools and homes."

"What happened to the Shadow Thief?" asked Nicolas, who was now trying not to think of what it must be like to be burnt alive.

"Necessary alliances have always made throughout time," Aldus explained, "and each overlord dragon has eventually been overcome. At long last, the Shadow Thief, too, was overcome. It was outwitted and trapped by a very powerful Wisp, who entombed the dragon inside the granite outcrop of the Timekeeper's Finger. This victory, however, occurred amid much destruction and grief," said Aldus, sadly.

"I don't understand," said Nicolas. "The Shadow Thief didn't die?"

"Well yes. In a way it did. Actually, it slept, or *smoldered*, you might say, like a hot cinder buried in the ashes of a doused fire. You see, my boy, an overlord dragon cannot *die*—it cannot be utterly destroyed—unless the dragon is destroyed from *within*.

There is something dreadfully extraordinary about the fire inside these dragons. If this fire could be extinguished, they can truly be destroyed. But that, as you might imagine, is quite a trick."

Nicolas frowned thoughtfully. "Were the other overlord dragons destroyed? Did they die?"

The old man sat still for several seconds. His milky white eye stared sightlessly at Nicolas, while his blue eye stared intently at the coppery leaf on Nicolas' lap. "Külon Tuz, the second generation, and King Liar, were both destroyed and their fires eternally extinguished. However, Komor Herceg," he said softly, "was only *locked* away."

The look on the old man's face seemed clear. He did not want to say anything more about the first overlord dragon.

For what seemed like a long time, Nicolas and the Laird of the First Gate sat quietly, each lost in their own thoughts.

The fire was warm, and Nicolas realized how truly tired he felt. His eyes were heavy, and the over-stuffed chair was coaxing him into falling asleep. With some reluctance, he finally broke the pleasant silence. There was one more thing he wanted to know—perhaps it was the most important thing to know—but he was afraid of what Laird Ward's answer might be. "May I ask something?"

"Of course, Master Bennett. It is a good time for a question."

Nicolas cleared his throat and spoke slowly—piecing things together in his head as the words came out of his mouth. "You have said I was 'invited' here, and that I've been 'expected' to arrive, but that my invitation is actually a dreadful warning of terrible things which might be going on or which might soon go on."

The old man did not say anything, so Nicolas continued.

"I guess what I'm getting at is I think I understand *where* I am now. I'm just not sure *why* I'm where I am." He looked directly at the old man's keen blue eye and asked, "Why am I here?"

The Laird of the First Gate nodded his chin understandingly and shifted in his seat. "A fine question," he began. " 'Tis a fine question, indeed." He took a deep breath and pointed a long, bony finger at the coppery leaf. "Before having seen *that*, I would have thought the Shadow Thief still remained buried deep in its tomb. But now…" The old man leaned back, shaking his head and puffing determinedly on his long-stemmed pipe. He seemed to have forgotten to finish his sentence.

Nicolas looked at the strange leaf in his lap. He said shyly, "I still don't think I understand what this means." He turned the leaf over with one hand, feeling as if he might have missed something.

Aldus gently laughed. "That's because I haven't *told* you what it means, Master Bennett. I humbly apologize. In Telluric Grand there is a special type of tree. This type of tree is said to be the first tree which sprang out of the earth when this was still a young world. These trees are called Eldur trees. They are rare and usually hidden deep within dense forests. They are much like Oak trees in your world, both are strong and magical, although your Oaks are more common. And, like most other trees, Eldur leaves change with the seasons. They are a bright copper colors in the summer and fade into deeply tarnished bronzes in the winter, but they *never* fall. Well," he grimaced, "almost never."

Nicolas looked again at the leaf on his lap. "Did *this* one fall?" he asked.

"Yes. I believe it fell. Its stem is not torn or broken. I suspect others have fallen as well. These leaves are special, like the Eldur tree itself. They are made of metal and earth and life. The only time the leaves fall, Master Bennett, is when a truly terrible darkness—the darkest of horrors—is at loose on Telluric Grand. When all kingdoms are at risk, and when the End of the world waits impatiently around the corner."

"Oh," said Nicolas quietly. He didn't know what else to say.

The Laird of the First Gate leaned forward. In a whisper, he said, "And *you* are here to stop it."

———◆———

The moment this was said, the great black raven vaulted off the high back of the old man's chair and flew into the air, ferociously beating its immense wings to gain height. It cawed loudly, quickly spiraling upward in a storm of sharp talons and dark feathers. Before Nicolas or Aldus could recover from their surprise, the bird flew out of a high, narrow window and soared away.

"Confound it!" shouted Aldus, waving a gnarled fist in the air. "Confound that bird! I nearly fell off my chair and into the fire."

Nicolas had also almost fallen out of his chair with fright. His heart was beating fast, and it beat even faster when a terrible thought occurred to him. "Where do you think it's gone? Was it spying on us?"

Aldus arched an eyebrow over his good eye, which was now a deep blue—almost black—color. "No, Master Bennett," he said softly. "I don't think we've been betrayed by Kaha, although I do think he has left us to visit… someone else."

Whether it was the lateness of the hour, or the strangeness of the day's long journey, or the dreadfulness of tales about dragons which consumed iron and brought gruesome death and ruin, Nicolas suddenly felt jumpy and fearful. He felt homesick.

"Why?" he demanded. "Why am I here to stop it?"

The old man did not respond. Instead, he got up from his chair and ambled over to one of the dark corners of the room. Nicolas could hear him lifting and moving books and occasionally grunting from the effort. Several minutes passed, and finally, the old man walked back into the firelight. One hand was tugging on his beard and the other held a roll of old and heavy parchment.

"This," he said, waving the scroll in the air like a wand, "this is a poem of old called 'The Ruin.' It is written in an ancient tongue which is no longer spoken, and which can only be translated by very few. It chronicles the history of Telluric Grand, its kingdoms and races and cities. It tells of its tragedies and wars. It recounts its songs and folklore and legends. And, it speaks of *dragons*. This poem," Aldus continued gravely, "even tells of things which had not yet occurred when it was written. Things which might be. Things which could be."

Aldus pointed the scroll at Nicolas. "This scroll originally came from *your* world, just as things from this world have passed to your own." He sat down and partially unrolled the stiff scroll in his lap. Nicolas could see fantastic drawings surrounded and interwoven with words written in a graceful, but bold, script he did not recognize. "Years ago, your grandfather brought this with him through a secret door, hoping, I think, to help us. Here," said Aldus, tracing his finger along a long and wide burn mark which ran along the edge of the scroll, "is where the poem's record now ends. The rest of it has been lost. Years ago, it was burned by the Shadow Thief in an attempt to destroy it."

Hearing something about his grandfather caused Nicolas' ears to perk up, but in spite of this, his eyelids had grown heavy again, and the warmth in the room was covering him like the old quilt in his bed back home. "Why did it try to destroy the poem?" Nicolas asked weakly.

The old man's answer came in a hushed voice. "Because the poem told of its downfall. And when it spoke of its downfall, the poem also spoke of a *boy*."

The Laird of the First Gate moved the end of his long finger over the last bit of graceful script, until it touched the burn's rusty brown scar. "But instead of giving the boy a name, the ancient who wrote these things down, simply referred to the boy as a *Wren*."

Much, much later, when Nicolas found a quiet time to think, he would try his best to recall those last few moments he spent in Laird Ward's private study, sitting in front of the firebasket, staring at the strange scroll, and listening to the lullaby sound of the old man's voice. But, try as he might, those last moments always remained stubbornly unclear to him. It was like trying to see through the haze of a thick bank of early morning fog.

Shortly after Aldus had revealed the poem's prophecy, Nicolas fell asleep, and his memory rapidly faded into a deep, impenetrable blackness.

His sleep was troubled and plagued by a dreadful nightmare. A terrifying and tormented dream.

Late the next morning, Nicolas awoke near a great fireplace in another much larger room, which was decorated with finely threaded tapestries, enormous candle chandeliers, and the stuffed heads of giant elk and wild boar. He was alone, lying on a make-shift pallet of thick quilts, and tucked warmly under the weight of a massive bearskin. Straw-colored sunlight, forming rectangular columns, streamed into the room through narrow windows high in the walls above.

Nicolas had barely opened his eyes when Master Brooks, the studious older boy from the night before, appeared, carrying a deep bowl of salted porridge and a piping hot cup of tea, which smelled of honey and jasmine. The older boy waited patiently as Nicolas hungrily worked his way through all the porridge with occasional interruptions to savor the delicious tea.

When the last bite had been eaten and the last gulp swallowed, the older boy announced, rather awkwardly, unaccustomed to giving orders, "The Laird of the First Gate has said you're to come with me, if you please. He has instructed that today, Master Bennett, you're to enter the City of Relic."

CHAPTER 12

ΠΕШ FRIΕΠDS

In the western Highlands of Scotland, surrounded by snow-peaked mountains, amid the black tidal pool of three ancient lochs, there is a lonely, rugged island dressed in green heather and a few scrappy pines. Atop this wild island there sit the ruins of a castle, hundreds of years old. Legend says the castle was built by the first son of a Highland clan chieftain as a stronghold against warring Viking invaders. The chieftain's son was renowned for his success at business and his shrewdness for war. It was said he possessed the peculiar, magical gift of being able to communicate with birds.

When Nicolas was eight years old, Mr. and Mrs. Bennett took him to see the castle's remains. Its windswept and scoured walls, its narrow paths, its blackened stones, and its wild grasses left an enchanted impression on Nicolas. As he and his parents walked toward the castle along the narrow neck of a curving stone bridge, Nicolas had a strange sense of both sorrow and wonder, as if he were walking back in time into a world of legends, folklore, and ancient kings. Once inside the castle's walls, his family wandered about until Nicolas had found himself standing in front of a large pocked and pitted square of green-grey iron, which, his father quietly told him, recounted the names of Clan Macrae's dead sons—men who lost their lives in the Great War fought many years before. A foggy Highlander wind stung Nicolas' face as he stood there, silently reading the names of the long-dead Scotsmen. Engraved below the solemn lists of names were a few lines of a poem written by a Macrae clansman after he had buried his best friend in the midst of a horrifying battle.

We are the Dead. Short days ago
We lived, felt dawn, saw sunset glow,
Loved and were loved, and now we lie
In Flanders fields.

Now, four years later, Nicolas had again seen the large square of iron with long lists of dead men's names. But he did not see the square of iron in the windswept castle atop a lonely island in the Scottish Highlands.

He saw it in a dream.

While fast asleep within the vast walls of St. Wulf's-Without-Aldersgate, under the weight of a thick bearskin, Nicolas the Wren had dreamed a dark and terrible dream. He dreamt of a massive door and lock as large as the Tower of London. Behind the great door was an awful, deep, and gloomy cavern. And somewhere in the abyss of this hellish cave, an immense and evil creature lay hidden. It was chained in huge shackles of bronze and steel. The creature's hideous breath felt unbearably hot and smelled of gruesome rot and fleshy decay. Nicolas dreamed of wounded, maimed, and dying men who lay outside the massive door and lock. He dreamed of a great curtain of fire and a great war. And in this dream, he saw a large square of iron, covered in strange writing and hung with thick, leaden bolts on the face of the door. The language was unfamiliar to him, and he could not read the words on the iron square, but he knew they spoke of slaughter and torment and destruction. They spoke of the names and histories of those who had already died—and those who were going to die.

We are the dead, he heard a legion of mournful voices say.

It was a horrifying, grisly dream.

Nicolas now stood blinking and shivering in the bright, cold sunlight of a late morning.

Master Brooks had led him out through the heavy gates in the back wall of St. Wulf's-Without-Aldersgate and onto a high causeway of cobbled stone which led to the great City of Relic. Long ages before, the City of Relic had been built on a kind of vast island, almost entirely surrounded by the natural defense of a wide and deep ravine. At the bottom of the gorge flowed a violent and rock-infested river. The gatekeep's arched causeway—and five other similar causeways, stretching out of five other massive gatekeeps—were the only means of entering the City.

Now, standing in the light of the sun, Nicolas rubbed the chill out of his arms and silently watched. Crowds of men, horses, donkeys, goats, sheep, and rickety carts piled high with hay, chicken coops, baskets of vegetables, spun cloth, and shouting children were led by their mothers and fathers over the long bridge of stone and into the shadow of the City's gate.

"You've arrived on a holiday," said Master Brooks cheerily. "Today is the three hundred and fifth day of the year. It's 'Dragon Dead' Day."

Nicolas involuntarily shuddered, trying not to think of his nightmare—of the shapeless creature in the dark and the screams and cries of dying men. "Why is it called Dragon Dead Day?" he asked.

The older boy looked slightly confused, as if no one had ever asked him that question before. "Well," he said, "it's called that because of all of the people the dragons killed. My mum used to tell me it's the one day when their lost souls are at rest, and we're supposed to honor their memory." He walked over to an elderly woman sitting on the ground near them with a large wicker basket full of scarlet-red flowers, and he tossed her a small coin. With a toothless smile, she handed Master Brooks two flowers. He gave one to Nicolas, and the other, he tucked into the colored cord around his waist. "These are Dragon Poppies. People wear them on Dragon Dead Day," he said simply.

Nicolas touched the soft petals. They felt like small swatches of velvet. Carefully, he threaded the flower's thin stem into his woolen sweater. The two boys watched the crowd surge by for several moments. "What am I supposed to do?" he finally asked.

Master Brooks straightened up, and as if reciting specific instructions, said, "The Laird of the First Gate has kindly asked that you go to the Iron Quarter and find a giant named Straight Hammer. Tell him who sent you, and show him the coin in your pocket. Let him know you'll be going on a journey and that you'll need some armor."

"A giant?"

"Yes, a giant," replied the older boy. "The giants who live in the Iron Quarter are peaceful giants. They are mostly black-smiths, bladesmiths, and armorers. Straight Hammer has a small blacksmith shop in an alley off Broken Blades, which is the main road through the Iron Quarter." Master Brooks handed Nicolas a weather-stained roll of cloth he had held tucked under his arm. "Here is a weather cloak and belt. M'lord said it would be wise to wear it over your clothes," he said kindly.

Nicolas took the gift and put it on and loosely cinched the worn leather belt in place. "Thank you," he said. Without knowing what more to say, Nicolas gave the older boy a clumsy wave and stepped out onto the causeway of cobbled stone and toward the great City of Relic.

"Be careful!" shouted the older boy as Nicolas disappeared into the throng of people and creaking carts. "And be back by nightfall!"

A few minutes later, the stream of people, carts, and noisy animals, all bumping together across the causeway's long expanse, flowed into the City's own gate, beneath its vast walls, and out again into the near-noon light of the sun.

Nicolas the Wren had finally arrived, unnoticed and uncertain, within the ancient, great City of Relic.

Most of the flowing traffic continued to surge straight down a main thoroughfare, which sloped gently toward the City's "open lands," a spacious area of short-grass fields near the middle of the City where herds of cattle and sheep usually grazed in peace. Today, however, on Dragon Dead Day—the second day of the City's three-day festival of Haligtide—the herds of cattle and sheep had been penned, and the open lands were anything but peaceful.

All across the plain, reaching almost to the King's Castle rising up in the center of the City, Nicolas could see what appeared to be an endlessly chaotic jumble of multi-colored stalls, tents, arcades, and pavilions, set up along several muck-filled and straw-strewn lanes. Snobbish merchants, serious tradesmen, talkative shopkeepers, and honest farmers just arriving from the Outlands were all busy announcing the sale of their wares, goods, produce, and meats. They haggled with frugal customers over prices, and squabbled with each other about having enough space, stealing each other's business, and the unparalleled quality of their merchandise. Barefoot farm boys herded pot-bellied milk cows into mud-spattered pens where squealing pigs, braying donkeys, bleating sheep, and unruly goats were busily being bought and sold at auction by sweaty fat men, who were calling out buyers' bids in quick snippets of words, which to Nicolas sounded like gibberish. Groups of laughing girls ran around excitedly, hunting for merchants selling colorful silk ribbons and unusual hair garlands, or lardymen selling fresh-baked strawberry tarts, sugared plum pies, and apple rings fried in sticky batter. Ensembles of minstrels, playing simple harps, fiddles, flutes, mandolins, and kettledrums, competed energetically with daring jugglers, troupes of dancers, and wandering poets for a few of the crowds' coins. Muscular servants shouldered temporary pathways through the crowds for wealthy landowners and titled nobles who trailed behind them on horseback, while pairs of the City's bailiff men, wearing high boots and carrying nasty-looking truncheons, marched about looking for men who had drunk too much ale and for pilfering scoundrels who'd filled their pockets with stolen things. Everyone, even the bailiff's men, wore bright red Dragon Poppies. Some in their hair, some in their vests, some in their belts, and some in wreaths woven round their necks which, from a distance, looked like the crimson wound of a throat that had been cut open.

Lively music, bawdy merriment, noisy animals, and the bubbly sound of thousands of voices mingled.

Amid the boisterous hustle and bustle, Nicolas suddenly heard an angry shout followed by a short scream.

He looked down a grassy lane running off to his left, pocked with messy mud puddles and bent grass that had been sadly pressed into the sod. There, next to a wobbly string-puppet stage, stood a wide, low stall. From out of the stall there came more shouting, some cursing, and the muffled sound of a sharp slap or two landing on someone's face. Nicolas heard another short scream, and this time it seemed to be infused with anger as well as pain. Quickly, a crowd of curious onlookers began collecting around the stall's entrance, craning their necks in hope of seeing what was causing the uproar. Through the jumble of arms and legs and moving bodies, Nicolas was able to spot several rough-hewn tables set up inside the stall, each piled high with dozens of loaves of different kinds of bread. There were round loaves, long loaves, and square loaves. There were loaves with raisins, loaves sprinkled with seeds, and loaves with nuts and dates. There were dark loaves of oats and rye, and there were lighter loaves of barley and wheat. Some of the loaves looked as hard and as rough as unfinished wood, while others were as glossy and as shiny as lacquered furniture. Some of the loaves had splits running down their length, while others had neat crosses slit into their sleek, curved domes. The stall smelled slightly sour and sweet at the same time, and irritated clouds of flour dust billowed out of its entrance.

Somehow, out from the muddled mix of feet and legs at the front of the stall, popped a smallish-looking boy. He was crawling rapidly on hands and knees with a large, oblong—and apparently stolen—breadtwist wagging from his mouth like an engorged, doughy tongue. For a split second after clearing the swarm of legs, the boy looked about, clearly looking for a suitable escape. His eyes—a stormy grey with tired half-circles underneath—landed on Nicolas. The two boys stared at each other, and in that fraction of a second, the smallish-looking boy gave Nicolas an odd, but friendly, look. For reasons which Nicolas was never able to properly explain, he motioned slyly to the boy with a quick snap of his wrist and lifted his weather cloak. Without missing a beat, the boy smiled and popped to his feet and rushed at Nicolas, who promptly dropped the discolored cloak over the boy like a sheet over a ghost. The boy stood behind him and hugged Nicolas' waist from the back. After adjusting his outer belt to accommodate his new guest, Nicolas did his best to stand still. Before anyone took notice, the boy-thief had disappeared from view.

A Place with Dragons

A moment later, a blubbery fat man burst through the crowd of onlookers, snorting and huffing, and sending angry sprays of frothy spittle flying out of his frog-like mouth.

"Where is he?!" the blubbery man spewed. "Where is that lice-infested, rat-kissing, pig-farting thief?" His bulbous head swiveled wildly from side to side, slinging more globs of sputum onto innocent bystanders. His mean eyes glowered briefly at Nicolas, but quickly looked away without having caught a glimpse of the pair of dirty bare feet hiding behind Nicolas' boots. Shiny rivulets of sweat poured down the man's fat, froggish face, while his slug-like fingers kept rolling up into plump fists. They reminded Nicolas of ten chubby snails, retreating back into their shells.

By this time, several of the onlookers lost interest. Their initial excitement at seeing a thief caught and punished—perhaps having a few fingers smashed to a pulp by one of the City's bailiff men—had disappeared when they realized the thief had made an escape. As most of the gathered men and women began turning to walk away, a young girl about Nicolas' height stalked out from the shade of the stall's interior. She was wearing a thin white smock, covered by a simple but dirty kirtle—a type of dress which combined a fitted bodice laced at the sides with a skirt pleated at the waist seam. A homespun surcoat of indigo blue was draped haphazardly over one of her forearms, and a single Dragon Poppy bounced at the tail-end of her hair's long braid. With her free hand, she held together one of her smock's freshly torn shoulder-seams. She was covered from head to toe in flour dust, and Nicolas could see slender wet trails of fresh tears on her soft cheeks. A purplish, ugly welt was beginning to swell to the right of her mouth, but her pink lips were shut together tightly, and her face had more of a look of anger than pain. A miniature goat, dappled in white and black

143

splotches, was trotting loyally at her heels like a pet dog.

Stamping her wooden shoe-clogs into the mucky grass, the girl circled around the sweating fat man. She stopped in front of him and spread her wooden clogs apart in defiance. Her shoulders squared back in an obvious challenge, and her tiny goat took a supporting position by her side as it bleated out an indignant "*baaa!*" The few bystanders who had not yet moved on, paused to see what might happen.

With cruel eyes, the fat man scowled down at the young girl. "And you!" he shouted, pointing at her with one of his slug-like fingers. "You're a worthless, motherless whelp of a ..."

Before he could finish his insult, one of the young girl's wooden clogs abruptly shot forward and cracked hard against one of the froggish man's shinbones. He immediately howled in pain and surprise, but before he could do much else, the girl's wooden clog shot out again and connected with his other shinbone in an equally loud crack of hard wood and bone.

"By the gods of crows and grackles!" he gasped as tears shot out of his eyes. He tried his best to lean over the huge curve of his disgusting belly to grasp at his throbbing shins.

"You'll not hurt me anymore!" shouted the young girl, bravely fighting back her own tears, and just as the froggish fat man managed to finally clutch one of his tender shins, she kicked him again, smashing the solid wood of her shoes against his soft, plump knuckles. The fat man jerked his hand up violently as if he'd been bitten by a snake and shook it back and forth, moaning and blubbering and whimpering.

The young girl spun on her heel to leave, and gingerly touched one of her delicate fingers to the painful bruise on her face. She winced, and instead of walking away, she angrily spun back again, and with a vicious "*Aargh!*" she crashed her thick wooden shoe into the froggish man's aching shins several more times. This new assault caused him to leap into an absurd dance to try to avoid her well-aimed blows. But, from the sound of several more loud cracks, the fat man's efforts were in vain. Somewhere off to the side, someone clapped in approval. Finally, her immediate fury having been satisfied, the young girl stalked off down the lane with her little dappled goat trotting happily behind her.

And in the process, the smallish boy-thief was entirely forgotten.

Several minutes later, Nicolas found himself trying to keep up with the smallish boy as he weaved in and out of the slow-moving mobs of people, animals, and farmers' carts. The boy-thief clutched his stolen loaf of bread under his arm like a rugby ball as his bare feet darted deftly around the crush of boots, hooves, and heavy wheels. It only took a minute or two for the two boys to come within sight of the young girl.

"Adelaide!"

The young girl turned at the sound of the familiar voice.

"Adelaide!" the boy-thief shouted again and waved. The young girl waved back, and soon the three of them were huddled together next to the tent wall of a farmer who was selling thick wheels of smelly cheese.

"I'm so glad to see you, Benjamin," she said to the boy-thief. In spite of her injury, her face was pretty, and her smile was warm and genuine.

"Thanks," he replied, and then lowered his eyes apologetically. "I didn't mean to get you in trouble. If I'd known he was goin' to hit you again, I'd never have let you give me the bread."

"Don't worry your little head about it," she said reassuringly, wincing slightly as she smiled. "I'm *not* going back. That's the last time. That sack of pig lard won't hit me anymore." Her eyes looked sad, but her voice was calm and firm. She was still grasping the torn shoulder-seam of her smock, and suddenly, Nicolas had an idea. He fished around in his pocket and pulled out the short bit of braided string he'd taken from the trunk in his attic bedroom.

"May I?" Nicolas asked politely, motioning toward the torn shoulder-seam.

Without saying anything, the young girl looked at the boy-thief, who nodded in approval. She looked back at Nicolas. "Okay," she said, and she turned her slender shoulder toward him. Thinking quickly, Nicolas pried a large splinter from the tent pole beside them and poked several small holes in the young girl's smock. He then took his string and unbraided it, separating out the blue string, the red string, and the gold string. He tied each string end-to-end and threaded it carefully through the holes.

"I think that'll work," he said, admiring the rough stitches.

"Thank you." She ran her fingers over the colorful threads. "My name is Adelaide Ashdown, and this," she said, pointing a finger at the little goat sidling by her ankle, "is Cornelia."

"I'm Nicolas Bennett," he said timidly, suddenly aware of the shabbiness of his weather cloak.

"And I'm Benjamin Rush," said the boy-thief, who was play-fully waving and grinning at them both like a rascally jack-o'-lantern. "This little lad is with me, m'lady," he said jokingly to Adelaide. "I saved him from your foul toad-of-a-boss." Benjamin looked up at Nicolas and gave him an extravagant wink. Nicolas couldn't help but smile.

The girl laughed and hid her injured mouth with her hand. "Benjamin," she chided, "Don't make me laugh. It hurts when I smile."

"You're not goin' back, are you?" Benjamin asked with a brief look of worry on his dirty forehead. "He'll kill you after the brilliant beating you gave his fat legs."

"No," she reassured him quietly, "I won't go back. Although…" She looked toward the City's high walls. "I'm not sure where I'll go." A tear welled up in the corner of her eye, and she promptly brushed it away.

As much to distract her as anything else, Nicolas piped up. "I need to find the Iron Quarter." He looked earnestly at the young girl and politely asked, "Would you please take me there?"

The boy-thief and the young girl both stared at him. They were clearly curious and were struggling to hide their smiles. "Whaddya need?" Benjamin asked. "A new suit of armor?" And he and Adelaide began to laugh.

Nicolas felt his cheeks turn a shade red. "As a matter of fact," he said lifting his chin, "I do. Well, at least, I need some kind of armor." His face turned a bit redder. "Actually," he said sheepishly, "I'm not really sure what I need. I just need to find a particular blacksmith in the Iron Quarter. I think he'll know what I need."

"Well then," announced Benjamin as he laid one of his smallish hands on Nicolas' shoulder, "you're in good company. Neither of us have any place to go. We'll see that you get where you need to go, Nicolas." As he spoke, he fished out the big breadtwist and tore off a chunk for each of them. "And we'll all have a bit of a bite to eat, too."

With that, the young girl, her dappled goat, the boy-thief, and the Wren struck out together, chewing oversized chunks of warm bread, and joking and laughing, as the rest of the world went by them unnoticed.

CHAPTER 13

THE IRON QUARTER

Scattered throughout the Outlands of the First Kingdom—the kingdom of the City of Relic—are many small yet cozy inns. In fact, if a traveler plans a journey properly, he can find himself arriving at such an inn in the twilight of each day to enjoy a dinner of roasted mutton or ham, a glass of something refreshing to drink, and a safe, dry place to sleep by a warm fire, or for a few coins more, a straw-stuffed mattress and bed in a private room. Many times, in the late of night, while huddled around rough-hewn tables of forest oak with comforting mugs of muddled wine and frothy ale clutched in their hands, curious travelers will listen as motherly innkeepers' wives entertain them with stories of ancient battles, hordes of golden treasure, the madness of evil kings, and forests haunted by murderous spirits. For those travelers who are bound for the City of Relic, however, the legend of how the City first came to be is always a favorite.

The legend, as it commonly is told, begins with a sinister description of an old, wicked crone with stiff crooked fingers, eye-sockets as deep as pits, and crinkly skin that smelled like sickness—she is sometimes described as a forest witch, sometimes as a twisted beggar, and sometimes as a dark prophetess from the High Desert of Shadows far northwest of the City of Relic. The legend then goes something like this:

Once, long ago, when the winters were much longer and darker, a malevolent old woman had become lost in a furious blizzard. She wandered through the forest for days but saw no

148

one and came across no road. Hungry, she ensnared a gentle snow dove and bit off its head. As her chipped and rotten teeth crunched the bird's fragile bones, the old hag realized she was also thirsty. Her throat burned and felt parched and dry. About this time, she came across a small spring of water that had not frozen, bubbling up like liquid silver from the snow. Eagerly, she bent down and scooped her crooked hands into the clear liquid, hoping to catch a refreshing mouthful. Strangely though, no matter how she cupped her gnarled hands, the spring's water refused to stay in them, and she wasn't able to take a drink. Frustrated, she knelt down and placed her swollen, cracked lips against the bubbling water's surface. But even this did not work. Each time the old woman tried to drink, the water moved away from her sour breath and ghastly lips. Furious, the old witch finally conjured an ancient spell. She cursed the small spring of water, saying, "Just as you have left me wanting, you too shall forever want someone to come and taste you, but none shall come. You shall forever spill your water on the earth, and no one shall drink from you." The evil old crone then stumbled off into the snow and soon died of feverish thirst.

Many long years passed, and the cruel winters shortened. Water from the spring kept bubbling to the surface, yet no one, not even the animals, ever came to the spring or drank from its cool waters. Lonely, the spring's cursed water ran across the earth, searching in vain for someone to take a drink. The water ran through grass and over rocks, eventually carving deep into the earth where other lonely streams soon found it and poured themselves into it. Rushing together, they formed a fierce river which cut through stone and finally poured out into the Cold Sea.

One spring day, the long quiet of the woods was shattered by the sounds of a great battle being fought. Amid the awful shouting and screaming of struggling, writhing, and dying men, a mighty chieftain fell heavily to the ground with a mortal wound. He had wielded his great sword in the thickest of the fighting, cleaving the bodies of his enemies apart in brutal strokes of edged steel. But while still in the heat of battle, he had watched as his shield-bearer, a kind lad of only fourteen years of age, was struck cruelly in the back by the blow of a heavy war hammer. Incensed with rage, the mighty chieftain leapt at his shield-bearer's attacker and split the man's helmet and skull in two with a single swing of his sword. He reached out his armored hand and helped the boy to his feet, but as he did so, he unthinkingly exposed his side, and a treacherous enemy soldier thrust a poison-tipped knife between his unprotected ribs, piercing his heart. As the mighty chieftain lay dying, his injured shield-bearer ran to find a cold drink of water to slake his lord's death-thirst. The servant came upon the small spring of fresh water. Scooping its clear water up into a bowl, he ran swiftly back to his lord. The chieftain lifted his head and drank deeply. "It is good," he said, and with a skyward whisper, his last breath passed over his lips, and he went to his home in the endless heavens. In honor of the mighty chieftain's sacrifice, his clansmen built a strong tower over the spot where he fell.

"And that," the innkeeps' wives will say as they finish their late-night tale, "is where the King's Castle now sits within the great City of Relic. From its stone side—the 'rib stone'—pours the same spring's waters from which the mighty chieftain drank. Now all can taste the spring's waters. The chieftain broke the curse. After all, when a king says, 'it is good,' then so it must be."

"It's in there!" pointed Benjamin the boy-thief, jabbing a finger toward the King's Castle at the center of the City of Relic. "It's inside the castle. I've never seen it, but I've heard people say it flows up from inside some hidden chamber and then pours out of the castle's walls from that ditch over there."

Nicolas, Adelaide, and Benjamin had been walking along a broad, cobbled stone thoroughfare for a while, and were about to leave the grassy plains of the City's open lands. They were near the entrance to a warren of streets and alleys known as the Iron Quarter when Adelaide had said she was thirsty. With a grand sweep of his little arm, Benjamin jokingly offered to go get a "King's Drink" for her, after which she'd punched him light-heartedly in the shoulder. Confused, Nicolas had asked, "What's a 'King's Drink'?" The boy-thief eagerly began telling him of the legend of the spring, taking particular care when describing how hideous the old woman looked. Adelaide grimaced and said, "yuck!" when Benjamin claimed, "the old hag's huge nose was covered with lumpy warts growing out of other lumpy warts." Adelaide's reaction made the boy-thief's eyes twinkle in amusement. She gave him another punch to the shoulder.

When Benjamin pointed toward the King's Castle, Nicolas stopped and squinted his eyes against the brightness of the early afternoon's sun. He was just able to see a thin veil of clear water pouring out of the base of one of the castle's high walls. "The water follows a course of cut stone called the King's Spring across the open lands, and falls into the gorge outside the city walls," Benjamin explained. "It's said that only a king—a *true* king—can drink the spring's waters and make it fit for everyone else to drink. That's why it's called a 'King's Drink,' but when there's no king on the throne, even the cattle and sheep seem to leave the water alone." The smallish boy-thief crammed his last clump of bread into his mouth.

Nicolas looked, and except for a thin line of trees along its banks, he couldn't see anyone, man or beast, near the channel of cut stone. "There's not a king, then?" he asked.

"Of course not," replied Benjamin between chews. "There hasn't been a king ruling the First Kingdom since before I was born." He took a final swallow and frowned at Nicolas inquisitively. "Where are you from, anyway? How can you not know there's not a king?"

Nicolas hesitated. He could see that Adelaide was looking at him, too, and he wondered if he'd said too much. "Um, I'm... I'm not from here," was all Nicolas could think of to say.

Benjamin shrugged. "Well, you *do* seem a bit odd."

Adelaide hit him on the shoulder again, and, as if to bring the point home, her little dappled goat butted his leg.

"Ow," Benjamin said, dramatically rubbing his shoulder and leg as if they were actually hurt.

Nicolas thought of the tall man he'd met in the woods with the donkey. The tall man had said the same thing to the gatekeep's master Grimlock: that Nicolas was "not *from* here." Maybe that's why it had popped into his head.

"What're the 'Dreggs'?" asked Nicolas. He also remembered the tall man telling the huge Grimlock he was from the City of Relic—from a place called the "Dreggs."

"The Dreggs are home for someone like me," mused Benjamin half-heartedly. "They lay in the southeast part of the City, past that tall stone column in the distance called the '*Lech O'Wahanu*,' the Stone of Separation. It's where most of the poor folk and laborers live, and where those who have no membership with a guild are allowed to work without permission from Lord Sulla. He's the High Chancellor." Benjamin shook his head. "The Dreggs are *no* place to be if you don't have to. I've seen men slice open each other's bellies over nothing more than a spit of roasted pigeon," he said, waving his arm about in a mock sword fight. He then looked slyly at Nicolas. "Of course, they *do* roast some *fine* pigeon in the Dreggs."

"Stop it, Benjamin," said Adelaide, rolling her eyes. "You're so boorish. You haven't seen anyone slice anyone else's belly open over some roasted pigeon."

"Maybe," admitted Benjamin. Then, quietly, he added, "But I *have* seen them smash thieves' fingers and cut off the ears of liars."

The three marched on in silence as Adelaide's wooden shoes, and Cornelia's tiny hooves, thumping lightly on the roadway's cobbled stone.

"We're here!" announced Adelaide.

Directly in front of them, like an enormous keyhole, was a massive, quarried stone of iron ore. A hole, wide enough for wagons and men on horses to pass through, had been chiseled out of its center. Spidery veins of copper spelled out the following message in the stone's face above the road: *Iron Is Not Bravery. But Bravery Without Iron Is Foolish.*

Benjamin cupped a hand to his mouth and whispered to Nicolas, "'Tis called the 'Eye of Brutus.' I 'ave to admit, I've only been inside the Iron Quarter once before. Let's just say they don't take lightly to sticky fingers." For the first time, Nicolas noticed the little finger on Benjamin's right hand. It aimed away from the other fingers slightly, and looked a bit misshapen. Nicolas wondered if it had been broken.

A coal cart suddenly rumbled past them, carelessly leaving a haphazard trail of coal chunks scattered along the cobbled road. Not far behind it came two young boys, both wearing dirty, buttonless vests, and carrying large wooden buckets half their size. They hurried about, collecting the wayward chunks of coal.

Nicolas and his new friends were now well-away from the festivities taking place out in the open lands, and the merriment of music and laughter seemed to shy away from carrying too much further in the cool breeze. With eyes wide open,

Benjamin looked at Nicolas. "Why're we here?" he asked, as if what had begun as a lighthearted adventure was finally settling into the possibility of genuine danger.

Nicolas looked at Adelaide. She also looked a bit nervous, but she didn't say anything. Nicolas wondered what he'd gotten himself into. He wasn't sure of what to say. "Well," he finally ventured, "I need to find someone. A blacksmith." Somehow, he couldn't quite bring himself to say, *I need to find a giant.*

"Who?" asked Benjamin.

"His name is Straight Hammer."

The smallish boy-thief nodded back as if he understood. "Alright," he said, setting his chin in a look of determination. "I haven't got anything better to do. Let's find a fella named Straight Hammer." He paused and looked expectantly at Nicolas. "*How* do we find a fella named Straight Hammer?"

Nicolas shrugged. "I don't know."

Adelaide squared her shoulders again, but Nicolas could see hints of unease and apprehension in her sea-green eyes. "You boys are *silly,*" she said with some annoyance. She slipped on her blue surcoat and pressed her hands nervously over her bodice and skirt, smoothing out the wrinkles and re-creasing the folds. "Let's go *ask* someone." And with that, off she went with her little goat companion devotedly trotting at her heels.

The two boys looked at each other blankly. Then, quickly catching up, they followed close behind the tiny goat.

Behind the sharp strike of hundreds of hammers on fire-softened metal, Nicolas could hear the endless squashy *whoosh* of large billows being worked up and down, stoking dozens of blacksmiths' coal fires with bursts of leathery, hot air. The Iron Quarter felt warm. It felt shielded from the rest of the world's autumn coolness. The ember-glow of its sweltering fires cast queer shadows out onto the cobbled street in spite of the afternoon sun. Greyish smoke and dreary ash hung in the air, smudging out the weakened sunlight.

A place with dragons, thought Nicolas as he, Benjamin, Adelaide, and her goat walked cautiously along the road.

And it was black, too.

Nicolas saw shop after shop blanketed in layers of chalky black soot. Burly men and grim-looking apprentice boys strode about in blackened boots, with blackened leather aprons and blackened leather gloves, carrying blackened hammers, chisels, pincers, and thick bars of raw iron and steel. The thick muscles of their forearms were glossy with the smoothness of scores of burn scars, and their foreheads glistened with smears of black soot and sweat. Wooden carts, loaded with coal, jars of syrupy oil, and lumps of velvety black charcoal, rumbled along the street, hawking their loads of fuel to surly shopkeepers. The Iron Quarter reeked of ash, singed leather, and bitter cinders.

"Excuse me!" said Adelaide suddenly.

A brutish man with a stubbly beard and a long scar running from the corner of his mouth to his ear stopped and looked at the young girl. His broad shoulder was bent under the weight of several metal rods, and the whites of his eyes looked like full moons against the night sky of his coal-black cheeks.

"Hmph?" he grunted unpleasantly.

"Where, if you please, is a blacksmith named Straight Hammer?"

The man scowled and quickly glanced left and right as if someone might have heard and might be watching. Without saying a word, he raised a thick arm and pointed a dirty finger toward a narrow alleyway, leading off to the left. Before Adelaide could say *thank you,* he was gone, lumbering swiftly down the road under the weight of his metal load.

The two boys, the girl, and her little goat stood there quietly.

"Well," Nicolas finally said, feeling as if he ought to take the lead, "on with it." He threw the weather cloak's hood up over his head and reluctantly left the afternoon's weak sunlight for the alley's darkness.

Other than a few haphazard barrels of oil, some broken bricks, and a large bin of coal, the alley held little surprise and appeared to be empty. Shuffling along in silence, the companions soon reached its end, which was nothing more than a high wall. To their left, they could vaguely make out an immense jumble of barrels, which Nicolas thought looked oddly enough like a disproportionately large man because of the alleyway's strange shadows and mottled light. To their right was a very large open door, with a sign hung unevenly over its black frame, showing two blunt-faced hammers crossed at their hafts carved clumsily into its face. Smoldering heat radiated from within. This shop appeared to be their only prospect for finding Straight Hammer.

"Hallo!" Nicolas called out. Nothing. "Hallo!" he said again. Still nothing. "Hallo!" he shouted a third time. Except for desperately wanting to see an actual giant, Nicolas felt nervous, and he secretly hoped there'd be no answer.

"We're closed!" boomed out a gravelly voice. "Get gone with ya before I decide to sling a hot poker in yer direction." A hulking, broad-shouldered man suddenly appeared in the large doorway. He wore boots, leather pants with holes in them, and a ratty-looking, loose-sleeved shirt. His hair was greasy and slicked back, and he smelled of onions and boiled cabbage.

With a high, sharp bleat, Adelaide's little goat charged.

Its hard little head caught the big man in his ankle, and he snorted with contempt. "What's this?" he asked scornfully, kicking the toe of his ugly boot at Cornelia. "Get yer *dog* and get gone with ya 'fore I lose my patience!"

"She's not a dog!" Adelaide yelled back, protectively scooping the little goat up in her arms. "Her name's Cornelia, and she's a goat, you pig-headed pile of pea-mush!"

At just this moment, a tall boy appeared behind the big man. His feet were spread apart and he held a short-handled hammer in his hand. "Leave off, uncle," he said darkly.

The big man turned around, balling his meaty hands into fists. After a minute of staring at the tall boy, whose face was pale but stared right back at him, the big man grunted in disgust and stalked back inside. The tall boy waited a few moments until he was sure the big man was out of earshot. He let out a big sigh of relief. "I'm sorry about that," he said to Adelaide. He slipped the handle of the hammer into a loop stitched to the side of his leather apron. The fierceness had vanished entirely from his voice. "That was my uncle, Ragnuf. He gets a bit bad-tempered when someone interrupts his nap. Actually," said the tall boy, breaking into a broad grin, "that's not true. He's *always* bad-tempered. When he was born, I think the first thing he did when his mum slapped his wee rump was to smack her back." The boy laughed with simple enjoyment at his own joke, causing his unruly mop of hair to fall in his face. "Whew!" he said, catching his breath and wiping the tears from his eyes. "I kill myself sometimes."

The tall boy pulled his wild hair back behind his ears and wrapped it with a short cord. "My name is Ranulf," he said proudly. "Ranulf son of Renfry. I'm an apprentice here, and they say when *I* was born I bit the midwife and howled like a Fenris Wolf. Who are you?" he asked them.

"I'm Adelaide Ashdown. This is Cornelia," she said, motioning to the little dappled goat in her arms. "I'm from the Outlands by birth, and today, I kicked a fat lardyman in the shins," she said in a rush. "I don't want to be a baker's helper anymore. I—I want to be a Healer," Adelaide added quietly.

Ranulf crossed his arms over his chest. "Good!" he said. "And you?"

Benjamin smiled. "I'm Benjamin. Benjamin Rush. And," said the boy-thief as he suddenly flourished Ranulf's short-handled hammer in his smallish hand, "*you* may have your hammer back."

"What?!" exclaimed Ranulf, slapping a hand to the empty loop where his smith's hammer had been a few moments before. "How did you do that?" he asked with a look of amazement and delight. "Are you a magician?"

"No," said Benjamin, clearly pleased he had impressed the tall boy. "I'm not a magician. I'm just small and fast." Ranulf nodded admiringly at him. "And this," Benjamin said like an energetic herald announcing a knight to the lords-at-court, "is Nicolas!"

"Yes, I'm Nicolas Bennett." Having been put on the spot, Nicolas abruptly felt shy, just he did when he'd left the North Lakes School and moved to Hunter Hall two years before. He felt out of place. He also couldn't think of anything to say, which made him feel even more awkward, but the small boy-thief unexpectedly came to his rescue.

"Nicolas saved my life today," Benjamin said frankly. "And for no reason that I can tell. These two," Benjamin said proudly, "are my best friends, Ranulf son of Renfry, and we're looking for a fellow named Straight Hammer. Do you know where he might be?"

Ranulf looked at them curiously. "Straight Hammer?" he repeated.

"Aye," said Benjamin. "Straight Hammer."

"Yes, I know where he is," said Ranulf with a look of gentle bemusement. "He's the giant standing right behind you."

BENEATH THE SURFACE OF WORDS

From the corner of the narrow alley, out of blue-black shadows of the jumbled pile of barrels, a figure larger than Nicolas had ever seen or had ever truly imagined stepped into the weak light of the doorway where Ranulf stood with crossed arms. The enormous figure was easily sixteen feet tall—nearly three times as tall as Nicolas—but what immediately spellbound the boy was the giant's *width*—better said, it was the giant's proportional size. Instead of having overly long-looking limbs, great gawky feet, and elongated facial features, which might have made the giant look simply *stretched* instead of truly massive, everything on this giant was proportionally normal, only much, *much* bigger. For instance, the giant's hands were huge but not necessarily long, and they were at the end of amazingly thick arms which would have been a normal length if the giant had been a normal man. But he *wasn't* a normal man.

In fact, he wasn't a man at all.

A giant—a *true* giant, one who is descended from an ancient race born from the mingling of star-gods and mortal humans—is not simply a large man or woman. A true giant comes from a separate race of creatures. Aside from the immenseness of their overall size, there are, in fact, several, characteristically unique things about giants which, Nicolas would later learn, have only a few, occasionally terrible, exceptions.

However, the giant now facing Nicolas in a narrow alleyway in the Iron Quarter of the City of Relic was a mostly normal giant.

159

He was wearing the traditional clothing of his male kinfolk. Great boots with folded-down tops and low heels (each the size of a sack of flour) rose up to just below his knees. After this came thick leather leggings which then disappeared under an equally thick, but woolen, tunic that was buckled about the giant's vast waist with a braided belt of colored ox-hide. He also owned an enormous vest of oiled sheepskin, although, at the moment Nicolas saw him, the giant's vest still hung on its large iron hook inside the smithy shop.

The giant's fingers were, of course, large, but they were also rather flat-looking, like the flattish shape of an axe handle. Each of his legs was as round as Nicolas' entire body, and the giant's shoulders and neck were large enough they would have hardly fit inside a barleyman's plowing yoke. He had enormous, deep-set eyes, overhung by a heavy forehead and great, bushy eyebrows, like Nicolas might have imagined a lumberjack might have. His beard was also an enormous affair, full and thick, and hanging to his waist, and this giant, like most men-giants, had his beard neatly oiled and gathered all together with three tight bands of decorated bronze. The first band was engraved with common depictions and symbols of the endless heavens. The middle band was engraved with common depictions and symbols for day and night. And the third band—the lowest-hanging band, and to a man-giant, one of his most prized possessions—was engraved with a set of runes.

True giants, as a rule, do not care for written words. Indeed, they have never created a written alphabet for the "Første Ord," the name of their spoken language, and they are not a race interested in books or scrolls. Giants often repeat sayings which reflect on their lives and their culture, and one of their many proverbs is, "*A word unspoken has no life nor being.*" They are, as a rule, suspicious of written words and believe a word must be said aloud to give it genuine meaning. Yet the runes engraved on a man-giant's third band are a significant exception. These few runes, in fact, are the only written characters any giant ever cares to read. They portray a man-giant's "glød"—his spirit. Straight Hammer's third-ring runes were simple.

ᛗᛁᛉᛗᚱ

In the common tongue of Telluric Grand, this meant, "Elder."

If Nicolas had been inclined to ask, Straight Hammer would have likely admitted that his favorite color—like most giants—was a deep, royal blue, and his favorite stew was made of boiled potatoes, roasted mutton, and fresh garlic cloves. His favorite stories always involved mountains, and his favorite game was called *Stones*—the only game most giants ever cared to play—where competitors would see who could crush the largest stone just by squeezing it in their hands.

But Nicolas was not inclined to ask any questions.

Nicolas did not say anything at all.

"Good day," said the giant in the shadows. His voice caught Nicolas by surprise. It was not gruff or growly as he expected. It was almost musical, and it was deep, like the resonant roll of a huge kettle drum. "I am Straight Hammer," the giant said. "Let us go inside and see what this is all about."

With a single stride past Nicolas and his companions, Straight Hammer stepped through the large doorway, although he still had to duck his head to avoid hitting it on the frame. Benjamin, with wide but excited eyes, scampered after the great giant, followed by Adelaide and her little goat, Cornelia.

"Aren't you coming, Nicolas?" asked Ranulf. He had moved aside out of Straight Hammer's way, but he was still standing next to the large door's thick frame.

"Of course," Nicolas replied as lightly as he could. "Of course I am. I—I've just not seen a giant before."

Ranulf pushed out his lower lip and dipped his chin thoughtfully. "Well," he said, "if that's the case—and there are some who've not—then Straight Hammer is a good giant for you to see as your first. He's one of the more aged giants," said Ranulf. Then, a little more quietly, he added, "and wise and quite gentle, too—unless you get him riled up." Ranulf smiled. "But I don't suppose you're here to rile up a giant."

"Not at all," Nicolas quickly said. And he, too, stepped through the door.

Straight Hammer was what was called a "Chancellor's Black-smith," because his was a blacksmith shop officially registered with the City of Relic's High Chancellor, Lord Sulla. Each Chancellor's Blacksmith was a member of the "Smith Guild," which was an association of all the registered smithies—both blacksmiths and bladesmiths. Since the passage of the King's Law in the year 793 R.R. (which stands for "Relic Rule," the official calendar of time sanctioned during the short reign of King Widofell in 294 R.R.), only giants were permitted to own blacksmith shops and to be registered as Chancellor Black-smiths. Many men worked for Chancellor Blacksmith giants, and depending on their ambition, working toward owning a bladesmith shop which could be owned by giants or by men.

Straight Hammer owned one of the oldest blacksmith shops in the Iron Quarter, and he was one of the first giants to be-come a Chancellor Blacksmith. Ragnuf, Ranulf's grumpy un-cle, had learned the blacksmithing and bladesmithing trades as a young apprentice under Straight Hammer years before. Eventually, Ragnuf's skill earned him the opportunity to open his own bladesmith shop under the same roof as Straight Hammer's blacksmith shop. But while many men and boys competed for a chance to learn from Straight Hammer, Ranulf was the only one who was willing to put up with Ragnuf's grouchy temper and to become his apprentice.

The warmth of the two-crossed-hammers blacksmith shop felt good after having spent most of the day in the coolness of the late autumn air, and especially good after standing in the chilly shadows in the alleyway. Most of the shop's heat came from a large grated trough made of clay and brick, filled with mounds of coal which glowed reddish-orange. The air was slightly smoky and smelled of burned oil, charred wood, the tanginess of tanned leather, the buttery wax of tallow candles, and old sweat. Aside from the glowing coals and one or two hanging candles, the shop was unlit and rather dark.

Scattered around the large main room were work stations arranged around iron anvils of various sizes. An array of differently-sized hammers, tongs, and pincers filled several sturdy buckets. Large barrels of dark water, where the smithys would immerse flame-heated metal, stood in between the anvil stations. Close by were half-barrels stuffed with raw metal bars, waiting for a blacksmith apprentice or journeyman to hammer and twist and fold them into something useful. Two of the shop's walls were lined with wooden dividers, bins, and tables, holding some of the shop's finished products: horseshoes, andirons, parts of plowshares, kettles, chains for carriage suspension, nails and brads, shovel heads and spades, pitchforks, plain and ornate firebaskets, thick barrel hoops, rims for wagon wheels, heavy door hinges, and a variety of iron hooks. Along a third wall was a more interesting assortment of helmets, swords, daggers, axe heads, spearheads, arrowheads (including bodkins, which were heavy arrowheads used to pierce armor), and a diverse collection of chain mail, plated armour, and leather joints and buckles to fit almost every part of a man's body.

Nicolas did not see any boys or men in the shop, and Ragnuf had disappeared, too. *They must all be gone to the festival,* thought Nicolas.

When Straight Hammer had entered the shop, he'd strode directly to an enormous chair, which sat with several other chairs of more normal sizes along another of the shop's walls. To Nicolas, this appeared to be where the boys and men and giants who worked in the shop would take breaks from their labors. Footstools and small tables littered with mugs and pairs of playing dice made of sheep bone sat around and in between the chairs. Little mounds of pipe ash were piled on the stone floor.

"Ranulf," said the giant cordially, "why don't you take our guests and show them upstairs to your room. As I recall, you still have a bag of smoked venison strips from your trip to the festival this morning. This young lad and lass look hungry, and I'm sure you can find some kibbles for her goat. And you may take a skin of muddled wine to wash it down with."

Ranulf smiled. "Come with me," he said as he walked toward a staircase that wound up past the back of the large oven-chimney at the head of the trough of glowing coals. Adelaide scooped up her little goat and followed after Ranulf. Benjamin, momentarily fascinated by the sight of weapons and armor glinting in the candle light, eventually said, "Coming!" and soon hurried after the girl and tall boy.

Straight Hammer, however, held up a massive hand to Nicolas. "Stay here with me, boy," he said in his deep and resonant voice. He motioned to a chair much smaller than his own, where Nicolas sat down. "There is flour dust on the girl's clothes and in her hair, which tells me she works for a lardyman," he said, thinking aloud. "The small boy's clothes are patched and are not his proper size. He has no shoes, nor a proper cloak, nor a proper mother to make him wash his face or scrub his ears. This tells me he is one of the unfortunates who live without a home in the streets. But *you*…" Straight Hammer stared inquisitively at Nicolas, his bushy eyebrows coming together and his banded beard wagging slightly as he moved his jaws. "You wear a common, stained weather cloak, but the boots on your feet are very curious to me. Your leggings are curious to me. Your shirt of wool is curious to me. Your presence at my shop is curious to me. *You* are curious to me. I think you are the reason a baker's girl, a homeless boy, and a goat the size of a green pea have suddenly appeared at my doorway on Dragon Dead Day."

Nicolas swallowed. His throat felt dry. He was, after all, speaking to a real giant. "I have seen Aldus—Laird Aldus Ward," he corrected himself, "and he told me to come here to find you. He said to show you this." Nicolas reached under his cloak and shoved his hand into his trouser pocket where he could feel the two coins resting together against the coppery leaf and his grandmother's thimble. Suddenly, he realized he had not asked Master Brooks *which* of the two coins to show to the giant. He paused. Then—slowly—Nicolas withdrew both coins and held them out in the palm of his hand. He guessed the giant might know which one was important. "I need some armour," Nicolas said shyly, and he waited to see what might happen.

The rocking horse crown coin shone brightly even in the shop's dull light. Nicolas looked at it and felt fairly confident this was the coin he was supposed to show to Straight Hammer. It was big and valuable, and it had a picture of St. George and the dragon on it. It seemed like the logical choice. And, in fact, the giant looked at the crown coin. His immense hand moved to pick it up.

But then it stopped.

The giant was staring at the farthing coin. The side of the coin engraved with the wren was facing up. His picked up this coin. Pinched between his enormous thumb and forefinger, it looked like a mere flake of metal.

"Where did you get this?" the giant asked. There was solemn reverence in his voice.

"I brought it with me."

The giant looked quizzical. "You *brought* it with you?"

"Yes," said Nicolas. "I brought it with me." Nicolas wasn't sure how much to say, and he wasn't even sure *how* to say whatever needed to be said. "I—I brought it with me. I brought it with me through a door."

Straight Hammer leaned back in his chair and held the tiny coin up in front of his large giant face. "You came through a door," he repeated quietly, "and you brought this with you."

"Yes," said Nicolas again.

"It is yours?" the giant asked.

"Yes."

Straight Hammer nodded. His eyes took on a deep, penetrating look. "What is your name, boy?" he asked.

"Nicolas. Nicolas Bennett."

The giant's chest seemed to rumble, and he said aloud a number of things which Nicolas couldn't understand. The giant's words—if they indeed could be called words—rolled along together with low vibrations and different pitches and tones, and a variety of long vowel sounds from the back of his throat, such as "*ooooooo*" and "*uuuuuuu*," and certain consonant sounds made by rolling or holding his tongue, such as "*rr-rrrrrr*" and "*lllllll*." The sounds were so rhythmical, harmonic,

166

and soothing, Nicolas felt almost instantly sleepy. He forced his eyes wide open, fighting the sudden urge to take a nap. He didn't know it at the time, but he was listening to Straight Hammer speak the ancient language of giants—the "Første Ord." Because giants believe their language is sacred, speaking it in front of non-giants isn't something giants do very often.

After several minutes, Straight Hammer became quiet. He carefully set the coin back down into Nicolas' hand. "So," he said, "it is *you*."

For the next half hour, Nicolas and the giant spoke about several of the things Aldus Ward had discussed with Nicolas the night before. They spoke of crows and Eldur trees, and doors and Wisps, and star iron and dragons. They spoke of the Shadow Thief. Occasionally, Straight Hammer looked mildly surprised, and he would pause and speak aloud to himself in the peculiar language of giants. After the second or third time he did this, he finally explained to Nicolas that he was reciting portions of long-told legends and prophecies.

"Legends and prophecies," the giant said, "are like mountains. Over time, they can change and may look and sound different. But these changes lie on the surface of the words. When the words are spoken in my tongue, it is like finding your way deep inside a mountain where wind and rain, and light and time, do not reach. Beneath the surface of words, just as beneath the surface of a mountain, legends and prophecies tell us what is truly there—what has always been there and what will always be there." Straight Hammer looked at Nicolas closely, and he spoke slowly. "You, Nicolas, have always been a part of the history of this world. You—only it is 'you' in a different way—are in the legends and prophecies of old. But now, you are on the surface—visible—and moving like the sun across a winter's sky."

Nicolas nodded, but inside, he didn't feel entirely sure of what the giant meant.

"Aldus said there was a poem. He said the poem mentioned a boy."

"Aye," replied Straight Hammer, his voice slightly sad. "That is the poem of The Ruin. And this," he said, pointing a thick, flattish finger at the farthing coin, "and *you*," he said, then pointing at Nicolas, "are below the surface of its words. Come now. You have a long road ahead of you in a short period of time. Let us get you some of what you'll need and get you on your way." In a still-kind but deep voice which caused many of the coals to jump and bounce in their glowing trough, Straight Hammer said, "Ranulf!"

A moment later, the tall boy appeared on the stairs. "Yes, sir?"

"This boy and his friends are in need of our work."

***

Quickly, with instruction and direction from Straight Hammer, Ranulf gathered several items together from the shop's assortment of armor and weapons. To Nicolas, he handed a padded shirt and a shirt of chain mail which had been stitched and forged for squires and the children of noblemen. Ranulf told Nicolas to put them on over his clothes but under his weather cloak. He also handed him a small, flat dagger with a hole in its handle, which Nicolas could hang from a leather thong around his neck. To Benjamin, he also handed a padded shirt and shirt of chain mail. The chain mail hung to his knees and drooped from the end of his arms. Ranulf cuffed the long sleeves and held them in place with forearm-straps of stiff leather. He also gave the boy-thief a pair of worn hunting boots, a discolored weather cloak (Ranulf said it had once been his when he was younger), and a chipped hatchet with a sharp edge, which Benjamin slung over his back using a loop of black leather. To Adelaide, he gave much the same thing: a padded shirt (this one was embroidered with purple flowers and a blue jay), a shirt of chain mail to wear under her surcoat, and a weather cloak with a fox-fur lined hood. Ranulf then ran back to one of the tables, piled up with a number of odd pieces of metal. He picked one out and handed it to Adelaide.

"What's this?" she asked, looking at the slender pin of grey metal about six inches long.

"It's a hair dagger," he said matter-of-factly. "Thread it into the middle of your hair braid. The curled end can act as a handle, and the sharp point can act as…well, a sharp point," he said with a smile.

After this, Straight Hammer looked at Ranulf. "And you, Ranulf son of Renfry. You are no longer your uncle's bladesmith apprentice."

Ranulf looked surprised and a bit uncertain. "What do you mean?" he asked.

"You are hereby released from your obligation, boy. Go and get your kit," said the giant quietly but firmly. "You now have a *new* apprenticeship to which you must attend."

A dawning look of realization came over Ranulf's face. He looked at Nicolas and Benjamin and Adelaide. Then, with a dutiful nod to Straight Hammer, he ran back up the stairs to gather his things. Ranulf would be joining them.

When he returned a few minutes later, he found the other three gathered in front of Straight Hammer's immense chair, listening to him speak to Nicolas.

"Take heed of your dreams, Nicolas. They live inside the mountain of your soul. You have dark days ahead of you, but the star-gods have chosen good companions for you. If ever there are giants you encounter, tell them the 'Elder' is your friend." Straight Hammer looked at them all, and in his kind and rich voice, bestowed a blessing.

May your words be true, and your hearts find comfort.
May your steps be sure, and your eyes find light.
May your cloak be warm, and your stomachs find food.
And if the earth be your blanket,
may it lay upon you lightly,
so the endless heavens may find you quickly and take you home.

The giant held out one of his immense hands. For some reason, Nicolas placed his hand on it, and the giant uttered something musical in his own language. He then said, "Now *go*! The day is late." He turned to Ranulf. "Take them straight-away to St. Wulf's-Without-Aldersgate, but do not take the main road. Stay close to the City walls and avoid others as best you can. Hurry, and speak to no one!"

With this, the four companions quickly disappeared into the darkness of the alley.

And Ragnuf, who had been sitting on a hogshead barrel of autumn ale in a dark corner of the shop, unseen and silently eavesdropping quietly hopped off his secretive seat and slipped out a sidedoor.

On their way back to the gatekeep, the four companions said little to each other.

They did their best to hurry along, and only stopped once when Adelaide said her wooden shoes had begun to hurt her feet. When she said this, Benjamin quickly disappeared down a sidestreet, taking her hard, wooden shoes with him. A few minutes later, he returned. Her hard, wooden clogs were gone, and in their place, he presented her with soft leather ankle boots with low heels and decorative laces. Adelaide hugged them to her chest. "Thank you, Benjamin," she said softly and sweetly.

"Lace them up, Adelaide," said Ranulf with a grin and a nod toward Benjamin. "We still have a little way to go, and the light is failing." To help with the pace, he picked up Cornelia, and for the rest of the way, carried the tiny goat protectively across his broad shoulders.

———————

When they finally came to the gate in the City wall, which led out to the long expanse of the cobbled archway and back to St. Wulf's-Without-Aldersgate, Nicolas stopped and turned around. The open lands were now awash in the twinkle of a thousand lights and cooking fires. He could still hear the merriment of music and voices. Dragon Dead Day was coming to an end.

Nicolas reached under his weather cloak and the weight of his chain mail. He touched the soft petals of the Dragon Poppy threaded into his woolen sweater. He thought of what the blood-red flower meant, and for a moment, the terrible sounds he'd heard in his dream—the cries and screams of dying men flashed in his head. He thought of the poem, The Ruin, and what Straight Hammer had told him. *You are below the surface of its words.*

The sun, fading behind the City's walls to the west of the Iron Quarter, threw long shadows over the open lands, and moments later, left the City of Relic in darkness.

Nicolas shivered.

A smallish hand touched his arm. It was Benjamin. "C'mon, Nicolas," he said. His voice was oddly reassuring. "We've made it."

The three boys, the girl, and the little goat hurried over the causeway and vanished inside the gatekeep as night began to fall.

CHAPTER 15

A Chat by the Fire

M aster Brooks had been waiting for them.

The thin, bookish boy had been patiently standing just within the heavy gates in the back wall of St. Wulf's-Without-Aldersgate, but he was now urgently waving Nicolas and his companions to follow him inside as night closed in behind them. "This way! This way!" he insisted, holding a flickering torchlight aloft. There were only a few straggling travelers at this late hour of the day, and the gatekeep guards were about to lower the portcullis for the night. A few minutes more, and Nicolas and his companions would have been stranded on the cobblestone bridge high above the river, which churned angrily in the darkness far below.

As soon as they were all within the safety of the gate's archway, Master Brooks took the lead, taking them through the gloomy passage and out into the gatekeep's large courtyard. Just after entering the courtyard, Master Brooks turned to his left under another archway and opened a thick oak door, leading into a spacious corridor. The corridor was lined with different colored slabs of stone, and every few yards stood tall posts of twisted iron, each topped by fat yellowish candles, with brightly burning wicks and long beards of melted wax. Long leather swags engraved with forest scenes hung between wide, blue-glass windows with lead panes. The leather drapes sported finely etched stags with gigantic antlers, standing proudly in the refuge of sunlit clearings. Tusked boars charging menacingly at hunters whose spears were at the ready and whose arrows were nocked in longbows. Gentle waterfalls pouring into even gentler streams where silver perch were in mid-leap into the air with curved tails, open mouths, and showers of water droplets. And overgrown thickets of old forest trees hiding the vague outlines of prowling foxes and unsuspecting hazel grouses, peacefully roosting.

Master Brooks extinguished his torchlight in a clay pot near the corridor's entrance, and again in an urgent voice, said, "This way." At the far end of the corridor, he fumbled through the clutter of keys hanging from the braided cord around his waist, and unlocked another thick oak door, through which they all quickly passed.

Nicolas immediately recognized the room. This was where he had awoken earlier that same morning, wrapped in a heavy bearskin and shaking off the grim recollections of a terrible nightmare.

This evening, several heavy logs burned brightly in the great fireplace, and the candle chandeliers above created a warm glow of light throughout the large hall. Near the fireplace, a long table and benches had been set with several bowls and trays of food, and pitchers and mugs of warm drink.

"Please," said Master Brooks, "make yourselves comfortable. The gatekeep does not presently have any large parties of guests, so you'll be staying here for the night. The Laird of the First Gate will be with you as soon as he is able. Until then, he respectfully asks that you stay here and do not leave this room." With a slight bow, the boy opened the thick door. "I'll be back in short order," and off he went.

"Food!" exclaimed Benjamin as soon as he was gone. Practically jumping onto a bench, the smallish boy-thief grabbed a juicily roasted woodcock, five boiled and peeled eggs, a pork pie, a large cut of salted cheese, and more than a few slices of "lardy cake," a rich fruit bread traditionally served at harvest time. With one of the eggs quickly stuffed inside one cheek, and a bite of the pork pie inside the other, he tried to say, "please pass something to drink," but it came out more like, "peas pass somebing to dwink."

Laughing, Ranulf threw off his weather cloak, his chest plate, and the chain mail. "Slow down!" he said merrily. "Now I know why your last name's 'Rush,' my little friend. Try to leave at least a nibble of stale bread for the rest of us." But after pouring Benjamin a generous mug of honeyed tea, Ranulf was not to be outdone, and had piled his own plate high with folded slices of cold beef, a chunk of warm bread with oats sprinkled on top, half a shepherd's pie, and a few pickled onions.

"Yuck!" said Adelaide, sticking her tongue out as she watched the boys stuff themselves. "Let's have tea," she primly said to Cornelia, who was nibbling gently at her finger. Adelaide also took off her weather cloak, her chained mail, her padded shirt, and her surcoat, but she took care to fold each of them nicely into a stack on one of smooth benches. She then sat down with her back straight and set her little goat beside her. She daintily poured some of the honeyed tea in her mug and poured a bit of thick cream into a bowl for Cornelia. Immediately, the tiny goat shoved her velvety lips into it, spilling it across the table and onto the floor. Innocently, Cornelia looked up at Adelaide with its round, brown eyes as if the bowl has spilled on its own. "Crabapples and crickets! You're as bad as Benjamin," fussed Adelaide. She poured some more cream and held the bowl firmly as her little goat lapped it up.

Nicolas stood near the fire, looking around at his three new friends, and a smile gradually spread across his face. *Maybe it's a day late*, he thought to himself happily, *but this is the most unique birthday party I've ever had.* A few moments later, with his own outer clothing lying in a messy heap on the floor, he was laughing and competing with Benjamin and Ranulf to see who could stuff the most lardy bread into their mouths at one time.

◆━

About twenty minutes later, Benjamin was the only one left at the table. He was slowly shoving one last boiled egg and a buttered biscuit into his mouth. Ranulf was rubbing his full belly with one hand and walking around the great room, staring up at the collection of stuffed animal heads.

"Oh my," Adelaide said quietly. She had already finished a large bowl of rosemary, mutton, and carrot stew, and she was now softly rubbing her hands across the remarkable needlework of one of the room's immense tapestries. It depicted an ocean-blue lake surrounded by snow-peaked mountains and shorelines garlanded in a profusion of strange flowers whose petals were dressed in shades of white, orange, red, blue, and yellow. After spending several minutes lost in her own thoughts, she found a comfortable chair near the fireplace's great hearth and sat down, tucking her legs under herself and holding Cornelia in her lap. She sang softly to the tiny goat, which had worked its way through a large pile of radishes, onions, cut oats, and bread scraps after finishing two bowls of cream. It was now suckling sleepily on one of Adelaide's fingers.

Benjamin finally pushed back from the long table, wiped his face with the back of his hand, patted his crammed belly, and joined Ranulf. The two boys—one tall and muscular, and one short and scruffy—wandered about the room, trying to out-do each other with important-sounding advice on how best to skin a boar, or how to best roast a leg of venison, or how best to stalk a bull elk. Nicolas sat on one of the benches, savoring a third mug of honeyed tea with its hints of fresh mint. He had one hand in his pocket, tracing a finger around the edges of the coppery leaf, and for the first time in the past two days, he felt relaxed.

175

Suddenly, the thick oak door at the end of the hall slammed open, and a giant black raven swooped in and came to rest atop one of the wild looking boar's heads mounted high up in a far corner of the great hall. Aldus Ward, the Laird of the First Gate and the greatest among the Commissioners of the Forfeited Gates, followed the raven, with the oversized arm sleeves and decorative hood of a stately black robe billowing all about him. A thick golden chain hung around his neck, and from it hung a large golden key, beautifully inlaid with emerald jade, clusters of rubies, and a thin coil of shiny copper around its long shank. Tucked under his arm was one of the same books Nicolas had seen two days earlier as he'd climbed the stairwell to Aldus' private chambers—one of the same books held by each of the tall, grim-looking statues—a book with metal hinges and a dragon-head seal. Behind Aldus scurried Master Brooks, his skinny arms full of scrolls tied with saffron ribbons, and pieces of parchment bearing fat buttons of stamped wax.

"Welcome!" exclaimed Aldus. He laid the old leathery book carefully on the end of the table and stood there, looking at each of them out of his one good eye in such a peculiar way Nicolas thought he might be reading their minds.

"Well, well," said Aldus, sounding satisfied. "You've all made it." He gave a slight bow. "Welcome to St. Wulf's-Without-Aldersgate, Miss Ashdown, Master Rush, and Master Ranulf the son of Renfry. I suppose a bit of an explanation may be in order. Come, let's join Miss Ashdown by the fire, and I'll do my best to tell you what I can."

Nicolas and Ranulf drew a few chairs closer to the crackling fire, while Benjamin grabbed one last chunk of lardy bread to nibble on. By this time, Cornelia lay fast asleep in Adelaide's lap. The young girl gracefully ran her fingers along the little goat's back in a soothing rhythm.

Master Brooks set his armful of scrolls and parchments on a bench and dashed about, helping to lift the chain and great golden key from Aldus' neck, and then assisting Aldus as he stepped out of his oversized judge's robe. Underneath the imperious and commanding robe, the Laird of the First Gate was dressed in a plain coarse tunic of undyed wool. Master Brooks neatly placed the robe and the chain atop the thick old book on the table, while continuously pushing his wiry spectacles back up his long thin nose.

"It is my understanding that Straight Hammer—a truly wonderful giant, by the way—at least gave all of you the idea an adventure might be in the making." As he said this, he motioned toward Kaha, perched high up on the boar's head, and Nicolas realized the bird must've given Aldus some information about his venture into the City. "But, as is the way of most giants, he probably didn't say too much. Although," Aldus approvingly observed, "I can see he provided you with a few things you're likely to need." Aldus glanced at the piles of cloaks and chain mail and padded shirts. "As I'm sure Ranulf already knows, the giant's unique handiwork with metal holds a few secrets. Should it be needed, I imagine you'll find the chain mail to be as strong as plate armour, but my suggestion is to keep it hidden if you can. All of you are rather young, and others may think they can take advantage of you or even try to take things from you." At this, Ranulf's face darkened, and the muscles in the older boy's jaw rippled and tightened. Aldus gently held up his hand. "My advice is to use your wits whenever possible. Your true strength will always lie in what others *don't* know about you. Let them guess, and let them be surprised when they find out there's more to you than what they can see."

Aldus adjusted his tunic absently and stared down at his feet with his one good blue eye. He was delaying the rest of what needed to be said. "I have already spent some time with Nicolas. He and I have discussed many dark and troubling things, and if we had more time together, I would be glad to share most of that with the rest of you as well. But tonight will go by quickly, and there are other things which must be done. I dare say, Nicolas already has a good sense of what may lie ahead, and I'm sure he'll share what he knows with each of you." Aldus paused before continuing. "Nicolas has a... a special 'part' to play in those dark and troubling things, and it is no accident he is here. But he'll need help. He'll need *your* help, if you're able and willing to give it." He looked up at Adelaide, Benjamin, and Ranulf. "You must know, this *adventure*, if you'd like to call it that, will be difficult. It will, in fact, be perilous at times. Indeed," he said in a quiet, apologetic voice, "it may end in terrible loss. And, if all that you depend on fails you in the end, it may also end in *death*."

A log broke noisily in the fireplace. Aldus' words slowly sank in.

Ranulf still had a dark look about him, but he now appeared thoughtful, too. Benjamin, the smallish boy-thief—usually quick to smile and say something clever—sat quietly in his chair with an unexpressive look on his face, weighing what the old man had said. Adelaide's lovely face was pale. She had stopped stroking Cornelia's back, but her pinkish lips were pressed in determination.

She was the first to break the silence. "*I* want to help. Nicolas helped Benjamin for no reason, so I want to help him," she explained. "Besides," she quickly added—her voice sounded bleak—"I haven't any other place to go."

"I don't, either," said Benjamin. The harshness of the boy-thief's statement surprised everyone. Benjamin's face was still expressionless, but his young voice was filled with years of hard living and the misery of a hard-scrabble life. "I've *never* had any place to go. I'd rather leave on a dangerous adventure than spend another night in the gutters of the Dreggs." He stood up and defiantly straightened his smallish body. "Where I come from, people have to act first and talk later." He nodded toward Adelaide. "And she's right. Nicolas helped me when I was in a fix without even thinking about it. They would've smashed my fingers if I'd been caught," Benjamin said, forgetting that he was speaking to a judge of the King's First Bench. "I've seen them do it to other boys. They end up begging for pecks and fighting with twisted fingers over spilled kernels of barley in the City's 'Bampfylde Houses' for the poor." His fists shook at his sides. "They won't *ever* catch me!" The emotion seemed to suddenly drain from his body. As if it was just occurring to him to ask, Benjamin turned his head and said to Nicolas, "Why *did* you help me?"

Nicolas—still horrified by what Benjamin had described—now felt his cheeks blush slightly at being put on the spot. He hoped no one could see his discomfort. "I dunno," he said with a vague shake of his head. "You looked alone to me, I guess. I know what it's like to feel alone," he said quietly. "I thought I could help, and you had an honest face."

Benjamin stood there reflecting on that for a moment. "Well," he said with confidence, "I'm not alone anymore." His familiar smile quickly returned. "You're my friend, Nicolas. And friends are all I've ever had. I can't lift a mountain, but if you need someone to get through a mouse hole, I can probably do that."

"I can't lift a mountain either," Ranulf jokingly said as he leaned forward and playfully picked up Benjamin, "but I can lift a mouse out of a mouse hole." Going along with the joke, Benjamin put his top front teeth over his bottom lip and made a quick *thcth, thcth, thcth*, sound, which made everyone laugh. Ranulf put the smallish boy down and rested his hands on his knees. "As for myself, I've grown up with the sound of hammers striking metal," he said. "I've carried buckets of coal, hauled water, and shouldered countless bundles of iron rods." His eyes went sympathetically to the bruise on Adelaide's face. "Straight Hammer didn't allow his shop apprentices to be beaten, but my uncle was a hard and bitter man. After my parents were killed by a raiding party of War Crows, my uncle brought me to the City. I think he resented me as an unwanted burden, and," he said, raising his linen undershirt, "he found ways to remind me." There, in random places along his right side, were several knobby burn marks which looked like Ugly Milkcap mushrooms. "He would say he was 'prodding' me to do a better job." Ranulf dropped his shirt and blankly stared at the floor. "Straight Hammer has given me a new chance, I think." He looked at Nicolas. "Whatever it is, I'll help the best that I can."

Nicolas gave him a quick nod. Inside, Nicolas felt profoundly humble. He thought of his own life in the Bennett family's small cottage. He thought about the recent arguments between his mum and his father, and how disappointed he had felt over his birthday. But Ranulf, Benjamin, and Adelaide had faced much bigger troubles. Nicolas' own problems and desires didn't seem all that big anymore. Whatever nagging hesitation he might have still felt about ominous crows, coppery leaves, devilish shadows, or ancient dragons, was instantly gone. Whatever it took—whatever it meant—Nicolas decided he, too, would do the best he could. Telluric Grand—his new friends—deserved it.

"Well done, well done!" Aldus said, clapping his hands together. "I had hoped for one, and instead, we have three! A bladesmith, a 'snatcher,' and a baker!"

"I'm not a baker," interrupted Adelaide. "I've only worked for that fat lardyman since I ran—" She stopped herself. "Since

I *arrived* in the City," she said more cautiously. "He only gave me work since my mother had taught me how to make dough and to bake, but it's not what I *want* to do. This morning, he caught me giving a loaf of twistbread to Benjamin." She touched the tender, puffy bruise at the corner of her mouth. "I'd done it before, but he'd never caught me doing it. A lot of people are hungry, but that fat man just cares about coins and more coins." She placed a warm hand on Cornelia's little black head. "If Benjamin hadn't distracted him, I think he would have killed me," she said softly.

"I'm truly sorry, Miss Ashdown," Aldus said. His good eye had become the color of soft, deep blue copper. He cocked his head toward Kaha. "I heard of what happened today, and I also heard that beastly man now has a couple of bashed shinbones." He winked and broke into a big smile. "It might please you to know, the City's bailiff men have since put his thumbs in screws for cheating a customer."

"Serves him right," Adelaide said coldly. "The man was a pig." She again touched her bruise. "All I've ever really wanted to be is a Healer." She looked earnestly at Aldus. "A *Bendith Duw*," she said quietly.

The Laird of the First Gate looked closely at the young girl. "I see," he said. "A *Bendith Duw*."

Suddenly, he clapped his hands. "Master Brooks!"

"Yes, m'lord?" The older boy had nearly jumped out of his skin.

"Take our strapping bladesmith to the armoury and stables. He is to have anything he needs, and the use of one pack animal, but make sure that any requests are made in my name. I don't want any wagging tongues if we can help it, even here in the gatekeep. Also, take this fine young 'snatcher,' Master Rush, to the gatekeep's tailor. His weather cloak needs one or two unseen pockets sewn into it." Aldus winked slyly at Benja-

181

min with a steel-blue eye. "And finally, Master Brooks, please take the lovely Miss Ashdown to see Missus Harpins. Tell Missus Harpins that Miss Ashdown needs a fresh kit of dried herbs, tonics, potions, and remedies." He stroked his silvery grey beard and grinned at Adelaide. "She's a *Healer* after all."

Then, Aldus was on his feet, swinging open the thick, oak door, and shooing them down the long corridor in a babble of excited whispers. "Hurry back!" He called after them. "You'll need your rest. You're to leave before dawn. *And speak to no one!*"

Amused, the old man turned back to Nicolas and caught his breath. "Well now," he said, pouring a generous mug of the honeyed tea for himself, "you and I ought to have a brief chat."

For the next hour, Nicolas and Aldus sat by the fire and talked about the day's events and about what Straight Hammer had said to Nicolas.

"It seems you've made another friend," said Aldus with approval. "And Straight Hammer's no ordinary friend, Master Bennett! That giant is far older than he looks, and knows far more than he usually lets on."

"He mentioned the poem," Nicolas offered.

"He did, did he?"

"Yes, and he said several things in his own language. He said I was in legends and prophecies… but that it was 'me' in a *different* way." Nicolas frowned, thinking back on the giant's cryptic comments. "I don't think I understood him very well."

"No, no, you did, you did," Aldus reassured him. "That's good. Very good. The span of his memory is greater perhaps than all the books in my library, and many of the legends and prophecies he knows go back even before the Great War of Giants, Wisps and Men." Aldus sounded pleased and satisfied. "It's what I suspected, Master Bennett. I just wanted to make sure."

Nicolas stared at the fire. Most of the huge logs had broken by then into glowing chunks of golden amber, fiery orange, and red. "We're leaving in the morning?" he asked.

"Yes, you must all leave in the morning," Aldus said. He sat back in his chair and swirled the tea in his mug pensively. "Having you go into the City was a risk, but I needed a quick way to make sure you were the right one. Few remain in the First Kingdom who can be trusted. Straight Hammer is one of them." He drained the last swallow of tea in a single gulp and stood up. "Tomorrow morning there will be a group of Outlanders leaving the gatekeep to travel back to their farms," he said. "You and the others will need to leave with them. Some of the Outlanders are strangers to each other. They are only traveling together for safety's sake. You should be able to blend in and deflect any suspicion."

Having said this, Aldus gathered up his black robe, the golden chain and key, and the thick book with metal hinges. He looked around the empty room and then up at Kaha, who still sat quietly perched high in the corner on the boar's head. "You need to go see someone," Aldus said in a low voice. "He'll know exactly what needs to be done."

"Who?" asked Nicolas.

The old man's blue eye was vacant-looking—nearly as dead as his milky white one. "A 'Clokkemaker,'" he said simply and quietly. "His name is *Remiel*."

The Laird of the First Gate moved toward the thick, oak door and opened it slightly, peering cautiously out into the corridor. The large black raven alighted from the boar's head and flew down to land on the old man's shoulder. "You've already met him," whispered Aldus, just before he left the great hall. "He's the Wisp you met in the woods."

183

CHAPTER 16

Into the
Woodcutter's Forest

One by one, Master Brooks led each of Nicolas' companions back into the great room.

When Ranulf returned, he was shouldering a large burlap sack, with a smaller leather bag tucked securely into his belt. He was smiling and humming merrily to himself. When he dropped the burlap sack to the stone floor, it jangled and clinked and clattered. Benjamin, however, returned looking much the same way he'd left, but when he opened his weather cloak, Nicolas could see several new pockets artfully stitched inside; just the right kind of cloak for a "snatcher" to wear. Adelaide was the last of the three to return, her little goat following sleepily at her heels. She had a soft leather roll, decorated with stitched beads, slung across her back. "It's full of *everything*," she said eagerly when Nicolas asked what was inside.

With everyone back in the great room, they each began to quietly arrange their sleeping pallets near the fire. All of them were very tired and lost in their own private thoughts. They said very little to one another. Soon, the helpful Master Brooks brought in four bearskins to cover them, and before he was able to close the thick oak door behind him and turn a key in its large iron grimlock, Ranulf, Benjamin, and Adelaide were all fast asleep.

Nicolas, alone—but now among new friends—lay tucked under the heavy fur, staring distractedly at the faraway ceiling. "Remiel," he said softly to himself.

Soon after, he fell into a deep and dreamless sleep.

"Master Bennett."

The voice was muffled.

"Master Bennett," it gently said again.

Nicolas blearily cracked open one eye. It was dark and smelly, and he couldn't see anything. In fact, it smelled like Jasper, the Bennett family dog, when he'd try to curl up next to Nicolas while he laid reading on the floor of his father's study. Invariably, the dog always ended up lying halfway on top of him, with Nicolas trying to push paws and dog hair out of the way, so he could read the words on the page. "*Jasperrrrrrrr*," Nicolas complained drowsily.

"Master Bennett," the familiar voice said again.

Nicolas felt a gentle poke in his back. His mind felt fuzzy. *Why is it so dark?* he thought. Then, with a jerk, he remembered where he was and why it smelled so musty. With one arm, he pushed back the heavy bearskin. The older boy, Master Brooks, was standing above him, pushing his spectacles up his slender nose. Next to him stood Ranulf, grinning and gently poking Nicolas with the end of a gnarled walking staff. The light coming through the tall narrow windows high in the wall was hazy and grey. It felt early.

"Your breakfast is waiting, Master Bennett," said the bookish boy as he kept patiently pushing his dodgy spectacles back in place.

"Your breakfast *was* waiting. Now it might be *gone*," countered Ranulf. "Benjamin will bite your arm off if you're not careful. He's been over at the table eating for at least five minutes. You'll be lucky if you even get a spoon to lick."

Nicolas yawned so hard his eyes watered. "I'm coming, I'm coming," he said. He sat up and yawned again. Benjamin and

Adelaide were both sitting at the long table. On the table were two clay pitchers of cold water, a pile of green and red apples, and a brown-black pot, steaming with a simple potage stew of potatoes, ham, lentils, and pepper. The boy-thief, or "snatcher" as Aldus had called him the night before, was shoveling the potage into his mouth out of a trencher—a make-shift bowl made of hard, dried bread—as fast as he could. Nicolas vaguely wondered how such a smallish boy could constantly eat so much. Adelaide sat next to him daintily munching on a large red apple, while Cornelia nosed busily around the floor searching for fallen bits of dried bread and other scraps.

Nicolas wearily got up, put his boots on, and stretched his arms high over his head. He'd been warm all night, but even the padded quilts hadn't made the stone floor underneath very comfortable. He took a seat on the other side of Benjamin and playfully jabbed him in the ribs with his elbow. The smallish boy-thief simply smiled and tried to say, "good morning," but his mouth was full, and the words came out more like, "goo moaning." Nicolas grabbed an apple off the table and took a big bite.

He was just finishing his second apple when Aldus arrived.

"Good morrow!" said the Laird of the First Gate cheerfully. "I hope everyone slept well. It's good to see you all up and about." He gave a brief nod to his bookish aide. "Well done, Master Brooks." Aldus lifted his chin, wagging his thick beard. "The band of Outlanders you're to travel with is already gathering in the yard. I've had our stable master speak with one of the farmers and ask whether a few children could accompany them. He told the man your parents had been unable to travel, but that they'd sent you to the festival in the City to sell various odds-and-ends and homemade knick-knacks. Your story is flimsy, but it need only to serve you for a few miles. Then you'll be on your own." He clapped his hands excitedly. "You must hurry! The bell for the gatekeep's second watch has already rung! The cockle has crowed twice! Hurry, hurry!"

Quickly, they all busied themselves putting on clothing, chain mail, and weather cloaks. Adelaide tied hers securely at her neck and slung the soft leather roll she'd acquired the night before across her back. The boys cinched their belts and gathered up the burlap sack and leather satchel Ranulf had brought in with him the night before.

"Me and Brooks arranged for us to take a pony from the gatekeep's stables," Ranulf explained to Benjamin and Nicolas. "It can carry the burlap sack and whatever else is too big or awkward. Roll up those bearskins, too, and help me bundle some of that kindling and some of those larger sticks by the hearth. We need to look like we're returning home from the City with things we bought or need for a few days' travel. Be careful with that leather satchel, too," he added. "Brooks dropped a few coins in there, along with a fire kit, some rolled up wineskins, and a purse of cooking spices."

"Cooking spices!" exclaimed Benjamin with a huge grin. "Smashing! I'll be in charge of the cooking spices," he volunteered.

"When have you ever used cooking spices?" Ranulf asked with a laugh.

Benjamin bit his lip and looked up at the roof beams. "Ummmm." His eyes lit up, and he jabbed a finger in the air. "I use them every time I *eat* something," he said.

"Well, we need to use them every time we *cook* something," Ranulf replied, laughing. "Don't worry, Master Rush. My uncle made me cook his dinner and evening sup all the time. I'll make sure we put the cooking spices to good use."

"I'll fill the wineskins with some water," Adelaide suggested.

As the other two boys and Adelaide continued to make

preparations for their departure, Aldus motioned to Nicolas to join him privately by the thick, oak door. "I am hopeful that if you get on the road quickly, before anyone has much of a chance to spy or to whisper, your way might stay relatively free of danger," he said.

"Why would anyone want to spy or whisper?" Nicolas asked. He'd already felt his chest tightening with anxiety again, remembering what Aldus had told him the night before—they were off to see a Wisp. The thought of anyone meaning them harm, in addition to seeking out the same dark and terrible thing he'd met in the forest, made him feel especially unnerved.

Aldus placed his aged hand on Nicolas' shoulder and sighed. "Sadly, there are those who crave power, Master Bennett—men as well as other creatures—and power can sometimes come from fear. For many years, the First Kingdom, and even lands beyond its borders, have enjoyed peace, but it has been an unsteady and uncertain peace—it was a peace bought with a binding curse and the prison walls of a dark cave. No king sits on the throne, and the terror of the Shadow Thief's possible return has continued to stay alive in people's nightmares. That uncertain and delicate peace has now begun to unravel," Aldus said with misgivings. "There are already dark rumors ..." Aldus' voice trailed off. He snapped his mouth closed and shook his head, refusing to say anything more. Instead, he cleared his throat and steered his words back to what was presently at hand. "Your presence here in Telluric Grand, and the possibility you could bring a *true* peace, would threaten those who cling to the kind of power which thrives on people's fear. They *must* not know you are here, Master Bennett. They must not know until the Shadow Thief has been destroyed for good."

By this time, the boys and Adelaide had finished their work, and they gathered together with Aldus and Nicolas. The Laird of the First Gate looked at them all. "Now listen well—all of you. Several miles down the main road, you'll come to a cross-roads marked by a split tree. There, turn to the southwest. This will take you along the Lonely Road which runs through the heart of the Woodcutter's Forest. I doubt you will pass anyone on this road, but remain vigilant and trust no one. After leaving the forest, you will come upon the 'Hollow Fen.' This is a vast moor of treacherous bogs and strange mists. Once you enter the Hollow Fen, be careful to stay on the road no matter what you see. I must warn you, many souls who've entered the Hollow Fen have become lost forever in its black marshes. Keep to the road, and you should be safe."

Adelaide shuddered. She hugged Cornelia to her chest. "Why do we have to go in there at all?"

"Because," explained Aldus, "you need to help Nicolas look for someone, and this particular 'someone' lives in the Fen. It is very important that you find him as quickly as you can," Aldus said gravely.

"Who would want to live *there?*" asked Benjamin with a grimace. "You'd have to be mad to want to live in some boggish, marshy slag heap."

"That may be true," agreed Aldus, "or you simply might want to be left alone."

"Then which one are we looking for?" asked Benjamin smartly. "A madman or a hermit?"

"Both," Aldus replied without hesitation. "But the one you're looking for will also know what needs to be done next." His keen blue eye looked sharply at Nicolas. "He'll know what Master Bennett will need to do."

"Where in the Fen will we find this person?" asked Ranulf.

"He lives in a humble home built out of blocks of cut peat and sod. Once you're on the path through the Fen, you'll find it. Or what's more likely," Aldus added with a shrug, "he'll find you."

Little else was left to be discussed, and all of them quickly made their way into the main yard of the gatekeep.

"Today is the third day in the festival of Haligtide," Aldus had said to Nicolas moments before they said goodbye. Ranulf had been busy making sure the straps and ropes—which held their bedrolls, a deep cooking pot, two bundles of sticks, a small pack of dried sausages, yellow potatoes, flat-bread, a sugar loaf, beans, turnips, onions, and cut oats, and the large burlap sack—were secured tightly to the wooden cross-frame mounted on their pony's back. Adelaide had been holding Cornelia up out of the muck in the gatekeep's yard and trying to keep the little goat from nibbling her earlobes. Benjamin had been standing idly by their pony, staring across the yard at the same enormous armored bear which had met Nicolas inside the gatekeep's front tunnel two days before. The bear was sitting calmly by the entrance to the front tunnel, but even in a sitting position, it was a colossal sight of fur, claws, and cruel-looking armour.

"What happens on the third day of Haligtide?" asked Nicolas, trying to pay attention to the old man. In reality, he, too, was mesmerized by the sight of the bear, which made him wonder where the gatekeep's Master Grimlock or the giant dog, Basileus, were, but he asked Aldus a question because he didn't want to seem impolite.

"Well," said the Laird of the First Gate, "those who have slain a dragon are invited to gather at the King's Castle to renew their pledges of loyalty to the First Kingdom and to have the king—or the High Chancellor—pledge the First Kingdom's loyalty to them. Then, after a traditional game of Haxey Post is played by teams from each of the City's gatekeeps, a long table is set with the best food and wine in the winner's gatekeep, and those who have slain a dragon sit at the table and eat their fill."

Nicolas, now very interested, looked at Aldus. "There are people who have *killed* dragons? And what is Haxey Post?"

Aldus laughed. "Yes there are, and you'll have to see it for yourself sometime, Master Bennett. Haxey Post is—well, it's quite a unique competition."

Across the yard, the massive bear yawned, startling one of the nearby pack horses, which promptly dumped its cargo on the ground. The owner of the horse scrambled about, swearing and doing his best to calm the beast down and to put everything back atop its wooden cross-frame.

"How many people have killed a dragon?" Nicolas asked quietly.

"A few," Aldus answered in a more solemn voice, "and fewer than a few are still alive to participate in today's feast." He paused, then said, "They are called the 'Dragon Nightfall'."

Half an hour later, Nicolas once again found himself on the border of the treeless plain, which lay in front of St. Wulf's-Without-Aldersgate, about to follow the bend in the road back into the dark forest beyond. He stood to the side of the road and let the others pass by him. He wanted to take a last look back at the immense stone fortress. Beyond the gatekeep, in the grey of early morning, he could see very little of the City itself. Its high walls and the uppermost towers of the King's Castle lurked in and out of the gloomy bloat of low-hanging clouds. Some of the heavier clouds had actually settled into proper fog banks, making the gatekeep and the City look eerie and ghostlike. Unlike the day before, the weather had turned dreary, grey, and cooler. The sky was the color of cold ashes in the bottom of a fireplace, and it was threatening to rain. Even from this distance, he could hear the faint swell of thousands of cheering voices as teams of men from each of the City's gate-keeps began to fight each other in the game of Haxey Post. He wondered what the game was like and who would win. Nicolas wondered who would then sit at the long table—the Dragon Nightfall. *Fewer than a few are still alive*, Aldus had said. And Nicolas wondered who they were.

Pulling his weather cloak more closely around his shoulders and lifting its hood over his head, he turned to catch up with his friends and the small group of fellow travelers.

———————

He and Adelaide, Benjamin, and Ranulf had taken a place at the back of the traveling group. Ranulf had suggested this as a smart way for them to attract less attention and to be able to depart from the group more easily when the time came. To their relief, three boys, a girl, a miniature goat, and a pack pony didn't attract much attention in the first place. The group of fellow travelers mostly consisted of farmers who hailed from different Outlander villages. Most of them had traveled to the City of Relic on behalf of other farmers from each of their home villages, acting as selling agents who brought their villages' wagons of barley, oats, and beans in the hope their crops would fetch higher prices from the purchasing clerks at the High Chancellor's granaries. There were also a few alewives among them. They had accompanied their husbands and were returning home after having sold a variety of homemade trinkets, baubles, and spun cloth.

Among the travelers, there were also a couple of men who were not farmers. There was an old tinker with a crooked back, who said he'd lost his hand-cart of tinsmith tools and knick-knacks; at the last minute, he'd asked to join the group as it had made its way out of the tunnel entrance of St. Wulf's-Without-Aldersgate. And there was a lanky carpenter, who carried a bucket-pole over his shoulder with two sturdy buckets full of hammers, chisels, rasps, wooden clamps, and saws hanging from hooks on each end. The tinker said very little to anyone, and seemed foul-tempered and sulky. Unfortunately, his twisted back gave him a slow, lurching gait, and he kept falling to the rear of the group, which put him uncomfortably close to Nicolas and his friends. They did their best to keep to themselves and mostly ignored him. The carpenter, however, liked to laugh. He talked more and told more jokes than most of the other men in the group who either preferred to trudge along in silence or who chatted about the weather and the best way to temporarily repair a broken plow beam. Nicolas overheard the carpenter say he'd earned a month's wages in only a week by helping build many of the stalls and temporary shops set up in the City's open lands. He said he was from an Outlander village four days travel to the south. His village had the curious name of "Bagdel Blomst," which, the carpenter said to anyone who was listening at the time, meant "Bottom Flower."

"Why is it called 'Bottom Flower'?" Nicolas quietly asked Ranulf.

Ranulf looked at him oddly as if Nicolas had asked why rain is wet. "Must be because of the cabbage," Ranulf explained matter-of-factly. "Bagdel Blomst is famous for its crops of Curdle Cabbage."

"Hmph," said Nicolas. "I've never heard of 'Curdle Cabbage.' Is Curdle Cabbage also called 'Bottom Flower'?" Nicolas asked, still confused.

Ranulf grinned and gave a quick laugh. "You're a strange lad, Nicolas. I'm guessing his village is called 'Bagdel Blomst' because anyone who eats too much Curdle Cabbage will spend the rest of the day making some rather smelly 'bottom flowers'." He gave another quick laugh and shook his head. "They'll be farting so much it'll be like two angry geese having an argument."

For a split second, the two boys stared at each other. Then they both began to laugh uncontrollably, which caused Nicolas to snort. Adelaide tried to shush them, but she also made the mistake of telling Benjamin what they'd been laughing at. The smallish boy grinned wickedly, then purposefully let go of a distinctly thunderous bottom flower which ended in a high, shrill squeak, and smelled like dirty lentils and sour milk.

After that, the three boys laughed so hard tears ran down their faces. They all stood in the muddy roadway, leaning on each other and gasping for breath. Disgusted, Adelaide shook her head, grabbed the pack pony's lead rope from Ranulf, and stomped away with Cornelia trotting closely at her heels.

The noon-day meal was much less eventful.

The small group had stopped off on the side of the road in a clearing full of dahlia flowers, sporting red petals and yellow centers, and bronze-colored "Cottage Apricots," which Nicolas' pack pony found especially delicious. Adelaide gave each of them a piece of flat-bread and a cut of cold sausage to eat. Benjamin complained and asked for seconds, but she said no. They needed to be mindful of their food supply. Most of the farmers took brief naps, and the alewives sat in a circle sharing gossip about sick children and how loudly their husbands snored.

A light patter of rain soon began to fall, which got everyone back on the road.

Aside from a bit of grumbling about the turn of wet weather, the small group of travelers slogged on in silence—even the lanky carpenter was quiet—for several more miles. Nicolas remembered very little about the roadway they were on, but when he had last traveled it, it had been a dark night, and he and the tall man and donkey hadn't paused to take a look around. Eventually, the small group passed the "Cider Press

Inn." The inn was quiet today. Benjamin waved at the innkeeper's wife, who was sitting outside as they passed by. She had a small awning of oiled sheepskin over her head, and she was peeling apples into a large bucket. As he walked by, she smiled and tossed him an apple.

Almost a mile further down the road, they finally reached a crossroads, marked by a large Rowan tree.

———————————

The tree stood about forty feet tall, with a full crown of hundreds of branches, thousands of small leaflets, and small bunches of creamy white flowers. Its branches were heavy with clusters of soft and juicy fruit, much like berries, which the farmers, the alewives, and the carpenter, immediately began picking as a refreshing treat in the late afternoon.

Nicolas, however, remained standing in the road, gawking at the Rowan tree.

Because of his father, Nicolas knew what the tree should look like, but this was the most curious Rowan tree Nicolas had ever seen, for one small but extremely noticeable reason. On the east half of the tree, all of its berry-like fruit was white. On the west half of the tree, all of its fruit was red.

"The 'split tree'," said Benjamin, reminding them of what Aldus had described before they left. "Look!" he then said, pointing at the other members of their small traveling group. Everyone who was picking the tree's fruit was only picking and eating the white fruit from the east half of the tree.

"Excuse me," Ranulf said to the lanky carpenter. "Is there something wrong with the red fruit?"

The carpenter wiped his juice-smeared lips. "Of course not, lad," he said. "But yer only supposed to eat the fruit from the side of the tree in which yer headed. I'm goin' thatta way." He pointed a long finger down the road, leading in the easterly direction. "So I'm eatin' the white berries. If you an' yer friends are continuin' south, then don't eat a thing, but if yer headed in a westerly manner, then I'd suggest you each grab a handful o' the red berries. It'll keep away the bad spirits." With that, he gave Ranulf a friendly pat on the shoulder and popped a few more white berries in his mouth.

Nicolas and his friends were soon plucking the tree's red fruit and popping them into their mouths. He thought they tasted like a pear mixed with cherries. Minutes later, with a friendly wave of goodbye to the carpenter and one of the ale-wives who'd spent some time chatting with Adelaide about different herbs, they watched the small group of travelers fade down the crossroad to the east.

When they were almost gone from sight, Ranulf said, "Well, let's get on with it," and took hold of the pack pony's lead.

Before he could begin leading them in the opposite direction, Adelaide asked, "May Cornelia ride on the pony's back? She's tired, and I'm tired of carrying her. I don't think she'll weigh that much."

"Of course," said Ranulf. He took the little goat and tucked her in between the burlap sack and one of the bearskin bedrolls.

"Follow me!" exclaimed Benjamin, taking a quick skip to the front of their small band as they started walking down the Lonely Road.

Soon, the trees and underbrush thickened. The muddy road narrowed to the width of a single small wood-cart. The sun, which had finally triumphed with a ribbon of clear sky, hung low above the western horizon, painting the dim skyline a deep, rosy color. The waning light smoldered its way through the dense weave of branches and leaves like the glow of a huge, distant fire, but as quickly as it had appeared, peeking beneath the dome of heavy clouds, the sunlight began to fade. The fallow—the late twilight at the end of the day—deepened across Telluric Grand.

There was a disturbing denseness and murkiness to the closeness of the hardwood trees and to the crowding of the tangled undergrowth. Nicolas didn't feel like the Woodcutter's Forest would be a very safe place to have to spend the night. But in truth, it was not the darkness of the trees or the gloominess of the brambles and bushes which made the Woodcutter's Forest unsafe.

Instead, a misshapen body silently crept along behind them, cleverly hiding from view among the long shadows of dying light.

It was the old, crooked tinker.

CHAPTER 17

†HE LOПELY ROAD

L ook!" Benjamin had stopped and was pointing along a thin path through the trees. About fifty paces from the Lonely Road stood a small cottage. "It looks deserted. Maybe it could be a warm, dry place to roast some potatoes and spend the night." Given the dimness of the forest's motley shadows, Nicolas was amazed Benjamin had spotted the trail, much less the cottage, in the darkness.

They were about two miles from the crossroads and the Rowan tree. Night—with its dark sky and the cold breeze— was now fully upon them. Only minutes before, Ranulf had stopped to hang a small lantern from a stick he'd lashed to the pommel of the pony's wooden cross-frame. The lantern bounced and bobbed with each of the pony's steps, but under the canopy of the forest's crowded trees, its light was comforting and helped all of them see a little better. Each of them had moved closer to the pony as they plodded along, saying little, and mostly concentrating on placing and pulling their boots out of the muddy muck of the narrow roadway. The light drizzle of rain had let up shortly after they'd started down the Lonely Road, but the branches and leaves grew close enough together, and intertwined enough over the roadway, that water, falling in plump droplets, continued to thwack against the oiled hoods of their weather cloaks and to thunk into the squishy mud beneath their feet. A warm, dry place to eat and sleep would be welcome.

"We can't," said Adelaide quietly. She was facing the boys, but she was looking at the dark cottage out of the corner of her eyes. "We can't go in there. *I* won't go in there," she said with certainty.

"Why not?" Benjamin asked. "It doesn't look like anyone's there, Adelaide. We could have a nice fire and a dry place to sleep." He looked around. "It'd feel a lot better than sleeping in these miserable, cold, wet woods."

Ranulf looked at Adelaide with concern. "What's wrong?" he asked. "Did you see something?"

"No," she answered hesitantly. "It's just that—it's just that, it scares me."

"Why?" asked Ranulf.

She looked timid as she spoke, as if the boys might not believe her, but her voice was firm. "No one knows this, but I grew up in a small village not far from here. When I was little, several woodcutters lived in this same forest. My dad said they were fierce men, who drank too much ale and gambled. They'd cut trees to sell them at village markets for use as cooking barrels or charcoaling. Or, they'd take the wood to the City on long black sleds for new buildings and king-ships. One night, after me and my little brother Simon had gone to bed in the sleeping loft, a large, dark man came knocking at our door. The hour was late, but my dad was a kind man and let him come in and sit by our fire. The man seemed cold and wouldn't stop shaking. My brother said it made him look blurry. Mum served him some hot tea, but he didn't say anything for a long time, and my parents let him be to get back some warmth.

"Finally though, my dad asked the dark man who he was and where he'd come from. He said his name was Payne and that he was one of the woodcutters who lived in the forest. He said two days before, him and three other woodcutters had been working in a grove of Black Alder trees. He was a 'tree topper' and was high up in one of the trees when he looked below and saw a stranger approach his two friends, who were busy collecting the branches he'd been cutting down. He couldn't hear what was said because he was too high up, but suddenly, the stranger pulled a two-headed felling axe out of his cloak, swung it over his head, and slammed it deep into the skull of one of the woodcutters. The man's other friend tried to run, but the stranger chased him, chopping at his legs, then split his head open, too." By this time, Benjamin, Ranulf, and Nicolas had instinctively gathered close to Adelaide. The more she talked, the darker the forest felt, and the quieter her voice became.

"What happened to the man in the tree?" asked Benjamin. His eyes were wide as tea saucers. He stood there with his shoulders hunched over and with his arms crossed over his chest.

Adelaide glanced at each of the boys. "Well," she said, "the dark man said the stranger stayed in the grove for a while. He seemed to be *sniffing* around, and at one point, the dark man was sure the stranger had discovered him. He said the stranger stared up into the branches and seemed to look right at him. The dark man said he'd hugged the tree and stayed perfectly still, hoping the stranger would go away. He didn't. Instead, he began to climb—to *crawl*—up the tree. The dark man could hear the stranger breathing, but the stranger didn't say anything. The man thought he was going to die, but when the stranger had climbed within a few feet of the dark man's boots, he stopped and snarled something the dark man thought was a curse. Then he turned and crawled back down the tree... *headfirst*." Adelaide shivered again. "The dark man said the day was falling fallow by that time, and it had been too dark to see the stranger's face. After a minute or two more, the stranger suddenly left the grove."

"And—what happened?" Ranulf asked. He had an intense look on his face, and Nicolas noticed Ranulf's hand was gripping the head of his smith-hammer, which hung from the loop in his belt.

Adelaide took a deep breath. "The dark man told my dad he'd stayed in the top of the tree for the next two days. He thought the stranger might return or be waiting for him below, but at last, he couldn't feel his legs anymore, and he was dying of thirst, so he climbed down. He said he tried not to look at his dead friends, and he was ashamed that he'd left them there for the wolves to eat. He was afraid and didn't know what else to do."

Adelaide's voice dropped to a whisper, and the boys leaned in further to hear what she was saying. "As quickly as the dark man had finished telling his story, he stood up. My mum later said his skin looked pale and sweaty, and he hadn't stopped trembling. He loudly said that the stranger was still looking for him, and he couldn't stay very long. He said the stranger was looking for *all* woodcutters. Before my dad could calm him down, the dark man flew for the door and ran out into the night." Adelaide had a worried look on her face and shook her head like she was trying to forget what happened.

Benjamin suddenly put his hands up in protest. "Snipes and snips!" he said. "That ain't a pleasant story, Adelaide, but I still don't see why it means we can't sit by a warm fire in that cottage." The smallish boy-thief had a brave smile on his face, but his voice didn't sound quite as courageous as he meant it to be.

The young girl gave him a prickly look. "You're right, Benjamin Rush. It isn't a pleasant story, but I actually haven't told you the most unpleasant part of it yet."

Benjamin's chin dropped. "Sorry," he quietly apologized. "Go on."

Adelaide's face looked drawn and tense. She looked around nervously. "The most awful part," she said, "is that my dad found out there were *three* dead woodcutters in the Black Alder grove. The next morning, he and some men from our village went investigating to see what had happened, and they found three woodcutters with chop marks on their bodies and with their heads split open. They'd all been dead for days. My dad recognized one of the men. It was the same dark man who'd been inside our cottage the night before."

Nicolas had a quick shiver and glanced at Benjamin and Ranulf. The boy-thief's eyes were as wide as Nicolas had ever seen them, and his mouth was hanging open. He had moved even closer to Adelaide, and without realizing it, he'd grabbed ahold of her hand. Even Ranulf, who was older and always seemed cool as a cucumber, looked pale and somber. "Are you being level, Adelaide?" he asked quietly.

"I am," she said, "I really am. Cross my heart. My mum later told me and my brother that the dark man must've been the dead woodcutter's ghost, come to warn us about his murderer, the 'Dyn Glas,' a blue man who carries an axe and is said to cause woodcutters to have accidents and to die." She gave a quick nod in the direction of the empty woodcutter's cottage Benjamin had found. "There's *no* way I'm sleeping in that woodcutter's cottage and have the Dyn Glas come looking for *me*."

As soon as she said this, Benjamin screamed.

Nicolas, who was still terrified at the story Adelaide had told, stood there, and for a split second, was confused.

Like a Halloween fright, he watched as a withered hand came out of the surrounding darkness and wrapped itself around Benjamin's neck, and he saw a wrinkled and pinched face leering over Benjamin's shoulder in the lantern's weak light. It was all so unexpected, and he'd been so gripped by what Adelaide was saying, it took Nicolas a moment to realize that what was going on was real.

It was the tinker.

While the boys had been listening to Adelaide's tale, the old crooked tinker had inched his way toward them in the darkness. Silently, he'd wormed his twisted body closer and closer, until finally, he was crouching just behind Benjamin, getting ready to strike. In his left hand, he held a short, thin knife made of hammered tin—perfect for quick stabs and slicing flesh like a hot knife through warm fat. But when Benjamin had suddenly moved next to Adelaide to hold her hand, the tinker had been forced to change his plan of attack. Instead of a hard thrust with his left hand into the boy-thief's back, he instead leapt at Benjamin, grabbing the boy-thief by the throat with his left hand, while his right hand—which was his weaker and more misshapen hand—tried to awkwardly hold the paper-thin, tin knife.

Benjamin had screamed out of surprise and fright, but a moment later, he grunted heavily as the twisted little tinker drove his wafer-thin knife into the boy-thief's side as hard as he could.

Impulsively—even before he'd had time to really understand what was going on—Nicolas reached out and grabbed Adelaide's arm. He jerked her toward himself, away from Benjamin and away from the maniacally grinning tinker. As Nicolas did this, Ranulf lunged forward with a harsh yell. The bladesmith apprentice was madly grabbing for his hammer, trying to wrestle it out of the leather loop on his belt, but the soft leather tugged back at the hammer's shaft. Ranulf only managed to throw his weight into Benjamin's body, which then slammed into the tinker behind him. All three of them fell together and sprawled into the muck of the roadway in a frenzied tangle of arms and legs. Ranulf desperately tried to seize the tinker by the throat, but in spite of his physical debilities, the tinker reacted quickly, and he bit Ranulf's hand rabidly, causing the older boy to howl in shock and pain. A warm course of blood pumped out of his palm from where the tinker's sharp bottom teeth had ripped through the skin. When Benjamin had fallen, he had rolled on his side and lay on top of Ranulf's other arm, unintentionally pinning his friend.

The crooked tinker heaved himself out of the mud and hunched over the two boys, who were lying there helplessly. He was still grinning a toothy, mad smile, and a long drip of bloody saliva was hanging out of his malformed mouth. "Which of you pathetic pups goes by the name of *Nicolas?*" he sneered. The pony sidestepped, and the lantern light flickered wickedly across the tinker's cruel face. His tongue flicked out, licking up the strand of bloody spit.

Ranulf raised his injured hand to defend Benjamin and himself. But as he did so, the tinker's mean eyes suddenly bulged out, and with the sickening crunch of mashed bone, his head caved in.

The crooked tinker fell dead at Benjamin's feet.

The wafer-thin tin knife lay in the mud next to Tinker's twitching, bent fingers, and at the edge of the light, right behind the spot where the tinker had been standing a moment before, now stood a very large bear.

Nicolas thought the bear must have used its massive paw to crush the tinker's head, except when the bear moved a little closer, Nicolas realized the creature had a human, but bear-like face. "Dat's de end o' dat thievin', schemin', tin-peddlin' goat turd," said the human face, and it spat scornfully on the tinker's muddy corpse.

Adelaide, oblivious to the bear-like figure or the tinker's lifeless body, pulled herself from Nicolas' side and rushed toward Benjamin, dropping to her knees beside him. She helped hold the smallish boy-thief as Ranulf gingerly removed his arm from underneath Benjamin's weight. Nicolas could hear her muttering some kind of soft prayers under her breath as one of her hands brushed Benjamin's wet hair out of his face, while the nimble fingers of her other hand quickly loosened his weather cloak. She tenderly reached inside and probed where the tinker had thrust his knife. With a look of genuine relief, Adelaide sat back on her heels. "I can't feel any wound under his mail shirt, and there's no blood. The knife must not have gone in, but his eyes are closed. I think he must've hurt his head."

"Ha!" boomed the bear-like figure. "Dat little cub's made o' steel."

"Who are you?" Ranulf demanded as he slowly pushed himself to his feet.

"Bardölf," the bear-like figure said, and he laughed. His huge teeth flashed in the lantern light. "Bardölf es a *Jamba* keeper."

A few minutes later, Adelaide set their small lantern atop a rough table inside the woodcutter's cottage, and began giving all kinds of unnecessary directions to Nicolas and Ranulf, who were in the process of laying Benjamin down near the stone hearth. The boys politely said nothing and simply grunted and huffed their acceptance. Bardölf, when Ranulf asked if he was planning on staying for the night, had raised his large, thick hand and said, "No invite yet," and quietly remained outside. His broad shoulders and wide girth took up most of the room on the cottage's small front porch. Nicolas could hear the muted sound of raindrops slapping on the cottage's roof, thatched with bundled straw, water reed, and heather. A heavy downpour had finally begun to fall.

"I'll get a fire going," volunteered Ranulf as he disappeared back outside to find his fire kit.

"What can I do to help?" asked Nicolas.

Adelaide was on her knees by Benjamin, carefully removing his weather cloak and mail shirt. She had already taken off her own cloak, mail shirt, and her indigo blue surcoat. She now rolled the surcoat into a ball and placed it under Benjamin's head.

"Bring our bedrolls in, if you don't mind," she said. "We need to keep him warm, and we may as well have our own beds close by." Stopping what she was doing, Adelaide glanced at him. "Nicolas, wait." She lifted her eyebrows in an innocent way. "Thank you. For earlier. You—you thought of me."

"You're welcome." He felt awkward and self-conscious and didn't know what else to say. "I'm not sure what I was thinking," was all he managed.

Adelaide smiled and turned back to her patient. Nicolas stood there for a moment, then headed out the door to find the pony and Ranulf.

The older boy had already led their pony out of the rain and under a lean-to built against one side of the woodcutter's cottage. He'd found some old, but still-good hay, and the pony was happily munching away as Ranulf unloaded its wooden cross-frame. "How's our little snatcher?" he asked with a grin on his face. "Leave it to him to put Straight Hammer's chain-mail to the test on the first day."

"I think he'll be okay," said Nicolas, but he really had no idea. "Adelaide is taking care of him. Maybe his side's just bruised."

"I think you're right," said Ranulf. He handed Nicolas one of the thick bedrolls, then paused. "Can I tell you something?"

"Sure."

"I think I've seen that tinker before," Ranulf admitted.

"You have? Where?"

"Earlier this autumn." Ranulf tossed the other bedrolls to Nicolas, who held them by their leather cords. "About a year ago, my uncle started trading with a few 'Gammeldags,' gypsies. They usually live and travel in bands with large families, but these few had fallen out of favor with their kinfolk, and they traveled and worked alone. I had little to do with them. They were hard men, and they usually came at night. Once, when I asked what their business was at the blacksmith shop, my uncle cursed me and told me to keep my nose out of it if I knew what was good for me." Ranulf jerked a thumb toward the muddy roadway. "I can't be sure, but I think that tinker out there was one of those Gammeldags."

Nicolas thought about what Ranulf had told him. "It could be," he said. "I think Aldus was afraid someone might try to follow us or hurt us."

"Hurt *you*," Ranulf said with an arched eyebrow. "That dead tinker out there thought Benjamin or me was *you*."

Nicolas nodded grimly. "You're right," he said quietly. His heart was suddenly beating very fast. "I think he meant to hurt *me*." He glanced at Ranulf's hand. "Sorry about that. Are you okay?"

Ranulf laughed. "No worries, my friend. It's only a scratch. That thin knife would've made it a lot worse if he'd gotten his way. Thank the First Kingdom for Bardölf!"

"Yeah, who *is* he?" asked Nicolas, leaning back enough to peer around the corner at the huge bear-like man, who was still standing silently on the front porch.

"He's a Jamba keeper—a kind of shepherd for bears. They live with bears and train some of them. I've briefly met a few before, but I've been told they are wild men, who can break ordinary men in half and use their bones to pick their teeth." Ranulf smiled at the uneasy look on Nicolas' face. "Don't worry. This one seems okay. After all, he and his war hammer just saved us." Ranulf threw a blanket over the pony, hoisted the food sack over his shoulder, and took one of the bedrolls from Nicolas. "C'mon!" he said merrily. "Let's get a fire going and roast some potatoes with sausage and thyme. I bet the smell of that would wake up Benjamin even if he'd already gone to the endless heavens."

A JAMBA NAMED GRIEF

On that particular night, in the blackness of the Woodcutter's Forest, Nicolas came to a conclusion. It was one of those conclusions which seems absurdly small in the grand scheme of things, but which somehow stays with a person for the rest of his life.

At the moment he came to this conclusion, he and Ranulf were sitting near each other in two rather rickety old chairs. The boys were in their still-damp stockings with their feet propped on the stone hearth, and Nicolas could feel his toes just beginning to toast. Ranulf was happily smoking a short, clay pipe and doing his best to make decent smoke rings. Adelaide was sitting on one of the thick bearskin bedrolls with Benjamin's head in her lap. She was singing in a soft voice, a strange folksong about water sprites and green-eyed fairies who met on a beautiful spring day. On a loom made from a cherry blossom tree, they wove clouds of pink, purple, blue, and grey, and when all the clouds had been woven, a sudden spring rain began to fall; the fairies and water sprites then parted ways but promised to gather together each spring and weave new storms. With one hand, Adelaide was idly rubbing Cornelia's little goat-ears, and with the other, she was combing her fingers through Benjamin's messy hair. Both the little goat and the boy-thief were fighting to stay awake, and Nicolas watched as the goat and the boy took turns opening and closing their eyelids. Just as Ranulf had predicted, Benjamin, who now sported a small, egg-shaped knot on the back of his head thanks to cracking his head against a stone in the muddy roadway, had been roused awake with the smell of roasted potatoes being stewed in a broth of sausage, thyme, turnips, and brown salt. The young *Bendith Duw*—the newly practicing Healer—had put an exacting mix of herbs and chalky powder into the boy-thief's stew, greatly reducing his pain and bringing the color back to his cheeks. Bardölf the Jamba keeper—whom Adelaide had politely invited to join them inside the cottage, using a strange Outlands language she later told Nicolas was the "Old Tongue"—was sitting by the door in a third rickety chair, snoring and spluttering thunder-gusts, which sounded like three old, deaf men grumbling loudly over aching bones and cold, wet weather. The bear-like man, clad in leather-wrapped boots, an overly wide belt, and a bearskin cape—complete with the head of a bear resting on top of his head like some fearsome hood—had been equally polite, accepting Adelaide's proper invitation in the same strange language. He had barely fit through the cottage door, and Nicolas did his best not to laugh while the bear-like man huffed and puffed his way through the tight doorframe. When dinner was ready, Bardölf had slurped his soup loudly, hardly chewing either potato or sausage or turnip, and produced a woolly flagon of mead from inside his great cape, which he emptied in a series of noisy gulps. The mead spilled out of the corners of his mouth and trickled into the snarl of his beard. He polished off his dinner with two roaring burps, loud enough to make Adelaide wince, and then fell asleep almost instantly as he collapsed into the chair by the door. He said little and seemed worried about nothing.

The small room, glowing with firelight, smelled like sausage fat, mint tea, damp clothes, vanilla pipe tobacco, oiled bearskin, wet forest, and charred oak wood. And it was at this point, snug in an abandoned cottage in the blackness of the

Woodcutter's Forest, that Nicolas concluded this was the most pleasant moment in the world. He hooked his thumbs in the waist of his trousers, leaned back in his chair, wiggled his toes, and took in a deep breath.

He felt full, safe, and—once again—ready for adventure. Thoughts of the forest's dark trees, the Lonely Road's exhausting mud, and the sudden attack by crooked tinker had faded away in the warmth of the fire's homey cracks and pops. In fact, Nicolas felt more daring. He'd survived the strangeness, hardship, and danger of the past couple of days, and it left him feeling bolder and more sure of himself. He felt—happy.

"Adelaide," Nicolas said in a not-too-quiet whisper.

The young girl looked at him but kept singing.

"Are you okay with spending the night in here?" Nicolas' question was more the result of him having a sudden urge to talk than it was an attempt to make sure Adelaide approved of their lodging for the night. The fact that she had practically led the way into the cottage after Benjamin was hurt made the question feel like a safe bit of conversation.

Adelaide finished her folksong. The miniature goat and the boy-thief were both now soundly sleeping. "No," she said softly, shaking her head, "but he was hurt and needed to be warm, and I needed a place to mend him that wasn't soggy or dripping with cold rain." She glanced over at the substantial heap of bear fur and noise rumbling contentedly on the chair by the door. "I suppose if any Dyn Glas come looking to murder us, the Jamba keeper will put up a fight."

"*I'll* put up a fight," Ranulf quickly said with a stern look.

Adelaide smiled at him. "I know you will, Ranulf. I just meant that Bardölf might hit it with that hammer." She nodded her head slightly in the direction of Bardölf's stout war hammer, which was standing upended on its head next to the bulky man. The head of the war hammer was made of a thick stump of solid black iron. One end of the head was broad and slightly curved, meant for smashing and cracking and breaking, which it could do with enough force that its shock waves could carry through even the most hardened plate armour. It was this side of the hammer Bardölf had used to cave in the head of the misshapen tinker. Like dropping a stone on a hollow eggshell. On the opposite end of the hammer's head was a nasty-looking curved beak, with lengthwise grooves leading down to its sharp point. The beak could be used like a hook to drag a victim closer, or to pull a man's feet out from under him, or to punch through armour like an icepick punching through paper. The grooves helped the iron beak release more easily from whatever it stabbed through—and gave it a more sinister look. The shaft of the war hammer was about three feet long and made of a thick stock of hard ash wrapped in leather cords. Nicolas noticed the hammer's blunt end was dark and gummy-looking; with a hint of queasiness, he wondered if it was the tinker's blood and brains.

"You're right, Adelaide," Nicolas said, finally taking his eyes off the ruthless weapon, "I think we're safe with him sitting at the door." He looked at his friends. "Why do you think he helped us?"

Ranulf wiggled his sock toes and stared into the fire. "Jamba keepers are odd, and keep to their own ways and their own counsel. From time to time, one of his kind would come to the blacksmith shop for some work on a hammer or buckle. They would also ask for iron braces, which they fit their fingers through to make their fists like bricks of granite. I guess fighting wild bears and fenris wolves takes brutal force. Straight Hammer would speak to them in the Old Tongue, and he seemed to know each of them, or at least a great deal about them." Ranulf cocked his head as if trying to remember more. "He said he'd once owned two or three trained jamba-bears—which is not uncommon with giants—to carry heavy loads, and as pets. I'm not sure what happened to them." The older boy looked at Bardölf and quietly said, "The other blacksmiths would say Jamba keepers believe they come from the first man, who was called 'Jambavau.' He is said to have been born out of the earth with thick, black hair all over his body, and immense strength. Jambavau's first son was also hairy, and he had a snout with sharp teeth and claws for fingers. His name was 'Jambacai.' His children became a race of jamba-bears. Jambavau's second son had smooth skin, and a human-like face and fingers. His name was 'Jambabl,' and his children became the race of men." Ranulf shrugged, still staring at the huge, snoring man. "I think Jamba keepers are some kind of mix of bear and man, but I don't really know." He raised his eyebrows. "And I don't know why he helped us, but I'm glad he did."

"I'm glad he did, too," Nicolas agreed quietly.

"Me too," said Adelaide softly.

"Well," Ranulf said, taking a deep, fitful breath, "I'm as tired as a hedgehog trying to outrun its fleas." He yawned and stretched. "Dawn will be here before we know it. Best to get some rest while we can." Nicolas and Adelaide both nodded.

A few minutes later, they were rolled up inside their bear-skins, breathing peacefully, while the large log in the fire broke.

———◆———

Nicolas woke before anyone else.

A grey smudge of morning light was coming through the cottage's single window. The night's rain had stopped, but the cloud cover remained, although not as heavy or as dark as the day before. Nicolas kept his warm bearskin wrapped around his shoulders and poked at the fire, which had died during the night. Under the ash, he found a few hot embers peering out like gleaming eyes in an ashy fog.

Ranulf sat up, too. "Lemme fry a few slices of bread in the sausage grease," he said sleepily. "I saw a well outside last night. Why don't you go fill that kettle with some water for tea, and check the pony."

Nicolas nodded. He slowly rolled his head around, stretching his neck, and pushed his shoulders back. *Not too bad*, he thought to himself. *Not quite like my mattress at home, but not too bad.* He got up and laced up his boots, and with the black kettle tucked under one arm, did his best to sneak around the huge, bear-like man, whose snoring was now a much lower rumble. The air outside smelled fresh and thick, with the scent of pine and the deeper mustiness of oak and ash trees. The forest's litterfall of wet leaves, soaked twigs, and pine needles cushioned his footsteps as he stepped off the cottage's porch. The pack pony shouldn't have heard him approach, but it was already standing in its stall, snorting and twisting at its halter rope. It nervously stamped its hooves in the moldy hay and wood shavings. Nicolas stopped and looked intently inside the stall, wondering if some small animal had taken shelter in there during the night and was now worrying the pony. He didn't see anything, and he didn't hear anything other than the pony's own uneasy noises.

"Easy, boy," he said, letting the pony know he was there. "Easy now. What's all the fuss about?" he asked gently, hoping the sound of his voice would help calm the beast down. It didn't. And, out of the corner of Nicolas' eye, he discovered why.

An enormous, dirty brown mountain of matted fur rose up out of a thick hedge of Black Elderberry bushes and sat on its haunches. Its short snout and mammoth forepaws were smeared with blackberry juice, which looked disturbingly like a jellied sheen of dark blood. Its thick lips, pursed out like a set of nimble fingers, were busy plucking ripe berries and skillfully rolling them back into the bear's mouth. But for the lack of armour, Nicolas thought the gigantic bear from the gatekeep had followed them, and he froze in place, staring.

The bear, at first unconcerned, suddenly stopped its plucking and chewing. With sudden, brute force, it slammed one of its huge paws on the ground, laid its ears back, and let out a frighteningly loud *WHOOF!* which reminded Nicolas of the sound of a locomotive entering the train station at Penrith North Lakes station on Ullswater Road.

"Dat jamba is 'bout to add yer scraggy bones to its breakfast," said a low, thick voice behind Nicolas.

Nicolas could feel his heart pounding madly in his chest. He wanted to run. He wanted to melt into the leaves beneath his boots, but every part of him was frozen in place. He just stood there—unblinking—staring—and waiting for the gigantic locomotive of matted fur and teeth and claws to run him over.

As swiftly as Nicolas thought death would descend on him, a blur of fur and tangled beard rushed by him instead. "*Grief!*" boomed Bardölf. The Jamba keeper stood with his legs apart, but at a slight angle like a boxer. His great war hammer smashed into the ground so hard, Nicolas saw sticks and leaves bounce up, and he felt vibrations run through his legs. "*Grief! Stans venn!*" he roared at the bear. Like two woolly titans committed to battle, the jamba-bear and the Jamba keeper faced each other, each of them uttering a low guttural growl.

Then, with a sickening crash of broken branches and crushed litterfall, the two charged at each other.

Nicolas, sick with fear and expecting the inevitable slaughtering of long claws and teeth, squeezed his eyes shut and turned his head.

He heard the blow of the impact, then grunts and snorts and groans.

And laughter.

Nicolas eased his eyes open.

Bardölf—his great war hammer lying harmlessly in a mound of wet leaves—was rolling about with the massive bear, exchanging playful blows that would have left a normal man senseless. They were wrestling and clearly enjoying it. Even with Bardölf's own incredible size, he looked like a kid-bear next to the colossal bulk of the jamba-bear, but the massive man was surprisingly quick, compensating for the difference in their height and width. Within a short time, the poor hedgerow of Black Elderberry bushes was flattened by brawling hulks of fur, legs, paws, and hands.

Bardölf sat up gasping for air. "Whoa, ma friend! Whoa!" His beard was woefully entangled with broken twigs, shoots of berries, wet leaves, and tufts of moss. The gigantic jamba-bear sat back on its haunches, clicking its tongue, and grunted. It seemed to almost have a smile on its face and waved an enormous paw in the air. "Dat is one way to wake oop in da mornin'!" chuckled Bardölf. "Wid a jamba knockin' some air inta yer lungs."

Nicolas, having gone from certain death to a circus wrestling match, was almost at a loss for words. "It didn't kill you! It's your *friend?*" he asked in amazement.

"Dat 'e is," Bardölf said. "I asked 'im to join us, but I did no' expec' 'im so soon." He shook his hairy head violently. "Whew! I took a wallop to me ear an' I can hear de spirits singin'." The huge jamba-bear laid a paw atop Bardölf's head. "I'm not yer cub, ya lazy berry-eatin' bag o'-stinkin' fur," he said playfully, pushing aside the mammoth paw. He jerked his head toward Nicolas. "I neve' seen no man—mooch less a man-cub—stand

215

an' look at a jamba when da jamba is tellin' dat man to run."

Bardölf's compliment felt good, and Nicolas didn't want to admit he'd felt frozen in place. "I didn't know it was telling me to run. I wish I could have," he said sheepishly.

"But ya didn'. An' I t'ink dat earned Grief's respect. Dis is a rar t'ing fer a man. A mos' rar t'ing fer a boy," he said. The wild-looking man stared at him as if he knew something he wasn't saying. Nicolas began to feel uncomfortable.

"Its name is 'Grief'?" he said, hoping to change the subject.

"Aye. Grief is dis jamba's name. He's a chief among jambas, an' an ol' friend." As Bardölf spoke, the enormous jamba-bear yawned and gave a low grunt.

"May I touch him?" Nicolas asked before thinking.

"Ha!" laughed Bardölf. "Ye might if Grief lets ya. But don' be disappointed eff he doesn'. Jamba is shy o' men unless der eatin' dem fer brakefast." Bardölf gave Nicolas a wink and an excited grin of crooked teeth.

Nicolas took a hesitant step forward and looked up at the giant jamba-bear's face. Grief looked mildly interested in the boy, but didn't move. Nicolas took a few more steps, and still the jamba-bear's expression didn't change. Finally, standing next to Bardölf, Nicolas reached out a wobbly hand. He touched one of Grief's massive upturned paws. It was the size of a serving platter. The pads were black and wet with rainwater and blackberry juice, and they felt rough, like untreated leather. The claws were as long as steak knives, curved and yellowish with streaks of hazy brown and black. Nicolas looked up. The enormous jamba-bear was looking down at him curiously. The solid enormity of Grief's head reminded Nicolas of the cast-iron AGA stove his mum used in the Bennetts' kitchen. The jamba-bear's eyes looked kind and old.

"Hello, Grief," Nicolas heard himself say.

After a moment, the jamba-bear gave a small grunt.

"Well, well," Bardölf said admiringly. "Dis jamba seems ta lak ya."

———◆———

"I can't believe you just reached out and touched it."

Ranulf and Nicolas were now busy loading the pack pony. The bladesmith apprentice had run out onto the porch with his smith hammer in hand when he'd heard Bardölf yell out Grief's name. Like Nicolas, he'd felt frozen in place with fear when he saw the huge creature, but after the danger had passed, he'd watched as Nicolas had approached the gigantic creature.

"Yeah," Nicolas replied. "I don't know why I did it. For a second, I thought it was going to eat me."

"I'm glad it didn't," said Ranulf, smiling. "You'd just be a snack, and I'd rather that jamba not find out what a bladesmith apprentice tastes like."

"You boys are ridiculous." Adelaide was standing on the edge of the cottage porch with her hands on her hips. "*That* is a '*vennlig*' jamba. He's friendly. You can tell because he has a ring of white fur around his neck."

Ranulf laughed. "What do *you* know about jambas?"

Adelaide *hmphed* in exasperation. "I happen to know a *lot* about jambas. Or at least more than you do, Ranulf son of Renfry. A Jamba keeper stayed with my family for a month during the Long Winter six years ago. He used to tell us stories at night about *vennlig* jambas and *farlig* jambas, which are dangerous. He said the *vennlig* jambas have white rings of fur and *farlig* jambas don't. They're wild, and they'll eat cattle and sheep if they wander into the forest. But he said my father didn't have anything to worry about because we had two bear hounds—two *kombai*."

"I think *she's* a kombai," Ranulf whispered to Nicolas out of the side of his mouth. "Alright, alright" he said loudly with a grin. "You win, you win." He pulled the final strap in place and patted the pony's wooden cross-frame. "Go get our 'snatcher,' Miss Ashdown. We're ready to go."

A few minutes later, Nicolas had the pack pony in tow and was leading them back out to the Lonely Road. During the night, some wild animal must have taken the crooked tinker as food. His twisted body was gone, and only mud remained on the Lonely Road. Ranulf walked beside Nicolas, humming quietly to himself, as Adelaide followed behind the pony with Bardölf, whom she spoke with in the Old Tongue. Earlier, she'd told Nicolas and Ranulf that Bardölf said he and the *vennlig* jamba, Grief, would accompany them to the edge of the Wood-cutter's Forest and make sure they stayed safe until they reached the Hollow Fen. Bardölf had said he'd seen several *farlig* jamba in the forest the day before, as well as some other, darker crea-ture, but he wouldn't describe it to Adelaide or tell her what it was when she'd asked. Behind her trailed Benjamin, who was still quietly nursing his tender head, although he'd said he felt much better, especially after eating three thick slices of toast griddled in sausage grease and washing them down with two steaming mugs of honeyed tea. Cornelia trotted happily at the boy-thief's heels, not the least bit worried by the enormous jamba-bear which ambled along behind them in silence.

The clouds had thinned, and the morning sun kept at its work until it managed to burn through the sullen sky by mid-day. They ate a cold lunch in a sunny glade Grief led them to, which had several bushes loaded with thousands of bright red autumnberries. The enormous jamba-bear ate them by the gal-lon-full and sprawled on its back in the sun, as full and as sat-isfied as a nursed baby. The afternoon sky soon brought more clouds and the light patter of cool rain for about an hour. They hurried along as best they could, but the mud in the road was a slippery slurry of clay and dirt, and with each step, their boots slithered and glided about, making progress a chore. Only Cornelia seemed happy with the mucky mess. She pranced about, butting the boys in the legs, and bucking up little clods of muddy clay. Soon, everyone's legs began to ache from the slog through the mud, but after Adelaide gave them all a few Birch tree leaves to chew on, they felt better.

<hr />

"Dat is whar dis road ends," Bardölf said.

They had trudged to the top of a slight rise in the roadway, and about half a mile away, they could see the thickness of trees thin out. Beyond this lay a dull muddle of fog.

"Is that the Hollow Fen?" Nicolas asked.

"Aye. Dat is de 'ollow Fen."

They all stood there in silence. For the first time in a while, Nicolas shoved a hand in his pocket. His fingers bumped against the thimble and coins until he'd grasped the coppery leaf.

"I suppose you and Grief will stay in the forest," he said, half-hoping the Jamba keeper and the gigantic jamba-bear would choose to continue in their company.

"Aye. We will stay. Der is no' good ground in de 'ollow Fen. Jambas an' Jamba keepers sink lak fat toads on small lily pads." Bardölf smiled. "Mists an' bogs are fer little t'ings wid wings an' little feet."

"And snakes," Adelaide said with disgust.

"Aye, an' snakes too," he said.

"But we'll be fine on the path," said Ranulf, the tone of his voice carried a hint of doubt.

"I t'ink so," Bardölf said. "Bes' to stay on de path, an' keep dat pony on de short leash. Bogs are always 'ungry fer fat little ponies," he said with a chuckle.

Benjamin chimed in. "And I'm hungry for a fat little potato.

Will we have dinner soon?" He winced. "I think food will help my head feel better."

"Food will help your *belly* feel better, Benjamin Rush," Adelaide said. "And yes, we'll have dinner soon." She looked at Nicolas. "Right, Nicolas?"

"I think that's a good idea," he said, "but first, let's see if we can walk a bit further. Maybe we can make it to the Clokkemaker's home before night settles in."

Benjamin frowned and sighed, but bobbed his head in agreement.

"Nicolas is right," Ranulf said. "Let's see how far we can get before it gets too dark. I'd hate to spend a night on the open moors if we don't have to. Thank you, Bardölf," he said with a bow and a wave.

"Yes, thank you," echoed Nicolas and Benjamin.

Adelaide picked up Cornelia and turned to Bardölf. "*Holde deg trygg*, keep yourself safe," she said in a halting voice.

Bardölf smiled broadly. "Aye, little Healer." He leaned forward and laid one of his thick hands to the side of his mouth. "An' keep yer *Wren* safe too."

The young girl looked confused but nodded anyway.

<hr/>

Some way down the road, as the last trees gave way to the sphagnum moss and cotton grass of the vast moorlands, Nicolas looked back. He could still see the outline of the huge Jamba keeper standing next to the gigantic jamba-bear. He watched as Grief rose up on its hind legs, like an enormous oak tree pushing up from the earth. Distantly but clearly, Nicolas could hear it bellow a great *yawwwwp*! and sit back down on its haunches. He waved in return and turned back to the path ahead.

If he had kept looking—if he'd waited a moment and looked more closely at the grey smudge of the forest's tree line—Nicolas would have seen something else. He would have seen a darkness—a gloomy but distinct shadow—threading its way like a ghost out of the last stand of trees before disappearing quickly into the Hollow Fen's dusky mists.

But he did not.

CHAPTER 19

✝HE HOLLOW FEN

Light is a wonderful thing. It distinguishes night from day. It grows flowers and plants and trees. It reveals what is hidden. It brings things alive, and it gives hope. Light is safe.

But fog, fog does a funny thing to light.

Fog isn't as bold as dark thunderheads of a stormy sky. It isn't as impenetrably gloomy as a deep cave. It isn't as obscure as the floor of the ocean, and it isn't as thorough as nightfall. Fog isn't even as shadowy as a shadow.

Fog is dull. It is dreary. It is drab. It is somehow like turning on a light while the room remains doggedly dark—a false hope of being able to see when, in fact, almost everything is just beyond view. Everything is vanishing. Inside a fog's ghostlike paleness, light is broken. Inside a fog, light reveals very little. Light is an empty promise—one left unfulfilled.

In this way, fog also does a funny thing to Time.

There are hundreds of little things people see and hear and smell which tell them time is passing. The sound and sight of traffic may swell during the morning and late afternoon when people are traveling to and from work and school. Birds may coo and chirp more busily as they share gossip or conspire about plans for a new day. Dogs may bark as they shake off a night's sleep and warn their owners against the imminent attack of garbage trucks rumbling slowly down residential streets. Pedestrians may flood sidewalks and crosswalks, dodging past each other on their way to important meetings with important people about important events. Drivers may impatiently tap their feet on brake pedals,

222

wishing red lights wouldn't take so long and school bus stops weren't so numerous. Smells of coffee, baked goods, and diesel exhaust may fill the air while distinct whiffs of cologne and perfume hover over men and women like scented halos. Trains click and clack noisily away from their stations. Airplanes roar away from their runways. Ferries churn away from their docks, blowing brassy blasts from their loud horns.

But fog—the strange wraith of mist and chill and haze—distorts these things. The visible presence of school buses and garbage trucks and pedestrians disappear inside a fog. Birds and dogs and trains sound more muted, hushed, and far away. Freshly baked donuts and coffee and pretty perfumes do not percolate through a fog; they only exist in tight pockets of smell—here and then gone.

Fog does this. Fog distorts and deforms those little things people see and hear and smell which tell them time is passing.

And because the fogs of the Hollow Fen were full of broken light and distorted Time, it is where the Clokkemakers—the Wisps—the secretive Kohanim—had decided to live.

After a long time of silence, out of the blue, Nicolas suddenly told the others, "We're looking for a Clokkemaker."

He had a growing sense of being lost, and hoped conversation would help to drown it out. Other than Aldus' instruction to enter the Hollow Fen, Nicolas had no idea where or how to find the Wisp, Remiel.

They had been slowly making their way through the strange moorland for about half an hour, and the path was not very wide. It was like the Lonely Road, except it wasn't hedged in by thick groves of trees, only moss and heather and yellow-leafed crowberry plants. Nicolas, walking at the lead, had kept his head down, watching carefully for ruts made by occasional cartwheels and horse hooves, while little Cornelia, mud-spattered and increasingly tired, had decided to trudge along at his heels. Star-grass also grew on each side of the path in occasional clusters. Each flower had six yellow petals, like bright little footpath lights, which made finding the path a bit easier. Adelaide had already plucked several, telling the boys the cheery flowers would help them to stay well after they were steeped in a hot tea. Ranulf carefully and quietly led the pony, and Benjamin walked last in line, every once in a while touching his sore head tenderly.

"A Clokkemaker?" Benjamin asked with some reservation. He reached down and plucked a quick handful of purplish-black crowberries. "I thought," he said as he gulped them down, "that all Clokkemakers were evil ghosts which haunt empty castles and possess ravens. Maybe even little goats." He grinned at Adelaide, showing off his purple-stained tongue and teeth.

She stuck her tongue out and flashed him an annoyed look. "The fat lardyman I worked for said Wisps came in the night to steal flour and barley, but I never believed him," she said. "He was always trying to come up with excuses when customers accused him of cheating. I don't think he really knew what a Wisp is. Still, it makes me nervous to think we're trying to actually *find* one." The young Healer anxiously looked around. "Actually, this whole *place* makes me nervous. I wish there wasn't so much fog."

"I don't think they're *all* evil," Nicolas said, although he didn't sound certain. "However, I was told about one raven, the raven that followed Aldus into the room where we all slept; *that* one has a Wisp inside it, but I don't think a Wisp *'possessed'* it. Aldus said the raven was a special kind of raven that had 'room' for ghosts—and it just happened to give that room to a Wisp," Nicolas explained. "I don't think Wisps really 'possess' anything." He stopped for a moment and looked around. The fogbank they were in had thinned, but twilight was settling in quickly, and the day's light had become much weaker. "I don't think Aldus would have sent me—us—to find this Clokkemaker—this Wisp—if it was an evil one." Secretly though, Nicolas didn't know what to expect. He wanted to tell the others about his encounter with Remiel when he was with the tall man and the donkey in the forest, but he didn't want to scare them. Instead, he simply said, "Aldus thinks this Clokkemaker will help us."

While the other three spoke, Ranulf had been grunting and tugging at the pony's lead rope, trying to coax it or force it over a patch of soft earth. Aggravated with the stubborn pony, he took a break and said, "Straight Hammer actually liked Wisps, but I think that was unusual for a giant. I once heard Bragnof, a giant who owns one of the larger smithy shops in the Iron Quarter, tell Straight Hammer he'd rather eat hot coals and drink molten metal than have anything to do with a Wisp." With that, the older boy gave a firm jerk on the lead rope. "C'mon!" he said, urging the pack pony forward, but the pony wouldn't budge.

Suddenly, there was a soft sucking sound. And then another. And then another. It reminded Nicolas of how his father's wellies—his dark green rubber boots—sounded when he was walking across the sheep pasture next to the Bennetts' home after a good rain. Everyone stood still, listening, unsure of what was making the strange noise. It was coming from beneath their feet, and Nicolas, like Ranulf, Benjamin, and Adelaide, began to stare intently around them at the grey-green turf, but they didn't see anything peculiar, except a small swell of wavy hair grass gradually rising between Ranulf's boots. Abruptly, the swell of grass flattened out. Then, with the same soft sucking sound, it disappeared underground entirely, leaving a small hole.

Immediately, Adelaide shouted in a clear panic, "Don't move!" But even as she did so, Ranulf's right boot sank up to his knee beneath the surface of the pathway. Then his other boot vanished. And then, without making a sound, *he* vanished. Nicolas leapt toward the older boy, trying to catch a fistful of his weather-cloak. But he was too late.

Ranulf was gone.

"*Ranulf!*" screamed Nicolas, as he scrambled backward from the enlarging hole in the ground. But there was no reply. Only more of the soft sucking sound.

The pack pony, now free of any guiding hand on its lead rope, turned and bolted back in the direction of the Woodcutter's Forest, knocking Benjamin on his seat. Before anyone could do anything about it, the pony had disappeared into the mist with its load of kindling and bulging sacks clattering wildly against the wooden cross-frame.

"Benjamin! *Don't move!*" Adelaide was clutching Cornelia to her chest and tears were streaming down her face, but the insistence in her voice was firm and steady. The boy-thief slowly nodded and sat where he was, eyes as big as saucers, clearly terrified but ready, too.

Nicolas was shaking. "What just happened?" he asked, his chest heaving with deep breaths. "What just *happened*?!"

Adelaide sniffed and wiped her tears with the back of her hand. "We're in a featherbed bog," she said quietly, tensely.

"A *what*?"

"My uncle used to call it a featherbed bog," Adelaide explained, clearly frightened. She was still sniffing, but she'd kept control of her voice. "Some call it a blanket bog. There's wet hollows hidden beneath the surface. They can be treacherous to walk on, but sometimes there is something more—maybe..." Her voice trailed off, and she looked like she might be sick. Another tear fell down her face.

"Maybe *what*, Adelaide?!" Nicolas pressed. He was still in

shock over Ranulf's sudden disappearance. The little he knew of bogs and mires was what his father had once told him about the North York Moors National Park in Yorkshire. The Bennetts had been attending a Dark Skies Festival in Dalby, the Great Yorkshire Forest outside of Pickering, and his father had chatted on about the plants and animals and landscape of moors and bogs. But nothing his father had said included people disappearing into the earth. "Can we get Ranulf back?" he demanded impatiently. There was something in Adelaide's reaction which also frightened Nicolas. Something more than sinkhole bogs.

A fresh wave of tears rolled down Adelaide's cheeks. "I don't know," she cried helplessly. "I don't know." She sat there rocking her little goat back and forth and shaking her head.

"I'm going after him." Benjamin's quiet voice seemed small and faraway. Nicolas looked at the boy-thief, who was still sitting, trembling on the ground. His smallish face was as pale as the mist surrounding them, and his lips were quivering. "I'm small. I'll go in and get him," he said again, almost whispering.

Nicolas stared at him and suddenly heard a steady voice say, "Me, too." It was his own. It felt removed from the wild alarms crashing about in his mind.

Benjamin nodded and slowly turned himself around onto his hands and knees. His mouth was set in a grim line. Nicolas glanced at Adelaide. She was staring back at him, still shaking her head. Pretty locks of her hair bounced against her shoulders. "*Don't*," she pleaded quietly.

Nicolas tried to sound brave. Cool and calm. "Why not? It's just a bit of mud and muck, right?" The young girl just kept shaking her head, miserable.

And, like a nightmare that wouldn't go away, the soft sucking sound returned.

Situated along a short coastal stretch of southeastern England, in Devon County to the east of Cornwall, is the modest beachfront borough of Torbay. Torbay's quiet marine inlet is fringed by three seafaring towns: Torquay in the north, Paignton in the center, and Brixham in the south. Summer tourists on holiday there might visit a medieval abbey with gardens and a tearoom, Oddicombe Beach, the fortified manor house of Compton Castle, or the sixteenth century Berry Pomeroy Castle ruins. But this small area of England has another curiously unique distinction. It has been occupied by people ever since the Palaeolithic Era. Indeed, the oldest human bones in Europe were found lying in Kents Caverns in Torquay. But long, long before then—ages before prehistoric man gathered together to sharpen stones for tools, or to scavenge for wild animals, or to forage for plants—*worms*, giant worms over three feet in length, burrowed deep within the damp earth under the borough of Torbay. These prehistoric worms only came to the surface to drink—and to feed.

On a brisk, early spring morning a few years before, Nicolas' father, Peter Bennett, had been sitting quietly in his study when he suddenly waved his Sunday edition of the Cumberland and Westmorland Herald in the air, and loudly exclaimed, "They've found giant worms in England!" Nicolas, who was halfway through a second helping of grilled oat cakes, sausage, and fried eggs, dropped his fork and raced into his father's study, hoping to see graphic pictures of enormous, slimy creatures as if they had come alive right out of an old science fiction film. He was disappointed. There were no pictures, and Mr. Bennett merely stabbed an enthusiastic finger at a boring page of newsprint, which discussed a recent find of the worms' fossilized burrows.

"Just *imagine*," he'd told Nicolas excitedly, wriggling his fingers in front of him, "giant worms as tall as you are!" Nicolas had asked a few questions, still hoping for some kind of ghastly alien description, but after a few minutes, he lost interest and hurried back into the kitchen before his eggs turned cold.

Now, standing in the pale light of a cold fog along a narrow path somewhere within a perilous moor, Nicolas again thought of that long ago Sunday morning. He regretted not learning more about the prehistoric worms because out of the hole into which Ranulf had vanished a few seconds before was the bulging, swaying head of a gigantic bog worm. And out of the rubbery, wet flesh of the bog worm's mouth came the soft sucking sounds Nicolas had heard. They were the sucking sounds of a bog worm *feeding*.

Adelaide screamed and buried her face against Cornelia's little body. Benjamin, with his mouth hanging open in shock, back-pedaled as fast as he could on all fours. Nicolas, however, just stood there. A thick terror was beginning to paralyze his mind, and his thoughts were becoming stiff and dull. Yet a single thought remained stubbornly vivid and alive—the grisly knowledge that his friend had just been consumed by the repulsive mass of ribbed worm meat in front of him. His friend, Ranulf son of Renfry, had vanished inside that spongy, wet, sucking bog worm's mouth.

Nicolas' hand grasped for the small flat dagger hanging around his neck. He jerked it free from its leather cord, and without any plan or strategy, he shouted madly, "*We have to save him!*"

Nicolas, the boy who called himself a Wren, jumped at the hideous bog worm, slashing his small knife downward toward its squirming flesh.

And as he jumped, the grey daylight around him became

dark. It was as if someone had turned the lights off in a room, leaving it in the gloom of evening shadows.

And the air around Nicolas instantly chilled, biting into his skin the way the icy dampness of a hard frost had done on many dark winter mornings. The air also smelled—*familiar*—like almonds and burned earth. Something he'd smelled once before, in the woods with the tall man and Cherry Pit the donkey.

Meanwhile, the bog worm, which sensed Nicolas was close by, had swung its fleshy head toward him, hungrily searching. Its huge throat muscles and thousands of little tongues were sucking excitedly against rows and rows of knobby, bony teeth. But just as Nicolas sprang at the worm, he was thrown back violently and crashed to the ground with the wind knocked out of him. At first, Nicolas thought he'd been struck by the bog worm's writhing body, and the thought flashed through his mind that he was about to be pulled inside its mouth and eaten alive. There was a sound like the roar of an avalanche, and the massive bog worm began to violently twist and lurch upward, raising its fleshy body up. In Nicolas' dim mind, the worm looked like a snake about to strike.

But it didn't strike.

Instead, the bog worm gave a final furious spasm, and miraculously, as if the gloomy, icy air itself had seized hold of its squirming, bloated body, the gruesome worm ripped completely in half, hurling chunks of fatty tissue and bits of bony teeth out across the boggish moor.

And in the slippery, gooey mound of bog worm guts, Nicolas—on the edge of blacking out—saw a human hand.

So he grabbed it.

It was dark—past grimlock, the witching hour—when Nicolas next opened his eyes.

He was lying on the narrow pathway. Someone had thrown his bearskin blanket over him, and his first thought was that this was odd, since he remembered seeing the pack pony run away. Slowly, he sat up. Lying next to him, rolled inside another bearskin blanket, lay Ranulf. The older boy was breathing evenly, and he was sound asleep. He looked unharmed, although his skin looked very pale and his dark hair looked several shades lighter. A few yards further up the pathway, Nicolas could see the flickering flames of a small fire. Benjamin and Adelaide were sitting by the fire, and Adelaide was speaking in a low voice to someone else—a very little person, perhaps only half her size, who was kindly petting Cornelia. The little person looked quite old, and in fact, had a pointed and tidy little beard. It wore a fitted leather cap and was dressed in a boiler suit—a pair of earth-stained coveralls—with little round-toed boots on its feet. A few steps away from the fire, Nicolas could see the pack pony, munching contentedly on clumps of wavy hair grass. Next to the pony, but more difficult for Nicolas to clearly make out in the shadows, stood a very tall figure. It was dressed in a dark hooded robe and held a slender staff in its hand.

"*You're awake!*" Benjamin's voice sounded happy and good. It confirmed that Nicolas was alive and was not dreaming.

"Yes," Nicolas said weakly, his voice croaking like it might after a long night's sleep. He smiled. "Yes, I'm awake."

The smallish boy-thief hopped up and ran over to him, nearly knocking him over. "Thank the endless heavens!" he cried. "You dropped to the ground like a dead man right after you pulled Ranulf free, and we thought you both had died and had your souls collected by the tusk moon." Benjamin squeezed Nicolas' hand. "I'm so glad you're awake."

Nicolas shook his head, trying to remember what had happened. "Me too," he said. Nicolas looked around. "What happened? Where's the worm?"

"It was ripped in *half*," Benjamin said with a grimace. "And what was left of it slowly slid back into the hole." The boy-thief had a slightly sick look on his face. "We heard other sucking noises. I think another bog worm must've ate it."

Nicolas felt his heart thump hard in his chest. His foggy mind tried to make sense of what Benjamin has said. "It ripped in half? There are *other* bog worms?"

"Yeah," Benjamin said, as an answer to his second question more than Nicolas' first, "but not around here. Not any longer. Not after what happened," Benjamin said with smug satisfaction. He gave Nicolas a reassuring pat on his arm.

Nicolas wasn't sure exactly what had happened, but he suddenly felt tired again. He felt his mind slipping back to sleep, back to darkness. He let out a long sigh of relief. He glanced over at Ranulf. "Is he okay?" he asked weakly.

"I think so," Benjamin said. "Got all his fingers and toes, as they say. I tell you, Adelaide is great. She carefully cleaned him and gave him tea with some kind of potion mixed in it after the Clokkemaker revived him."

Nicolas struggled to pay attention. "A Clokkemaker?"

"Yeah," Benjamin said and pointed to the tall figure standing next to the pony. "The Clokkemaker. He says his name is Remiel."

CHAPTER 20

The Whisper of a Plan

The second time Nicolas opened his eyes, it was still dark, but he was no longer surprised to be wrapped in his bearskin bed roll. He realized he must have drifted back to sleep after talking with Benjamin. He'd felt tired, extremely tired, and the comfort of the nearby fire, the warmth of his bearskin, and the closeness of his friends lulled him back to rest. Nicolas heard the muted pad of footsteps on the mossy pathway, and he peered out of his snug cocoon to see what was going on.

The night air was taut and chilly, but it looked as if most of the fog, and even the clouds, had cleared off and the sky was brilliantly lit with thousands of star clusters. The small fire had gone out, and the bright starlight cast everything in pale shades of grey-white and bluish-black. He could see Benjamin holding the pack pony's lead rope, and that he was bent over with his hands resting against his knees, chatting with the same little fellow Nicolas remembered seeing the first time he awoke. He spotted Cornelia only because of her two stubby, round horns. She was a mere dark lump resting among the sacks and bundles on the pony's wooden cross-frame. Her young owner, Adelaide Ashdown, was standing near the tall, hooded figure, and appeared to be taking some kind of instruction, although Nicolas couldn't hear the tall figure's voice.

"You wouldn't happen to have a flask of water hidden in that bearskin, would you?"

Nicolas rolled on his side. Ranulf had just wakened, and he was smacking his dry lips together. "Of course, if it's a flask of mead, then I suppose that'll do, too," he joked. "I can't remember ever being this thirsty."

Nicolas grinned at him. "I'm glad to see you're awake, Ranulf—that you're alive. I haven't got any water or mead, but I'll go see what I can find." Ranulf nodded at him feebly and laid his head back down. Nicolas crawled out from his cozy shelter and stamped his feet. He was still fully dressed, except for his weather cloak, which he quickly threw over his shoulders, pulling it close around his neck and fastening its three short buckles. Nicolas rubbed his arms vigorously through his cloak and gave his face a few quick stretches. He shivered, but felt a little heat begin to circulate through his body.

He approached Adelaide and the tall, hooded figure. "Hello," he said. He still didn't hear the figure's voice, and he hoped he wasn't interrupting. "Ranulf's awake, and he's thirsty."

Adelaide smiled. She looked extraordinarily pretty in the starlight. "Wonderful," she replied. "I still have some tea I'm keeping warm in a flask underneath Cornelia." She flashed a smile. "That little goat is as warm as a brass bedwarmer." In less than a minute, she was kneeling next to Ranulf and helping him take a much-needed drink.

Nicolas, unsure of what to say to the tall, hooded figure, said "Hello" again and waited for a reply. Its face was in a deep shadow under its hood, and Nicolas couldn't even tell if it was looking at him. After several moments, the hood dropped forward as the tall figure dipped its head in greeting. They both stood there for several minutes in silence. Benjamin remained absorbed in his conversation with the little fellow, and from the little Nicolas heard, it sounded as if they were eagerly exchanging stories and advice about mushrooms—the best kind to eat, when to pick them, how to fry them, soak them in butter or oil, stuff them with bread crumbs and bacon, slice them into little sandwiches with a bit of cheese in the middle, and dry them out to make savory, smoky snacks. For a poor street scamp who scrapped out a harsh existence in the Dreggs, Nicolas was repeatedly impressed with Benjamin's knowledge about, and sheer dedication to, anything and everything that was edible.

"May I see the leaf."

Nicolas gave a slight jump. The tall figure's voice had been quiet and gentle, rolling out from within its hood almost as if it were an echo coming from a small, deep cave.

"Of course," Nicolas said respectfully. He reached in his pocket and touched the edge of the coppery leaf. It felt warm, and when he lifted it out, its shiny surface caught sparkles of stars like broken moonlight reflecting off of tiny ripples in a country pond. The tall, hooded figure bent over slightly, and Nicolas held out his palm, expecting the figure to take it from his hand. But he didn't. Instead, Nicolas felt the draft of a light wind as if the figure had blown on the leaf. Even in the muted colors of the starlight shadows, Nicolas watched as the surface of the coppery leaf seemed to stir with vivid pigments and dyes and shades of red.

"It's a terrible warning," the tall figure said.

Nicolas nodded. "Aldus Ward told me the same thing."

"But you—you, Nicolas, are an equally formidable answer." The tall figure's voice was still quiet and gentle, but Nicolas felt the air around him grow icy. It almost hurt his skin.

"I… I…" Nicolas couldn't think of what to say. He wanted to say, *yes I am. I'm a formidable, powerful deliverer.* But he didn't. He didn't say anything. The air around him went back to the late night's frosty chill.

The tall figure straightened up to his full height. He must've been seven feet tall. "You're a *Wren*," came the rolling echo from his dark hood, "and that's why you're the perfect answer. It won't see you until it's too late."

Adelaide took charge of their short journey to Remiel's home. The tall, hooded figure, which was Remiel himself, had told her to hurry them along. He had said they would make an easy target for spies now that most of the fog had cleared, but that his home was close by. They scattered the ashes from the small fire, buckled their weather cloaks, and struck out. Benjamin and the little fellow—an earth-gnome whom Benjamin said was called Agathon—led the pony and walked beside Nicolas. Adelaide led them, walking with Ranulf's arm over her shoulder for support.

Remiel stayed behind. They left him standing at the edge of the dark worm hole in the pathway, muttering something. Nicolas couldn't hear what he was saying, but his voice was unkind and sounded thick and crude. Remiel tapped the edge of the hole with his slender staff, and Nicolas caught the faint smell of Sulphur. And then, to Nicolas' surprise and slight horror, Remiel leapt into the hole and disappeared.

Dawn was just beginning to push a faint greyish-blue above the eastern horizon.

Half a mile away, the pathway climbed a gentle slope peppered with juniper, bog rosemary, and bunchberry plants growing beneath clumps of heather. It continued down the other side of the slope and off toward the south, but a hardly noticeable footpath forked to the west, and this is where Adelaide took them.

The blanket bog they had been crossing bordered a wet fen—a black marsh fed by hidden swells of ground water. The footpath took them along the fen's waterline, which was thick with a strange kind of carnivorous butterwort plant that fed on insects, small rodents, and skylark hatchlings. The air of the marsh smelled foul. It was saturated with the dense, fetid odor of rotting plants and pockets of methane.

After a short distance, they came to a small bridge which went across the brackish water and strange butterwort plants. They were already halfway across it before Nicolas realized the bridge was actually made of a compacted mass of heavy roots, even though he couldn't see any single plant or tree connected to the roots. It was as if the entangled roots had simply risen from the black water of their own will—or, perhaps, the will of something other than a tree.

Having crossed the bizarre bridge, they continued to a small grove of brown Celtic Maple trees and followed Adelaide under their branches. The trees actually formed a rough circle, or large hedge, about one hundred yards in diameter. In the center of the circle stood a large craggy stone, like a giant jagged tooth rising up out of the moss. A Merlin was perched atop the stone near a wicker nest, and it stared at them with its sharp falcon's eyes as they each came into view. The base of the stone appeared to be blackened by fire, and several smaller stones were spread around it, reminding Nicolas of seats in a classroom. Off to one side of the circle was a low-roofed house built from cut blocks of peat.

This was Remiel's home.

"C'mon," Adelaide said confidently. "He's invited us to put our things inside and to rest." She had small puffy bags under her eyes and a sleepy smile on her face. "So far, our journey's been as peaceful as a meadow."

Ranulf grinned weakly at her joke and staggered inside the peat house. Nicolas and Benjamin followed, while the earth-gnome offered to picket the pack pony near some sweet grass. The little fellow kindly asked Adelaide if he could play with Cornelia while they slept. He seemed to have a natural liking for the miniature goat, and she said yes, it would be quite alright. A small fire was already burning in the stone fire pit in the middle of the home's turf floor, and the four friends had each barely unrolled their bearskins around it before they were all fast asleep.

The morning's dawn was just beginning to pale into a dull-ish white as a fresh bank of fog settled calmly over Hollow Fen and the little peat home in the blackwater marsh.

Nicolas awoke to the high-pitched chirps of hundreds of Meadow Pipits settling into dozens of twiggy nests among the thick branches of the Celtic Maples. He was the first one to wake up, and he vaguely wondered what time it was. The light outside looked a little less bright than when he'd fallen asleep, and he realized the shadows outside were pointing in the op-posite direction from when they had arrived. It was fallow, the last light of day. He and the others had slept for the entire day. Stretching, Nicolas got up and went to stand in the doorway of the little house. The inside of the little peat home was warm but a bit smoky, and he wanted a breath of fresh air. The weak-ness of the night before was gone. He felt much better.

The Merlin was gone hunting for field mice and lizards, but Remiel was sitting on one of the smooth stones facing the tall, craggy rock. A small fire of dried peat burned at its base, throwing long shadows up its rough face. Because of his height, Remiel's knees were bent quite far up, and his slender staff rest-ed against one of his shoulders. He had his head down, and it looked to Nicolas as if he was drawing something on the ground with his finger. The finger was long, oddly long, and did not appear to have the usual bulges caused by knuckles. Remiel's deep hood was lying against his back, and Nicolas—among very few living humans—found himself taking a rare, long look at a real Kohanim, a Wisp, a Clokkemaker.

The Wisp's ears were curiously large and swept backwards into a point, causing Nicolas to think of two small wings. His head was entirely smooth and bald. He didn't even have eyebrows. His skin looked translucent, and from a distance, it made his head look like it was made of bone-white marble. He had a curved, hawkish nose and a pronounced but tapered chin. His lips were thin, almost non-existent. The Wisp's eyes were almond-shaped, slightly slanted toward his nose, and like his ears, they too were large.

"Come sit," said the Wisp.

Remiel had not looked up, but Nicolas knew he'd been caught staring. He crossed the short distance quickly, and carefully took a seat on the stone the furthest away from the Wisp. Remiel's lean lips lifted in a smile, but he still did not look up. "Closer, Nicolas. What needs to be said should be said so only these stones can hear." Nicolas nodded and moved closer, and Remiel rubbed out whatever he'd been tracing in the dampness of the spongy moss. They sat silently together for several minutes.

"Why did you go into the hole?" Nicolas finally asked. His curiosity had gotten the better of him and part of him was amazed Remiel was still alive.

"It is best to meet evil where it lives," the Wisp said. "Bog worms are remnants of an ancient wickedness—a gluttonous ruin. They are mindless creatures, driven by very primal hungers, and they can be difficult to find. My brethren have rooted out most of them, but some of them, especially the older ones, remain. This one, however, troubled me. It was a young worm and had not yet fully formed. After it was dead, a larger, more mature worm ate it before I could examine the body for eggs. We have not seen new worms in a long age."

Nicolas couldn't imagine what it must be like, dropping beneath the earth into terrifying darkness, looking for such monstrous, horrific things. He had to ask. "Were you afraid?"

The Wisp looked at him. "No," he said. A soft hiss flew out of his mouth's thin slit. The marble white of his face transformed to leaden grey. The air became icy, the peat fire diminished, and the Meadow Pipits suddenly fell silent. "To the worm, *I* am death," he whispered. Remiel's eyes were as black and as glossy as the crow's had been, and to Nicolas' surprise, the Wisp's teeth, barely visible in his dark mouth, were pointed and sharp.

As quickly as it had come, the moment passed. A small flame jumped back up, and the birds went back to their evening chatter. Remiel's face returned to a smooth, translucent color, and he bent over and again began tracing something in the moss with his long, wand-like finger. "Let us speak of a different worm, Nicolas," he said gently.

Nicolas shifted on his hard seat. "Do you mean the Shadow Thief?" he asked.

"Yes."

"Aldus Ward told me it was buried somewhere by a Wisp, um, by a Kohanim," Nicolas said trying to sound polite, "but he thinks it might have freed itself somehow."

Remiel gave a slight nod. "The Laird of the First Gate is correct. The Shadow Thief was buried—it was bound by a curse scroll."

"What's a curse scroll?" Nicolas asked.

"A curse scroll is a simple but powerful thing. It contains the name of its victim, and the name of the place where its victim is bound to remain. Once, a long, long time ago, they were used to imprison treasonous giants, but after the Great War of Giants, Wisps, and Men, few of them remained."

Nicolas instantly thought of Straight Hammer. He wondered what a treasonous giant was like and decided it mustn't be very pleasant. "If a curse scroll was used to bury the Shadow Thief, how could the dragon become free again?" he asked.

Remiel's face darkened. "The scroll was eaten," he said somberly.

"It was *eaten?*" Nicolas asked quietly.

The Wisp nodded. "Yes. If a curse scroll is found, it can be consumed by someone other than the victim, and if this happens, then that person commands the scroll's prisoner." Remiel lifted his head and stared into the last bit of light hanging in the western sky. The fog had thinned, and Nicolas could see the first few stars scattered in the east above the high branches of the Celtic Maples. "*Someone*—someone sinister, someone I cannot yet see—found the Shadow Thief's curse scroll and ate it. The dragon has been set free."

The last of the sunlight died in the western sky and everything felt a bit colder.

Nicolas, motivated by what he'd already been told, but uneasy about what it might mean, asked, "What should I do? Is there something *I* should do?"

The Wisp's face held a faint smile. He did not answer Nicolas directly. Instead, he looked up into the new night sky and quietly said, "The Kohanim come from the formless, endless heavens. Our beginning is unchronicled—unknown in man's Time or by the Rule of Relic. We have simply *been*, even before the sun smiled for the first time in the eastern sky. Our rightful place has always been in the background, behind those things which have unfolded among men, their histories, and their kingdoms. Our rightful place is to be silent, to be watchful, to help safeguard the age of man and mortal creatures, realms and nations, and the living earth. All of these things are born, they live, they die, and more are born. But not the Kohanim. We are not of these things."

He bent over and once again began tracing something in the dark dampness of the moss. "Yet I and some of my brethren have been elected to sometimes interfere, to sometimes walk in the sun and the moon's light, and to help guide and protect the ways and lives of those who live by man's Time. We can also cease to be seen—you would call this 'death'—but we then become 'uninterrupted,' once again part of the endless heavens. In the Great War, long ago, many of my brethren followed this path and returned to our true home. But there were also some who fell into disgrace and are forever lost in darkness and shadows. Only I and a few others now remain." Remiel stopped what he was doing and looked at Nicolas. The firelight made his smooth skin appear waxen, almost as if it absorbed some of the pale flame. "I would spare you the danger you now face, Nicolas. I would spare you this if I could. The Shadow Thief is exceedingly sly and crafty, and this dragon looks to destroy whatever lies between it and its ceaseless hunger. For twelve years, it has been imprisoned in the earth, unable to feed or kill, but now it is loose, and it stands like a fenris wolf over the cradle of a newborn. Few have been lived who could stop its madness or its need to eat, to consume iron, and to bring ruin."

"Can't you kill it?" asked Nicolas. He anxiously pulled his weather cloak tightly around his shoulders, feeling very much alone. "What can *I* possibly do?"

Remiel looked compassionately at the boy. "The Shadow Thief and I come from the same beginning," he explained, "and neither I nor my brethren have been given the power to send it back, back to the endless heavens. But *you* can," said the Wisp. "You are young. You are young like your grandfather was once young, and like he once was, it is your youth, with the confidence and hope undamaged by man's Time, which are your best weapons. These, Nicolas, are far greater than those weapons which are forged in steel or wielded by great men of war."

Remiel suddenly stood up. He took his staff in hand and raised his long arms above his head, lifting his pallid face up to the clear night sky now bejeweled with the light of infinite stars. In the same strange, faraway voice Nicolas had heard the night before, Remiel said, "For the Shadow Thief, for *Árnyék Tolvaj*, the dragon whose fire is so hot it even burns away shadows, its cunning and its triumphs have nurtured its pride. This has ripened into vain arrogance—a blind belief in its own immortality. Because of this, it will not be able to see—it will not *accept*—that you and your young companions bring an end to its death-dealing. That *you*, a Wren springing out from the cover of eagle's wings, will be its Dragon Nightfall."

The ancient Wisp looked down at Nicolas. The boy could see flames from the gentle peat fire reflecting in the black pools of Remiel's eyes. His pointed teeth glistened inside the thin, dark line of his mouth. The Clokkemaker hissed, "*Come now. I have a plan.*"

CHAPTER 21

Stones

W hat were you talking about?" Adelaide asked. She was sitting quietly between Ranulf and Benjamin, and looked up when Nicolas came back inside the earthy home.

The bladesmith apprentice was asleep, but even in the dim light from the firepit, Nicolas could see the older boy was looking much better. Benjamin was barely awake. His eyes were sleepy, and he kept slowly blinking, trying to stay awake. After Adelaide had awoken, she'd fretted over the two boys like a mother hen. She'd clucked about the tender bump on Benjamin's head and the bruise on his side. She'd cooed about how weak Ranulf felt and the need for him to stay still. She'd worried over a simple soup of carrot and onions with mutton broth, and clacked at both boys until they'd eaten and drunk all they could. She'd fussed with the coals in the firepit, keeping the little home warm and cozy, and she nagged at both boys until they agreed to try to go back to sleep and get some more rest. Nicolas was amazed at how resourceful, thoughtful, and brave Adelaide was. He felt lucky to have met her.

"Where did you learn to do all this?" he asked, avoiding her question. He didn't think any of the girls he knew could have done half the things he'd already seen her do—kick a fat lardyman, willingly march down mud-filled forest roads, speak to Jamba keepers, or bravely lead the way through a dangerous moor at night.

"All of what?" she replied, pulling the bearskin up around Ranulf's neck and trying to smooth out Benjamin's unmanageable hair. She pointed to a low bench close to the firepit. "There's a mug with some broth in it. I hope you like carrots and onions."

"I do," Nicolas answered. He picked up the mug and took a tentative sip. It was warm and tasted mildly sweet. "I dunno," he said, returning to her last question. "Everything, I guess. You just seem like you know how to do a lot of stuff."

Adelaide shrugged her shoulders. "I guess I've had to learn a lot," she said vaguely.

"What's a 'Healer' anyway?" he asked, remembering what she'd told Aldus before they had left the gatekeep.

She quietly cleared her throat. "A Healer is a woman who has become a *Bendith Duw*—I think it's supposed to mean 'a blessing' in the common tongue. I've heard there are a few wandering Healers, who are said to have magical powers, but I've never met one. Usually, each village has its own Healer. My village's Healer was named Brita. She was old and wrinkly, and smelled like candle wax and honey. A Healer is supposed to take care of people when they're sick, she helps with childbirth, she's wise, and she brings sorrow baskets when someone dies."

"What're 'sorrow baskets'?"

"They're small wicker baskets, brightly painted, and usually filled with white lilies and purple chrysanthemums, or lilac snapdragons. When someone dies, the Healer comes to the door of the family's home, carrying a sorrow basket in her arms. She sings a short song, and gives the flower blossoms to each person in the home. In return, they open their hand, letting their sadness fall into the sorrow basket, then the Healer takes it away."

"What does the song say?" Nicolas asked.

Adelaide looked slightly uncomfortable but in a shy way. Her pretty cheeks were rosy, and she brushed back a strand of hair which had come loose from the long braid she wore. "I've never sang it for anyone," she said.

"But do you know it?"

"Yes."

Nicolas smiled. "May I hear it?"

"I don't know if it should be sung in a home if someone hasn't died." Her soft eyes had a slight look of worry.

"It's just a song, right?" Nicolas asked.

"I suppose so," she quietly agreed. "Okay, but I can't sing it here. It must always be sung at the door." She got up, tugged her thin white smock smooth, and went to the little home's simple door. Adelaide turned and cupped her hands gracefully together. The rising moon cast a pale light through her threadbare garment and made her skin shine like fresh cream. Nicolas thought she looked like a ghostly angel.

In a delicate but clear voice, the young Healer mournfully sang a lament Nicolas would never forget.

You were dreamed
Before you were born,
You were loved
Before you were named,
And the light that you are,
Will ne'er be far
When you sleep in the home of the angyles.

You have lived
The life that is yours,
You have said
The words you have made,
And the soul that you are,
Will ne'er be far
When you sleep in the home of the angyles.

We will meet
Before the Great Storm,
We will sing
Before that last day,
And the star that you are
Will ne'er be far
When we wake in the home of the angyles.
May we wake in the home of the angyles.

As she finished, the cold night closed in behind her, and Adelaide stepped back inside. The peat fire was smoky, making the little home dim and shadowy. Neither of them said anything after that, and it wasn't long before they were all fast asleep.

The next morning dawned very cold but clear.

Nicolas had already been awake for at least an hour, huddled in his bearskin blanket, staring absently out of the little peat home's doorway. He had not slept well.

The echo of Adelaide's mournful voice the night before had followed him to bed, then pursued him in his dreams where he'd again had a nightmare of an awful, eerie cavern. The immense and evil creature was inside it, but this time, Nicolas dreamed the creature's chains of bronze and steel had fallen away. It scratched its long curved claws against the great door with the large square of iron, and breathed fire under its threshold. *We are the dead,* a multitude of sorrowful voices said. Nicolas saw a waiflike Healer standing outside the great door, although he did not recognize who it was. Her voice was pure and flawless, and her breath seemed like snow falling against the creature's dreadful, hot breath. *We will meet before the Great Storm*, she sang.

And Nicolas awoke.

247

During the night, a thick fog had blanketed the small hollow where Remiel's peat home stood. It had left a heavy, cold dew on the moss.

"'Tis the wedding veil of Seren Drist," Ranulf said softly. He had awoken on his own and sat up quietly by Nicolas. There was a weak smile on his face. The guts of the bog worm had bleached his skin and hair snow white, and the paleness made him look sickly, even though all the sleep had done him well. His bright eyes told Nicolas he was doing better.

"What do you mean?" asked Nicolas.

Ranulf cleared his throat. "I was still young when my mother told me the story, but I think about it every time I see dew on the ground. She told it much better than I can, but let me see what I can do," he offered. "When the world was still new, Seren Drist, an immortal princess of the endless heavens, fell in love with Seren Marw, a mortal who was a mighty hunter. It was said Seren Marw killed great horned and clawed beasts and made them into constellations for Seren Drist to wear as jewelry when she sat in the court of the heavens. As a wedding gift to his betrothed, Seren Marw decided to slay the fierce Blood Boar—a nasty and brutal creature which lived deep within the earth. When the Blood Boar became angry, it would gore and slash the heart of Telluric Grand so violently that fountains of glowing rock would spout from mountaintops and the ground would tremble and break apart." Ranulf coughed lightly and cleared his throat. "Wearing the skin of another dead boar as a disguise, Seren Marw entered a deep cave and stalked the Blood Boar in the darkness of the heart of Telluric Grand. Soon, the mighty hunter came upon the Blood Boar's lair, and without hesitation, he thrust his war spear into the creature's side. Fatally wounded, the Blood Boar rose up, squealing and screeching, and began crashing its massive tusks into the walls of its lair, trying to kill Seren Marw. But the mighty hunter escaped injury, and the Blood Boar fell dead. In triumph, Seren Marw tied a rope to the beast's leg and dragged it out of the earth. But Seren Drist had seen jets of glowing rock spewing from the mountaintops when the Blood Boar was in its death throes. When she saw a boar come out of the earth, she was afraid the Blood Boar had killed her husband-to-be. She did not know it was Seren Marw in disguise. In anger and grief, she threw a great rock of star-iron at him and killed him." After Ranulf said this, he became silent, seeming to have lost himself in his own thoughts.

Nicolas waited for several moments and asked, "Then what happened?"

"Sorry," Ranulf said. His eyes looked sad. "I was thinking about my mother," he said quietly. Clearing his throat again, he said, "When Seren Drist realized what she'd done—that she'd killed her true love, her betrothed—she lifted him up and took his body to the endless heavens. She gave him a place of privilege, and he became the moon. This is why, when the moon is shaped like a boar's tusk, it is called a 'Tusk' moon. It is said to gather on its tusk the souls of all those who have died to take them to their place in the endless heavens. The fog is said to be Seren Drist's veil, and when the stars chase the moon across the sky, the veil falls from her head and lays like dew on the earth, soaked with her tears." Ranulf became quiet.

"That's beautiful," Nicolas said softly, not quite sure if he meant to say that about the story or about the chilly autumn morning coming to life outside the little peat home. The dew drops were like tiny glistening diamonds scattered over the sphagnum moss and dark pink and purple clusters of bell heather. There was a slight breeze, and the air blew through the open door in cold puffs. "I wish he hadn't died," he said reflectively.

Ranulf gave another weak smile. "If he hadn't, we wouldn't have the moon, and who would catch each of us to take us to our place in the endless heavens? Sometimes death is the greater part of our lives, I think," he said.

Nicolas nodded. "I guess you're right." He liked the story Ranulf had told much better than what he'd learned in school about what causes the morning dew.

By mid-morning, their things were packed, and Nicolas was leading them back over the bridge of thick roots.

The pack pony's wooden cross-frame was again piled with various rolls and bags, along with a new sack of oats gifted by Agathon the kindly earth-gnome. The little fellow had graciously taken care of the pony and Cornelia, and both animals seemed happy and content. The small goat's coat was even shiny, and she seemed torn between following Adelaide and staying with the little fellow who'd so considerately befriended her. As Nicolas led them out through the hedge of Celtic Maples, they each turned and waved at Agathon. He sat on one of the low stones, smoking a short clay pipe and swinging his short legs back and forth. The Merlin had returned to his roost atop the craggy rock, but they had not seen Remiel. Before they left, Nicolas told them Remiel had said where to go next and what must be done.

"We're supposed to find the Moss People," Nicolas had said. "I think I've met one of them before. His name was Baatunde."

"Do they live in the ground like earth-gnomes?" Benjamin asked.

"No, they live in cottages in the trees, I think, and their real name is the 'Caledonii.' I'm not sure why they're called Moss People, and Remiel didn't tell me, but they live in a stretch of woods near an outcrop of rock called the Timekeeper's Finger," Nicolas explained. "Remiel said I needed to speak with one of them. He said he would have something I need." Nicolas took a deep breath and softly added, "I'm supposed to find the Shadow Thief." For some reason, it was unexpectedly difficult to say what came next. "I'm—I'm supposed to *kill* him."

Adelaide gasped and covered her mouth. Ranulf clenched his jaw, causing his pale cheeks to turn even paler. Benjamin, the smallest of them all, laughed and grimly joked, "Well, *that* makes the bump on my head seem like small potatoes." He then looked at the young girl and at the bladesmith apprentice, his eyes asking them an unspoken question. Adelaide and Ranulf looked back at him and each gave a barely noticeable nod. The boy-thief turned to Nicolas. "We're still with you, Master Bennett," he said firmly.

"Thank you," was all Nicolas could think of to say. He felt an awkward knot in his throat, and he didn't feel like explaining anything else. "Let's get on with it, then."

Their way out of the Hollow Fen was, thankfully, less eventful than their journey in had been.

By mid-morning, the sun had begrudgingly settled behind a rising line of thunderstorms in the far east. Flashes of lightening looked like faraway fireflies, and the distant sound of thunder was so faint, it was more like a far-off drum than a nearby crash of cymbals. A frigid wind blew through the Fen, which shooed away the fog and left the cotton grass waving wildly at their feet. The path they were on was winding, but it did not have any turnings, and it did not meet with any other paths. Other than a few Red Grouse and Lapwings, with their shiny green feathers on top, large black and white wings, and wispy green crests on top of their heads, Nicolas and the others did not see any animals. The far-off storm seemed to quiet the Hollow Fen, and they hurried along, stopping only once for a quick bite of salted pork, flat biscuits, honey, and hot tea with cinnamon.

While Benjamin walked with Adelaide behind the pack pony, Ranulf stayed at the front by Nicolas' side. Nicolas could hear that Ranulf's breathing was more labored than usual, but the older boy did not complain and always tried to smile when anything was said. Nicolas was afraid Ranulf had caught some kind of sickness from having been swallowed by the bog worm, but he did not want to bring it up. He noticed a leather bag hanging from Ranulf's belt, which seemed a bit heavy and constantly banged against the older boy's hip.

"Why don't you let me carry that?" Nicolas suggested. "I can sling it over my shoulder in a snap. That way, it won't bang against your leg so much."

Ranulf glanced down at the bag, and after a few seconds, said, "Sure. I guess so."

They paused for a moment, while Ranulf unbuckled the bag's strap and handed it to Nicolas, who looped it through a strip of leather and slung it over his shoulder. As they began walking again, the leather bag bounced against Nicolas' back. "What's in there?" he asked. "Feels like a bunch of rocks."

Ranulf smiled sheepishly. "It is," he said. "I know it sounds mad, but I've always loved rocks, and I've collected a few. For as long as I can remember, I've liked rocks. They can be plain and simple, or they can have glittering crystals, or they can be smooth as black glass." Ranulf smiled even more broadly. "When I was very young, before my parents died, I would run around our farm looking for rocks and driving my parents mad." He laughed. "One of the best memories I have of my mum is because of rocks. I remember her planting some potato tubers and onions in a small garden near the house one spring, and I noticed a few loose rocks in the dark soil. It was a dark patch of earth which had always grown big vegetables, and my dad used to say it'd been blessed by the earth-gnomes.

It was easy to dig in, and so I started digging, looking for more rocks, and I found several. They were different sizes and different colors, like cream, blue or grey, and green-brown, and they all had amazing little holes in them. The holes were very tiny, as small as a bed-bug, but in my little mind, I thought they were the kind of holes earth-gnomes lived in. I was so excited, I ran into our home shouting about how I found rocks with earth-gnomes in them." Ranulf laughed and coughed until tears welled up in his eyes. "The look on my mum's face was sheer horror," he said, still laughing. "I must've looked like a little earth-gnome myself, having crawled straight out of the wet ground. I was covered in dark, wet dirt from head to toe and hollerin' like a mad goblin, while hugging an armful of strange-looking rocks." Ranulf's laughter made Nicolas laugh. It was good to hear the older boy sound happy and healthier. "My mum grabbed her broom an' started swingin' it wildly at me, yelling and shouting for my dad to come help her cause '*a cracked gnome is invading our home!*'" Ranulf laughed so hard at the memory, he stopped and bent over, wiping the tears out of his eyes. Finally, he caught his breath, and let out a loud "*whooo!*" The pack pony bumped them from behind with its velvety nose, and the two boys started walking again.

"What happened after that?" Nicolas asked with a snicker.

"Well, my dad whupped me pretty good for scaring the snowflakes outta my mum. But," Ranulf said triumphantly, "he let me keep most of the rocks." He pointed at the bag over Nicolas' shoulder. "You know, giants like stones, too. They play a game with them. Maybe working with Straight Hammer made my interest in them seem to make sense." He shrugged. "I managed to hang onto a few of them through the years, and I've picked up a few others along the way. I don't really know why I like rocks. Maybe because they come in all different shapes and colors and sizes, and maybe because they're strong and come from the earth. Or, maybe because they make me smile," he said wistfully, and Nicolas could tell he missed his parents.

"Were they pumice stones?" Nicolas asked, thinking about what kind of rocks have small holes in them.

"What're pumice stones?" Ranulf looked confused, and Nicolas realized that might not be what they're called on Telluric Grand.

"Oh, well, they're—they're rocks that come from volcanoes," he tried to explain.

Ranulf looked even more confused. "What're volcanoes?"

"Nevermind," Nicolas said. He looked at Ranulf. "Thanks for telling me about your mum. That's a great story."

Ranulf smiled and nodded. He wiped a last tear out of his eye. "Yeah, I miss her," he said quietly. "She was a great woman."

The sun never appeared again that day. By fallow-time, the storms to the east had subsided, leaving behind bulging, bruised clouds, heavy with unfallen rain.

They had all chewed on some more Birch tree leaves, but their legs had grown tired, and even the pack pony seemed to be plodding on a little bit more slowly. Their route had taken them northward, and as Nicolas and Ranulf came to the top of a low rise, they could see a thick, dark line stretching across the northern horizon.

Ranulf squinted in the dull light. "What's that?"

"It's the Black Forest, I think," said Nicolas quietly.

Benjamin came up beside the two boys. "What're you looking at?" he asked.

Nicolas pointed.

Benjamin also squinted. "What is it?"

"The Black Forest," said Ranulf.

"Is that where we're going?"

"Yes," said Nicolas quietly. Remiel had told him the path they were on would take them out of the Hollow Fen and into the heart of the Black Forest, and just beyond that, to the rocky outcrop of the Timekeeper's Finger. Now, as Nicolas stared at the grim charcoal line of ancient oak trees, he suddenly didn't want to leave the Hollow Fen. As wild as it had been, with its dense fogs and treacherous bogs, the open country of the Fen had begun to feel familiar.

"Is anyone hungry?" he asked, hoping they'd all vote to stay put for the evening. Perhaps the forest could wait until the next day.

"I could eat," piped up Benjamin.

"You can *always* eat," said Adelaide. She'd finished putting Cornelia on top of the pack pony and had joined them.

"That's true," said Benjamin, lifting his eyebrows as if he were really thinking about it. "I can always eat."

Adelaide rolled her eyes. "Well I don't think we should make camp in the open," she said, decidedly. "If it rains, I think we'd be better off if we were out of the Hollow Fen."

Ranulf pointed north. "Nicolas says we're headed there, to the Black Forest." Adelaide looked where he was pointing. "Have you ever heard anything about the Black Forest, Adelaide?"

Adelaide gave a shrug and shook her head. "Not really. I remember my dad telling us it was a very old forest and a forest with dark magic, but when we asked him for a story, he wouldn't say much, but he did say the Moss People live there."

"That's what Nicolas says," said Ranulf. He coughed but squared up his shoulders. "I think I agree with Adelaide. I think we should try to make it under the cover of those trees before the light is gone. The Fen makes me uncomfortable—or at least the thought of bog worms makes me uncomfortable—and the

Black Forest doesn't sound too bad or Adelaide would've heard something about it." He tried to look encouraging. "It can't be more than a mile."

Nicolas screwed up his face, but nodded in agreement. "Okay," he said. "Let's go."

"*Awwww!*" said Benjamin. "My stomach thought we were staying *here*."

"Your stomach does *all* your thinking for you, Benjamin Rush," Adelaide said, trying to sound exasperated. "Let's get going if we're going to make it before it gets too dark."

"No, it doesn't," Benjamin muttered back sullenly. "It just does *most* of my thinking."

Without much else to say, the four tired friends, their pack pony, and Cornelia, who was already sound asleep among their rolls and bags of luggage, trudged northward, and before long, they disappeared into the distant grim grey line.

CHAPTER 22

A WASHER WOMAN

The Black Forest is not as dense or as thick as the Woodcutter's Forest, but it has rightly earned its name.

Enormous black oak trees—ancient and undisturbed—have grown together in great groves, stretching out branches and leaves as thick as thatch on a cottage rooftop. The forest's leafy canopies are of different heights, creating great cathedral naves with the lattice-work of thick boughs and tree limbs. There are occasional small meadowed spaces which briefly open the canopies to the sky, like murder holes in the ceilings of castle gates. They are strewn with coarse, woody debris, and filled with long grass as tall as a man's waist. In other places, there are copses of dead trees which haven't yet fallen. These are "standing snags," and their giant upright carcasses—charred by lightning-fire and greyed by countless winter frosts—look like silent congregations of old, broken, and silvered men. And in other places still, there are tree-falls of wrecked timber—mostly hollowed by decay, wet-rot, and wood worms—causing pits and mounds where displaced root masses have left perilous depressions in the loamy earth. These decaying trees give off the scent of soggy wood, and are slowly consumed by the creeping green moss which carpets the entire forest floor.

Roe and red deer bucks rut competitively with the clack and rattle of sparring antlers, while solitary elk and small herds of antelope move like brown ghosts through the gloomy trees. Spotted owls, small woodlarks, brown long-eared bats—hanging like thousands of overripe plums from shadowy maternity trees—and nightjars, with their silent nocturnal flights and eerie but charming, churring sound, inhabit the Black Forest's damp air, hunting for black darter dragonflies and blue-tailed damselflies. Orange-tip butterflies lay eggs in garlic mustard weed blooms and bob along the forest's unpredictable wind drifts, while fisher cats (which aren't cats at all but much more like weasels), wily red foxes, striped badgers, and grey squirrels scamper along high branches, or trundle along the forest floor, tracking hapless insects, lizards, and forest rodents. Fat-bodied adders, with brownish-black scales and short curved fangs, lie among swells of fallen leaves and under the shadows of tree roots, breeding large litters of young snakelings. Shiny woodlouse spiders eat their fill of swollen woodlice, as newly hatched lace weaver spiders murder and eat their fill of their mothers. Walnut-orb spiders, with leathery skin and flat tick-like bodies, patiently hide under loose bark until twilight before spinning their gluey three-foot webs.

For ages, the Black Forest and its inhabitants have remained mostly untouched and unsettled by human hands, and untrodden by human feet. Occasionally, slave traders and dark travelers move quickly through its shadowy trees, or groups of pioneering families naively invade one of its quiet meadows, thinking they can start a woodland village. But in time, they all disappear, and there are very few who have lived to tell any tales about the Black Forest.

In part, this is because the forest lies in a lonely place between the Hollow Fen to the south and the High Desert of Shadows to the north. But this is also because the Black Forest has a secluded, fateful life of its own—an odd, menacing sense of dread. A traveler who might spy a Black Forest badger catching a hedgehog, or preying on a ground-nesting bird, would be disturbed by the way the badger mercilessly ravages its victims, crushing fragile bones with abnormal ferocity and pulping its meals into excessive messes of blood and tissue. A passing slave trader who might spot an unsuspecting mouse stumbling across an adder's nest would be sickened to watch the viper strike repeatedly at the small mammal, cruelly injecting it with an unnecessary amount of deadly venom before it dislocates its jaws and begins to swallow its victim while the mouse is still kicking its back legs. A wayward vagabond who might hear the muted click-clack of footsteps through the underbrush might become hysterical upon discovering the footsteps belong to a thick-legged, hairy bird spider—over a foot in length and weighing a few pounds—scuttling down a dark, damp burrow to kill and loudly consume a blind mole-rat. The trapped rat's squeals of agony and fright would leave even the bravest man shivering in disgust and dismay.

Indeed, the Black Forest seems to have a uniquely savage nature—breeding uniquely savage things—and those who venture under its tall black oaks count themselves lucky if they ever leave.

Nicolas and his friends had a hint of this as they entered the Black Forest the night before.

Benjamin, who was getting back some of his daring and who was eager to add a bit of flavor to supper, had scrambled up a tree shortly after they had walked under the forest's darkened shade. His sharp eyes had spotted a finch's nest, and with a lively promise of returning with a fresh egg or two, the boy-thief had nimbly climbed and clawed his way up the oak's thick trunk, until he lay stretched out along the branch which cradled the twiggy nest.

"Well," said Ranulf, peering up into the shadows, "what do you see, Benjamin?"

259

The boy-thief didn't reply, and they thought he might be busy, warily plucking the eggs from their nest.

"Benjamin!" Ranulf echoed. "Are there any eggs?"

Again, Benjamin didn't reply. Instead, they all watched as the smallish boy slowly pushed himself backward along the branch and lowered himself to the ground. His cheek was scuffed from where it'd been rubbed by the rough bark, and his usually cheery face was drawn and cheerless.

Adelaide put one of her slender fingers under his chin to look him in the eyes. "Did you find any eggs, Benjamin?" she asked gently.

He unhappily shook his head. When it was clear he didn't intend to say anything, Ranulf wagged his head and confidently said, "No bother! We've got plenty of foodstuffs to cook up tonight. Let's find a place to sleep and get a fire started!" He put a friendly arm around Benjamin and led him further up the path until they'd found a small clearing, soft with leafy moss and mostly clear of bumps and swells.

Nicolas helped Ranulf gather armfuls of fallen branches and sticks and twigs, and soon, they had a merry blaze going. The two boys then took some time arranging an awning with several strips of leather, a large goat hide, and some stout branches. Ranulf didn't think it smelled like rain, but the forest had queer odors, and he admitted he couldn't be sure. Adelaide busily hummed away, putting together a broth of onions, cabbage, and mutton, and fussing over Cornelia and the pack pony, which happily munched some the oats and armfuls of forage grass she quickly gathered together.

Benjamin, still acting dejected, just sat down, and once the fire was hungrily licking its way among the kindling, he stared into it with a brooding look on his face. Nicolas and the others left him alone, but Nicolas felt a little worried. The boy-thief still hadn't said anything, and he'd kept to himself as if something were troubling him.

Finally, when they were all sitting on their bearskins, chewing on the last bits of stale-bread trenchers soaked in the hearty broth, Nicolas gently prodded. "Benjamin, you okay?"

Benjamin nodded but kept his eyes on the fire.

Adelaide laid a soft hand on his small shoulder. "Something's bothered you," she said. "What was in the nest, Benjamin?"

He gave a quick shudder. "It was awful," he finally said.

"What was awful?"

"The chicks," he said quietly.

"What about the chicks?" asked Ranulf.

"They were dead. A large-bill crow was sitting on the other side of the nest. It'd killed them all."

"I'm sorry," Adelaide said wistfully. "I guess that happens sometimes."

"No, it doesn't," said Benjamin defensively. "It doesn't happen. A crow doesn't kill finch chicks like that." Tears were welling up in his eyes, and his hands were balled into tight fists. "It didn't just kill them. It ripped off their heads." As quickly as he'd said this, he let out a deep sigh as if all the anger had gone out of him. He stared into the fire again. "It'd ripped off their heads," he repeated faintly, wiping his nose, "and left their bodies lying in the nest. It was eating one of the heads when I saw it. It stopped and looked at me, and then just kept eating." He quivered. "It was evil. Evil."

Adelaide pulled him close and pressed his head against her chest. She waved a hand at Nicolas and Ranulf, motioning them to not say anything else. She began humming again and running her soft fingers through Benjamin's wild hair. After a few minutes, he slumped down in her lap, and a few minutes after that, he fell asleep.

"I've never heard of anything like that," Nicolas whispered.

"Neither have I," Ranulf said. Adelaide shook her head in agreement and gazed at the surrounding press of darkness. "I don't like the feel of this place," the older boy said. "Tomorrow, let's do our best to wake early and move along quickly. I don't have my full strength back yet, but the longer we take, the stranger this place feels." They all agreed. The Black Forest felt *unhealthy*.

The next morning, they ate a quick breakfast of oat porridge and berries, packed the pony, and doused the fire's coals. A cold breeze was blowing through the trees. Overhead, the leaves rustled like water babbling over river rocks. Adelaide found a few blossoms of wild Mugwort. She plucked them and gave a few to each of them, telling them it would help protect them from evil spirits and wild animals. Cornelia even ate a few.

Thankfully, the morning passed by uneventfully. Except for one peculiar thing.

Adelaide, who'd been walking behind the pony with Cornelia at her heels, suddenly screamed and began shouting and stamping around. The boys had raced back to see what was the matter and found her angrily staring down a rather large, rough-looking hare. The hare was sitting on its haunches several feet from the path, staring back at Adelaide and chattering at her with its long front teeth.

"What happened?" Ranulf asked.

"That, that *thing* attacked Cornelia," Adelaide gasped, trying to catch her breath. "Shoo!" she shouted at the mad hare, but it just sat there, malevolently twitching its scarred nose.

"Are you sure?"

"Of course I'm sure!" she'd said curtly. "It came out of nowhere and slammed into Cornelia, and tried to bite her." The little goat was on her feet. She didn't look hurt, but kept maneuvering to keep Adelaide between herself and the strange hare.

"That's weird," said Ranulf. He picked up a stone and threw it at the hare. "Go away!" he shouted. The hare backed up a step or two, but didn't leave. Nicolas found a stick and waved it at the strange animal, while the boys continued shouting at it to go away. Finally, the hare turned, and after a final, malicious look over its ratty-looking shoulder, hopped away into the underbrush.

Once Adelaide was sure Cornelia was alright, she'd put her little goat among the baggage on the pack pony, and they had continued on their way, saying very little. For Nicolas' own part, he kept anxiously glancing into the surrounding forest, and for the first time in his life, he felt uncomfortable among trees.

━●◆●━

They decided not to stop for lunch. Instead, Ranulf passed around chunks of peasant bread sprinkled with cornmeal and thick slices of smoked ham. When it was his turn, Nicolas drank deeply from the flagon of honey mead and felt his insides warm.

Benjamin had decided to walk out in front. He still seemed a bit shaken from the night before, but, as he put it with a wily grin on his face, "A snatcher is quick, and if something's amiss, I'll be quick to run to the back and let *you* deal with it." This made Ranulf laugh and cough, and Nicolas felt a little better. Adelaide walked between Nicolas and Ranulf and quietly kept them entertained with stories of when she was young, before she'd left her village for the City. Nicolas wanted her to sing again, but he was too shy to ask.

After a while, Benjamin stopped and appeared to be waving his arms in the air, trying to clear away what looked to be a gauzy cloud of brownish-grey smoke hanging above his head.

263

"What is it?" shouted Ranulf.

"Moths!" Benjamin shouted back.

Adelaide stood with the pack pony, while Nicolas and Ranulf walked up to where Benjamin was. The smallish boy had caught one of the moths in his hands and opened them to show it to the other two boys. The moth was large, perhaps two inches across. It had a rounded, oval shape with black mandibles and reddish-brown wings and pale yellow markings. It had settled near a scabbed scrape on one of Benjamin's fingers, and the moth appeared to be gently sucking or feeding on it.

"That's disgusting," said Nicolas, staring at the moth in morbid fascination.

"Does it hurt?" asked Ranulf.

"No," Benjamin said, pushing out his lower lip. "It kind of tickles." He waved at Adelaide with his other hand. "Adelaide! Come look!"

When the young girl walked up, she took a look at the moth feeding on Benjamin's sore, and blanched white. "Yuck!" she said and began nervously glancing around them.

Ranulf looked at her quizzically. "What're you looking for?"

"A carcass," she said quietly.

"Why a carcass?"

Her pretty face was ashen. "That's a *grease* moth," she said with a strained voice, which made Benjamin look worried.

"What's a grease moth?" he asked.

"The year I was born, there was a sickness—the Grey Death—which came to my village," she said.

"I remember that!" Ranulf interjected. "People were dying by the droves in the City and the gatekeeps were closed for weeks."

Benjamin slowly nodded his head. "They said dead bodies were burned in great piles in the open plains."

"Yes," she said, nodding, "well, many people also died in the Outlands, and my parents told me half our village died in the span of only a month. My dad was afraid I would die, so he locked my mum and me in our cottage. My parents said many people thought the Grey Death was caused by grease moths."

"Why?" Nicolas asked, confused. "I've never heard of a moth causing anyone to be sick."

"Because they feed on the *dead*," she whispered.

The boys looked at each other. After a moment, Ranulf said, "Well Benjamin's not dead."

"I know he's not dead," the young girl replied, exasperated. "But look what it's eating." She pointed to the sore on Benjamin's finger. Benjamin shook his finger violently, frightening the moth away. "Since there was a cloud of them," she said, "I thought some dead animal might be nearby."

They all looked closely at the dark oaks and underbrush surrounding them. Nicolas couldn't see anything. No carcasses. No animals. No moths.

"I don't see anything," he said quietly. "I think they're gone."

And for the second time that day, Adelaide screamed.

———————

Nicolas, on edge from the night before and the mean-looking hare and the flesh-eating moth, nearly jumped out of his skin. Had he not been so scared, he might have laughed at Benjamin, who shook like a leaf in a storm and opened his eyes so wide, they seemed to push the rest of his face downward.

"What!?" shouted Ranulf, who was also as pale as a sheet. "What're you screaming for?!"

Adelaide had one hand over her mouth and with the other, she pointed a finger through a space between some trees to their right. Nicolas looked hard in the direction she was pointing and didn't see anything. Well not at first, anyway. Squinting, he finally made out the snaking shape of a small brook of water. It was perhaps three feet across, shallow, and even in the gloom of the forest, appeared to be running swiftly and clearly along its course.

"The stream?" he asked hoarsely. "I don't understand. You're screaming at the stream?" He asked this last question more harshly than he'd intended, and looking at Adelaide, he instantly felt badly about it. Her eyes were wide and the blood had left her face. Her knuckles were white, and she was breathing in shallow puffs. "The *woman*," she gasped, clearly terrified. "The *woman*."

"What woman?" he asked.

"The woman," she whispered and gulped for air.

Nicolas looked into the shadows. *What woman?* he thought. His muscles suddenly ached with tension, and he felt aggravated in spite of himself. *What is she talking about?*

"The *washing woman*," Adelaide hissed. "I saw a woman washing clothes in the stream."

Nicolas felt more confused than ever, and he was about to say something when he caught sight of Ranulf's face. The older boy, still pale, looked intense. Afraid.

"What?!" Nicolas asked, now unsure of what was going on. "I don't see a woman! What's going on?"

Ranulf gently but firmly put a hand over Nicolas' mouth and looked over his shoulder at the stream. "I don't see anything, Adelaide," he said quietly. Desperately.

Adelaide didn't reply. She just kept pointing.

Firmly, Nicolas grabbed Ranulf's wrist and pulled the older boy's hand away from his mouth. "What is it?" he whispered. "Tell me what's going on."

Ranulf looked at him. "Be quiet, Master Bennett." With a sure but gentle calmness, the older boy stepped to Adelaide and circled his arms around her. She crumpled into his embrace, let out a sob, and was quiet. With a jerk of his chin, Ranulf directed Nicolas to the blackened teapot slung on top of their luggage. Without saying anything more, Nicolas and Benjamin went about building a small fire, and a short time later, had the teapot glowing merrily among bright coals. When Nicolas had gone to the stream to fill it with water, he'd looked carefully around, but he'd seen nothing. No woman. Nothing.

They stayed there, along the path, for the better part of an hour. Ranulf made some cinnamon tea and placed Cornelia in Adelaide's lap while the young girl drank a cup. She'd composed herself by then, but she still looked shaken, and every once in a while, she'd steal a glance over her shoulder toward the stream. Squatting together several yards away, the boys held a small council.

"I don't understand," Nicolas said quietly. "What happened?"

Benjamin looked at Ranulf, clearly wanting him to explain. The smallish boy-thief's forehead was wrinkled with worry.

Ranulf pressed his lips together hard, then sighed. He shook his head. "Seeing a washer woman—" the older boy glanced at Adelaide, making sure his voice was low enough. "Seeing a washer woman is a sign of *death*," he whispered.

Nicolas looked quickly at Benjamin and back at Ranulf. "What? What do you mean it's a sign of death?"

The older boy remained quiet. Benjamin had the saddest look on his face. The smallish boy-thief softly said, "If a person sees a washer woman, it means they're going to die."

Nicolas felt sick. "No!" he said stubbornly, more loudly than he meant to. "No one is going to die. That's ridiculous. I didn't see anything." Benjamin and Ranulf said nothing. Nicolas peeked at Adelaide. She was sitting cross-legged with Cornelia in her lap, sipping her tea and singing softly to the little goat.

"No," he said again in a more hushed voice, "*no one* is going to die." He suddenly felt a surge of strength and anger knotting in his chest. "Let's get going! Let's get out of these cursed woods."

Ranulf nodded approvingly and smiled weakly. He looked exhausted. "Okay," he said, as if Nicolas had settled the matter. "No one's going to die. Let's get going, Benjamin."

The boys stood up together and tightened the belts and buckles around their weather cloaks. Nicolas turned back to the pack pony, the little goat, and Adelaide.

Nicolas the Wren had yet to learn there are certain times in life when you are faced with terrible situations. Situations that offer only pain to yourself or pain to someone else you hold dear. In such a time, a person discovers where his heart lies, and in this particular moment, Nicolas discovered his heart was greater than himself.

He felt it break inside him when he turned and saw Adelaide dying.

CHAPTER 23

✝HE FALLS OF CADGAMLAN

Ogres—real ogres—are nasty, awful things.

As a rule, they're brutish, gullible, and dull-witted, but they can be cunning when it comes to laying traps and ambushing prey. Some say they are the accidental offspring of giants and stone-demons. Others say they are the result of ancient sorcery and twisted spells intended to mix the race of trolls with the race of men. This might explain why ogres can be extremely superstitious and are afraid of magic. They are simple-minded and magic confuses them. Magic is one of the few things which scares them.

Most ogres—except for a small breed which learned to live in holes in the ground and hunt earth-gnomes—have disproportionately big heads and are very large—both fat and tall—and they have coarse, matted hair on their legs, forearms, shoulders, and ears. Their skin is tough and calloused. This is partly because they tend to bite themselves when they are very distressed or very hungry. They have bizarrely long arms and are bow-legged, but they're still able to move extremely fast in a kind of skipping, sideways-hopping motion. Ogres usually keep their teeth and nails filed sharp by rubbing them on rough rocks. As a general rule, they live alone in lonely caves or crude stone houses near or under old bridges or waterfalls. In fact, it is rare to find more than one ogre at a time because they have the ghastly habit of frequently fighting and eating each other, sometimes while the loser is still alive.

Outlanders who live in the northeast, between the Black Forest and the mountains of Dolmen Tombs, are said to build their cottages with small windows for fear of one particular ogress, an awful creature named Black Annis, who they say uses her long arms and sharp, curved nails like fish hooks to reach through cottage windows at night and snatch babies and small children out of their beds while they sleep. In point of truth, ogres are constantly, relentlessly, and forever hungry. While they will kill and eat any kind of meat—the fresher and bloodier, the better, even though ogres have also never been known to refuse a rotting, moldering carcass—their favorite meal is human flesh, straight from the bone, preferably little children or soft babies. They simply crave the taste of humans. They've even been discovered scavenging after newly fought battles, eating their way through fallen men, and not caring if they find one whom is only wounded. Apparently, screaming is not very upsetting to an ogre.

Perhaps because of this peculiar and hideous taste for human flesh, an ogre will sometimes almost starve itself mad, waiting until a human victim comes along.

And this is precisely what Sulten, the ogre who seized Adelaide, had done.

―――――◆◆―――――

While the boys were standing off to the side of the path, discussing what Adelaide had said about what she'd seen by the stream, Sulten, who'd been spying on them for the better part of an hour—his empty belly gnawing angrily at his thick ribs—finally saw his opportunity and sprang out from the hollowed trunk of a great, black oak near the water and leapt at the unsuspecting young girl. He was half-crazed with hunger and was not as crafty as he otherwise might have been.

The last bite of human flesh Sulten had eaten had been a

skinny farmer who'd kicked a lot and was stringy and tasted like dirty cabbage. The unlucky farmer had gone into the Black Forest, desperately looking for his lost children after they'd been kidnapped by slave traders several days before. He was afraid they'd been sold to sand tribes in the High Desert of Shadows, and that is probably what happened to them. As for him, a quick drink from the stream's cold waters had cost him his life. And Sulten had sucked and gnashed the last bit of marrow from his bones over a week before.

Now, the ogre, frantic to snatch Adelaide before anyone could put up a fight, used his long, hairy arms to swat Cornelia out of Adelaide's lap, sending the poor little goat tumbling across the turf like a broken ragdoll. Thick strands of foul-smelling drool swung wildly from the corners of Sulten's wide mouth, as the large ogre then curled his fetid fingers through Adelaide's sweet hair and hurriedly drug her into the brush, all the while, slashing his razor-sharp fingernails at her face, hoping to gouge out her eyes and blind her. He, like many ogres, did not like anyone to see where he lived and fed, and Sulten had learned to begin his attacks by stabbing one of his long nails through his victims' eyes or scratching them out of their sockets. Besides, blind victims were less trouble.

But when the hungry monster had lunged forward to thump Cornelia out of the way, one of his calloused, bony knuckles clipped Adelaide on the edge of her jaw and knocked her senseless. Because of this, she didn't even have time to scream. And, as good fortune would have it, she also avoided having her pretty eyes gouged out. As she hung limply by her long hair, being roughly drug along the forest floor like some lifeless figurine, most of the ogre's swipes with his mean fingernails flew harmlessly through the air and missed her eyes. His efforts only managed to leave one deep cut above Adelaide's right eye, which bled freely over her porcelain face like a wet, red mask.

And this is what Nicolas saw. A blood-soaked, lifeless Adelaide Ashdown. The sight broke his gentle heart.

"*Nooooo!*" he screamed in helpless panic and agony, instantly leaping forward to run after her. It happened so swiftly that Benjamin and Ranulf, who'd been facing the other way, barely had time to see the last bit of Adelaide's soft leather ankle boots before she disappeared between two dead black oak trees. Ranulf immediately ran after Nicolas, with little idea of what had happened, while Benjamin took a moment to tenderly lift Cornelia on top of the pack pony's back and to make sure the pony was tethered securely to the base of a scrubby bush. He, too, then took off in the direction the other two boys had run.

———◆◆———

Sulten's stone house was a simple, putrid affair. It had a wide opening with no door, no windows, and no hearth or chimney. Its floor consisted of gnawed bone chips, tufts of old hair, ogre dung, and soggy dirt clumped with saliva and snot. There were no candles or rugs or blankets or beds—any of the things which might make a home a home. Instead, there were knotty ankle bones, snapped rib bones, and bits of neck bones chiseled with marks from Sulten's gritty knife. There were a few black pots in which the ogre would boil severed heads, a large one for adults and a small one for children. There was also one shiny belt buckle he'd kept from a blubbery merchantman who'd tried unsuccessfully to pass through the Black Forest a year before. Indeed, it wasn't really a proper house at all. Sulten had simply built a wall of stone under a high embankment of sour, dark earth next to the Falls of Cadgamlan, the Falls of Massacre, which was a wide waterfall of perhaps twenty feet across, spilling into the forest stream Adelaide had first spotted.

The Falls were well-known to slave traders who passed

through the Black Forest, and it was likely those evil folk who'd first named them. Before Sulten had made the Falls his grisly home, generations of forest hares had lived quietly nearby. Instead of living solitary lives as most hares in the wild will do, families of brown-jacketed hares and long-eared jackrabbits raised their litters, and lived and died near the Falls, sleeping peacefully in grass nests, chewing happily on cowslips and dandelions, and chasing each other through sun-dappled bracken on warm summer mornings. But when Sulten arrived many years before—some say he'd fled the mountains after having been stalked by an especially murderous and jealous pair of ogre brothers named Hongrois and Hongrid—he'd sat sullenly by the Falls, muttering miserable things to himself, catching the nearby hares, throttling them by their necks, and devouring them whole. To pass the time in between waylaying random travelers, he would sometimes toss a bloodied ear, or a bit of nose, or a few torn eyelids toward one of the more curious hares, and after a long while, the once-gentle hares became dark and violent, and developed an unnatural taste for blood, meat, and bone. It was, in fact, one of these same hares which had attacked Cornelia earlier that same day.

On this particular morning, Sulten, almost gleeful at having caught a tender young girl, rambled back to his stone home, not realizing the three boys had followed him. Survivors usually bolted, running away as fast as their frightened legs would carry them. Sulten grated his yellowed teeth together—a sure sign of an excited ogre—and dropped his hold on Adelaide's hair once he'd reached his wretched hideout. The Falls splashed nearby, splattering and striking a rabble of stones and old skulls below, like tumbling links of a never-ending chain. Wispy clouds of grease moths, busily sucking the tiny morsels of congealed fat and tissue off the lanky farmer's splintered thigh bones, made the air dark and hazy. The ogre's home stank. It smelled of rotted muscle, putrefied flesh, and decomposing gristle.

Nicolas, Ranulf, and Benjamin hid behind the dense hedge of a hawthorn bush, trying their best to breathe quietly and to not gag at the awful smell. They watched as the large ogre stupidly pranced around, banging together his dented iron pots, and in a lurching, harsh voice, sang,

Dweedle, dwāddle,
Where's my ladle?
Dwiddle, dwengle,
What's to mangle?
'Tis a chil' I see!

Dweedle, diddle,
Why so little?
Dwiddle, doddle,
Half a potful!
'Tis a chil' for me!

Dweedle, duddle,
What's ta cuddle?
Dwiddle, daddle,
It won't tattle,
Once inside o' me!

Having finished this hateful ditty, Sulten picked up his short, curved knife and waved it over his huge head. A stiffened string of sinew hung from its notched edge. "I shall eats the skins first!" the ogre spluttered gleefully, licking his froggish tongue against his thick, wet lips. "Skin it first, skin it first!" he blubbered, squatting over Adelaide like an enormous toad.

"*Stop!*" Nicolas shouted.

Ranulf had pulled at Nicolas' weather cloak, trying to keep him in place, but Nicolas wrenched free and jumped out from behind the hawthorn bush. He didn't have a plan. Down to his boots, he was terrified of the huge ogre, and he knew in his heart that Adelaide was dead—darkened blood covered her face and had soaked into her homely kirtle and surcoat—but he couldn't bear to see her cut up and devoured by the sickening, nasty thing crouching over her. Even in death—behind a mask of deep scarlet and twigs and dirt—Adelaide was still beautiful. *When you sleep in the home of the angyles.* Nicolas could hear her haunting voice in his head and pictured her in her poor white smock, glowing in the moonlight, and singing the sorrowful song of a Healer. He had to *do* something. And, at the spur of the moment, the best he could come up with was to shout, "Stop!" and stand up.

Sulten, with a twisted handful of Adelaide's hair in one hand and the pitiless knife in the other, straightened, squinting his wide-set eyes at the hawthorn bush. "What's this?" he snarled madly. "It's another bag-o'-bones, I see." The ogre let go his hold on the young girl's hair, and before Nicolas knew what else to do, Sulten scuttled over to him, waving his long arms and whipping the edge of the knife through the air in ragged zig-zags. "Another bag-o'-bones! Another bag-o'-bones!" The ogre howled joyfully at his good luck, slathering Nicolas with droplets of greasy spittle.

"I'll—I'll—I'll *crush* you!" screamed Nicolas. His neck was as tense as a bow-string, he was shivering, his hands were balled into fists at his side, and he felt like his legs were rooted to the ground. For some mysterious reason, '*I'll crush you,*' was the first, and only, thing he could think of to say.

Sulten's wild gyrations jerked to a sudden stop. "It crushes me?" he asked, bewildered. "It crushes *meeeeeee?*" he repeated. The nasty ogre had never had anyone, much less a child, threaten him before. Usually, his victims screamed and yelled and wept, and called out for mercy or help, but no one had ever threatened him. No one had ever said "I'll crush you." Sulten quickly lowered his bulging, round head, huffing and grinding its teeth, to look Nicolas in the eye. His breath smelled like rotten eggs and vomit, and Nicolas swallowed hard, trying not to breathe and doing his best not to throw up. "What's it *mean*, it'll 'crush me'?" the large ogre stupidly grumbled.

"I'll *crush* you," Nicolas firmly said again, scrambling to think of what else he could possibly say. What he could possibly mean.

Sulten raised one thick bony finger and poked Nicolas sharply in the chest with the end of his cruel fingernail. "What's it *mean*, it'll 'crush me'!?"

Nicolas jerked back from the force of the ogre's push, thankful he was wearing his chain mail shirt. The leather bag of Ranulf's stones banged against his back, and he nearly slipped on the soft moss underfoot, but his mind remained a frustrating blank.

"What's it *mean*?!" howled Sulten, spitting in Nicolas' pale face angrily.

"I'll—I'll *crush* you," began Nicolas again, his voice cracking and not as fierce as he wanted it to be. "I'll crush you like—like …," His eyes suddenly lit up. "I'll crush you like a *stone!*" he yelled furiously at the leering ogre.

Sulten slumped back on his bow-legs with its reeking mouth hanging open. He didn't understand this at all. He folded his long arms against his chest and used the gory knife to pick a chunk of rotting meat out of his front teeth. "What's it mean," he whined in confusion, "to crush Sulten likes da stones?" The large ogre's mind hurt. He was trying to think, trying to understand what this strange boy had said. Sulten wasn't sure, and it bothered him. It gnawed at his cramped and slow-witted brain.

"I'll crush you *like a stone!*" Nicolas said again bitterly, and as he did so, he unslung Ranulf's leather bag of stones. He opened it, and with a snap, spilled its contents on the spongy turf. There was an assortment of rocks, some smooth, some rough, some glittering with minerals, and some black as a crow's blind eye. Nicolas bent over and picked up one of the grey stones with tiny holes in it. "I'll crush you like *this* stone!" And to the ogre's everlasting shock and amazement, the defiant boy clenched and gritted his teeth, squeezed his fist tight, and burst the rock into powdered dust and small fragments.

The horrified ogre reeled backward. *Curses! Magics! Plagues!* He dropped his knife, howling in confused fear and rage. "*It crushes stone!*" he screamed, pointing at Nicolas. "*It crushes stone!*"

"*Aargh!*" Nicolas screamed back at the shocked creature. Tears of frustration and rage and fear welled in his eyes. He wanted to take advantage of the ogre's sudden fear, so he picked up another grey stone and took a threatening step toward the frenzied ogre. "I have powerful *magic!*" he announced madly. He took several more steps, pressing the bewildered ogre back toward the open door of its stony home. "I have powerful magic!" he screamed again. "I can crush stone! I can crush *you*! I can *drown* stone, I can drown *you*, or I can make stone *float!*" Nicolas flung the grey stone into the bubbling cascades of the Falls of Cadgamlan. Now, in truly terrified astonishment, the panicked ogre watched the stone float on the water's surface, bobbing along, pushed by the current, and winding its way down the swift running stream like a powerful sorcerer's trick. "You killed her!" screamed Nicolas, shaking his fists. "I'll kill *you*!" He felt exhausted, afraid, enraged, and lost. Hot tears fell freely down his face.

Sulten, genuinely horrified at the strange boy's strength, savagery, and witchery, thought some kind of dark magic was at play. The ogre stumbled rearward in raw fear. "It don't crush me!" he pleaded in a sick, croaking voice. "It don't crush me!" He scuttled along, tripping over his hairy, long arms, rushing inside his stinking stony home and cowering in its shadows, sniveling and whimpering like an injured animal.

Nicolas kept a wary eye on the gloomy door of Sulten's home as he kneeled next to Adelaide. His salty tears fell on her wilted body, mingling with her blood, and he tenderly scooped his arms underneath her. With a grunt, he picked her up. "I'll crush you!" he shouted again at the moaning ogre and took a step backward. Then another. Then another. Until he felt a firm hand at his back.

"I've got you," said Ranulf, quietly. The bladesmith apprentice stepped out in front of Nicolas, his smithy hammer in his hand. He eased Nicolas behind him and stood at the ready in case the hungry ogre had a change of mind. Benjamin stood up and helped Nicolas with Adelaide's body.

Within seconds, the three boys disappeared behind the hawthorn bush, leaving Sulten, a half-starved, confused, and frightened ogre, mumbling miserably to himself in his vile, dark, and stony home.

"Quickly," Ranulf said nervously.

Together, the boys carefully hoisted Adelaide's lifeless body on top of the pack pony, tucking her gently next to Cornelia. Her skin was cold and clammy, and they affectionately covered her with one of the warm bearskins. Benjamin, bravely sniffing back tears, kept one of his small hands on Adelaide's cool shoulder, while Nicolas untied the pony and quickly started them off down the path.

Nicolas felt numb and couldn't stop shaking every few seconds. "I'm sorry about your rocks," he mumbled blankly to Ranulf.

The older boy shook his head. A stream of warm tears coursed down his cheeks. "I can't think of a better use," he said softly.

The Black Forest closed around them, and an hour later, night fell cold, silent, and for Nicolas the Wren, infinitely sad.

CHAPTER 24

A Welcome Rest

Grief is one of the strangest things.

Grief *weighs* something. It's heavy. A weight that pulls down inside a person like wet clothing. It tugs downward with a stubborn grip, like sticky-thick mud sucking doggedly at each footstep. Like the ocean deep dragging down on a swimmer's tired legs. It feels lonely, empty, and suffocating. It drains and fills a person's mind all at the same time. Grief is, indeed, a strange thing, and it can cover the living like an unstoppable floodwater.

Much, much later, Nicolas would remember little about that afternoon in the Black Forest. He had trouble recalling the raindrops striking his bare head or rolling down his temples. He couldn't recall how the pony's damp lead rope rubbed his skin raw. He didn't remember the gentleness in Ranulf's quiet voice. "Nicolas. Nicolas," the older boy would say, trying to reach out to him somewhere in the depths of the suffocating feeling inside his chest. He didn't even recall when they finally stopped, enclosed by the greying light of the dying day.

A short figure, clothed in a red-dyed goatskin, had stepped into their path. "Master Bennett," it said softly, taking the pony's lead rope from him.

Nicolas didn't remember Adelaide's crumpled body, lying silently under the thick bearskin on the pony's back. In fact, his only memory wasn't real. It was of Adelaide's sweet face, looking at him and saying, "When someone dies, the Healer comes to the door of the family's home, carrying a sorrow basket in her arms. She sings

279

a short song, and gives the flower blossoms to each person in the home. In return, they open their hand, letting their sadness fall into the sorrow basket, then the Healer takes it away."

Nicolas wanted a Healer—he wanted *her*—to come and take away his sorrow, the merciless grief filling his insides.

But she didn't come.

Late the next morning, Nicolas woke up with sunlight finding its way through a small, stained glass window, speckling his bearskin with subdued colors of red, blue, pink, yellow, and dark green. He lay there, utterly exhausted and drained. He didn't make any movement to get up. His insides felt shaky and fragile. He didn't want to move.

Nicolas wanted to go home.

"Stand up, son," he suddenly heard his father's voice say. "Stand up. A great man is passing by."

Three years before, Nicolas sat with his father and mother in the dark walnut pews of St. Andrew's Church in downtown Penrith, England. They were toward the front of the long sanctuary, which was unusual, but on that day, Nicolas' grandfather, Paul Douglas Bennett, was being buried. It was a blustery February afternoon. Squalls were blowing out of the east, threatening to litter a fury of snowflakes across the purple sky. Only a handful of mourners were present, mostly family. The balcony seats were entirely empty.

Nicolas' four uncles, and the churchwarden—a mustached fellow by the name of Argyll—and a local pub owner acted as his grandfather's pallbearers. They carried his simple black coffin slowly up the aisle and placed it on a draped stand in the church's chancel with his grandfather's feet nearest the altar. The parish priest, a kind man with a sincere smile and thin, silver glasses, sprinkled the coffin with holy water and incensed it with the fragrant smoke emitting from a gold censer. Candles were lit, prayers were said, and absolution was given. But because of the storm, his grandfather's body stayed in the church that evening and was buried the next day.

The next morning, Nicolas sat by himself on a small folding chair, waiting as the pallbearers approached the aproned grave. His father, Peter Bennett, stood behind him. Gently, he touched Nicolas' shoulder quietly saying, "Stand up, son. A great man is passing by." Somehow, standing up had helped. Nicolas was still sad, but standing—having the strength to show respect for a man he'd only known a little—had made him feel better. Nicolas' heart had swelled with pride though it was still heavy with grief. He'd loved his grandfather, although he'd not seen him very often before he died. The older Mr. Bennett had lived in a small farmhouse on the Isle of Walney, an island off the west coast of England at the western end of Morecambe Bay, and for some reason unknown to Nicolas, family visits had been few and far between. But as he stood at his grandfather's burial, he somehow felt closer to him than when he'd been alive. It was as if something had been passed between them—some mantle or heritage.

Now, three years later, in the Black Forest of a mysterious, hidden land his grandfather had once known and been to, Nicolas could again hear his father's softly spoken instruction. "Stand up, son."

So he did.

His bare feet touched a smooth-worn, wooden floor, and Nicolas let the bearskin slide off his shoulders. He was dressed in only his pants and woolen sweater, and his mouth felt dry and unpleasant. Nothing wondrous or magical or miraculous suddenly happened when he stood up.

Except that Nicolas was upright and ready when Adelaide Ashdown came back from the dead and walked into the room.

The young girl opened the door cautiously and quietly slipped inside. Her sandy-colored hair was clean and bright, and braided in fantastic swirls and designs. There was a thin, clean bandage above her right eye, but her cheeks were rosy, and her wonderful eyes sparkled. She was dressed in a new weather cloak made of goatskin dyed a deep red. Her polished mail shirt glittered underneath, and even her soft ankle-high boots were clean. She looked at him and practically rose up on her toes. "Good morrow, sweet Nicolas!" she yelped. He was stunned and couldn't move. She impatiently leapt at him, knocking him back on his bed, and gave him a spirited hug.

Adelaide showered his forehead and cheeks with playfully loud kisses, and Nicolas, still too stunned to do much of anything in return, did the least manly thing of all. He cried.

"*You're alive!*" he gasped, each syllable catching in his throat. "You're alive, Adelaide!"

"Of *course* I'm alive, you silly bird," she said, sitting up with her hands on her hips. She brushed his tears away. "What else would I be?" she asked, teasing him. Nicolas threw his head back and laughed. A few tears still came, but he laughed, and like a rolling wave, warmth and joy and strength filled his heart.

"Please," he said when he'd finally caught his breath, "tell me what happened? I thought you were dead." They sat beside each other on the edge of the bed. Her braided hair smelled like vanilla and peppermint.

"Well, I *was* almost dead," Adelaide said softly. "I don't remember much of anything, which is probably on account of this bruise." She turned her chin toward Nicolas, pointing a finger at a blue-ish bruise running along one side of her slender jaw. "It must've hit me and knocked me out right away," she said. "I don't even remember what the ogre looked like, although Ranulf and Benjamin said it was hideous and huge."

"It was," said Nicolas vacantly. "I think it's the worst thing I've ever seen."

"Then I'm *glad* it knocked me out," she said, "and other than the bruise, I only suffered a cut above my eye."

"But you were covered in blood," Nicolas protested and involuntarily shivered. "I thought that thing cut your throat or something."

"It bled a lot," she said, gingerly touching the bandage and wincing. "The cut went deep. I guess I'll have some kind of terrible scar." Her eyes lowered and she played nervously with a tuft of fur on the bearskin. "They said it was like the cut *poisoned* me. My skin was turning black, and apparently, my body was really cold even though my heart beat very fast. My breathing was quick, too, but faint, so faint, Ranulf said he couldn't hardly hear it when he put his ear to my mouth. And, I lost a lot of blood, I suppose. I still feel dizzy if I stand up too quickly." She shrugged. "Ranulf said Obasi fed me some kind of yellow broth made of chicken bones and garlic, and packed the cut with a sticky poultice that smelled like tar. I really don't remember anything until I woke up about an hour ago, but I already feel *much*, much better."

"Wait," said Nicolas, holding up a hand to interrupt her. "Who's Obasi?"

"Oh!" she said, giggling. "Sorry, I thought you knew. This is his home. He's one of the Moss People."

"Oh," replied Nicolas. He looked around the room. It was clean but a little cluttered. There were little shelves packed with little books, and scattered randomly around the room on little brass candlesticks was a litter of melted candles of all different shapes, sizes, and colors. A small fireplace—a bit smaller than the one in Baatunde's cottage—was in one corner of the room furthest away from the bed, and a small rocking chair sat next to it near a little table on which sat a jumble of pipes, matches, a short stack of books, a pair of wiry spectacles, and a tall goblet made of emerald green glass. A gnarled little walking stick leaned on the wall next to the door, and a small cloak of red-dyed goatskin was hanging on a peg next to it.

"Is Obasi like Baatunde?" Nicolas asked aloud.

"Who's Baatunde?" asked Adelaide curiously.

Nicolas gave a quick shake of his head. "Nevermind," he said. "I was just thinking about someone I met."

"Oh," she replied, pursing her lips. "Well I don't think Obasi or any of his family is like anyone *I've* ever met. They remind me of earth-gnomes, only bigger and much more talkative and silly, and they have a peculiar accent, too." Adelaide laughed at herself. "Maybe they aren't much like earth-gnomes after all!" She smiled warmly at Nicolas. Suddenly, she cupped his face in her hands and looked him squarely in the eyes. "I know what you did for me, Nicolas Bennett," she whispered solemnly. "I don't know what made you do it, but it's the bravest thing anyone's ever done for me." She tilted his head forward and gave him a gentle kiss on his forehead. "Thank you," she said.

"You're—you're welcome," Nicolas stammered, feeling awkward and not very brave. "Ranulf and Benjamin were there, too. I just happened to hop up first, I think."

"No," she said, slowly shaking her head. "Ranulf told me what you did, and he said he's never seen anything like that, either." Adelaide looked at him inquisitively. "There's something special inside you, Nicolas. You're so quiet and thoughtful, but there's also this... this... *thing* inside you. You're more than what you appear to be." She hugged him, and without saying anything else, he hugged her back.

Later that afternoon, Nicolas found himself sitting comfortably in the crook of a dark oak tree's enormous exposed roots, which were upholstered in a layer of deep, cushiony moss. He was conversing with Obasi, who, like Nicolas, was also sitting in a natural seat of tree roots, wagging his legs over their thick limbs and lazily smoking a long clay pipe. Its smell of roasted hazelnuts and sugary peaches floated dreamily through the cool autumn air. Nicolas, for the first time in what seemed like a very long time, felt genuinely relaxed, at peace. He had this unwarranted good feeling that everything—even what was to come—would be okay.

I'm a wren, he thought boldly and smiled in spite of himself.

Obasi, as it turned out, was Baatunde's younger brother, although, by Nicolas' estimation, both of them were at least several hundred years old, which made it strange to think of Obasi as 'young' in any sense of the word.

Like his older brother, Obasi was bald, but instead of a single eyepiece, he wore the wiry silver spectacles Nicolas had earlier seen in his room. His nose was large and friendly-looking, and it, too, presided over a fantastic moustache. The ends of Obasi's moustache were actually braided together across his round but muscled stomach, and one fantastically engraved silver bell was tied to the end of the braid. It rang whenever Obasi walked about, bouncing against his firm, curved belly. Like his brother, Obasi was shirtless, and like his brother, Obasi had an intricate, colorful, compass-like tattoo across his belly, just above his thick leather belt. He sometimes wore the red-dyed goatskin cloak which Nicolas had seen hanging on a peg in the room—in fact, he had been wearing it when he'd encountered Nicolas and his friends the day before.

"Aye, ye were in a sad fog, laddie," Obasi was saying. "Ye were stumblin' along, yer face wet w'th tears an' yer feet 'eavy w'th grēēf. I dinnae think ye knew whār ye were goin'," he said compassionately.

"I—I thought Adelaide was dead," Nicolas said. He suddenly felt a sharp stab of the same sorrow he'd borne the day before, and his voice trembled slightly. "I don't really remember much, except feeling like I'd led her to her death."

At that moment, several of the Caledonii children—all with round noses, curly hair, and curious tattoos across their little round bellies—scampered by, shouting and waving their arms. They were chasing a large, greyish-green Common Emerald moth and prattling together in a language which sounded like old Gaelic to Nicolas. From where he sat, he could see Ranulf across a small grassy meadow, sitting cross-legged together with a few Caledonii adults, all much the same as Obasi, both men and women. Nicolas couldn't hear what the older boy was saying, but he seemed to be telling them about the bog worm. He pushed one of his hands up through the other, with which he had formed an imaginary hole. The Caledonii all leaned back, gasping and looking at each other with concerned amazement. Nicolas could also see Benjamin, squatting together with an especially old-looking Caledonii man, who sported an especially large nose and mustache ends which curled about his feet like two grey-haired sleeping kittens. They were both intently staring at a large black kettle, hung over an open fire and bubbling with what looked like chunks of potato, bay leaves, onions, and large brown mushrooms. Off to the side, on a rickety set of steps which led up to one of the tree cottages, sat Adelaide with Cornelia at her feet, speaking softly with one of the Caledonii women. The little woman, who had long grey hair and a wrinkly, squished face, was wrapped in a particularly dark red-dyed cloak with soft deerskin boots on her feet. She was touching Adelaide's forehead with one of her wrinkled thumbs, and the two of them seemed to be lost in a close and quiet conversation. The young Healer had her eyes closed as they spoke, and Nicolas wondered what they were discussing.

"Thar are so few of them," said Obasi quietly, waking Nicolas out of his musings. The little man was waving his pipe at the passel of passing Caledonii children. "I'm afred we are fadin'," he said reluctantly. "One ba one, goin' home ta the endless 'eavens, inta ta Great Forest whār our forefaders wait fer us." Obasi tapped the ash out of his pipe and refilled it carefully, gently pressing a wad of cut moist leaves inside its bowl. "All t'ings in time," he said, drawing a first full puff of fragrant smoke, "are meant ta travel, ta dance, in a *circle*. An' that," he said as he pointed a fat finger skyward, "is whār *all* circles begins an' ends." Obasi, lowering his finger, now pointed it at Adelaide. "An' dinnae worry abōōt yer Healer. She is slowly learnin', she has great magic inside o' her. She is a wandering *Bendith Duw*," he said approvingly.

Nicolas nodded slowly, and as he did so, Adelaide opened her sea-green eyes and caught sight of him looking at her. She waved.

"What yer doin'," Obasi said, "is also what *she's* meant ta do, too. Ye 'ave friends, Master Bennett," said the little man, motioning toward Ranulf and Benjamin, "an' friends dinnae walk *behind* ye, they walk *with* ye. Concentrate yer mind on what lies *ahead*. Dinnae fret abōōt who walks beside ye."

"And what lies ahead of me?" Nicolas quietly urged.

Obasi looked closely at him for several moments and puffed vigorously on his clay pipe. Finally, he arched an eyebrow and said grimly, "Shadows an' darkness, Master Bennett. After that, I cannae see. Thar is the light o' a sunrise, an' the dark o' a sunset."

"Will—will I live?" Nicolas asked hesitantly. Obasi said nothing. Instead, the little man looked off into the shadowed trees, and for several minutes they sat in silence, watching stiff brown oak leaves shiver in the autumn sun. "Remiel said you have something for me," Nicolas finally said.

Obasi pushed his thick lips out, took a deep breath through his nostrils, and smacked his lips together. "I dew, I dew," he said, remembering. He reached inside a small leather pouch which hung from his belt and pulled something out of it, waving his closed fist at Nicolas, who opened his palm. Obasi dropped a large, talc-like stone into it. The odd-looking stone was uneven, but its edges felt almost soft, as if it were made of hardened soap. It had smoky swirls of grey and white and was cool to the touch, but not cold.

Nicolas was baffled. "This is *it?*" he asked.

Obasi laughed. "It's yer answer, Master Bennett. It's what I 'ave to give ta ye."

"A stone?"

"Aye, a stone."

Nicolas looked at it closely. His first thought was how much Ranulf might like it, but he didn't see anything special about it. Secretly, he'd been expecting some kind of incredible weapon, or some enchanted potion, or, even better, a powerful sorcerer's wand which he could use to strike the Shadow Thief dead. But *this*. This just seemed like a stone.

"What am I supposed to do with a stone?"

Obasi looked at him, bemused. "Ta Clokkemaker dinnae tell ye?"

"No," Nicolas said emphatically. "He said you'd have something to give me. He had a plan—a dreadful plan—but I thought... I thought," Nicolas didn't know what else to say. As surely as he'd felt at peace before, as surely as he'd felt like everything might be okay, he now felt as appallingly certain it could only end in ruin. In death.

"*Giants*," said Obasi mysteriously, lowering his eyes and

lowering his voice, "fall victim ta small *stones.*"

"I don't understand," said Nicolas, feeling frustrated and confused—feeling lost and defenseless. "I need something to fight the *Shadow Thief*, not a giant."

Obasi looked slightly disappointed. He said, "I know, I *know*, Master Bennett. Ye face a dragon, an evil few can face an' fewer can dafēēt. An' *it* es yer 'giant,' an' *giants fall victim ta small stones.*" The little man looked carefully at Nicolas, as if Nicolas should now understand what he was saying. But Nicolas didn't, not really. Or maybe he didn't want to understand.

The little man leaned back and let out a big sigh. "This dragon desires *iron*, Master Bennett." Obasi slammed a ham-sized fist onto his leg and flared his large nostrils, "*So*, when da time comes, give 'im a *stone of star-iron!*"

Gradually, like a weak winter sun stubbornly pushing its way through cold, dense snow clouds, a thought abruptly occurred to Nicolas—an awful thought, but a practical thought. And like a tombstone settling into place, he realized what Obasi was saying, and it finally made what Remiel had told him make sense. He understood why Remiel's plan needed to be so dreadful—dreadful yet necessary. "So this," he said reluctantly, lifting up the soft stone into the yellowed forest light, "is what I'm supposed to use."

"Yes," Obasi replied solemnly, once again puffing the smell of roasted hazelnuts and sugary peaches into the chilly autumn air. "Yes, *that* is what yer supposed ta use."

Nicolas swallowed hard against the lump in his throat. He looked desperately at Ranulf son of Renfry, Benjamin the boy-thief, and Adelaide Ashdown, the wandering Healer, and quietly, he finally said, "Okay. I understand."

The memory of his grandfather's casket popped into his head. "I'll do it," he said.

And he meant it.

CHAPTER 25

✝HE ✝IMEKEEPER'S
FINGER

They do not happen often, but on occasion, there are those intensely personal, distressing moments when all goodbyes have been said, well-wishes have been wished, and blessings have been given, and all that remains is the painful moment when grasping hands part, hugs release their hold, and the sounds of words fade away. When what you hold dear, you let go of. You say farewell, and you take a first step away from everything that is safe, everything that is sheltered, everything that is trustworthy.

And through a small break in the Cornish hedge of stone, turf, moss, and "ironwood" Hornbeam trees of the Caledonoii's magical home deep in the Black Forest, Nicolas, for the first time in his twelve years, experienced this moment—a uniquely despairing sense of forever parting ways, from the Caledonii, and from Obasi.

From the boy Nicolas had always been to what he must now become.

Obasi, his family, and the Caledonii—the ancient Moss People of the Black Forest—had been remarkably kind to them all. Their isolated Haven—a place the Caledonii called their "*Mahali Salama*," their *Safe Place*—filled with laughter, good food, encouragement, and peaceful rest, had been exactly what Nicolas and his friends had needed. And like discovering an oasis among the dry dunes of a barren desert, making the decision to leave had been a very difficult one.

For several days, Adelaide, Benjamin, Ranulf, and Nicolas had reveled in the company of the Caledonii, nestled securely under thick bearskins in cozy tree cottages with bright red doors, playing day-long games of "Chords and Secrets" with curly-headed Caledonii children, and gobbling down roast joints of meat, shoulders of pork (with the pink skin scored, salted, and roasted *hot* so it turned into crispy crackling), and generous cuts of mutton, accompanied by apple sauce, mint sauce, and bread puddings, as well as roasted potatoes, seared parsnips, and other vegetables and herbs, laid by an ever-present large jug of warm gravy made from meat juices, spring water, salt, and rosemary. And in the late, cold autumnal evenings, as enormous Walnut Sphinx moths fluttered above them, they would gather around large bonfires of hickory, alder, and ash logs, listening to the Caledonii tell tales of long ago—of giants, sorcerers, Gammeldags (gypsies), Realm Knights, Wisps, and War Crows—as they chewed on bits of brittled bacon, caramelized with butter and sweet sorghum. For a while, Nicolas had even forgotten the miserable thoughts which afflicted his soul—the thoughts of where he must go, what he must do.

But now, the time had come.

Early one morning, Nicolas had awakened and quietly stepped outside into the chilled air, still wrapped snugly in his bearskin blanket. The dawn was a light grey along the rim of the sky, and the forest around him was silent. A single snowflake suddenly appeared in front of him, wavering and searching among the careless breezes to find its way to the ground below. It jogged left and right, and once, it even bobbed upward for a brief moment, but eventually, it fell. Persistent and silently resolute, the snow crystal was inevitably drawn downward, and with a final, imperceptible caress, it landed on Nicolas' bare toe.

He stared at it for several moments and felt something inside him also fall. "It's time," he whispered to the snowflake.

Nicolas' own path lay inevitably in the direction of the Shadow Thief, and no amount of delay would change that.

It was time.

"May all evil sleep! May all good awake!" shouted Obasi, waving both hands in the air as Nicolas and his three friends left later that day.

When Nicolas had told them it was time to go, they'd each nodded, said nothing, and quietly went to gather their few things. Cornelia had *baa'ed* mournfully at Adelaide, but was held in check with a braided grass rope by one of the Caldonii children—a round-faced girl with purple Fairy Slipper petals in her soft, curly brown hair. It had been grimly decided the faithful little goat and the pack pony were to be left behind. The danger which lay ahead was no place for miniature goats or pack ponies, but the decision had been a hard, hard one to make. The four friends would travel together without their animal companions.

Adelaide bravely did her best to hide her tears, but Benjamin, convinced he wouldn't see another genuine meal anytime soon, looked utterly distraught and kept saying maybe they ought to stay for another day or two. Ranulf, grim, white and not yet at his full strength, looking older than his few years, rested his hand on his smithy hammer and motioned toward Nicolas. "Lead on," he said gently, and the company of four stepped forward onto the path leading them out of the Black Forest and toward the Timekeeper's Finger.

It is not normal for a twelve-year-old to feel as if he is walking to the ends of the earth, but on that day—among the shadows of those dark oak trees, with the chill of an early winter's breeze chaffing his face—this, in fact, is what Nicolas felt in his heart of hearts. The end of the world loomed ahead. And little hope remained.

Pushing aside the coins and leaf in his pocket, Nicolas clutched the soft stone in his hand. "I'll do it," he steeled himself to whisper. "I can do it." And on he went. A wren. A king of birds. But also a young boy.

At the southern end of the High Stile Ridge, which is part of the Western Fells dividing the lonely valleys of Ennerdale Water in the Lake District of Cumbria and the Buttermere Lake in the northwest of the English Lake District, stands a place called the High Crag.

The High Crag's great scree slope of Gamlin End drops for over seven hundred feet and then rises again, another two thousand feet, up to the treeless bluff of Scarth Gap. A century ago, it's said that two men lived in a small hut and mined the plagioclase crystals of the High Crag. After some time, the men stopped visiting the local hostel, and an investigation was conducted to determine what had become of them. When one of the men's bodies was found with suspicious bruises around his neck, lying face-down in a dark tidal pool at Warnscale, it was determined one had murdered the other. Because of this, Nicolas' father, Peter Bennett, had always said the High Crag was a haunted place. A mournful, lost place. A place, his father had said, "that leaves the earth and touches the sky."

The Timekeeper's Finger was just such a place.

A few hours after leaving Obasi's home, Nicolas and his friends walked out of the last few dark oaks of the Black Forest and could now see the high spines of rocky hills and stony headlands which separated the aged forest from the High Desert of Shadows to the north.

"Is that it?" Benjamin whispered.

Nicolas gave a nod. "That's it."

Like the high fin of an immense sundial, the Timekeeper's Finger was a series of several dark bluffs, forming a jagged ridge which generally ran for about a mile from the southwest to northeast, throwing long shades of gloom out into the desert's vast wastelands. A few scrubs of ragged pine trees—fairly short with blue-green leaves and orange-red bark—dotted its lower slopes, and wild, thin grasses bravely climbed a thousand feet higher, but beyond that—where raw rock had pushed its way to the surface, swept cold and naked by countless storms, gales, and nature's furies—there was nothing but morose black stone and surly grey sky.

And it was here, deep within the iron-feldspar of the Timekeeper's Finger, that a prison had been burrowed twelve years before—a prison meant to lock away a dragon. An overlord dragon. *Árnyék Tolvaj*, the Shadow Thief.

"Somewhere up there," Nicolas pointed.

"We've got to climb those hills?" Adelaide asked nervously. Her voice shook, but it also could have been the wintry wind.

"Yes," he said.

"And then what?" asked Ranulf earnestly.

"Then," Nicolas said, taking a deep breath. "Then, we find the dragon."

The four of them—fastly-made new friends—stood there as sharp flurries of bitter wind flapped noisily among their weather cloaks. Try as he might, Nicolas was hollow inside. The secret he carried felt unbearably heavy.

"What did Remiel say?" Adelaide quietly asked as if she sensed his uneasiness.

Nicolas sighed, keeping his eyes on the high, barren escarpments. "Nothing much, except that he'd meet us there."

"Well *that's* something!" Benjamin said, all smiles. "I think that tall, dark fellow might have something 'unexpected' in store for that mean ol' dragon."

"Yes, yes, he might," replied Nicolas distantly. "Remiel said something of that sort."

"And Obasi," Ranulf ventured hopefully, "Obasi gave you what you need?"

"Yes, yes he did."

"Well then," said Ranulf, rubbing his hands together in committed anticipation, "then let's get as far as we can in this light, make camp, and in the morning, we'll put an *end* to this curse once and for all."

Adelaide and Benjamin eagerly agreed. Nicolas shrugged. At this point, he felt like any reason to interrupt their journey was a good excuse. So they picked up their pace, and within the next hour, before the sun had fully settled into its western grave, they'd found a purchase of some sheltered ground, sitting at the foot of the first scarp of the Timekeeper's Finger. It had a bit of a grassy swell, and green earth to protect them from the night's chilly breeze. Before long, they were boiling a small black pot full of carrots, green sprouts, and sugared ham, and were huddled around the fire in their bearskins like four small jamba-bears.

"What do you think it looks like?" Benjamin asked. The boy-thief was intently stirring the pot with a large, rough wooden spoon, causing the stew's fragrance to fill the air. Nicolas wasn't hungry, but the broth still smelled comforting. Soothing, and like home.

"What does *what* look like?" Ranulf asked.

"The Shadow Thief," said the smallish boy matter-of-factly.

Adelaide, who was leaning back against her furry bedroll, re-braiding her long locks of supple hair, said, "I've heard it looks like black granite, like scorched star iron, with ribs of stonework and eyes of blue flame."

"Straight Hammer says overlord dragons are dark as night and as large as storm clouds," said Ranulf as he threw another stick of hickory on the fire.

"What do you think, Nicolas?" Benjamin asked. He slurped a mouthful of the thick stew from his spoon and sat back on his heels.

"I don't know," Nicolas said weakly. "I guess it looks like... like a dragon."

Benjamin laughed and wagged his head. "I hope so!" he said, slurping another spoonful of broth. "I'd hate to journey all this way to kill a little Yellow Wagtail bird."

Nicolas couldn't help but grin. "You always make me smile, Benjamin." There was an unusual tenderness in his voice.

"Well then," said the boy-thief, with a look of mock seriousness, "I guess you'll have to keep me around."

Nicolas nodded, laughed, and pushed hard against the lump in his throat. He leaned his head back to stare at the first evening star flickering on the eastern horizon.

"What's troubling you?" asked Adelaide quietly.

"Nothing," Nicolas said. The eastern star's light flickered, then shone brightly, as the sun waved its last before disappearing entirely behind Telluric Grand's rose-colored horizon.

"Okay," she said generously, finishing her braid and knotting it with a short loop of blue ribbon. "We're here for you when you need us," the young girl said and pulled her bearskin up around her shoulders.

Nicolas nodded, and hoped that in the gathering twilight, she couldn't see the tears welling up in his eyes.

They spent that night eating stew, drinking muddled mead—a kind of honeyed, spiced wine—and laughing. Benjamin was in rare form, fully recovered from the knock he'd taken during their night in the Woodcutter's Forest, and he kept them in stitches, telling jokes and silly stories, until Adelaide pled for him to stop before she peed herself. Ranulf—with his hair still white as a cotton-puff—had said it was too late, he'd already wet his breeches. This brought even Benjamin to tears, and Nicolas, like the rest of them, had laughed until his stomach hurt and his eyes were blurred with tears.

From somewhere in his small pack and out of the folds of carefully wrapped cheesecloth, Benjamin produced a loaf of rich, fruity bread he'd made the day before with the old-looking Caledonii man, whose name, he told them, was Akachi. Together, he and the old man had cold-brewed orange tea, then used flour, mixed spices, brown eggs, and mixed fruit soaked in honey and ginger to make a thick batter, which they'd baked in a black, butter-smeared, covered kettle underneath a pile of glowing coals.

"And now," Benjamin proudly announced, while warming the glistening loaf on two sticks over the fire, "we can smother it in lemon marmalade and cinnamon honey!" Like a pleased parent, he'd cut each of them a thick slice of the dense bread, and with all the showmanship of a circus ringmaster, he then squeezed extravagant amounts of marmalade and honey all over the slices, until, it seemed, everything was sticky and sweet. And they ate every sticky crumb. They ate every crumb and licked every finger, until every last bit of bread, fruit, and honey was gone.

Then, with full stomachs, syrupy lips, and content smiles, the four friends had laid back in their warm bearskins, watching the constellations shift slowly across the clear night sky. Nicolas felt at home—at home in a way you can only know among friends, true friends, camped out under a limitless night sky near the sputter and snap of a comfy fire. He felt truly at home, but finally drifting off to sleep, he also felt troubled, anxious, and unsure.

A few days before, while gathered around the crackling blaze of an evening bonfire, Nicolas had listened to Ayomide, Obasi's chubby wife, tell the unusual story of the Fortingale yew tree. Holding a clay mug of tea, steaming with the syrupy scent of sea buckthorn, Nicolas had huddled together with other Caledonii children and he'd listened as the age-worn little woman had spun a tale that tremored in his bones and echoed of one his father had once told him.

"'Tis an ancient tree," Ayomide had said, spreading her short, plump arms in the air, "always green, æven in the winter, with Snow Buntin' birds chatterin' among its lush boughs. It grew high on ta Timekeeper's Finger," she'd said, "alōne but brave, since the beginnin' of ta world. Older than Dellin', ta god of ta dawn, ta Fortin'gale tree pushed it roots inta' the 'arth, makin' a place fer itself, an' waitin' ta see what Time would bring. It waited an' waited, as ta 'arth formed itself beneath its shade. As mountains, an' 'ills, an' crops sprang up, strong an' new. As giants chipped at ta rock, an' as ta foamy sea bloomed waves an' storms. Ta Fortin'gale tree 'eld fast," she'd whispered, "keepin' its root-feet planted in ta stone o' ta Timekeeper's Finger. An' one quiet, snowy day, it looked down, an' dar, amōōng its gnarled roots slept a wee chick. 'Twas a baby bird, all fluffy an' brown. 'Twas a wren, ta simplest o' birds."

"Was it mighty?" the Caledonii children had eagerly asked. "Was it powerful?"

"Nay," she'd said, shaking her round finger, "ta little bird 'twas not mighty, nor powerful. 'Twas simple, plain, an' alone. But it spread its little wings, an' in a gust o' wind, it took flight."

The Caledonii children gasped.

"It took flight, an' flapped an' fluttered as best it could," she'd said, waving her hefty arms in the dark night air. "An', usin' a gust o' wind, it sailed across the sky. An' when it 'ad flapped an' fluttered as best it could, it found an *eagle*."

The Caledonii children's eyes had widened and their little mouths dropped open.

"An' ta little bird tucked itself 'neath ta eagle's wings. Higher an' higher it flew!" she'd gestured. "Higher an' higher, an' when ta eagle could go no higher, ta little brown bird leapt from its wings an' rose up ta meet ta sun!"

Ayomide then bent forward, spreading her arms over the children, and Nicolas, who'd been innocently swept up in the story of the tree and bird, leaned toward her. She caught his eye and looked straight at him. "An' ta little bird, born under ta Fortin' gale tree, flew higher than all ta other birds," she whispered. "An' became a *king*."

<hr />

When Nicolas opened his eyes the next morning, he wasn't sure if he'd dreamed about Ayomide's story, or if, in the haze of waking up, he was simply remembering her having told it. He fumbled under the weight of his bearskin and shoved a hand inside his pocket. He felt around, ignoring the crown coin, the coppery leaf, and the smooth grey stone, until he clenched the smaller farthing coin.

Today is the day, he thought uneasily. He pressed the coin hard into his palm. *How am I going to do this?* he wondered. He wanted to stay buried in his bearskin. He wanted to go back to sleep. He wanted to… to…

And just when doubts and fears and disaster were about to drown his mind and paralyze his legs, a fantastic, strange, and sudden burst of honest conviction exploded inside him. It seemed to come out of nowhere, but Nicolas Bennett—the twelve-year-old boy from Plumpton Head, England—now knew *exactly* what he truly wanted. He knew exactly what he wanted and exactly what he needed to do, what he *must* do.

Hopping up, he threw off his bearskin, quickly shoved his feet into his boots, buckled his weather cloak, and in the bracing, frosty air of early morning, Nicolas the Wren began stalking up the long, slow rise of the Timekeeper's Finger. *A place with dragons.*

CHAPTER 26

A Wicket Keeper

There was a single path up the Timekeeper's Finger, long unused and wild.

In certain places, the footing was gravelly, while in others it was slick and moist, spongy with dark earth and loamy moss. At first, the slope of the Finger was fairly shallow, and Nicolas took long strides, wanting to move away from the shelter of their camp as quickly as he could, before anyone discovered he was gone. He wanted to be far away before he could rethink his decision, before the surge of strength he'd felt in his heart receded. Before the anxiousness, and the burden he'd been silently bearing, could replace it like weighty stones strapped around his ankles.

If he was, after all, a *Wren*, then he wanted to do this on his own.

He wanted to leave his friends alone.

He wanted to leave them safe, wrapped warmly in their bearskins by the grey coals of last night's fire, probably wondering where he'd gone, but *safe*. Safe from *it*.

Safe from *him*.

Nicolas hurried up the slope. When the ground levelled for a stretch, he jogged along, and when it steepened again, he scrambled, took longer strides, and did his best to keep moving at a quick pace. He was breathing heavily and his legs began feeling rubbery. The cold air thinned out a bit—raking the inside of his lungs with each sharp breath—and before long, he was lightly sweating. After cresting a slight rise, Nicolas paused for a moment, unbuckled his weather cloak in spite of the early

301

morning's dampness, and quickly made it into a roll he could sling over his shoulder. This exposed his mail shirt, *but who cares*, he thought. *It's not as if a mail shirt will make any difference to a dragon anyway.*

The sky was a mottled grey and the clouds were a deep, deep blue. Short, hardy grass rippled on the empty slopes of the Timekeeper's Finger, with an occasional sprinkle of purple and yellow flowers clumped together. Nicolas didn't see any wildlife, but couldn't help but think, *how beautiful!* The magnificent view thrilled him. With the indifferent abandon of a man climbing to the gallows—to no more of a future than a hangman's noose—nothing else seemed to matter to Nicolas in those moments he spent scrambling up the Timekeeper's Finger. No other thoughts or memories or feelings cluttered his mind, just the path in front of him and the majesty of the view displayed around him. It was if he was dashing to the top of the world; to a place where the bruised sky came to rest on a green-stubbled and stone-capped earth—where the world finally stopped and the endless heavens were within reach.

Nicolas' heart beat in his ears. Other than noisy gusts of chilled wind, the only sound was his labored breathing. He huffed and puffed, and climbed and climbed, until his Malham boots carried him beyond the dark earth and wild grass, and began scraping against grainy, weathered rock. Any semblance of a path was behind him now, and there was little underfoot to tell him where to go. But stony heights lay in front of him, jumbled with boulders and pebbles and shingles of flinty stone, so he kept going higher, and as he'd round the base of a huge, jagged rock, or mount the rise of another slope, another bluff of stone would always appear ahead of him, beckoning him on.

So on he went.

Close to an hour after he'd leapt out of his bearskin and begun his rush up the Timekeeper's Finger, Nicolas had finally reached the height of its long spine. He was out of breath, his legs burned, and he felt light-headed. For the moment, he hadn't any strength left, so he dropped to his knees, sat back on his heels, lifted his chin in the air, and let his mouth hang open, gulping in the thin mountainous air. The clouds, cold and deep blue, against a colder and blue-grey sky, looked closer than before. He didn't know if a storm was moving closer, or if he'd moved closer to the clouds, or both.

Nicolas' last bit of energy, his last sprint, had brought him over a stony bank and through a messy string of large, blackened rubble. And now, like a hidden rooftop garden, a small field of stout grass spread out before him, sheltered by a large but shallow depression worn into the rocky terrain. On the far side of this grassy meadow—a mere hundred yards away—the gritty rock of the Timekeeper's Finger again rose out of the bluish-green grass, like an immense, dead grey tooth, and sloped upward toward a massive stack of several sharp-looking and thick plates of dark stone, which violently jutted out of the earth at steep, slanting angles. And there, bored into the base of these gigantic slabs of angular stone, was a large but crude-looking hole.

It was a cave.

The mouth and rim of the cave appeared to be chalked with fire-blackened charcoal, and this collar of soot made the mouth and the inside of the cave even blacker still. Nicolas strained to see inside of it but he couldn't.

A place with dragons, he thought despairingly. *A kingdom without a king. A place of coppery leaves, grim tales, menacing crows, and—and... dragons.* His thoughts felt as weak as his legs. He wished he was home again. He wished he was in his attic bedroom, beneath the weight of his old tattered quilt, with Thomas the cat curled at the foot of his bed, and his mum singing an airy, Irish melody in the kitchen below. He wished he hadn't seen the footpath. He wished… he wished. He wished he could've spoken with his grandfather.

Yet here he was. And *there*—there across the windswept pasture of swaying grass—hid a dragon. The Shadow Thief.

Where is Remiel? Nicolas desperately thought. *He said he would be here. He said—he said…* Nicolas thought back to the evening he'd spent on the smooth sitting-stones, the peat fire, the tall, craggy rock, and the hissed words of the Wisp, the Clokkemaker, listening to the Wisp's dreadful plan. "I'll come," Remiel had whispered darkly, his pointed teeth clicking behind his thin lips. "I'll stand with you. But when the time comes, Nicolas, when the time comes, you must—you *must*—betray me. The dragon will never see it coming." Remiel had then stood, stretching his arms up to the star-littered heavens. "The dragon will think it has won. It will never suspect that you—so small and insignificant—are its doom. And then—at *that* moment—feed it the false iron."

Feed it the false iron, Nicolas thought. He rubbed his thighs vigorously, trying to ease the ache and tiredness in his muscles. *Feed it the false iron*, he thought again, *How? Where is Remiel? Where is the Shadow Thief?* He sat there silently, vaguely wringing his hands together.

And it was then that Nicolas finally took note of the cow. Or perhaps it was a bull.

There, standing in the middle of the high meadow was an enormous, shaggy bull. It was larger than any bull Nicolas had seen, at least five feet high at its wide shoulders—a brindled, dun color with long, ropy-looking hair, and horns which curved up and forward—slowly chewing thick clumps of the meadow's rangy grass. The cold wind tousled its mangy coat, but other than this, the great ragged beast looked peaceful, undisturbed and content. Nicolas listened, bemused as it cropped the grass with hard tugs and pulls of its teeth, and he watched as the bull lazily chewed each mouthful as if it was contemplating something enjoyable. Nicolas wondered if the bull had somehow become separated from a herd on the lower slopes and had wandered up here, looking for food. Perhaps, but the bull really did seem unconcerned. In fact, it seemed quite content, unthreatened, and gladly absorbed in the untouched bit of grassy food at its feet. It hadn't even seemed to notice Nicolas, kneeling exhaustedly at the edge of the empty meadow, and for a moment, this all made Nicolas think of the gentle sheep pasture, stretching out from the Bennetts' farm cottage to the woods beyond his home. The thought relaxed him. His breathing seemed to calm and the ache in his legs began to subside. Perhaps the dragon was gone. Perhaps the burden in his heart was needless. Perhaps.

And this is when he finally saw *it*.

On the far side of the quiet meadow, Nicolas suddenly saw *it*.

Like an enormous chameleon, grey with ash—a pebbled hide, rippling with sinewy muscle, jointed ligaments, and cruel, almost skinless-looking ropes of muscle—Nicolas saw the *dragon*. In the cunning camouflage of shingly wings and flinty claws and teeth, it rose up from the gravelly slope where it had laid silently like a slab of lifeless rock, as if it was part of the stones of the Timekeeper's Finger—cold, hard, unyielding. Its massive jaws came open, with thick lumps of snarled muscle pulling back from rows of black teeth, and its eyes—now open and glowering—were like splinters of woody embers buried beneath the folded hoods of its forehead's heavy flesh. The dragon had two contorted forelegs, tipped with claws like broken glass, which it used like meat-hooks fastened in carpet, pulling along its serpentine body, which slipped silently down the grey slope and into the innocently swaying grass.

Nicolas stopped breathing.

His heart flushed his muscles with oxygen and blood, and all his senses, readied with a primeval reaction of a hormonal cascade, were tensed to respond—to run, to flee back down the Timekeeper's Finger. To save himself from the slithering, creeping, barbaric predator slinking its monstrous way through the waving grass.

But the giant, shaggy bull—naively unaware of the tragedy moving toward it, calmly chewing mouthfuls of pleasant grass—paid the butcher's bill. With the speed and ruthlessness of a viper, the dragon ambushed the quiet bull. It suddenly reared up and closed its hideous, knife-like teeth over the beast's large back and instantly drew them together, slicing effortlessly through hide, muscle, and bone. Geysers of bright blood spurted high in the air as the bull frantically mewed in a pathetic frenzy of terror and pain. The dragon seemed angry, needlessly ferocious. Like a wild dog, it violently shook its beefy prey back and forth, loudly cracking vertebrae and bone, and pulverizing cartilage like bits of dry rice. Flaring its thick wings above its ugly head with a quick gust of chilled wind, the dragon abruptly snapped itself forward. It was so forceful, it literally carved the bull into two grizzled pieces of mangled meat, broken bone, and hairy hide.

Nicolas, stunned by the savagery and swiftness of the attack, remained motionless, stiffly frozen on his heels. He dared not breathe. He dared not move.

Where is Remiel?! Nicolas' mind screamed in panic. He *knew*—he knew as surely as a condemned man trembles at the last seconds of light he'll ever see—that he wouldn't survive.

A Place with Dragons

He knew he was dead. The dragon would finish the bull and then see him. It would slither across the grass, and alone, atop a barren backbone of grey rock in a distant land of dark forests and ancient castles, Nicolas Bennett would die, consumed in an unspeakable butchery of teeth and hunger and evil.

One of the cold blue clouds, hanging low overhead, suddenly burst in a fantastic fury of battle-thunder and blinding light. And at this moment, when the executioner's axe felt so close, when the hangman's noose was cinched tight, is when Remiel appeared. An ancient and terrible Wisp lightening down from the endless heavens.

When the cloud burst in noise and light, Nicolas thought the great thick slabs of stone across the meadow were breaking apart. Involuntarily, he clapped his hands to his ears to keep out the deafening racket, even as the dark cloud, which was not really a cloud at all, gathered itself into a dense shadow and descended on the earth. Almost immediately as it did so, acrid billows of burned grass curled out from underneath the dragon's claws and the slaughtered remains of the bull. In a blur of thought, Nicolas assumed a bolt of lightning had struck the ground—that a storm had come—and indeed, a storm *had* come.

Here, it is worth noting that there are very few records of a Wisp unleashing the full breadth of its powers. Such moments are catastrophic, utterly terrifying, and most often, shockingly destructive. It is as if the stars have turned their backs on the earth, and the sun has refused to rise in the east. A furious Wisp in its full glory, shedding the stature and cloak of a human-like appearance, is a tragic thing to behold. In fact, after the Great War of Giants, Wisps, and Men, traveling bards and songsmiths had little evidence, and even fewer firsthand accounts, of what a Wisp's unleashed fury looked or sounded like. Descriptions

307

of such events were widely unpopular in the First Kingdom, as if any retelling might invite the disintegration of the endless heavens and the Great Storm which prophets of old foretold would signal the end of the time and of Telluric Grand. People would rather hear tales of brave Talön Knights, ferocious fenris wolves, invading War Crows, and evil giants, than listen to a wordsmith try to recount the awe and dread of an enraged and unfettered Wisp. This, in fact, was the kind of unreasoning terror most good folk associated with a *Shedu*, a storm demon—a Wisp, once fallen into disgrace, existing in a nightmare of evil vengeance and retaliation.

Nicolas, alone in living memory, was, perhaps, the only person who experienced a sense of genuine relief, even if still mixed with terror, at the sight of a Wisp unveiled—unbound—unrestrained.

Remiel had come. And he was *angry*.

He lit upon the horrid dragon the way a stalking hawk lights upon a cowering field mouse. There was an awful, deafening impact, followed by dragon screams, and rips and gashes and ruptures, and claws and teeth, and darkness and ice-cold shock waves of compressed air, booming across the gentle meadow and rippling across the grim stone of the Timekeeper's Finger. The dragon writhed and twisted, roaring and snarling in rage and fear as the Wisp began peeling off its rough skin and tearing the dragon's muscles from its black bones. The dragon tried to bite. It tried to slash. But the Wisp brutally ripped its two forelegs from their sockets, and tore the dragon's powerful jaws apart at their hinges. In a tortured, thrashing agony of death, the dragon's thick wings, each tipped with a long, sharp talon, lashed out at the Wisp, trying to find some weakness, something to hurt and injure. But they found none. Instead, with merciless judgment, Remiel's long fingers—now like thick oak roots—curled around the base of each wing and wrenched them out of the dragon's shoulders.

The horribly dismembered monster fell dead.

The once-again quiet meadow was a great pool of dark blood. The remnants of the bull were now covered by the pieces of its butcher. And Remiel, still clutching the wings by their broken joints, stood like a giant, frightening statue over the mauled chunks of the dragon's deformed corpse, uttering ancient, foul curses, still seething with unbridled battle-fury and righteous rage.

———◆———

A smallish hand suddenly landed on Nicolas' shoulder, nearly giving him a heart attack.

"Nicolas!" Benjamin gasped. Close behind him came Ranulf and Adelaide. Slung over Benjamin's back was the chipped hatchet he'd received when they were in Straight Hammer's shop. Ranulf held his smithy hammer in his hand, and Adelaide was holding her hair dagger. They were all out of breath, and the smallish boy-thief quickly dropped both hands to his knees and bent over, panting heavily. "We thought—we thought we lost you," he wheezed in between big gulps of air. "We thought you'd left us for good."

"What's the matter with you, Nicolas?" Adelaide asked. Her voice was shaking and her hands trembled. "Why did you leave without waking us? Why'd you leave without saying anything?" The reddened rims of her eyes shimmered with unfallen tears. Ranulf just stood there, looking closely at Nicolas, his strong chest heaving in and out.

"I—I wasn't sure *what* to say," Nicolas replied quietly. He felt completely spent—tired, but desperately thankful to see his three friends. Slowly, easing his weak legs underneath him, he stood up and gave each of them a tight hug. "I'm so glad to see you," he whispered. And he was glad. It was over. Somehow Remiel had come at the right time. The Shadow Thief was dead. Nicolas hadn't had to… to… He didn't want to think about it. He didn't want to think about any of it anymore, not for a long while. He gave a quick laugh. "Let's go home," he said, grinning at Adelaide. "Let's go home. It's done. Remiel killed it."

"Nicolas."

The voice was gentle. It reminded Nicolas of the first time Remiel had spoken to him, how the Wisp's voice had rolled out from within its hood as if it were an echo coming from inside a deep, small cave.

Nicolas turned and looked back into the meadow. Remiel was still standing among the carnage. He still held the dragon's wings in his hands, but now his face was calm and translucent white. He didn't seem as big as he'd been moments before, but he was still very tall, straight, and—and there was something else, too. Nicolas tilted his head. Remiel almost looked sad.

Over Remiel's shoulder, beyond the meadow, up the slope of coarse rock and beneath the massive stack of angled, dark stone, Nicolas could see the cave. He could see its soot-blackened entrance and its coal-black mouth. And within that hellishly dark maw, Nicolas could now see something which made everything inside him turn cold and empty and hopeless. He could see the slivered violet-green glow of two eyes.

"Nicolas," the Wisp said again, dropping one of the withered wings onto the blood-soaked ground. "*This* was only a wicket-keeper dragon. A brutish dog protecting its ward." The Clokkemaker lowered his great head. A cold flurry of wind moved across the long folds of his cloak. "The time has come," he said, almost too softly to hear. "*Árnyék Tolvaj—the Shadow Thief—awaits.*"

CHAPTER 27

ΠICOLAS THE BETRAYER

In a small bookcase in a corner of Nicolas' attic bedroom, among a dozen or so tattered books which Nicolas always pretended were the equivalent of his father's downstairs study, rests a slim hardback with a dark blue spine and a cover picture of a ghostly white man atop a horse with a young girl in a red raincoat slumped in front of him. Its title is simply, "Storm," and when he was younger, Nicolas loved to say the author's last name, "Crossley-Holland."

On a late Sunday afternoon, hardly a year before, Nicolas' father, Mr. Bennett, had been sitting in his study, reading a wrinkled copy of The Daily Telegraph, while Nicolas was spread out on the floor, thumbing through a comic book. "Right-o!" Mr. Bennett suddenly exclaimed, loudly thumping the newspaper with his finger. "That chap, Crossley-Holland, has it square to rights!"

"What?" asked Nicolas, startled by his father's sudden outburst, but interested because he instantly recognized the name.

Mr. Bennett peered over the lip of the newspaper at his son. "Some writer named Crossley-Holland says *you*, and all the rest of England's schoolchildren, ought to be taught Greek mythology, and I most certainly agree."

"Why?" Nicolas asked, now propping himself up on an elbow.

"Because," Mr. Bennett said in a tone he always used when he considered the matter already settled, "Greek mythology teaches you 'what it is to be civilised humans.'"

"Oh," said Nicolas, no longer very interested. Shrugging his shoulders, he again picked up his comic book.

It wouldn't be for quite some time before Nicolas would read about things such as Mount Olympus, nymphs, dryads, satyrs, and the dark agony of the Greek underworld, ruled by a god named Hades. But when he finally did read about them, icy shivers would run up his spine, and Nicolas would wonder if anyone else noticed the strain of guilt haunting his face. Nicolas, in a very personal and painful way, would understand the meaning of the five rivers encircling the hellish agony of the Greek underworld. He would understand why, in a well-known, medieval poem, the River Kokytos, the "River of Wailing," was described as a frozen lake reserved for *traitors*. Where three of the most contemptible sinners in all history—three men who'd betrayed a person they were supposed to love—spent eternity being gnawed and chewed to death.

Nicolas understood this because *he* knew what it was like—that hollow, sickening feeling inside. He knew what it was like to hurt someone who was good. To turn his back on someone who had protected him, who'd trusted him. To sacrifice someone else, while he still lived.

Nicolas understood this because he had done those things. Nicolas had been a betrayer.

With his head still bowed, Remiel slowly turned his back to Nicolas and faced the cave beneath the great stones of slanted rock. Nicolas watched his wide shoulders rise and fall as if the Wisp was taking deep breaths.

A dreadful voice roared out from the cave's darkness. "*Watcher!*" it thundered, sounding like heavy stone scraping across stone.

Remiel, with his head still bowed, let go of the wicket-keeper dragon's other wing, and slowly raised his arms until they were spread out, the sleeves of his cloak snapping in the cold wind like a pair of great wings. Nicolas waited for the Wisp's fury—the violent rage he'd seen tear apart the wicket-keeper—to manifest itself, to swell into a noble wrath, and to crash head-long into the center of the blackened cave, forever silencing the dreadful thundering voice.

But nothing happened.

Remiel just stood there, arms held out, head bowed, and silent. Nicolas felt sick inside. He'd hoped, he'd ached, he'd *prayed* for this moment to not come. After the death of the wicket-keeper, he'd been *sure* there would be another way, another choice. But now—*now* he felt it; he *saw* it slipping away. He felt sick.

"*Watcher!*" Again came the hoarse, other-worldly accusation, and the sliver of violet-green eyes grew larger, lurching wildly toward the cave's black mouth. Nicolas, having forgotten about the three friends standing by his side, now watched in dreaded fascination as *Árnyék Tolvaj*—the fourth generation of overlord dragons, a demon from the endless heavens—crawled out of its prison, rising from its once-intended tomb.

The great dragon's jawbones emerged first into the grey light. They were like a crow's beak, curved and pointed at their tip, with enormous teeth rising straight out of the jaw bones. And, to Nicolas' everlasting horror, its incredible jaws were like a crow's beak in a more bizarre way—there wasn't any *skin* on them. In fact, as the immense dragon come out of the blackened hole, Nicolas realized it had very little, if any, skin on its entire body. The Shadow Thief was made of hard, cruel-looking, and razor-sharp bones—or some kind of terrible, counterfeit stone—and grainy ropes of muscle, tendons, and ligaments. Its eyes burned out of lidless carved sockets. Its legs and enormous claws flexed inside powerful joints. Even its wings—incredibly vast and thin, and sharp on all sides—appeared to somehow be shaped from a devilish mixture of

strained black muscle and polished flecks of rock. As the dragon moved, its body screeched and shrieked, like a thousand
blades striking together against thousands of shards of flint. Its
spine, a deadly row of glass-rock daggers each as tall as Nicolas,
piercing through ligament webs, arched and bent together in
sprays of dull sparks. The overlord dragon was elemental iron,
and Nicolas could see a hellish glow of blue flame burning and
flaring between visible gaps in its enormous rib bones.

Remiel, unmoved by the horror surging out of the cave, remained where he was in the middle of the lonely meadow. The
hem of his cloak was now discolored, soaked in the dark blood
of both the wicket-keeper and the bull. The grey light of the winter sky shone dully on his bowed head. And then, as if he were
standing peacefully next to Nicolas, Remiel whispered, "*Now!*"

Nicolas, sick but reaching for strength from a place deep inside his soul—a place which he'd never known, which he'd never
used before—abruptly ran forward. He felt his boots thud into
the grass and pound on the thin soil underneath. He heard the
winter wind whistling mournfully in his ears, and he *ran*. He ran
like he was being chased by Mr. Wolf. He ran like he did the day
the ogre took Adelaide. He ran like his life hung in the balance.

And it did.

Within moments, Nicolas had reached the motionless Wisp,
the soles of his boots slipping and wheeling about in the miry
sludge of slaughtered meat, torn flesh, and blood-jellied grass.
His small dagger, quickly ripped from the leather cord hanging around his neck, was gripped in his right hand, and—and
with a loud cry of pain and anger and fear, Nicolas *stabbed* it
as hard as he could through the Wisp's cloak and deep into his
upright back. Nicolas felt Remiel flinch violently and grunt as
the narrow blade sank inside his body, glancing off rib bone
and driving as deeply as Nicolas could force it.

Remiel, still standing but now taut with the suffering of white-hot pain, slightly turned his bowed head toward Nicolas. "Finish it," he said gently. So Nicolas stabbed him again. And again.

The ancient Wisp, with his long cloak now drenched in his own blood, finally sank to his knees. He gasped and put his arms out in front of him as he fell forward. Nicolas stood over him, his knife glistening with dark murder, and he choked back a sob and quietly—so softly even the wind at his lips couldn't hear it—Nicolas said, "*I'm sorry.*" Through sheer will, Nicolas kept the tears that filled his eyes from falling down his face, and without another word, he watched Remiel collapse into the blood-filled grass. For a brief second, the Wisp's skin glowed a soft yellow, then gradually darkened into a lifeless, pale grey. He stopped breathing.

The Clokkemaker was dead.

Doing his utmost to compose himself, Nicolas lifted the knife over his head. "Come look!" he screamed miserably into the cold wind. "The filthy Watcher is *dead!*" Faintly, from far away, Nicolas could hear Adelaide's cries of fear and grief.

The Shadow Thief—only a moment before, having been an oncoming force of revenge, punishment, and furious death—came to an abrupt halt. The great dragon, suspicious and dark-minded, crouched, unfurling its enormous wings, expecting some trick of treachery and deceit.

"Come *look!*" Nicolas shouted again and pointed down at the Wisp's silent shape. He felt dizzy, and his head felt light, almost unattached to his body. Nicolas the Wren stared blankly at the dragon, into the face of timeless Death, and no longer cared. In fact, his thoughts drifted away from the torment wracking his chest and went back to the Saturday morning when he saw the crow. He remembered throwing back his quilt, walking to his frosted bedroom window, and coming face to face with the shadowy bird. He thought of it striking the icy glass, and he thought of the coppery leaf it left behind. And, in that small moment, he knew—he *knew*—he had truly become a *Wren*. The king of birds.

The colossal dragon of star-iron and hellish blue flame poked its sharp head forward. Its hollow nostrils snorted and drew in a deep breath, sparking the glowing flame in its iron belly. It smelled the pleasant smell of death. It smelled cold blood and useless tissue. The Wisp was dead. And the small, strange boy had killed it.

The sound of stone grated across stone, and the winged demon said, "Who *are* you?"

"I'm the Wren," said Nicolas, as steadily as if he was ordering a meal at the Four and Twenty eatery at 42 King Street.

"The *Wren?*" repeated the Shadow Thief suspiciously.

"Yes," Nicolas said, "and I've come to make a *deal*."

The Shadow Thief lifted its great iron head. It looked past Nicolas, coldly staring at his friends, huddled together, horror-struck and afraid. The dragon disgorged a thunderous clout of white hot flame from its throat and spewed it into the grey air, screeching like a lamb being butchered.

Nicolas stood there. He still gripped the wet knife in his hand, but it trembled, yet his face remained the same, empty and emotionless. "I've come to show you a *door!*" he shouted. And the world around him instantly fell quiet.

The Shadow Thief lowered its skinless face, its violet-green eyes flickering like the jets of an old gas heater. "What door?" it demanded.

"An *iron* door," Nicolas said. He took a deep breath and dug into the center of his soul. "I care *nothing* for this world; I care nothing for my own world, either. The ancients prophesied your doom, but I want your *power!* I am not here to destroy you. I'm here to make a deal."

The dragon, trying to entice Nicolas into a trap, seductively replied, "And your friends? Those sniveling, frightened *things* over there?"

"Eat them!" shouted Nicolas belligerently. "They're stupid *fools*. Fools and food," he exclaimed, tossing his head arrogantly. "Eat them. They mean nothing to me. Test my truthfulness."

The dragon looked from Nicolas to Adelaide, Ranulf, and Benjamin. The smallish boy-thief was weeping and Adelaide was holding him close, sobbing with him. Ranulf, ever the protector but as pale as a ghost, held out his arm as if he could somehow ward off the dragon's dark teeth.

"Iron," the Shadow Thief said sternly with a starving look in its cold eyes. "I want *iron* as proof. Then I'll eat your pitiful friends, little one."

Nicolas slowly nodded, and dropping the knife, dug desperately into his pocket. He fumbled past the coins and past his grandmother's thimble. His fingers found the soft stone Obasi had given to him, and just as Remiel previously told him he would, he also felt the chalky ashes of the coppery leaf. Still staring into the dragon's burning eyes, Nicolas withdrew his hand and held out the soap-like stone. It felt light in his hand, and was now colored black by the coppery leaf's ashes. "Here," he said, lifting it up. "A token of what is to come. My world has more iron than even you could consume in *two* lifetimes."

The Shadow Thief lowered its mammoth head and glared at the little black rock. "Star iron?" it asked greedily.

"*Star* iron," Nicolas replied proudly, and suddenly, as hard as he could, he hurled the stone straight at the dragon's black-boned jaws.

Jerking in reaction, the Shadow Thief hungrily snapped at the flying stone, crashing its teeth together with an ear-splitting shudder of bone cracking against bone. Immediately, it swallowed, and dark blue flames spouted from its thick ribs in explosions of appetite and desire.

The cold wind picked up and threw great waves of chilled air across the soiled meadow.

"How does it taste?!" screamed Nicolas in an uncontrolled burst of anger and frustration. "How does *death* taste?!"

The dragon, unfamiliar with the feeling of confusion, paused. Suddenly, one of its black ribs cracked loudly. One of its giant legs tremored, stiffened like a corpse, and in a violent rupture of splintered stone, burst away from its enormous body.

"*Betrayer!*" the demon roared in instant rage and anguish. With a fearsome beat of its flinty skeletal wings, the Shadow Thief reared back convulsively as the poisonous soap-stone began consuming its guts. The dragon inhaled so hard, Nicolas rocked forward in the violent vacuum of air and fought to keep his balance. Now screaming and writhing, the dragon dug its remaining claws into soil and rock, wildly grasping for control of its mortally diseased body. It thrashed and stabbed and beat its hard bones against the earth, biting and tearing at the air and ground in a blind, maddened frenzy. And suddenly, as if the Shadow Thief had gained a split second of terrible, helpless clarity, it stretched out its long, spiny neck and glared malevolently down at Nicolas, its violet-green eyes flashing bright red embers of molten fire. "*My doom*," it whispered, like the faint scratching of stone on stone, and in thunderous waves of sun-burst explosions, its stony body shattered into millions of pieces, then collapsed back together as if they were all sucked at once back inside the dark cave.

The meadow fell silent.

Soundlessly, the deep blue clouds moved overhead. A light rain began to fall.

Nicolas the Wren—Nicolas the Dragon Nightfall—dropped

heavily to his knees. With a shaking hand, he reached out and weakly clutched a fistful of Remiel's cold, wet cloak. He wept. He wept while the early winter's rain kept falling.

CHAPTER 28

Uncertain Promises

The way back down the Timekeeper's Finger was cold and wet, and for Nicolas, it felt numbing and lonely. Ranulf led the way, keeping his thoughts to himself. Adelaide wrapped a steadying arm around Nicolas' waist and walked with him, sometimes resting her head on his shoulder but staying quiet, while Benjamin came along behind them several strides back.

As Nicolas had kneeled next to Remiel, he'd wept all the tears that would come, and he now felt exhausted as they made their way back to their small campsite. His eyes were tired and bleary, his muscles felt weak, and his boots were too heavy to keep lifting for much longer. Adelaide said nothing, and occasionally, he could hear a sniffle coming from Benjamin trudging along behind them. His three friends still surrounded him, but Nicolas could sense their doubts, their mistrust, and their worry.

He'd turned his back on them. Offered them as unsuspecting victims. *Fools and food*, he'd said to the dragon. *They mean nothing*, he'd said. When, in truth, they meant *everything*.

Before racing after Nicolas earlier that day, Ranulf had the foresight to quickly roll up each of their bedrolls and toss them under a cape of oiled sheepskin. The rolls were still dry, and Adelaide put Nicolas' bearskin around his shoulders and motioned for him to remove his boots and pants. She gathered them up, and without a word, walked off to a nearby exposed boulder where a rivulet of rain water ran down a crack in the coarse rock face, providing a quick way to wash the blood from his clothes.

Ranulf busied himself with building another fire, and in spite of the wet weather, he soon had brightly crackling flames flickering up between stout sticks of Hornbeam wood. Benjamin, with an uncharacteristic lack of enthusiasm, rustled together a handful of chopped turnips, an onion, some thyme, and a few dried meaty mutton bones to put into a pot and hang over the fire on a black hook he'd jammed into the ground. For his own part, Nicolas just stood there watching his friends, and anxiously—desperately—wanting to find the right words to say—a way to explain what he'd done, what *had* to have been done.

"Pass me that, would you?" Ranulf asked, pointing to a larger piece of wooden deadfall lying in the grass behind Nicolas. Nicolas quickly handed it to Ranulf. The older boy gave a brief nod but didn't say anything else to him. Nicolas tried to think of something to say but couldn't. He felt so lonely and so terribly, awfully sorry.

By this time, Adelaide had come back and was in the process of putting together a crude loom over which she could drape Nicolas' wet clothes next to the fire. The cold rain thankfully stopped, and each of them put on dry changes of clothes from out of their rolls. Soon, they were all sitting around the fire, sipping an herbal tonic tea Adelaide had made, and quietly watching the thin stew begin to bubble and quiver in the little black pot.

Benjamin poked his finger at a small rock sitting in front of him. "The first memory I have is of my mother," the smallish boy-thief quietly said, breaking the long silence. "It's the best memory I have. I don't even remember her face really well, but in my mind she is a beautiful woman. I at least remember that she had dark hair and slender fingers. Her voice was merry and soft, and she smelled like warm goat's milk. She was laughing, and I think I was trying to dance some stupid little dance or something like that. I was acting up, and I think she found it funny." Benjamin didn't look up. He just kept staring at the little rock. "But the second memory I have is my very worst one. It's also of my mother. I remember her crying and saying my name over and over again. 'Benny,' she called me. She was hugging me tightly, but I wanted to play, so I remember squirming and trying to get away. I remember her finally setting me down and pulling my favorite blanket around me, pinning it together under my chin like a cape. She took my hand in hers, and we walked for what seemed like a long time. Eventually, we went through one of the gatekeeps and over one of the arched bridges to a City gate. I remember being amazed and a little afraid at how big they were. I remember her saying to not ever be afraid of big things." Benjamin paused and picked up the little rock, rolling it slowly between his fingers. "My mother had me sit near one of the guards and told me to stay there. She said she'd be back in a bit, so I waited." He closed his hand over the little stone and looked up at Nicolas. "My mother never came back for me," he said quietly. "She left me there, and I never saw her again. For a long time, I hated the thought of that day. I wanted her to pick me up and to hold me again. I wanted to hear her laugh and to see her face. I felt miserable and alone and abandoned by the one person who was supposed to love me and care for me." Nicolas looked at Benjamin's clear, young face. Tears muddled the lower lids of Nicolas' eyes, and he wanted to grab the smallish boy and hold him close, but he sat there, waiting for Benjamin to finish.

"But then one day, about a year ago," Benjamin said, "I happened to see a brown-headed Cowbird in one of the small trees growing next to the ditch of stone which carries the water from the King's Spring. The Cowbird was sitting on a limb near a thrush's nest and seemed to be waiting for something. When the thrush flew away, I watched as the Cowbird hopped into the nest, where I could see it lay a single, small egg, then fly off to a higher branch in the same tree." Benjamin opened his hand and looked down at the little rock in his palm. "After a little while, the thrush returned. It looked like it rolled the Cowbird's egg around a little, but soon it settled down and nestled on top of it, treating it like one of its own eggs." Suddenly, the smallish boy-thief smiled. "I think the Cowbird cared enough to make sure its egg would be raised safely by the thrush. I think it gave away its egg because it hoped its chick would have a better life, a life it couldn't give to it." Benjamin looked around at Nicolas, Ranulf, and Adelaide. "My mother leaving me is my worst memory, but I understand it now. I think she loved me enough to bring me to the City, to try to find a better life, one she couldn't give me, *and*," the smallish boy-thief said, "I think I understand why *you* did what you did, Nicolas." He tossed the little rock across the fire for Nicolas to catch. "You gave up something, too, because you knew that was the *only* way to make everything better. Giving us up, giving up the Clokkemaker, was the only way to save us."

Nicolas couldn't say anything. He was too stunned. He tried, but the words lumped together in his throat, and instead, a tight sob puffed out. The well of tears in his weary eyes finally rolled down his cheeks. He looked at Ranulf, who was also wiping tears out of his eyes. Ranulf nodded at him and reached over to give his arm a good, firm grasp. Adelaide, whose pretty face was also wet with the warm relief of tears, quickly hopped up and kissed Benjamin in his messy, curly hair. Everyone cried except Benjamin. He'd already shed his tears on the walk back down the Timekeeper's Finger. Instead, the smallest of them all just smiled and looked at each of his friends with a wonderful, big grin on his face. Soon, Adelaide laughed and Ranulf laughed and Nicolas, with the redemptive feeling of a huge, monstrous weight lifting off his shoulders, rocked back in his bearskin and laughed until he was out of breath, out of tears, and free of the dark regret which had plagued his heart.

—◆—

The next day, the cold wind hurried a school of heavy clouds across the grey sky and kept the rain at bay until late in the day when the four friends arrived back at Obasi's home, the Caledonii's *Mahali Salama*, under the eaves of the Black Forest's dark trees. Obasi, his wife, Ayomide, and all the other Moss People greeted Nicolas and his friends warmly with welcoming hugs, happy chatter, and, to Benjamin's personal delight, a great feast, which was spread out on a soft, mossy dais surrounded by three large fire pits. There were flaky filets of trout and sturgeon cooked in vinegar and parsley, roasted haunches of tender venison, an aromatic stew of rabbit, rosemary, carrots, and nutmeg, bowls of pickled cauliflowers and toy onions, trays of barley cakes with raisins, sugared plums, and tart seeds of pomegranate, deep mugs of sweet cream and huge strawberries, boiled yolks of egg sprinkled with spices, figs with cinnamon, and an entire wild boar, with crisply fried skin glistening in a thick glaze of cherry sauce. Everyone laughed, talked, ate, rested, and then ate some more.

Giggling Caledonii girls played with Adelaide's long hair, while she held Cornelia on her lap, popping sticks of celery and sprigs of parsley into the happy little goat's mouth. Ranulf sat with some of the Caledonii's "mid-men"—what Nicolas thought of as adults but not yet elders—examining their sets of simple arrow heads and sharpened throwing sticks and wood axes, and, like some old, time-worn blacksmith, he commented on how best to keep their edges sharp and how a simple forge might be set up to make some better-crafted weapons and tools. Benjamin, almost too busy eating to talk to anyone, reclined next to the same old-looking Caledonii man he'd been cooking with two days before, whose large nose and mustache ends were now dressed in stains of shiny grease and globs of brown gravy.

Obasi sat next to Nicolas, off to the side of most of the hubbub, kindly observing how little Nicolas seemed to be eating.

"Et 'urts, doesn't it?" Obasi said to Nicolas softly, while sucking a bit of sugar from his finger.

"What hurts?" Nicolas asked.

"Yer heart," Obasi replied matter-of-factly.

"Oh," said Nicolas quietly. "Yes, I suppose it does."

Obasi reached for another sugared plum and unceremoniously licked some of the caked sugar from its deep purple skin. He then popped the whole plum in his mouth and chewed it in silence.

Nicolas looked down at the half-eaten barley cake he held in his hand. He felt happy and greatly relieved, but deeper down—deep in a place where Nicolas thought he could hold his pain like a forgotten penny in his pocket—Obasi was right. His heart still hurt. Nicolas didn't want to, but he thought of the high meadow, of how the deep blue clouds almost touched the earth, and of how the simple weave of Remiel's cloak had looked after it'd been soaked in dark blood.

The air seemed to leave his lungs, and his shoulders slumped down. Nicolas slowly put the uneaten barley cake back on the tray in front of them. "Will it always hurt?" he asked hesitantly. Nicolas wondered what had caused Obasi to guess at how he still felt deep inside. Since returning, no one had asked what had happened, and neither Nicolas nor his friends had volunteered to tell anyone. It didn't seem like a secret, but it felt like an unhealed wound, something still too tender to touch.

"Aye," the little man nodded gravely. He swallowed the last

bit of plum, wiped his mouth, and stared at the gaggle of girls, who were now all eagerly showing Adelaide their collections of grass and twig dolls. The young Healer was laughing and laying them all out in front of her, like little babes in a nursery.

"Aye," Obasi repeated with a sigh. "It'll always 'urt. Yer heart'll always be a bit 'eavy w'th grēēf." The ancient Caledonii elder folded his hands across his round, tattooed belly and leaned back against the gentle, mossy slope. He looked at Nicolas with kind eyes and softly said, "A king's heart always 'urts a bit. Dat es part o' bein' a king, ma boy."

They spent the next day and night with the Moss People, sleeping, eating, and laughing, but on the second day, they knew it was time to go. Their little pack pony contentedly stood still while its wooden cross-frame was again loaded with their bags, bed rolls, carrots for Cornelia, and sacks stuffed with generous gifts of food and flasks of cold water and spiced mead. One of the "mid-men," with a braided moustache hanging down to his knees, had been charged to escort them safely out of the Black Forest.

They waved their goodbyes, buckled their weather cloaks against the chilly winter drafts, and set off toward the mists of the Hollow Fen.

"Agathon!" shouted Benjamin. The smallish boy-thief rushed ahead of everyone with Cornelia keeping close at his heels, and dropped to his knees in the spongy moss to greet the smiling earth-gnome. Cornelia licked at the little man's fingers and nibbled at the oats he pulled out of his tiny pockets as he and Benjamin laughed and then spoke in serious tones about the benefits of mushrooms, mushroom soup, stuffed mushrooms, sautéed mushrooms, and "mushroom bits," something Benjamin said he'd invented which involved smoking mushrooms with hickory wood, drizzling them with a syrupy vinegar, and drying them out in the sun.

They camped for the night on the edge of the Hollow Fen after saying goodbye to the brave Caledonii "mid-man," who trundled quickly back into the Black Forest amid a brief flurry of large snowflakes. Ranulf kept their campfire hot, and after a substantial dinner and a fitful night's rest, bundled deep in the warmth of their heavy bearskins, it was especially hard to wake up and continue on. Adelaide mothered over each of them, brewing some hot black tea with mint and serving toasted oat cakes for breakfast with a bit of cherry jam she said one of the Caledonii women had given to her the day before.

"What's a little fog among friends?" Ranulf joked as he'd strapped their luggage back atop the pack pony. "But this time, let's see if we can avoid becoming bog worm burps." He laughed and winked at Nicolas.

Agathon shepherded them carefully through the Hollow Fen, and they were glad for the little fellow's company. Most of the day was spent hedged in by dense fogbanks, which ebbed, then rose up as if they were in competition with each other, with minds and dark purposes of their own. The chilly wind did its clever best to push back the fog, but as soon as it cleared the mists a little, another would creep in behind, and leave them all in an endless haze of gauzy white. The little earth-gnome, however, seemed unbothered by any of it, as if his rounded feet, stepping lightly across the sphagnum moss, could find their way just by the touch of earth underfoot. By the time fallow fell, they were on the far side of the Fen with the Woodcutter's Forest in sight. Exhausted from the day's travel, they made camp and built a peat fire, and Benjamin and Agathon made a thick stew of fat mushrooms, parsnips, onions, and roasted eels, which Agathon proudly pulled out of a scuffed leather pouch looped over his shoulder. In truth, the stew was wonderful and warmed Nicolas to his bones, but he did his very best not to think of the fat eels as baby bog worms.

The next day dawned clear. A few gloomy snow clouds conspired together in the western sky, but in the east, the sun stretched its rays up into clear blue.

"Maybe the Lonely Road won't be such a mucked-up mess!" Benjamin said hopefully.

"*You're* a mucked-up mess, Benjamin Rush," joked Adelaide, which made all of them laugh, as Benjamin, playing the ham, scampered around like an organ-grinder monkey, throwing bits of wavy hair grass and moss beards into the air and scratching at his armpits.

Almost tearfully, the smallish boy-thief soon bid a touching goodbye to Agathon, who in return, as is the traditional way of earth-gnomes, bowed so low, the little fellow's beard brushed the ground for several seconds. And, as their small troupe headed toward the dark line of trees of the Woodcutter's Forest, Cornelia, not wanting to leave behind her benevolent source of oats, anxiously stood there with Agathon, stubbornly bleating loudly at Adelaide, until, finally convinced the young Healer was going to keep going anyway, it scampered after her as fast as its little legs would carry it.

Nicolas and his friends, blessed with a window of dry weather, determined to move quickly through the forest, only stopping to eat a hasty lunch in the same glade which Grief, the jamba-bear, had led them to, but then hurrying on, passing silently by the trail to the woodcutter's cottage, with each of them keeping to their own thoughts about the twisted tinker and the murderous spirits of the *Dyn Glas*. With much effort, and occasional tugging at the pack pony's lead rope, they were able to reach the split Rowan Tree before nightfall and joyfully clapped each other on the back, happy to be out of the dense copses of oak trees and onto the final leg of their journey back to St. Wulf's-Without-Aldersgate. It seemed an eternity had passed since they'd last stood at those same crossroads.

Late that evening, with bellies full of a special treat of pan-fried bacon, grease-fried onions, and grease-griddled loaves of flat barley bannock bread, Adelaide, who was lying close to Nicolas, whispered, "What will you do?"

Nicolas didn't answer, but instead, propped himself up on an elbow, and for a moment, just stared at her. The memory of her dressed in her thin white smock, singing the Healer's lament in the doorway of Remiel's simple peat home, came to his mind with a refreshing sense of joy. The joy that she was alive—the joy that they were *all* alive—and it filled his heart.

"What do you mean?" he asked quietly.

"Well, what now?" she asked. "Now that the Shadow Thief is dead. What will you *do*?" Adelaide looked up at him. The cold clarity of the moonlight made her eyes appear bright grey and blue, like the surface of a midnight ocean.

"Well," he said, unsure of how to answer her. "We'll go back to the gatekeep, and I'll speak to Aldus, I guess."

"I know that, silly. But *after* that. What will you do?" she asked again.

Nicolas stayed silent for a moment, then laid back down, pulling his bearskin up to his chin and crossing his hands underneath his head. He stared up at the cold, clear night sky. The star clusters were especially bright, and for several minutes, the Wren and the young Healer watched the constellations navigate soundlessly across the endless heavens.

"You said you cared nothing for your own world," Adelaide said gently.

Nicolas winced at the memory. The echo of his own terrible words, shouted in anger and in a moment of necessary betrayal, crowded his thoughts, and he was glad for the dark. "I did," he answered.

"What did you mean, 'your *own* world'?"

Nicolas let out a peaceful sigh. And suddenly, he had a vision of his mum, sitting quietly on the edge of his bed at night, tucking him in, and gently asking him how his day at school had been. It was shortly after he'd moved from the North Lakes School to Hunter Hall. She'd asked him how he was doing, but he'd hesitated to answer. He didn't want to tell her how out of place he'd felt, how lonely he was without his old friends. Sensing this, she'd said, "The nighttime keeps all secrets, Nicolas." So he told her, and Sarah Bennett had hugged him tight, kissed his forehead, and told him it would get better. And it did.

The nighttime keeps all secrets, Nicolas thought to himself. "I—I come from somewhere else, another world," he whispered to Adelaide. "I guess I'll go home soon... but—but I'll return, I think."

After a long pause, the young Healer softly replied, "Okay." She reached over and found his hand, squeezed it, and held it tight. "Okay," she said again.

And with that, the young boy and girl said nothing else and kept watching the constellations sail high above shift silently across the vastness of the endless heavens.

CHAPTER 29

HOME AGAIN

S hall we begin with answers or questions?"

The Laird of the First Gate and the greatest among the Commissioners of the Forfeited Gates was sitting much as he had been so many days before in one of the high back chairs, nestled close to the firebasket, surrounded by the marvelous sight and smell of thousands of books which cluttered his private chambers. Aldus Ward was, in fact, wearing the same linen tunic and a dark green woolen cloak, with silver leaves and vines embroidered along its hem and collar, as he had been the day he met Nicolas. His right eye—bright blue and sparkling with flecks of gold and emerald—was wide open with anticipation.

"Oh, I like answers," Nicolas said with a laugh. He was sipping a hot cup of lemon tea Master Brooks had brought in, and his lap was littered with the crumbly remains of shortbread biscuits. "They're tidier than questions because answers know where they belong."

Aldus clapped his hands together and laughed. "Well done! Well done, Master Bennett!" He took a few thoughtful puffs from his remarkably long pipe. "Answers it is," he said pleasingly as he stared into the fire.

Nicolas sank back into his overstuffed chair and took a last swallow of tea. "The dragon's dead," he said quietly. "I suppose the poem you showed me was right."

Aldus pushed out his lips and blew a few undulating smoke rings into the air. "Yes, yes," he said.

Nicolas took a deep breath. "Remiel had a plan, an—an

awful plan… but it worked."

"Yes, yes," repeated Aldus, who sent a particularly large, thick smoke ring flying right into the fire. "It worked."

Nicolas snuck a look at Aldus, but the Laird of the First Gate appeared to be quite content to let him continue. Summoning the courage, Nicolas whispered, "I—I had to *kill* him." He lowered his head. Saying it aloud made him feel like there was a dead weight inside of him. It was terrible and made him feel as if he'd done something wrong. No matter how he explained what happened, Nicolas couldn't make it feel right inside his heart. He set down his empty cup and looked at his hands. "I killed him, Aldus. He said I had to. He said it was the only way."

"It was," the old man said simply.

Neither of them said anything more for a while. Nicolas stared through the fire at the decorative metal fireback with its raised impression of a large tree, half full of leaves, and half barren. He looked at the strange words written beneath it.

"Nicolas," Aldus said softly. "Nicolas, do you know why your grandfather was here? Why he was in Telluric Grand?"

Nicolas shook his head, but didn't look up.

"He was *here*, Master Bennett, as a shield-bearer. He was young—a little older than you, but still young."

Nicolas looked up.

"Your grandfather was here long, long ago. Long before this gatekeep stood here. Even before the King's Castle or the City of Relic were built." Aldus knocked the ash out of his pipe and repacked it delicately, using his little finger to make sure the walnut-colored leaves were snug but not too snug in the pipe's bowl. He found a long splinter of wood among the kindling, sitting in an iron hoop near the firebasket, and held it in the orange flames until it caught fire. "You see," the old man said as he suspended the match's flame over his pipe bowl, "your grandfather first arrived in Telluric Grand when there was little more than warring clans, when there were still hordes of evil giants living in the frosty peaks of the Dolmen Tombs, when sorcerers and witches wandered about unchallenged, and when fenris wolves roamed the hills in large packs, and sleuths of farlig jambas infested every forest. Those were dark and evil times, indeed. A time when coppery leaves were falling from Eldur trees.

"Your grandfather—just fourteen that first time, I believe—came here amid the violence and uncertainty of chaos and disorder. He found a place as a shield-bearer with a great chieftain and proved himself to be a kind and thoughtful servant, one the chieftain came to admire and love as he might his own son. Your grandfather always stayed close by his lord's side, and, disregarding his own fear or safety, he often followed him into cries, and screams, and sudden death of battle." The Laird of the First Gate rested his elbow on the arm of his highback chair and leaned closer to Nicolas. "During one especially violent engagement, your grandfather was hurt—struck, I think—by an enemy soldier, and the great chieftain came to his rescue, but in doing so, the chieftain was mortally wounded by another enemy soldier. Your grandfather, still hurting from his own wounds, rushed to his lord's aid, and in his dying moment, served him a cold drink of water."

Nicolas abruptly looked at Aldus—his face was an intense, almost distressed, cloudburst of realization. "I *know* this story!" he said. "I know this story! Benjamin told me about a shield-bearer—about a spring, some old witch, and the King's Drink!"

"Yes!" said Aldus, poking a bony finger into the air in smug satisfaction. "It's *that* story, Master Bennett. Your grandfather was *that* shield-bearer."

"But how can that be?" Nicolas asked. "Benjamin made it sound as if that was a legend, something that happened a long time ago."

Aldus gave a friendly laugh. "Have you learned nothing, Master Bennett? Time—you might remember—is more about *where* you stand than *when* you stand. Of course, it was long ago—it was ages and ages ago—but your grandfather was *there* just as sure as you're here now."

Nicolas collapsed back into his chair and slapped a hand to his forehead. "I can't believe it."

"Well you'd better believe it," Aldus said, and the old man also collapsed into the depths of his chair. He began briskly sucking on his pipe again, sending smoke rings chasing smoke rings up through the cluttered room's shadowy eaves. After a minute or two, Aldus leaned forward, his single eye's gaze lost in the dancing flames. His voice was low. "*Your* grandfather—your 'second father,' Nicolas—became the *first king* of the First Kingdom. He established and built the King's Castle over the King's Spring, and the City of Relic was eventually built around it. And *you*," Aldus said in a curiously soft way, "were built around *him*. You have a king's blood inside you, Master Bennett."

Nicolas, now stunned beyond words, just sat there, also staring into the fire. *How could he not have known? How could his grandfather have never said anything?* He closed his eyes and shook his head. "I didn't know," he said quietly. "No one ever told me."

"Of course, you didn't know, Nicolas, and even if you had, it wouldn't have made any sense to you. Your grandfather spent most of his life in our service—the service of Telluric Grand—as if he was one of the ancients, passing silently between our two worlds when our need was most dire. He came to us just as you've come to us." Aldus, in an almost shy voice, said, "I know you must go now. You've got a home to return to, but I *do* hope, my dear boy, that one day—one day soon, perhaps—you and I will sit here again, and we'll fill in all of our questions with wonderful, wonderful answers. Answers which know where they belong," the old man said with a kind wink.

Nicolas nodded his head. "Me, too," he said.

A charred log cracked in two, sending up a brief shower of sparks in the firebasket. As he had once before, Nicolas could see the decorative metal fireback, which had been forged with an impression of a large tree, half full of leaves and half bare. He looked again at the strange words written in a strange script below the tree. *Llawenhewch, yn Dod y Brenin.*

"What does that mean?" Nicolas asked, pointing at the fireback.

Aldus broke into a grand smile. "It means, 'Rejoice, the King Comes,'" he said, and suddenly, the old man sat straight up, his back as rigid as a Queen's guard, his chin held high, and his bright blue eye looking intently at Nicolas. In a loud, sure voice, the Laird of the First Gate and the greatest among the Commissioners of the Forfeited Gates said, "He was a *king*, Nicolas. A true king! And *you*—you, the little Wren, the friend of giants, the bane of ogres, the *Dragon Nightfall—you* shall be even greater than he was."

<hr/>

The next morning went by in a blur for Nicolas.

He awoke early, surrounded by his three friends in the same great hall in which they'd slept the night before they'd set out on their journey. Far more quickly than he liked, they had eaten a hasty breakfast and had walked with Nicolas to outer gate of St. Wulf's-Without-Aldersgate. To his surprise, there stood the tall man, Abrec Westenra, and his donkey, Cherry Pit. They would be taking Nicolas back along the road to the Cider Press Inn, and after that, he would be on his own. On his own to find the hollow in the tree.

"Well, Nicolas," said Ranulf, as stoutly as he could. "I guess we'll be seeing you again." The older boy looked closely at him, a little less stout. "That's right, isn't it? We'll be seeing you again, won't we?"

Nicolas grinned. "Yes, I think so," he said and gave Ranulf a tight hug. "My friend," he said, muffled against the older boy's shoulder.

"My friend," the older boy gently replied.

Nicolas felt a tug at his sleeve. It was Benjamin.

"Here," said the smallish boy-thief, the snatcher. He held out his quick little hand, and inside it, a bit crumbled and with one bite missing, was a barley cake from breakfast. "I want you to have this," Benjamin said.

Nicolas smiled at him and laughed. "I tell you what, Benjamin Rush. You eat it for me, and when I see you next time, I'll ask you for two."

Benjamin smiled back. "Alright," he said and shoved the cake back inside his weather cloak. For a second they stood there grinning at each other, then Benjamin, with a sudden jump, wrapped both his smallish arms around Nicolas and squeezed tight.

"Alright, alright," Nicolas said. "Let me breathe!" And he hugged the younger boy back.

"Don't leave," Benjamin said quietly.

Nicolas laid a hand on his messy hair. "My friend," he said earnestly.

"My friend," Benjamin replied.

"You boys are all silly birds," Adelaide interrupted, lightly tapping Benjamin on the shoulder. The smallish boy-thief let go his grip and took a couple of steps back. Trying to act like he'd seen something fly by, Benjamin looked away and quickly rubbed a tear out of his eye.

Without saying anything else, the young Healer wrapped her slender arms around Nicolas' neck, and he hugged her close. They stood like that for several moments. Nicolas could feel the warmth of her breath in his ear.

"Thank you," she said to him, softly so no one else could hear. "The star that you are," she whispered.

"My friend?" he asked just as softly, smelling the vanilla and peppermint in her hair.

"Always," Adelaide Ashdown whispered back.

Finding the dark tree hollow—amid the long shadows of a fallow sky—took Nicolas a bit more time than he expected, and try as he might, he couldn't quite remember the pace count he'd first taken, but eventually he found it, and stepping into it, he let himself plunge back into the icy waters of the ancient River Eamont.

Baatunde and Magnus the thrush were both sitting much as he'd left them.

The little man's eyes lit up as Nicolas walked back up to the hearth and stood there, warming his hands by the fire and imagining the cheery flames popping and cracking in the fire-basket in Aldus' cluttered chambers.

"Well?" Baatunde asked, excitedly smoking his pipe.

"Well," Nicolas said quietly. "I'm a Wren."

"Haha!" laughed the elder Caledonii, and he danced wildly about as if someone had given him a surprise present.

By the time Nicolas made his way back and found Mr. and Mrs. Bennett, it was a little after 5 o'clock.

The sun was just settling into its western bed, and everyone who was left at the fair was moving toward the Lancaster Castle stage, chatting eagerly as they awaited the Piper's Procession

---

and the sacrifice of another year's pumpkin heads.

"Where've ya been, lad?" Peter Bennett asked. His son looked a shade more *worn*—aged, perhaps—than when he'd left them a few hours before.

Nicolas gave his dad a quick smile. "Oh, I've been talking to giants, and walking with bears, and outwitting ogres."

Mr. Bennett laughed and paused. With a questioning look on his face, he smiled back at his son. "Walking with bears, you say?"

"Yes, dad. I've been walking with bears." Then, a bit more quietly, Nicolas said with a wink, "In a place with *dragons*."

His parents asked Nicolas if he wanted to stay for the Piper's Procession, but Nicolas said no. He told them he was tired, gave them both an unusually long hug, and asked if they could go home. Peter Bennett looked at his wife, and Sarah Bennett smiled her wonderful, Irish smile. "Sure!" she said. So off they went.

"Dad?"

"Yes, Nicolas?"

"Would you mind if we visited Grandfather's grave soon?"

Peter Bennett turned to glance at his son, who was sitting in the backseat, staring out the window. Mr. Bennett wrinkled his forehead in mild concern, and he looked at Mrs. Bennett to see if she knew what this was all about. She raised her eyebrows and gave a quick shrug. "Sure," Mr. Bennett said slowly and turned his eyes back to the dark road. "Anything wrong, Nicolas?"

"No," Nicolas answered with a shake of his head.

The boy turned and pressed his face against the cold glass of the window and watched the trees fly by as they drove along Earl Henry's Drive, over the River Eamont and northwest on the A6 toward Bridge Lane.

"I just want to see the grave of a king," Nicolas said softly to himself.

Made in the USA
Coppell, TX
30 November 2020